When th... come their way, Donovan Chance's and Gage Reynolds's lives get complicated!

MEN TO MARRY

Two fantastic, passionate, page-turning
romances delivered to you by two
award-winning and bestselling writers

We're proud to present

MILLS & BOON®

SPOTLIGHT

a chance to buy collections of bestselling novels by favourite authors every month – they're back by popular demand!

MEN TO MARRY

The Groom's Stand-In
GINA WILKINS

Good Husband Material
SUSAN MALLERY

MILLS & BOON®

This collection is first published in Great Britain 2007
Harlequin Mills & Boon Limited,
Eton House, 18-24 Paradise Road, Richmond, Surrey TW9 1SR

MEN TO MARRY © Harlequin Books S.A. 2007

The publisher acknowledges the copyright holders of the
individual works, which have already been published in the UK
in single, separate volumes, as follows:

The Groom's Stand-In © Gina Wilkins 2002
Good Husband Material © Susan Macias Redmond 2002

ISBN: 978 0 263 85679 8

064-0707

Printed and bound in Spain
by Litografia Rosés S.A., Barcelona

The Groom's Stand-In

GINA WILKINS

GINA WILKINS

is a bestselling and award-winning author who has written more than fifty books. She credits her successful career in romance to her long, happy marriage and her three 'extraordinary' children.

A lifelong resident of central Arkansas, Gina sold her first book in 1987 and has been writing full-time since. She has appeared on numerous bestseller lists. She is a three-time recipient of the Maggie Award for Excellence, sponsored by Georgia Romance Writers, and has won several awards from the reviewers of *Romantic Times*.

Chapter One

Donovan Chance had done a lot of favors for his friend and employer, Bryan Falcon—some involving actual risk to life and limb—but he had never served as a babysitter. While that wasn't exactly what he was doing on this Sunday afternoon in early April, the description felt uncomfortably accurate.

He had reluctantly agreed to escort Chloe Pennington—Bryan's current girlfriend—from her Little Rock, Arkansas, apartment to Bryan's vacation home on Table Rock Lake in southwest Missouri. It would be a little more than three hours in the car with a total stranger, a trip Donovan wasn't anticipating with any enthusiasm.

With a sigh, he reached for the door handle. He owed Bryan a lot more than a few favors—regardless of his personal feelings about this one in particular.

The apartment he'd been directed to was on the

ground floor, opening onto a covered sidewalk. Rain was in the forecast—lots of it—and the air was nippy. Hunching a little against a brisk breeze, he rang the doorbell.

From the photograph Bryan had shown him, he immediately recognized the woman who opened the door. Medium-brown hair cut in a smooth bob to her collar. Large, long-lashed hazel eyes set in a fair-skinned oval face. Straight, smallish nose. Soft mouth, the lower lip fuller than the top. More pretty than beautiful. Dressed very casually in jeans and a long-sleeved red T-shirt.

He wouldn't have thought she was Bryan's type—but then, this whole situation had been a surprise to him. He wished he could say it had been a pleasant one.

He was quite sure no emotions were revealed in his expression when he introduced himself. "Ms. Pennington? I'm Donovan Chance, Bryan Falcon's associate."

Rather than make him feel welcome, as he'd expected, she gave him a cool once-over that left him feeling like something she'd spotted floating in her soup. "Associate?" she asked. "Don't you mean flunky?"

His eyes narrowed in response to the unveiled insult. *This* was the woman Bryan wanted to marry? The one he'd described as sweet, warm, funny, a little old-fashioned? If Donovan hadn't seen a photograph, he would be certain he'd come to the wrong apartment. "You *are* Ms. Pennington, aren't you?" he asked just to be sure.

"Yes. May I call you Donnie?" Her honeyed tone was pure insolence this time. Donovan had always believed that no one could deliver an insult more effectively than a woman of the South.

"Not if you want me to answer." He hadn't been prepared to like her particularly, but he'd thought she'd at least make a show of being pleasant. He'd bet she never talked this way in front of Bryan. He'd had a great deal of experience dealing with difficult people, so he was able to keep his voice blandly polite. "I suppose we should get on the road. May I carry your bags for you?"

From babysitter to bellhop. Bryan could well owe *him* a few favors after this. Especially if Ms. Pennington's attitude didn't improve significantly. Soon.

"If it were up to me, no one would be getting in a car with you," she said, and her expression now seemed to be an odd mixture of frustration and disapproval. "Then your rich boss could go shopping elsewhere for a suitable partner for his ridiculous marriage of convenience."

Now he *was* confused. He'd thought Chloe Pennington was a willing participant in this whirlwind courtship—too willing, actually. He'd been certain she was as attracted to Bryan's money and power as to Bryan himself—as too many other women had been during the past few years. But this woman wasn't even pretending to be looking forward to the week she would be spending with the man who had been courting her so persistently. Did she really think it didn't matter how she spoke to Bryan's closest associate, as long as she behaved properly in front of Bryan himself?

Because he'd long since appointed himself Bryan's protector, he spoke sharply, "Look, if that's the way you really feel about this, let's just forget it. Bryan doesn't have time for a vacation now, anyway, especially with someone who would rather be elsewhere. And to be honest, I have plenty more important things to do than babysit a…''

"Grace? I saw Mrs. Callahan in the laundry room, and she asked me to tell you…" The woman who had entered the room, wearing khaki slacks and a mint-green sweater and carrying a load of folded laundry in a round plastic basket, came to an abrupt stop when she saw Donovan standing in the open doorway. "Oh," she said, looking suddenly flustered. "You must be Donovan Chance. You're early."

Donovan wasn't usually caught completely off guard, but it took him a moment to respond. "Actually, I'm exactly on time."

The woman set the laundry basket on the couch and approached the door. "I'm so sorry. My watch must have stopped again. It's been doing that lately."

Though their appearance was almost identical—the only difference being that this woman wore her brown hair slightly longer and straighter—the newcomer's voice was warmer than the one who had opened the door to him, her expression friendlier. "Grace, haven't you even invited Mr. Chance inside?"

"Actually, I had almost convinced him to leave without you." Her face resigned, Grace stepped out of Donovan's way.

Sighing, Chloe stepped forward to extend her hand in Donovan's direction. "I'm sorry if my sister was rude. Perhaps we should start from the beginning. I'm Chloe Pennington, and it's very nice to meet you, Mr. Chance. Bryan has often spoken of you."

Donovan remembered now that Bryan had mentioned that Chloe owned a business with her sister.

He had neglected to add that the sisters were identical twins. Donovan would have to discuss that with his friend later.

He shook Chloe's hand briefly. "It's nice to meet you, Ms. Pennington," he said, because etiquette demanded it of him.

"Please call me Chloe. And you've already met my sister, Grace."

Meeting Grace's glittering hazel eyes, Donovan nodded. "Yes, I've had that pleasure."

She flashed him a challenging smile.

Looking suspiciously from one to the other, Chloe shook her head. "Now I'm even more convinced that an apology for my sister's behavior must be in order."

Turning his back on Grace, Donovan looked at Chloe—the woman Bryan had chosen, he reminded himself. "Are you ready to leave?"

Chloe glanced at her watch, shook her wrist, then slipped it off and tossed it to her sister. "See if you can have that repaired while I'm gone, will you?"

Catching it easily, Grace replied, "You could always stay and see to it yourself."

"Don't start with me again." Chloe picked up the laundry basket and turned toward the doorway that led to the back of the apartment. "Five minutes," she promised Donovan. "Make yourself comfortable in the meantime."

He nodded, watching Grace a bit warily out of the corner of his eye.

Maybe Chloe sensed his uneasiness. "Grace, why don't you come help me get everything ready," she said, and her tone made it clear it wasn't a suggestion.

"I'm sure Mr. Chance won't mind waiting by himself for a few minutes."

"Not at all," he assured her.

Grace crossed her arms over her chest. "You can handle everything in there. I'll keep Falcon's chauffeur company."

Donovan was going to let it pass, but Chloe spoke sharply on his behalf. "Mr. Chance isn't a chauffeur, he's an executive in Bryan's company. He's doing Bryan a big favor by giving me a lift today because Bryan was detained in New York."

"An executive. Is that what they're calling errand boys these days?"

"Grace!"

Holding up a hand toward Chloe, Donovan focused on her sister. "You might as well get it off your chest. What other insults would you like to throw at me before I leave?"

He was a bit surprised to see her blush. She kept her chin high, defiance overcoming embarrassment. "I suppose I should apologize for the things I've said to you. You're only doing your job, I guess. It's my sister who needs some sense knocked into her."

"You don't approve of the engagement?"

"Bryan and I aren't engaged," Chloe said quickly. "We're still in the preliminary stage of our relationship. That's why we're taking some private time at his vacation home this week—to discuss the future in private. We were both disturbed when the press got wind of our friendship and started dropping hints about a possible marriage."

Grace whirled toward Donovan. "Do *you* approve of this ridiculous arrangement?"

He shrugged. No way, of course, was he going to

admit that he agreed with Grace Pennington—about anything. "It's none of my business."

"So you *are* just an employee and not a real friend of Bryan Falcon."

His eyes narrowed at that. "Bryan Falcon is the best friend I've ever had. But I don't tell him how to run his personal life."

Which didn't mean he wouldn't give his opinion when asked, of course. And if Bryan asked him, Donovan was going to suggest that his friend think a lot longer before making himself a part of *this* family.

"I wish you would teach that trick to my sister," Chloe said. "Not getting involved in other people's business, I mean."

Donovan doubted that there was anything Grace Pennington would be willing to learn from him. "We'd better get going," he said to Chloe, looking pointedly at his own efficiently accurate watch.

"I'll hurry," she replied. "Come on, Grace."

With a show of reluctance, Grace followed her twin from the room, leaving Donovan to exhale slowly and wonder what on earth Bryan had gotten the two of them into this time.

Strapped into a luxuriously soft and comfortable leather seat, Chloe looked through her lashes at the man behind the wheel of the expensive sedan. The passing scenery was lovely. Though it was a bit chilly due to a midnight rainstorm the night before, the past couple of weeks had been quite warm, coaxing new leaves from trees and bringing out daffodils, Bradford pear blossoms, and a few early azaleas. As much as she enjoyed the first signs of spring, Chloe found herself unable to stop surreptitiously studying her driver.

Bryan had described his second-in-command as the classic "strong, silent type"—tough, blunt-spoken, ruthless when necessary. He had then added that Donovan Chance was the most honest, loyal, reliable friend he'd ever had. Chloe had expected to be a little awkward with Donovan. She hadn't anticipated that she would be totally intimidated by him.

He wasn't as handsome as Bryan—not in the traditional sense, anyway. Donovan's features were more rugged than Bryan's. She would bet he'd had his nose broken in his youth; just enough to keep it from being perfectly straight. His jaw was square, his cheekbones broad, and his unsmiling eyes were such a pale, cool green they looked almost metallic. Nice mouth—but she doubted those firm, intriguingly etched lips curved into a smile very often.

He wore "business-casual" clothing—a thin, V-necked cream-colored sweater over a navy-and-cream checked shirt with navy chinos and loafers—but he looked as though he'd be more at home in a denim shirt, jeans and a pair of boots. He'd apparently made an effort to comb his medium-length, chestnut-brown hair into a conservative style, but it showed a tendency to tumble rebelliously onto his forehead.

On anyone else, she might have referred to that errant lock as "boyish." But not this guy. There was nothing boyish about Donovan Chance.

Because she knew that Donovan was Bryan's best friend as well as his employee, and since she figured she'd be spending a lot of time around him in the future if she and Bryan did marry, she decided that now was as good a time as any to try to get to know him. After all, that had been Bryan's intention when he'd sent Donovan to escort her to the resort, though she had assured him she was perfectly capable of traveling alone.

"Bryan told me you and he have known each other since high school," she said to kick off the conversation.

Donovan replied without taking his eyes off the road ahead. "Yeah."

"Were you neighbors?"

"No."

Okay, no more questions that could be answered in monosyllables, she decided. Whether he was just naturally averse to small talk, or was still smarting from Grace's rudeness, she didn't know, but they would never get anywhere this way. "How did you and Bryan meet?"

After a rather lengthy pause, he said, "Four guys were doing their best to beat me to a pulp. Bryan jumped in to help me."

Chloe felt her eyebrows rise as she tried to picture always-immaculate, elegant Bryan Falcon engaged in a vicious fist fight. On the other hand, she had no trouble at all imagining Donovan taking on four challengers. "Did you and Bryan win the fight?"

"Actually, they beat us both to a pulp."

Chloe was startled into a laugh. "That's terrible."

What might have been a smile—it was hard to tell with this man—quirked one corner of his mouth. "We recovered."

"So you and Bryan have been friends ever since?"

Another long pause—followed by another monosyllable. "Yeah."

Chloe stifled a sigh and sat back in her seat. Looked as though this was going to be a long, quiet trip. She might as well enjoy the view.

* * *

It was with effort that Donovan kept his gaze focused on the road ahead instead of the woman sitting in the passenger seat. Something about her kept drawing his attention her way.

A sideways glance let him see that she was gazing out the side window at the passing landscape, a somber look on her face. Her fingers were twisted in her lap so tightly that her knuckles gleamed. She didn't give the appearance of a woman on her way to a romantic getaway with the man she was planning to marry. Which made him wonder again why she was going along with this very businesslike courtship.

The most logical answer, of course, was that she had several million reasons—all green.

He was lousy at small talk, but he searched for something to say, a way to get her talking again so he could try to figure her out. "Bryan told me you're in the retail business."

She seemed relieved to be drawn out of her thoughts, even with such a lame conversational gambit. "Yes, Grace and I own a shop in Little Rock's River Market district. We call it Mirror Images—a shameless play on our being twins, I'll admit. We specialize in decorating accessories—unusual mirrors, mostly, but also pottery and sculpture, candleholders, carved boxes, blown-glass pieces. Many of the items are handmade and one-of-a-kind."

Hearing the enthusiasm in her voice, he could tell her heart was in her work. Bryan had always said that no business could be successful if the owner had no passion. It was probably Chloe's enthusiasm for her shop that had drawn Bryan to her in the first place. And maybe her smile…

He cleared his throat rather forcefully. "How's business? Making a profit?"

Her eyebrows rose. "We're doing all right," she said, her tone a bit cool now.

Did she think he'd gotten too nosy? Or did she simply not want to admit that the shop wasn't making money? He knew how difficult it was for a small business to survive. More than half folded within their first year of operation. It required a good deal of start-up capital to acquire stock, hire competent employees, purchase enough advertising to catch the buying public's attention....

He shrugged. "You'll do better once Bryan's involved."

Everyone knew that Bryan Falcon had an almost magical way of making every business he backed turn a sizeable profit. Donovan was sure Chloe was well aware of her new boyfriend's business talents—not to mention his notorious talent for charming women.

When she spoke this time, her tone was almost cool enough to deposit ice on his eyelashes. "I don't expect Bryan to be involved with my business in any way. My sister and I are perfectly capable of running it on our own."

"I see," he said—which didn't mean he believed her, of course. There was no way he'd accept that the financial advantages of marriage to one of the most successful venture capitalists in the country had never crossed her mind.

She frowned at him. "You think I'm only interested in Bryan's money?"

"I didn't say that."

"No—you didn't say it." But apparently, she'd interpreted his words that way anyway. She sat back in her seat, her face turned away from him, her posture stiff enough to let him know she'd taken offense.

He thought about trying to apologize, but decided to let it go. For one thing, he was lousy at apologies—hadn't made enough of them to get good at it. For another—well, hell, of *course* he figured she was interested in Bryan's money. He'd met few women—or men, for that matter—who weren't. And since her own sister had made it clear she didn't consider this a love match, then Chloe had to have more prosaic reasons for considering marriage to Bryan.

An eminently practical man himself, Donovan supposed he couldn't blame Chloe for keeping her eyes on the bottom line, but he still didn't approve of this whole arrangement. Bryan deserved better than to be married for his money.

Donovan believed his friend was overreacting to his last failed romantic relationship. Bryan had been burned by a woman who had convinced him that she wanted him for himself, not his money. The truth of that ruse had been revealed when she'd gone ballistic at the first mention of the rather strict prenuptial agreement that Bryan's team of attorneys had drafted years earlier. She hadn't been a good enough actress to convince anyone that the extent of her outrage couldn't be measured in dollar signs.

Because it hadn't been the first time Bryan had been deceived, he had come to the conclusion that the only way he could be certain of a potential mate's motives was to have everything spelled out from the beginning. He wanted children, and he wanted to raise them in a conventional two-parent family. He'd decided he should approach marriage the same way he started a new business—with legal contracts, long-term planning, calculated risks and clearly defined benefits.

Donovan had tried to point out that one didn't choose a wife the same way one hired a financial officer, but Bryan had shrugged off the admonition. To him, it had seemed like a perfectly logical plan.

He'd told Donovan about the day in February when he had wandered into Chloe's shop while on a break from a day-long meeting being held nearby. They'd started talking, then had somehow ended up having coffee together at the popular River Market pavilion. Bryan claimed to have known very quickly that Chloe was exactly the sort of woman he'd been searching for since he'd made the decision a few months earlier to enter into a practical marriage.

Donovan had never been accused of being even remotely romantic, but Bryan's plan seemed too cold and calculated even for him. He couldn't help wondering if someday Bryan was going to feel that he'd settled for less than he could have had, if he would always be aware that something important was missing.

Since he himself had no strong desire to reproduce, Donovan figured his way was easier—he didn't plan to marry anyone. Any relationships he entered into were strictly short-term and no-strings, so motives didn't really matter.

He was convinced that his strategy was the most practical of all.

They'd been on the road for almost an hour when Donovan realized that Chloe's posture was still unnaturally rigid. Her hands were still laced tightly together, her short pink nails digging into skin.

"Are you okay?" he couldn't resist asking. "My driving isn't making you nervous or anything, is it?"

His question brought her head around. "Of course not. You seem to be an excellent driver. I'm not nervous about anything at all."

Definitely a lie, he decided, glancing again at her telltale hands. "You just seemed a little tense."

"I'm fine." She looked straight ahead again as she spoke. "What is it you do in Bryan's organization, exactly?"

He shrugged. "Whatever he needs me to do."

"Such as escorting me today?"

Since the answer to that seemed obvious, he allowed it to pass.

"You've been out of the country for the past few months," she tried again. "In…Italy?"

"Venice. I was there for almost three months."

"That must have been very nice."

"It was business."

She twisted in her seat, tugging at the seat belt to allow her to look at him more closely. "Surely you took some time off for sightseeing."

"Not much," he admitted. "I was only supposed to be over there a couple of weeks. Problems kept cropping up to detain me. I was just trying to get everything settled so I could get back to the States."

"You must have missed your family."

"I don't have family. I had a lot of work piling up here that I needed to attend to."

"I see." She settled back into her seat again.

Because he knew Bryan wanted him to keep Chloe entertained, Donovan tried to think of something interesting to say about his weeks in Venice. "The food was good."

"I'm sure it was."

"And the sunrises were nice," he added. "I had a balcony, and I would sit out there and have coffee early in the mornings while I read through paper-work."

The enthusiasm of her response to that made him glad he'd gone to the extra conversational effort. "That must have been spectacular!" She lifted her clasped hands to her chest as she apparently tried to visualize the scene he'd described so sparingly. "I've always wanted to travel. To see some of the places I've only read about until now."

"When you marry Bryan, you'll be able to travel as much as you want." As he was sure she was aware.

She lowered her hands slowly to her lap. "*If* I marry Bryan," she corrected him, her voice a bit cool again.

"The gossip columnists seem to think it's all been decided." And he imagined the rumors were correct. Despite her affront at implications that she would marry Bryan for his money, why *wouldn't* she want to marry a multimillionaire who could take her to all those places she'd always wanted to visit?

She wrinkled her nose. "That's something I'm still having trouble getting used to—being in the gossip columns, I mean."

He shrugged again. "You'd better get used to it. For some reason, people seem to be fascinated with Bryan. Everything he does makes the papers."

Money, he thought, had a way of drawing attention. Combine a lot of money with Bryan's good looks, impressive family background, unerringly shrewd business decisions, personal charisma and single status, and the result was that he was included on every Most Eligible Bachelor list published in North America.

Just the hint that Bryan's name might soon be removed from those lists had the gossips all abuzz with curiosity, despite Bryan's efforts to keep his personal life private. Someone had apparently tipped off the tabloids about his interest in Chloe, much to Bryan's displeasure.

That was another reason Bryan had asked Donovan to play escort on this trip. He'd been concerned that Chloe might find herself annoyed by reporters. Donovan rarely had that problem. For some reason, they took one look at him and quietly put away their notebooks.

"One of the so-called reporters called me Zoe," Chloe muttered, "and another said it was Grace that Bryan's been seeing."

Donovan wondered if her disgruntled tone was because she'd been in the papers at all—or because they hadn't gotten her name right. "The way your sister was talking earlier, I doubt that she appreciated seeing her name linked with Bryan's," was all he said.

Chloe winced. "No, she didn't."

"What does she have against Bryan, anyway?" Maybe Grace was jealous that *she* wasn't the one poised to marry a multimillionaire.

"It isn't Bryan, exactly. She's just worried that I'm making a mistake. Grace has a little trouble trusting people—especially wealthy, powerful men. She's convinced herself I'm going to end up bitter and humiliated. Unlike *some* people," she added pointedly, "my sister knows I want more from a marriage than financial security, and she doesn't believe I can find those things with Bryan."

"And why is that?"

"She suspects that Bryan is playing me for a fool, and that he has no intention of settling down and raising a family."

"Bryan does what he says he'll do."

"You're very loyal to him."

Because she could never understand how much he owed Bryan—and because it wasn't any of her concern, anyway—he let the comment pass without remark.

They fell quiet again then. Donovan had run out of things to say, and Chloe seemed to have relaxed, if only marginally. Or perhaps even riding in uneasy silence seemed preferable to making stilted conversation with him.

He supposed he couldn't blame her for that.

Chapter Two

They'd been on the road for almost two hours when Donovan nodded toward a small convenience store ahead. "We're just past the halfway point of our trip. I could use a cold drink. How about you?"

"A cold drink sounds good."

He flipped on his turn signal, automatically glancing in the rearview mirror as he did so. A big, extended-cab pickup was right on his back bumper, followed by a blue, soccer-mom minivan. The van had its signal on, too—no surprise, since there wasn't another convenient place to stop for several miles ahead.

Because his gas tank was still more than half full, he drove into a parking space on one side of the small store. The only open space available, it lay in deep shadow. Though it wasn't a particularly cold day, Donovan felt a chill go through him when he turned off the motor. He'd learned to trust feelings like that;

he looked around before opening his door. Everything looked fine—a couple of older-model vehicles, several work-weary pickup trucks, and the soccer-mom van, which was parked at one of the three gas pumps.

Chloe eyed him quizzically. "Are you supposed to be my bodyguard?"

That whipped his head around, his eyes narrowing as he stared at her. "What makes you ask that?"

"Something about the way you checked out the place just now—all tense and alert, like a Hollywood version of a secret service agent."

His reply was more curt than he had intended. "I'm no bodyguard. Do you want to go in with me or wait out here?"

She reached for her door handle. "I'll go in."

He followed close on her heels as they stepped out of the shadows and around to the front of the store. She glanced over her shoulder at him when they entered. "If you'll excuse me a moment," she said, motioning in the general direction of the restrooms.

He nodded and turned to a wall-size cooler filled with soft drinks. He found himself watching the restroom doors during the brief time Chloe was out of his sight, though he couldn't imagine why he was suddenly so antsy.

This whole situation probably had him unnerved. Bryan was supposed to be making this trip, but he'd been detained in New York and had arranged to meet them at his Ozarks vacation home. He'd asked Donovan to make sure Chloe got there safely. In a couple of hours, Bryan would become Chloe's companion, and Donovan could get back to his own life—which, admittedly, consisted mostly of work.

Chloe joined him at the cooler, reached inside and

selected a diet cola. They carried their selections to
the register, setting them side by side on the counter.
Chloe started to open her purse, but Donovan already
had his money in hand. "I've got them."

She looked as though she wanted to argue, but his
expression must have let her know there would be no
point. The purchases paid for, he handed her the diet
cola and motioned toward the door.

A cloud passed in front of the sun just as they
stepped outside, plunging the parking lot into even
deeper shadow and making the brisk breeze that
skipped around them feel suddenly colder. Once
again, Donovan found himself moving closer to
Chloe's side.

Chloe looked at him curiously. "Is something
wrong?"

He was being foolish, of course. This wasn't one
of the rare operations during which he had to flinch
at every sound, search every shadow, or suspect every
bystander of being armed and dangerous. All he was
doing was escorting Bryan's girlfriend for a few
hours. Not an assignment he would have chosen for
himself, but certainly not a hazardous duty.

Chloe found herself sneaking glances at Donovan
again during the remainder of the quiet ride. She regretted that he had slipped on a pair of dark sunglasses when they'd left the convenience store. His
face had been difficult enough to read when she could
see his eyes, as little as they revealed. Now, all she
could see was the hard line of his jaw—which wasn't
encouraging conversation.

He would probably be perfectly happy if they completed the rest of the trip in silence. Even when he'd

tried to make small talk, he hadn't been particularly friendly. Maybe she shouldn't take it personally. Maybe he was this way with everyone, although she found it hard to believe that charming, congenial Bryan Falcon's closest friend had the personality of granite.

She couldn't say this trip was starting out promisingly. But, at least, she had never had any trouble talking to Bryan, she reminded herself. Just the opposite, in fact; they'd chatted almost like old friends from the first time they'd met.

If Bryan felt more like a good friend than a potential lover—well, that was something she was hoping to overcome during the next few days. Bryan was handsome, personable, intelligent, amusing, attentive—everything a woman could want. She was quite sure that once they were alone, away from the pressure of public scrutiny, their relationship would progress naturally.

She wasn't looking for blazing passion in a marriage, she reminded herself. She wasn't expecting to fall desperately in love—nor to be blindly adored in return. She'd sought those romantic myths before, only to be repeatedly disappointed. She would be content now with security, respect, affection and, most of all, children—and Bryan had almost convinced her he wanted exactly the same things.

Why couldn't Grace understand how appealing his offer sounded?

As for Donovan—Chloe risked a glance at the stern-faced man behind the wheel. He'd made his disapproval clear enough. Did he really think of her as a scheming gold digger, or was he, like Grace, completely turned off by the businesslike way Bryan and

Chloe were going about this courtship? She doubted that Donovan harbored any romantic illusions about love and marriage. She would bet he was convinced she was only after Bryan's money, that Bryan was the one being used.

Well, that was Donovan's problem. She wouldn't waste her breath trying to explain her motives to him. For one thing, it was none of his business. For another, he would never believe her anyway, not if he already had his mind made up about her.

"How much farther is it to Bryan's vacation house?" she asked.

"About another hour."

She nodded and adjusted her seat belt, mentally preparing for another awkward hour. "Will Bryan be waiting for us there?"

"He hoped to arrive about the same time we do— maybe an hour or so afterward if he got held up in New York."

"And will you be staying with us?"

Even though she couldn't see his eyes through his dark glasses, she felt the dry humor in the glance he shot her way. "Don't worry, I won't interfere with your plans. I'll be on my way as soon as you and Bryan are settled in."

She didn't know why his words embarrassed her. There was nothing overtly suggestive about them. But still she found herself averting her face to hide her expression, gazing fixedly out the passenger-side window.

She was an adult, she reminded herself—closing in fast on her thirtieth birthday. She didn't owe Donovan, Grace or anyone else explanations or justifications for her actions. She didn't have to tell them that

Bryan had promised not to rush her, that they had agreed they would spend the next few days talking in private about what they both wanted for their futures.

She'd tried to convince Grace that this was the primary purpose for this intimate retreat, but Grace hadn't accepted it. She was convinced that Bryan was going to pressure Chloe into sleeping with him for a few days. Then, when he grew bored with her, he was going to announce that he'd changed his mind about marriage, leaving Chloe feeling used, betrayed and deeply disappointed.

Chloe suspected that Donovan harbored similar unflattering suspicions about *her*.

She was relieved when Donovan turned off the main highway onto a winding lane that he said led to Bryan's Table Rock Lake vacation home. The sooner this uncomfortable journey was over, the better, as far as she was concerned. She much preferred Bryan's easy charm to Donovan's brooding disapproval.

He made several more winding turns, seemingly taking them miles from anywhere. It occurred to her suddenly that she was being awfully trusting, going blindly into the wilderness with this taciturn man she hadn't met before today. But Bryan had told her she would be safe with Donovan, and she trusted Bryan implicitly. She wouldn't have agreed to spend the next week with him if she didn't.

She had expected Bryan's vacation house to be nice. She already knew he wasn't the type to settle for less.

She hadn't expected anything quite like this.

Looking more like a lodge than a private vacation home, the sprawling structure was built of rock and redwood. Big windows and roomy decks allowed for the enjoyment of the beautiful surroundings—the thick woods, the rolling hills, the glistening lake that lay in the distance behind the house, which perched at the top of a tall bluff. Though tasteful and inviting, there was no question that this place belonged to someone with a great deal of money.

Chloe's family had never been poor, but they would definitely have been categorized as "working class." She'd never been to a place like this that wasn't a public resort.

"Looks like we've arrived before Bryan," Donovan commented, parking in front of the house. "He should be here soon. I'll help you get settled in."

Now that she was actually here, Chloe was unexpectedly hesitant about going inside. Maybe it was because the house was so much more impressive than she had expected, emphasizing the differences between her lifestyle and Bryan's. Or maybe it was a result of the uncomfortable hours she had just spent with Bryan's associate. Or maybe it was because the full magnitude of what she was doing was just hitting her.

This wasn't dinner and a movie, or a night at the symphony—the type of outing she'd shared with Bryan until now. This was a full week with him. Days…and nights. That was enough to daunt her, since going away with a man wasn't something she had done very often. But she couldn't even mark this off as an impulsive fling; the primary purpose of the next few days was to discuss the future. Marriage. The rest of her life.

All the lectures Grace had given her during the past ten days or so suddenly replayed in her mind. Ironically, it wasn't Grace's gloomy warnings that Bryan wasn't serious about marriage that made Chloe so nervous; it was her own deep certainty that he *was* serious.

"Something wrong?" Donovan asked, breaking into her somber introspection and making her realize how long she must have been sitting there without moving.

She swallowed. "No. Nothing's wrong."

Except that she abruptly wanted to go home. Now. As much as she wanted children, as often as she had told herself that there were more sensible reasons to marry than the passionate love of fantasy and fiction, she suddenly found herself suddenly longing with all her heart for the fairy tale. She wanted it *all*—why was she even contemplating settling for less?

Donovan seemed to be studying her intently through his dark glasses. "Changing your mind?"

She lifted her chin and reached for the door handle, determined that he wouldn't see her irrational panic. "Of course not. I was just…admiring the view."

He made a sound that might have expressed skepticism, but she didn't bother to try to convince him further. Before she could change her mind, she opened her door and stepped out of the car.

She hadn't committed to Bryan yet, she reminded herself. He had promised not to pressure her, and she trusted him to keep his word. And who knew? Maybe she *would* fall in love during the next few days. Stranger things had happened.

She wasn't doing a very good job of hiding her reactions to Bryan's Ozarks vacation home. Donovan was aware of the irony in his observation that the woman he suspected of trying to dupe his friend into a marriage-for-money didn't appear to be a particularly skilled actor.

Carrying her bags inside, he watched her face as she took in the professionally contracted decor. Her expressions ranged from impressed to slightly intimidated as they passed through the glass-walled great room, up a curving flight of stairs and down a long hallway to the bedroom suite Bryan had selected for her use.

The luxurious guest suite was located at the farthest end of the hall from Bryan's master suite. Bryan had told Donovan that he and Chloe planned to spend most of this secluded week-long retreat engaging in serious discussions about the future. But Donovan doubted that Bryan intended Chloe to remain at the far end of the hallway throughout the entire week.

"Is, um, something wrong?"

Chloe's hesitant question made Donovan realize that he'd frozen in the doorway of the guest suite, his eyebrows lowered into a heavy scowl. He made a deliberate effort to smooth his expression. He didn't know why he'd been frowning, anyway.

"Just wanted to make sure this room's okay with you before I set your bags down," he bluffed.

Standing in the center of the sitting area that led into the large bedroom, Chloe glanced around at the painstakingly selected antiques and accessories and the invitingly comfortable-looking furnishings. "This looks fine. Perfect."

Maybe it was only nerves that made her sound less than enthusiastic. Maybe just the awkwardness of standing in a bedroom with a near-stranger. Maybe it was that same awkwardness that had his own stomach suddenly tied into knots. "I'll just set these bags beside the, uh, bed,'' he said, then cursed himself for the uncharacteristic verbal fumble.

Chloe nodded and tightened her grip on the bulging tote bag she was holding, as if she were afraid he might try to take it from her.

This was stupid, he thought irritably as he deposited her luggage. While he'd never possessed Bryan's silver-tongued charisma with the ladies, he wasn't usually reduced to stammering. This whole situation was awkward and weird—which must account for the sense of impending catastrophe he'd been fighting ever since they'd stopped at the convenience store.

Leaving Chloe to settle in, Donovan went downstairs to the kitchen. At home there, he opened the refrigerator door and pulled out a soft drink. Popping the top, he downed a third of it in one long guzzle. For some reason, his throat suddenly felt parched.

He would be glad when Bryan arrived so he could get the heck out of this kooky courtship.

As if in response to his fervent wish, the telephone rang. Out of habit, Donovan scooped up the kitchen extension before it could ring a second time. ''Donovan Chance,'' he said automatically—the only way he ever answered a call.

The caller spoke without bothering to identify himself. ''I wasn't sure you'd be there yet. I tried your cell phone. Did you forget to turn it on?''

Donovan reached automatically for his belt. ''Forgot to bring it in. I left it in the car.''

''You didn't have any problems getting there, I hope? The weather's good?''

It wasn't like Bryan to stall with small talk. ''Where are you, Bryan? How long will it take you to get here?''

The sound of a throat being cleared was the only answer, making Donovan's frown deepen. "Bryan? What's going on?"

"Something's come up, D.C. I'm not going to make it there today."

"Damn it, you haven't even left New York, have you?"

"No. The deal here started unraveling this morning and I've had my hands full trying to keep everything together. This is the first chance I've had to even give you a call. I kept hoping I could slip away late this afternoon, but noon tomorrow's going to be the earliest I can get out. I hope to be there by early tomorrow evening."

"And what am I supposed to do with your house-guest in the meantime? Leave her here by herself?"

"I don't think that's a good idea, do you?"

Donovan sighed. "Damn it, Bryan."

"Look, I know you have things you'd rather be doing…"

"Things I *need* to be doing. Like work. Isn't there any way you can hop on a plane tonight and I could take care of things there?"

"I'm afraid not. Trust me, Donovan, this isn't my choice. I'd much rather be there making plans with Chloe than fighting it out here with Childers. I feel like a heel for bailing out on her like this after she's made that long trip. I hope she won't be too angry with me."

"I'm sure she'll get over it," Donovan muttered. Bryan had a way of charming women into forgiving him. Who was he kidding? Bryan's magic even worked on Donovan. He should be steamed over being stuck here like this, but instead, he was agreeing to extend his babysitting services for another twenty-four hours or so.

"So what do you think of Chloe? Is she everything I told you she was?"

"Yeah. She's nice."

The bland words seemed to echo through the phone lines for several long moments before Bryan spoke again. "You have a problem with Chloe?"

"Of course not."

"Something's bugging you, I can tell. What is it?"

"Nothing. I'm just wondering how I'm supposed to entertain her until you get here. She didn't agree to come away on a cozy vacation with me, you know."

"Just keep her company. Take her for a walk or a boat ride or something. Make dinner—maybe throw a couple of steaks on the grill. There's a good selection of DVD movies in the media room, and some new books in the library. Or there's always Scrabble or Monopoly if you get desperate, though I know you're not much of a game player."

With another heavy sigh, Donovan nodded. "We'll get by somehow."

"I'm sure you will. Despite your own glaring personality shortcomings, you'll find Chloe's great company. Maybe she was a bit nervous during the car ride—let's face it, pal, you've been known to intimidate tougher souls than Chloe—but once she's comfortable with you, you'll see how interesting and amusing she can be. Just keep in mind that she's already taken."

"You don't have to worry about that." Donovan hadn't forgotten for one moment that Chloe planned to marry his boss.

"I guess I'd better break it to Chloe that I won't be there tonight."

"She's in her room, unpacking. I'll get her for you."

"Thanks, D.C. I owe you for this."

"You sure do," Donovan muttered, setting the receiver on the counter. "Big time."

She really should have listened to her sister.

Wearing a green satin nightgown and a matching robe, Chloe stood outside on the balcony of the dauntingly elegant guest room. It was a beautiful night—clear, mild, gilded by a bright, nearly full moon—but chilly. Her breath hung in front of her as she leaned against the railing and gazed somberly at the landscape of mysteriously shadowed hills and the glittering lake in the distance. It was a night made for romance and intrigue.

Yet she was spending it alone, wishing she was back in her simple Little Rock apartment.

Grace had warned her that this was a bad idea. She had predicted from the beginning that it wouldn't work out the way Chloe hoped. Little could she have known just how right she would be.

From the moment Bryan had gracefully and effusively apologized for standing her up this evening, Chloe had sensed the plans she'd made disintegrating around her. Or maybe it had all started crumbling even before that—maybe when she'd walked into her living room and found Donovan Chance and her sister glaring at each other.

She wanted to believe she would feel differently now if Bryan had been available to pick her up at her apartment and drive her here himself. If he had been the one to spend the day with her, to dine with her, to bid her goodnight. Instead, she found herself trying to summon a clear mental picture of him. For some strange reason, his image kept metamorphosing in her mind—his thick, glossy black hair and brilliant blue eyes changing to rebellious chestnut-brown strands and metallic-green eyes.

It was obvious that she kept thinking of Donovan because she'd spent so much time with him today. It certainly wasn't anything more than that; she couldn't even say that she liked the man very much. It had been all she could do to make conversation with him during dinner, since he still showed that irritating tendency to answer with a monosyllable any time he could.

The main problem was that at this point, she couldn't say that she particularly wanted to be with Bryan, either, no matter how much more articulate and entertaining he could be than his friend.

She sighed.

"Dreaming of anyone in particular?" a gravelly voice drawled from somewhere beneath her, making her start.

Her heart pounding, she peered tentatively over the balcony. "Donovan?"

On the ground below her, a figure stepped out of the shadows of a bushy tree and into the range of a motion-triggered security light. The resulting yellowish illumination exaggerated the angles and planes of Donovan's firmly carved face, making him appear even more a stranger than he had before. He'd changed from his conservative clothing into a black pullover and black jeans, and he looked very much at home in the darkness.

"What are you doing down there?" She hadn't even realized he was outside, having assumed he was asleep in one of the other bedrooms.

"Just patrolling the grounds."

"So security guard is also on your job description?"

She wasn't surprised when he responded with one of his laconic shrugs, then changed the subject. "Couldn't sleep?"

Leaning her arms against the railing, she looked down at him. "I guess I wasn't as tired as I thought I was."

After a slight pause, he asked, "Want to come outside for a walk?"

"Thanks, but entertaining me *isn't* on your job description."

"Actually, it is. I promised Bryan I'd make sure you aren't bored until he gets here."

Because he made her sound like a cranky toddler he was endeavoring to humor, she replied a bit coolly. "I'm not at all bored."

Bryan had commented often on his second-in-command's commitment; when Donovan Chance took on an assignment, he gave it his full attention. Apparently, he considered her his latest assignment. He was grimly determined to keep her entertained until he could hand her over to his employer. A depressing thought, she discovered, though she didn't care to analyze why.

"I believe I'll turn in now," she said, taking a step back from the rail. "I'll see you in the morning."

He nodded. "Call out if you need anything."

"I'm sure I'll be fine." She couldn't imagine any

reason she would be calling for Donovan Chance during the night.

A shiver went through her as she reentered her bedroom and locked the balcony door. It felt strangely like a premonition—which only reinforced her belief that she was stressed-out about being here at all.

She really should have listened to her sister.

Chapter Three

Donovan didn't require much sleep, but he managed even less than usual during that night. He kept being awakened by the nagging feeling that something was wrong. Or that there was something he should be doing. Because his instincts were so often right, he'd tested all the locks—twice—and he'd patrolled the grounds. He could find nothing wrong, nothing pressing he needed to attend to before morning.

He had to assume he was simply overreacting to the unusual situation he found himself in that evening.

He would be glad when Bryan arrived and he could turn Chloe Pennington over to him—or at least, he *should* be glad. After spending several hours with Chloe, he could understand what had attracted Bryan to her. Had she not already been claimed by his best friend, Donovan might have considered making a move on her, but since Bryan was involved, that, of course, was a line he would never cross.

As for this marriage plan…he still couldn't approve. While he wasn't quite as certain now that Chloe was only after Bryan's money, he still doubted that she had any deep feelings for his friend. There had been some warmth in her voice when she'd talked about Bryan during dinner, but it was almost as if she'd been speaking of a distant acquaintance that she rather liked, rather than someone who should be far more important to her.

He didn't know what her motives were, exactly— whether they were money, security or social connections—but he would bet Chloe wasn't planning to marry Bryan for love. And while Bryan might insist that he wasn't looking for that sort of bond—just as Donovan wasn't interested in falling under some romantic spell—it still seemed that there should be something more to a marriage than amiable companionship.

Shifting restlessly in the bed he usually occupied during his frequent stays here, Donovan told himself he really should mind his own business when it came to Bryan's matrimonial plans. What did he know about marriage, anyway? His own parents had probably considered themselves in love when they married, and that had been a disaster. Bryan's parents could hardly stand each other, but they were still together, apparently content with the arrangement they'd come to during the past forty years.

If Bryan wanted the same sort of cool, convenient alliance, who was he to interfere, even if Bryan would allow him to do so?

Donovan rolled over again in the bed, telling himself to go to sleep and stop fretting about things that were beyond his control. And then he found himself remembering the sight of Chloe standing on that balcony in the moonlight, wearing her floaty nightclothes and looking pretty enough to make a man almost forget how to think.

Donovan was not in a good mood.

Chloe didn't know if he hadn't gotten enough sleep or if he was just bored, but he'd been all but snarling at her ever since she'd joined him in the kitchen. She'd risen early, but he'd already had coffee made and breakfast cooked.

"I hope you like oatmeal," he'd said. "It's one of the few things I know how to cook."

"I like oatmeal," she had answered, warily eyeing his stern expression.

"Good."

She didn't think he'd said a complete sentence since, she mused as they stacked their bowls and spoons in the dishwasher a short time later.

She glanced at the clock on the wall. It wasn't even 9:00 a.m. yet. "What time did Bryan say he would be here?"

If anything, the question only seemed to make Donovan grumpier. "He didn't know, exactly. Late afternoon—early evening, maybe."

The hours in between stretched ahead of her like a gaping hole she had no idea how to fill. She'd packed a couple of books, but it seemed rather rude to close herself in her room for the rest of the day. Or maybe Donovan would prefer that she do just that, freeing him from the responsibility of entertaining her.

After closing the dishwasher door, he ran a hand

through his hair. "It's a nice day out, even though it's cloudy," he said abruptly. "Why don't I show you around the place? You'll probably be spending a lot of time here. It's Bryan's favorite retreat when he needs to get away from the everyday grind."

He seemed to be again assuming that she and Bryan would be married, despite her reminders that she hadn't made that decision yet. Since it didn't seem to serve any purpose to continue reminding him, she merely nodded and said, "All right. I'd enjoy a tour."

He glanced at the thin, coral-colored T-shirt she'd donned with khakis. "You'd better grab a jacket. It's still a little cool out."

For some reason, his words evoked an image of being on the balcony last night, her breath forming silvery clouds in front of her, Donovan gazing up at her from the shadows below. She took an involuntary step backward, as if she could physically move away from that oddly unsettling memory. "I'll be right back."

At least a tour of the grounds would give them something to do for a little while, she reasoned as she pulled on a heavy denim shirt in lieu of a jacket. She was probably growing increasingly aware of Donovan because they had been confined to such tight quarters for so many hours—first in his car, and then in this house. Maybe it would help to be outside.

Donovan was waiting by the back door. He wasn't wearing a jacket, apparently thinking his long-sleeved black pullover and black pants would be warm enough. He'd shown a predilection for black clothing since they'd arrived here, she mused as she stepped outside ahead of him.

Studying him through her eyelashes, she decided it was a good thing he hadn't been dressed this way when he'd arrived at her door to pick her up yesterday. Her over-protective twin might have been tempted to throw herself across the doorstep to prevent Chloe from leaving with this stranger.

Donovan Chance looked just a bit dangerous in black.

As he'd warned her, the air was nippy—though not as cold as it had been last night. The grounds around the house were beautifully landscaped, the plantings lush and natural so that little maintenance was required. Rock and hardwood mulch had been used for pathways through the trees and beds, and several inviting seating areas offered choices of breathtaking lake views, peacefully shaded alcoves or sunbathed clearings. Fountains, waterfalls, birdbaths and feeders added more sensory input.

Chloe was so enthralled by the sheer beauty surrounding her that she almost forgot to watch her feet. She might have taken a tumble if Donovan hadn't reached out to catch her arm, bringing her to an abrupt stop. ''Drop-off,'' he said with his usual brevity.

She glanced down to discover that she stood at the top of a series of flagstone steps that had been carved out of a rather steep hill. The steps were set to one side of the rocky bluff that overhung the lake a hundred feet below. ''Do these lead down to the lake?''

''Eventually—in a roundabout way. It takes a bit of exertion—especially coming back up—but Bryan and I go down that way fairly often. Want to check it out?''

She looked cautiously over the edge of the bluff.

It was a long way down—and she'd never been particularly fond of heights. "How steep does the path get?"

Donovan shrugged. "Steeper in some places than others. But it's safe. Bryan wouldn't take any risks with his guests' welfare."

She didn't doubt that. If there was one thing she had learned about Bryan, it was that he was a stickler for details. "Then I'd like to go down to the lake."

"Hang on a second." Moving around her, he walked down a couple of steps, then turned to look up at her. "The stones are still damp, so watch your step."

He was always so conscientious about taking care of her. Donovan really took his assignments seriously, she mused as she moved cautiously onto the first step.

She was glad she was wearing sneakers for the extra traction they provided. Whether because of them, or because she was enjoying the scenery so much, or just because Donovan hovered so protectively nearby, she felt perfectly safe during the descent.

The area was filled with wildlife—birds, chipmunks, rabbits, deer. Two playful squirrels chased each other across the path, oblivious to the two-legged trespassers in their playground. Laughing at their antics, and perhaps a bit overconfident in the traction of her sneakers, Chloe nearly stumbled when her foot slipped on the uneven edge of a stone step. Donovan steadied her instantly, displaying impressively swift reflexes.

"Thanks," she said, embarrassed by her clumsiness. "I guess I've lived in town for too long."

He didn't immediately release her, but kept a loose grip on her arm as he guided her down another short flight of steps to the next sloping walkway. "Did you grow up in Little Rock?"

"No, I'm from Searcy, originally. Our parents still live there, though they left two days ago for a tenday-long Caribbean cruise. Grace and I moved to Little Rock eleven years ago—right out of high school. We worked days and attended night classes at the University of Arkansas at Little Rock until we earned degrees in business. We always wanted to go into business for ourselves, but we had to wait until the time was right. We opened our shop ten months ago."

It was more than he had asked, of course. Maybe in reaction to Donovan's customary terseness, she tended to babble when he made conversational overtures.

"You and your sister have shared an apartment for eleven years?"

She didn't know whether he found it hard to believe that any two people could cohabit for that long, or if anyone could live with her sister for eleven years—Grace had hardly made a positive first impression with Donovan. She quickly set him straight. "Grace and I don't share an apartment. We did for a while when we first moved to Little Rock, but we found our own places several years ago. Grace was there yesterday to, um, see me off."

"To see you off...or to try one last time to talk you out of going?"

She smiled wryly to acknowledge the hit. "Yes, well..."

Moving ahead of her, Donovan stepped over a large boulder in the path and then turned to offer her his hand. "Careful here. It's slippery."

She hesitated only a moment before placing her

hand in his. His fingers closed around hers, providing support as she made her way carefully over the boulder. He did have a competent air about him. She certainly understood how Bryan had come to depend on him so much.

As soon as Chloe reached the foot of the trail, she decided the trip down was worth the effort. A driftwood-littered gravel beach was shaded by trees that leaned out over the water. On one side of the private inlet sat a neat metal boathouse and a covered wooden deck lined with benches.

"Oh, this is nice." She made a slow circle, peering up the face of the bluff. The back of the house above them was just visible from where she stood. The sun glinted off the many big windows that overlooked the lake. She turned again to study the boathouse and dock. "I suppose Bryan keeps a boat here."

"Two—a ski boat and a pontoon boat. Would you like to go for a ride?"

"Not now, thank you."

"Saving yourself for Bryan?"

The apparent double entendre made her turn to look at him in surprise. Had that actually been a lame joke? If so, it was the first time she'd heard Donovan even attempt to be amusing. Now, how was she supposed to respond? Had she been with Bryan, she would have shot back some similar wisecrack, but with Donovan, her usual wit seemed to get tangled around her tongue.

He didn't wait for her to come up with something to say. Instead, he turned, reached down to scoop up a pebble, and sent it skipping frenetically over the surface of the water.

"Very impressive." She feigned applause. "I

could never do that. Grace, now, is a champion rock skipper.''

He looked skeptical. ''You can't skip a rock?''

''Nope,'' she replied cheerfully. ''I've tried since I was seven, and I've never managed more than a sorry bounce or two before my rock sank straight to the bottom. My dad was convinced I just wasn't trying, but I really did try—until I finally gave up in sheer frustration.''

''Everyone can skip a rock.''

''I can't,'' she said with a shrug. ''Just never figured out the trajectories or whatever.''

''*Everyone* can skip a rock,'' he repeated, looking down at the ground.

''Not everyone.''

He bent to pluck several stones from the ground, then rattled them in his palm as he straightened. ''Here. Give it a try.''

''I'm telling you, Donovan, it's a lost cause. I cannot skip rocks.''

''Of course you can.'' He placed a flat stone in her hand. ''Now, just skim it over the water's surface.''

''Easier said than done,'' she muttered, then obligingly tossed the rock at the water. As she'd expected, it sank with a splash.

''No, you threw it into the water, not across it.'' Donovan handed her another stone. ''Think of the water as a solid surface and let the rock hit it at a glancing angle.''

''Oh, sure. No problem.'' She sighed and threw the second rock, watching in resignation when it immediately disappeared beneath the surface. ''Okay. Have I convinced you yet?''

''You're not trying.''

"If only you knew how many times I've heard that—in exactly that same tone."

He gave her another stone. "Try again. And remember, your object is to skip the rock, not sink it."

That rock made a half-hearted attempt to bounce before it was devoured by a hungry ripple. Chloe turned with a disgusted shake of her head. "I told you. I can't—"

He folded her fingers around another rock. "Try again."

She frowned a little. She didn't quite like the grimly determined look on Donovan's face. He had decided, for some reason, to teach her how to skip a rock—and he didn't seem inclined to give up until she had learned to do so. Because she had a sudden mental picture of herself standing there throwing rocks until sundown, she shook her head. "I'd really rather not. I just can't—"

Her words stumbled to a halt when he moved behind her and covered her hand with his own.

"Like this," he said, pulling her arm back and tilting her hand to a position that satisfied him. "Bring your arm forward and release the rock exactly at that angle."

She had to clear her throat before she could speak. "You're not going to give up until I learn this, are you?"

His low voice rumbled unnervingly close to her ear. "It's just a matter of convincing you that you want it."

"It's, um, not that important a skill to learn."

Without releasing her, he shrugged. "I don't like hearing anyone say, 'I can't.'"

There had to be some significance to that statement,

she mused, trying to distract herself from how closely he stood to her. Something in his past or his psyche made him doggedly stick to a task until it was completed to his satisfaction.

The distraction technique wasn't helping much. She was entirely too aware of the warmth that seemed to radiate from him, and the strength of the hand that held hers. She was definitely spending too much time alone with this man.

She tossed the rock quickly, hoping it would skip so he would move away. It sort of bounced once before sinking.

Sighing, she turned her head to look at him, intending to tell him to forget it. To mark this project off as a lost cause. She couldn't skip rocks, didn't even want to skip rocks, and she saw no reason to waste any more time trying. She was simply going to politely, but firmly, tell him....

Her gaze locked with his cool green eyes...and whatever she had intended to say fled from her mind. His arm was still partially around her, and he stood so close she could feel his breath on her cheek. A quiver of reaction rippled somewhere deep inside her.

It was no longer possible to deny a fact she'd been trying to ignore since she'd first met Donovan Chance. She was very strongly attracted to him. She still couldn't say she liked him—but she was physically drawn to him in a way that worried her.

Though she had tried to tell herself the attraction was simply circumstantial, the rationalization just didn't ring true anymore. She certainly didn't fall for every interesting man with whom she spent time. Which made it even more perplexing that, for the second time in a short period, she found himself intrigued by a strange man.

She moistened her suddenly dry mouth. "Um…"

So abruptly she nearly stumbled, Donovan released her and backed away, shoving his hands into his pants pockets. "Maybe Bryan's the one who should help you with this," he said.

It demonstrated exactly how far her thoughts had wandered when she gaped at him and asked, "What do you mean?"

His left eyebrow lifted fractionally, "Bryan's better at teaching things than I am. He explains things more clearly. He could probably show you how to skip a rock halfway across the lake."

She managed a weak, decidedly fake smile. "I doubt that."

Motioning toward the path they had come down, he moved another step backward. "Ready to head back up to the house?"

"Sure. Bryan could be trying to call us."

His face could have been carved from the same hard rock that made up the bluff behind him. "I have my cell phone. He'd call that number if he wanted to reach us."

Nodding, she made a sign for him to proceed her. "I'll follow you."

"It would probably be better if you go first. Just in case you slip or anything."

She stepped onto the path, but asked over her shoulder, "Still playing bodyguard?"

"I told you. I'm not a bodyguard."

The word always seemed to annoy him. Something else from his past, perhaps. Another little psychological quirk she would probably never understand because she didn't expect to get to know him that well.

She started up the path with as much speed as she could safely manage. She had no intention of falling into his arms, or making a fool of herself in some other way with him.

It seemed the best thing for her to do when she reached the top was to lock herself in her room with a book—rude or not—and try to put Donovan Chance out of her mind. While she was in there, it wouldn't hurt her to do some thinking about her true feelings for Bryan. After all, she'd come here to consider marrying him—only to find herself inordinately fascinated by his best friend.

Definitely something wrong with that picture. Something she should consider very seriously before she made any commitments—to anyone.

It was beginning to look more and more as if Grace had been right all along, she thought somberly, and then winced at the thought of her twin saying, "I told you so."

Donovan hesitated outside Chloe's bedroom door, his hand half raised to knock. For some reason, he was having a little trouble following through with that motion.

After making her way up the path with a speed that had left him almost breathless, she'd closed herself in her room for the remainder of the morning. She'd murmured something about having brought some paperwork along. Rather unexpected, considering this was supposed to be a romantic getaway for her and Bryan—but then, it wouldn't surprise him at all if

Bryan brought a briefcase full of paperwork with him. Maybe Chloe and Bryan really were two of a kind.

Scowling, Donovan rapped on the door more sharply than he had intended.

Chloe opened it quickly. "What is it?"

"It's nearly one o'clock. I thought you might be hungry."

She looked surprised, as if the morning had slipped away from her. "I didn't realize it was so late. I hope you've already eaten."

"No."

"Then you must be starving. Since you cooked breakfast, I'll fix something for lunch."

"Too late. I've already prepared lunch. I hope grilled chicken and vegetables sound good to you."

"That sounds fine, but you really shouldn't have gone to so much trouble. I let the time get away, but I certainly don't expect you to cook for me."

He shrugged. "I had to eat, anyway. I'll meet you in the kitchen when you're ready."

"I'll wash my hands and be right down."

He really hadn't minded preparing lunch; it had given him something to do other than think about Chloe. He had the table set and the food ready to serve when she joined him.

"This looks delicious," she said, taking her seat. "Don't even think about doing dishes after we've eaten. Cleaning up is the least I can do."

He wouldn't argue with her. If doing dishes made her feel like she was pulling her weight, then he wouldn't try to stop her.

"You're a very good cook," she said a few minutes later.

"I get by as long as I've got a grill and a micro-wave."

Glancing toward the state-of-the-art, chef's dream kitchen attached to the sunny nook in which they were eating, she replied, "You have a lot more than that here."

Following her glance, he nodded. "Bryan always goes top-of-the-line."

"Does Bryan like to cook?"

"He knows how, of course. Even though he's always been able to pay for services, he believes everyone should know ordinary living skills like cooking, doing laundry and basic home and car maintenance."

"That's a very practical point of view. If he ever loses his fortune, at least he'll be able to take care of himself."

Donovan knew she was joking. He knew she doubted—as did he—that Bryan Falcon would ever have to count his pennies.

Donovan had no doubt that *he* would still be there if Bryan lost everything. His loyalty to Bryan had nothing to do with fortune or social position. He wasn't confident that Chloe could say the same. If her relationship with Bryan wasn't based on love but on the promise of financial security, then bankruptcy would certainly put an end to that connection.

When he failed to respond to her quip, Chloe changed the subject. "You told me a little about your recent trip to Venice. Has your work with Bryan involved a lot of travel?"

"At times."

"Do you enjoy it?"

"My work or the travel?"

"Either."

"I like the work. I tolerate the travel because it's part of the job."

She looked vaguely dismayed, reminding him that she'd told him she dreamed of travel.

"I didn't say I dislike the travel," he said, feeling almost as if should apologize for disappointing her. "I enjoy it sometimes."

He must not have convinced her. She changed the subject again. "Have you worked with Bryan since you finished college?"

He stabbed his fork into a cauliflower floret. "I never went to college, actually. I went into the army after high school."

"I didn't realize that. Bryan said you'd been with him since the beginning."

"We've been friends for a long time. Stayed in touch while he went off to college and I went into the military. When he broke away from his father's company a few years ago to start Bryan Falcon Enterprises, he brought me on board."

"Were you still in the army then?"

"No. I'd been out for a while."

"What did you do in the interim?"

"This and that." He didn't want to talk about those years in between.

He knew she was only trying to keep the conversation flowing, trying to avoid those awkward lapses between them. Lapses during which they both became self-conscious and tongue-tied, when stray glances tended to lock and hold for long moments—until Chloe looked away, her cheeks turning pink and her voice becoming a little breathless. He didn't try to convince himself that she was fighting the same inappropriate attraction he was, but there was definitely an awareness between them.

They'd spent entirely too many hours alone together. It would be better for everyone involved if Bryan arrived soon.

Leaving Chloe to clean up, as she had insisted, he went into the smaller of the two offices in the house, the one he always used here. He turned on his computer and spent an hour replying to the most urgent of his e-mails, trying to keep himself occupied. When the phone rang, he answered it absently.

"How's it going there?"

Bryan's voice brought Donovan's attention away from the computer monitor. "Tell me you're in transit."

"Problems there? You and Chloe are getting along okay, aren't you?"

"Well enough. But she didn't come here to spend time with me. Right now she's probably wishing she'd stayed home."

"What have you been doing today?"

"I've been working most of the day. Parker in L.A. wants an answer by tomorrow morning. And Hamilton's got a proposal she wants us to look over soon."

"You can take care of those things later. I'd rather you keep Chloe entertained now. I don't like to think of her bored and lonely while I'm stuck here for the rest of the afternoon. I know you can be entertaining company when you make the effort, so give it a try, will you?"

Donovan made certain his exaggerated sigh carried clearly through the phone lines. "I really do have more important things to do than to babysit your girlfriend du jour, you know."

The words had barely left his mouth when he happened to glance toward the open doorway. Chloe stood there holding a steaming mug. Her face was completely expressionless, but Donovan knew she had heard his cranky complaint. The set of her shoulders let him know she hadn't liked it.

He cleared his throat. "Er…"

"Let me guess," Bryan drawled, as eerily perceptive as always, "Chloe just walked in."

"Yeah."

"Put her on the line, will you? And, Donovan—after you pry your foot out of your mouth and apologize, be nice to her, okay?"

"Bryan wants to talk to you," Donovan said, holding the receiver toward Chloe without bothering to respond to his friend.

She nodded coolly. "I brought you some coffee. I just made it."

"Thanks. I'll drink it out on the deck while you talk to Bryan."

After swapping the mug for the phone, Chloe turned away from him. Pointedly.

Wincing, Donovan carried his coffee out of the room. It wasn't easy walking with both his feet in his mouth, he decided wryly.

Chapter Four

Though Chloe wasn't watching him, she knew Donovan had left the room by the time she spoke into the receiver. "Hello, Bryan."

"I'm glad you're still speaking to me."

"I'm sure you couldn't help being detained there."

"No. Believe me, I've done everything I can to resolve this mess in a hurry so I can join you there, but it's taking longer than I expected. I can't tell you how sorry I am."

"Does this mean you won't be here tonight, after all?"

"No. I still believe I can get away in time to be there this evening. It could be very late, but we can start our vacation first thing tomorrow morning."

It seemed oddly apropos that a cloud crossed in front of the sun at that moment, darkening the room for a moment. What might have been a frisson of

premonition coursed through her. Maybe because the
week had started so badly, she had a sudden feeling
that she really should suggest to Bryan that he stay
in New York.

She'd always believed that when something kept
going wrong, perhaps it wasn't meant to be. Grace
had said repeatedly that Chloe was making a mistake
coming here this week. And then Bryan had been detained. Now Chloe's reactions to Donovan were getting all jumbled and confused—and he thought of her
as a gold digger.

Things were definitely going wrong.

It was only her hesitation to ask Donovan to take
her home, her reluctance to look wishy-washy or pet-
ulant to him, that kept her from canceling everything
with Bryan.

"Chloe—about Donovan," Bryan said, as if he'd
sensed the direction her thoughts had taken.

"What about him?"

"Don't take him too personally. He doesn't mean
to come across the way he sometimes does."

"You're not going to try to convince me his bark
is worse than his bite, are you?"

Bryan laughed softly. "No, I'm not going to try to
tell you that. But he doesn't bite very often—and
never without provocation."

His words weren't particularly reassuring.

Still, she didn't want to seem ungracious, especially since Donovan had been going out of his way
to entertain her. His comment about babysitting
Bryan's "girlfriend du jour" still stung, though. She
hated the idea that he thought of her that way.

She and Bryan chatted for another few minutes,

and then Bryan said he had to go. "The sooner I get back to work, the sooner I can get away," he added.

Chloe hung up the phone, then glanced toward the open doorway. She wasn't looking forward to rejoining Donovan after the crack he'd made to Bryan. She was sure he'd try to apologize, and then they'd get all awkward and embarrassed. It was a scene she would rather avoid, if possible.

She found Donovan in the kitchen, rinsing out his empty coffee mug. "The coffee was good," he said. "Thanks."

"I was making some for myself, anyway."

He set his mug in the dishwasher, then turned to face her. Braced for the awkward apology she expected, she was surprised when he said, instead, "I'm going into town for a few supplies. Want to come along?"

She would like to get out of the house, actually, but there was still that irritating comment hanging between them. "I'm sure you'd like to spend some time by yourself. I have some more paperwork to keep me busy here while you're gone."

"Actually, I'd like you to come along, if you don't mind. I need to buy some groceries, and it will be easier if you're there to help with the selections."

If this was his idea of an apology—or an olive branch, perhaps—it was a strange one. But then, Donovan was definitely a different sort of man from anyone she'd met before.

She still resented being called Bryan's "girlfriend du jour." And she still suspected that Donovan questioned her motives for getting involved with Bryan—and she didn't like him seeing non-existent dollar signs in her eyes. But he *had* given up two days of his busy life to spend time with her in Bryan's absence. He had cooked for her and had done his best to entertain her, she supposed, even though there were things he would admittedly rather be doing. The least she could do was try to be gracious in return, especially since he'd placed her in the position of doing him a favor by going with him.

She kept her reply just a bit cool, because she wasn't going to forget that babysitting crack *too* easily. "Then of course I'll come with you. Just let me get my purse."

She felt him watching her as she left the room, so she kept her chin raised to a regal angle, her back very straight. She intended to make it quite clear to him that she was perfectly capable of taking care of herself. She didn't need a "babysitter"—and that certainly wasn't the way she wanted Donovan to think of her.

Donovan was relieved when Chloe agreed to his plan. He'd concluded that it might be easier to control his thoughts about her if they got out of the house. Out in public with other people.

He probably should have apologized about that babysitting remark. He was fully aware that it still rankled with her. But, damn it, he did feel as if he were babysitting—or bodyguarding, which was even worse.

He didn't know what was wrong with him today— since yesterday, actually. Specifically, since he and Chloe had left her apartment. First there was that itchy sense of impending disaster that had been bugging him for no reason. And then there was his growing physical awareness of Chloe.

It wasn't so strange that he would notice her attributes, of course. She was attractive, if not as stunningly beautiful as most of Bryan's women. Donovan was a normal, healthy male. They'd spent several hours close together. He could still almost feel her slender body brushing lightly against his when he'd stupidly attempted to teach her how to skip a rock. It had seemed like a good idea at the time—something she might consider fun—but he'd quickly realized his mistake.

Standing too close to her—watching her wrinkle her nose in self-derision when she repeatedly sank her stones—hearing her chuckle in resignation at her perceived ineptitude…she'd been entirely too appealing then. Had it been just the two of them involved, with Bryan completely out of the mix, he'd have kissed her there by the water. He doubted that he'd have wanted to stop at kissing.

He *was* sure he would have stopped before discussing marriage—no matter how much he might grow to admire her. He was beginning to strongly suspect that, where Chloe Pennington was concerned, Bryan was thinking with the wrong part of his anatomy.

Not that he blamed his friend entirely for that, he mused, eyeing the slight sway of Chloe's softly rounded hips as she left the kitchen with her shoulders defiantly squared.

To his annoyance, the itchy feeling increased at the back of his neck again the moment he slid behind the wheel of his car. In automatic reaction, he scanned the grounds around them. He saw nothing but trees, brush, rocks, a couple of fat squirrels—nothing to cause him the slightest alarm.

He was beginning to believe he needed a vacation. He hadn't actually taken one in several years.

All during the quiet twenty-minute ride to the nearest town, he tried to ignore that sensation, though he stayed vigilant. There wasn't much traffic in the area, but he found himself studying each battered pickup and late-model sedan that passed them.

Shaking his head in self-disgust, he looked ahead. "Are you in the mood for something sweet?"

"I beg your pardon?"

"There's a little diner near here that serves the best pies I've ever eaten. Want to try it out before we head for the grocery store?"

"Sure. It sounds good."

Though he suspected she was agreeing more for his sake than her own, he nodded and turned right at the next light. The diner wasn't crowded since it was mid-afternoon, too late for lunch and too early for dinner. There were only a couple of vehicles in the small gravel parking lot, which was heavily shaded by the building and several large trees. It was warmer now than it had been earlier, yet, as he pulled into a deeply shadowed parking space, he felt a chill go through him.

He wondered if he was losing it.

"Is your neck bothering you?" Chloe asked from across a small table a short while later.

Realizing he'd been squeezing the back of his neck as if he could make that nagging itch go away, Donovan lowered his hand. "Yes," he said, but he saw no need to elaborate.

"I have ibuprofen in my purse, if that would help."

"It wouldn't. But thanks, anyway."

A waitress with angelic blue eyes and a devilishly

dimpled smile approached their table. "Well, hi, Mr. Chance. Haven't seen you around in a while."

He returned her smile with genuine warmth. "Hello, Judy. It's nice to see you."

"You, too. Mr. Falcon's not with you this time?"

"He's flying in later. I'm sure you'll be seeing him in the next few days. He'll be wanting his pie."

Judy chuckled. "Mr. Falcon does love our chocolate-chip pecan pie. I swear he could eat it every day if he had the chance."

"I'm sure you're right." Donovan nodded toward Chloe. "Judy, this is Chloe Pennington."

"I've seen your picture in the paper," Judy said after studying Chloe a moment. "You're Mr. Falcon's fiancée, aren't you?"

"Well, I…"

"I told Mama your hair was brown. That picture we saw wasn't very good and she was sure it was red, but I told her I doubted Mr. Falcon would be getting involved with another redhead after that last one. Mama never could figure out what he saw in that—"

Donovan cleared his throat. He noted that Chloe looked a bit dazed, but he was accustomed to Judy's chattering. It was her mother who made the pies he and Bryan were so fond of. They'd long since decided that the pies were worth the mostly harmless gossip. "I'll have the coconut pie, Judy. Have you decided what you want, Chloe?"

She glanced at a hand-written list posted on a blackboard near the register. "The lemon meringue, please."

"You want coffee with your pie?" Judy asked, switching easily from gossip to business.

They both accepted, and Judy bustled off.

"I guess I should have warned you that Judy knows everybody's business."

Chloe smiled weakly. "Apparently so."

"Don't let her rattle you. She means well."

"She seems nice."

"She is."

Judy returned and slid two enormous slices of pie in front of them. She looked as though she wanted to stay and talk a bit longer, but a telephone call interrupted her, to Donovan's relief.

Donovan tried to think of something to say to Chloe, but since nothing came to him, he turned his attention to his coconut pie with three-inch-high lightly browned meringue—the diner's specialty. He enjoyed the food—but the itch at the back of his neck didn't go away.

The only conversation between them while they ate consisted of Chloe telling him that he'd been right about how good the pies were here. He replied that he'd been sure she would like them, and then they fell into silence again. Donovan was aware that Judy kept giving them questioning looks, as if wondering why they were there together, and why they were being so quiet, but for once the waitress stayed discreetly in the background. He assumed she had realized that he wasn't in the mood for chitchat today.

There were no other customers in the place when he and Chloe paused at the cash register so he could pay the tab. Judy took his money with a hearty invitation for them to come back soon.

"The grocery store is only a couple blocks away," he said, turning to Chloe just inside the exit door. "If there's anything you particularly want, don't hesitate to say so."

"I would like some fresh fruit," she admitted. "And tea—oolong or Ceylon, if possible. Anything but Earl Grey. I've never developed a taste for that blend."

Donovan rarely even noticed the brand of the tea bags he occasionally dunked in water to make iced tea in the summertime—much less the blend of the leaves encased in the bags. "We'll see what's available."

She reached for the door handle. He beat her to it. With one hand at the small of her back, he opened the door and guided her through it, scanning the nearly empty, gray-shadowed parking lot as he did so.

"You're doing it again," Chloe murmured, eyeing him quizzically. "Acting as if you're guarding me from some supposed danger."

He hesitated a moment, then shrugged, knowing it would do no good to deny that he was on alert. He tried to come up with an explanation that would satisfy her—without revealing the extent of his odd paranoia. "You're involved with a wealthy and powerful man. There are inherent risks in that association, not to mention the possible annoyance of the paparazzi."

"Paparazzi?" She laughed. "I hardly think I'd be of any interest to them."

"You might be surprised," he murmured, noting the way her laughter made shallow dimples appear at the corners of her soft mouth.

As if on an impulse, she patted his arm when they stopped beside the passenger door of his car. "I think it's rather sweet that you're taking such good care of me," she said, her tone gravely teasing.

He surprised himself—and undoubtedly her—by chuckling. "Just doing my job, ma'am."

"I'll be sure and tell your boss to put a commendation in your employee file."

"Do that." He opened her door for her, his faint smile fading at her mention of his boss—the man who *should* be teasing with her in this parking lot. As he headed around the back of the car toward the driver's side, an image of her smile stayed in his mind.

Despite his earlier vigilance, the attack caught him completely offguard. Maybe it was because he'd been so close to getting in his car and driving away. Or maybe because he'd finally talked himself into discounting those nagging, apparently groundless premonitions.

He should have known better. His instincts had always been very accurate. They'd only betrayed him once before—and that, too, had led to disaster.

Something cold and sharp punched into the back of his neck. Someone big and solid pushed him against his car, pinning him there so tightly he could hardly breathe.

Donovan wasn't a small man—six feet tall, a hundred and eighty pounds—but whoever was behind him dwarfed him. Even then, he might have had a chance in a fight—he'd been well-trained in hand-to-hand combat—but whatever had been injected into his neck was already taking effect, blurring his vision, making his stomach lurch.

His legs started to shake, no longer supporting his weight. He would have crumpled had he not been pressed against the car.

He heard a vehicle pull up close to his own, and

got a peripheral impression that it was a van. A side door opened.

"Chloe," he said, but his voice came out only a gasping croak. *Lock the doors,* he wanted to yell. *Blow the horn, do something to get attention.*

Everything went black before he could make his unresponsive tongue form the words.

"Wake up, Donovan. Oh, please wake up." Chloe spoke the words softly, but urgently, trying to penetrate the drug-induced stupor he'd been in since they'd been taken outside the little diner. She was concerned that he'd been out so long, and by his pallor and his very shallow breathing.

What if the bastards had given him an overdose of whatever sedative they had used? What if he didn't wake up at all? She risked speaking a little louder. "Donovan? Can you hear me?"

He lay on his back on a bare blue mattress, both his arms stretched above his head. His wrists were secured by a pair of handcuffs that had been looped around one vertical bar of a black iron headboard. Chloe was on her knees beside him. One end of a pair of cuffs encircled her right wrist, the other end locked around another of the iron bars. She'd never worn handcuffs before, and the metal felt cold and heavy against her skin.

Since she wasn't wearing a watch, and Donovan's had been taken away, she had no idea how much time had passed. She only knew that panic was building steadily inside her with each passing minute.

Hearing a noise from somewhere else in the house, she spoke again. "Donovan? Please open your eyes."

A sound rumbled low in his chest—a cross, she

decided, between a growl and a groan. Whatever it was, she'd never heard a more welcome noise. It proved that he was alive—and, she hoped, beginning to rouse. She laid her hand on his chest, just above the spot from where the groan had emanated. "Donovan?"

His eyes opened to bloodshot slits, focusing immediately on her. His voice had a ragged edge when he asked, "Where are we?"

It amazed her that he seemed to wake almost fully alert. No apparent confusion or disorientation. "I don't know where we are. They brought us here in a minivan with the back windows covered, so I couldn't see out."

"How long have I been unconscious?"

"I'm not sure, exactly. It seemed like hours. We were on the road in the van for a long time."

She watched him test the cuffs that bound him as he asked, "Smooth roads? Like highways?"

"No, rough. Like gravel. Lots of turns and hills."

He nodded, then gave the room a slow once-over, apparently noting the one small, grimy window, the dirty wooden floor bare of any furniture except the iron bed, the single closed door. He was still pale, and his eyes didn't look quite right to her, but he wasn't giving in to any aftereffects he might still be suffering. He seemed wholly focused on assessing their situation and figuring ways to get them out of it.

Having taken thorough inventory of his circumstances, he turned his attention to her. "They didn't hurt you," he said, and it wasn't a question. She suspected he'd come to that conclusion after his first glance at her. Typically, his first thoughts had been about business.

"No. I'm not hurt."

"How many of them were there?"

She almost shuddered as she replayed the scene in her mind. "Three. Two attacked you, while another ripped the car door out of my hand before I could close it and lock it. It happened so fast—before I even knew what was going on."

"Did anyone see them grab us?"

"I don't think so. We were parked in that deep shadow and the van pulled up right next to your car, blocking the view from the road or the restaurant. And they moved so quickly...."

"Did you have a chance to scream?"

"They told me they would kill you if I screamed. You were unconscious and the big man held a gun to your head. I couldn't risk your life."

His left eyebrow rose. "So you just got in the van?"

"I didn't have any other choice."

"You saw their faces?"

"They made no effort to hide them."

What might have been a frown flashed across his face. After a moment, he ordered, "Tell me everything they said."

"They said very little. The whole operation seemed to have been carefully worked out ahead of time. They didn't discuss anything. I tried to find out who they were and what they wanted from us, but they just told me to shut up. I rode sitting in the back of the van with your head in my lap and a gun pointed at me." She somehow managed to keep her voice steady despite the lingering terror of that ride.

He glanced at her lap, as if visualizing the scene, and then he said, "I think it's fairly obvious why they grabbed us."

"Is it?" she asked dryly.

"C'mon, Chloe, your name and your photograph have been in the society pages linking you to Bryan. The gossips have the two of you all but married. Even Judy at the diner recognized you. And I'm Bryan's best friend and closest business associate. This is a simple kidnapping with ransom as the objective."

He was confirming a theory she'd already developed. She'd been aware that there were drawbacks to being involved with a man as wealthy and powerful as Bryan Falcon, even before Donovan had pointed them out during the past couple of days, but she'd considered gossip the most troublesome. She had honestly never imagined her personal safety was at risk. Now, of course, she realized she'd been naive not to consider it.

Bryan obviously hadn't made the same mistake. After all, he'd sent Donovan to escort her to the lake house because he hadn't wanted her to make the drive alone. "Did you and Bryan suspect something like this would happen?"

"Of course not." Donovan's reply was sharp and instantaneous. He looked irritated that she had asked. "We didn't have a clue. If we had, do you honestly believe I'd have been so careless?"

Hearing the self-recrimination in his voice, she shook her head. "But you weren't careless. You were so alert that I even teased you about acting like a bodyguard."

"Some bodyguard," he muttered, flexing his hands within their bindings.

He blamed himself. Chloe made another effort to reassure him. "It happened so fast. It was all so well-planned and executed. They had us before either of us could react."

She could tell that he found no comfort at all in her words.

Another sound penetrated the closed door—a muffled thud that might have been another door slamming shut. The sound of a car being started and driven away followed.

"Do you think they're leaving us here alone?" Chloe asked, looking toward the closed door, not certain if she would be dismayed or relieved if their kidnappers had abandoned them.

How long would it take to die of dehydration? But if their kidnappers were going to let them die, wouldn't they have just killed them already? They'd been rough and abrupt, but neither she nor Donovan had been injured.

Donovan didn't seem to share her concern about the possibility of being stranded. "We should be so lucky," he muttered.

She swallowed. "What do you think will happen now?"

Even as he answered, she could tell he was busy studying the room again, and considering their options. "They'll probably wait a few hours before contacting anyone, just to make sure our absence is noted and people have started to worry about us. When enough time has passed, they'll get in touch with Bryan, give him the standard threats if he should contact the authorities, and then offer him their deal for our safe return."

"What do you think he'll tell them?"

Donovan's mouth twisted into his odd half-smile—the one that held little, if any, humor. "What he'll say initially should probably not be repeated in mixed company. After that, he'll negotiate."

"Will he contact the authorities?"

After a quick glance at the door, Donovan merely shrugged.

Was he worried that they were being monitored? Watched, perhaps?

Biting her lip, Chloe glanced quickly around the room, searching for any evidence of a microphone or a video camera. She saw nothing, but then she wasn't exactly an expert on covert surveillance. She didn't know why, but she had a feeling Donovan was more experienced with such matters.

He shifted on the mattress, making her aware that her hand still rested on his chest. She knew she should move it, but she was reluctant to do so. There was something reassuring about the warmth that seeped through his black shirt, and the steadiness of his heartbeat against her palm. She was disinclined to break that fragile connection.

Without thinking, she tried to lift her right hand to brush back her hair, which had fallen into her face. The handcuff jerked her to a stop, rattling loudly against the iron bar of the headboard. "Damn," she muttered, letting her shackled hand fall to her side.

Donovan looked at her tumbled hair. "Your hair was up this morning."

"They took all my hairpins. As well as my purse, your watch, everything in your pockets, both our belts and our shoes." She shivered as she remembered the rough, impersonal pat-down she'd been subjected to while the biggest of the three kidnappers had held her arms behind her back. His grip had been so tight it had brought humiliating tears to her eyes.

"They seem to have covered all the bases in that respect."

She eyed the heavy metal links skeptically. "They thought we could actually use hairpins to pick the locks on these cuffs?"

Donovan moved one shoulder in a semi-shrug. "They might have been right."

The comment brought her eyes quickly back to his face. "You could do that?"

"I could damned well try."

"In that case…" She reached beneath the denim shirt to the coral, pocketed T-shirt she wore beneath, fumbled around for a moment, then produced a sturdy metal hairpin, which she held in front of him.

Chapter Five

Donovan's eyebrows rose. "You always keep hairpins hidden inside your shirt?"

"When I'm wearing my hair up, I do. My hair's fine and it tends to crawl out of restraints during the day. I usually stash an extra hairpin or two in case I need them. I had this one tucked into my T-shirt pocket. It had fallen down into the seam, which must have kept the guy who patted me down from feeling it."

He opened his right hand. "Let me have it."

She placed the pin in his palm, then frowned when he hid it in his own hair instead of setting to work with it. "Can you see it?" he asked.

The thick hairpin was completely hidden in his brown hair. "No. But aren't you going to try to escape?"

"I'll give it a try when I think it's safe to do so."

"And when will that be?"

He glanced toward the little window, which was so dirty that the light from outside barely penetrated it. "Later."

Was he waiting for nighttime? How many more hours would that be? It had been about four-thirty when they'd left the diner. She estimated that they'd traveled for more than an hour in the van, and then perhaps another half hour had passed while she'd waited for Donovan to wake up. It would be dark soon, but she wasn't sure how much longer she could sit here, bound at the wrist, waiting in dread for that closed door to creak open. It had to be worse for Donovan, flat on his back with his arms fastened over his head.

"Maybe we should try now, while we're alone in here. Maybe they assume you're still unconscious. Maybe we could get out through the window before they realize we've gotten free."

"And maybe someone would come in while I'm fumbling with the cuffs and take away the only potential tool we have. I didn't say I *could* pick the lock. I only said I would try. Even if I succeed, it could take a while."

She had to acknowledge his point, as well as the need for caution, but she hated the thought of spending hours here. In frustration, she tugged at the cuff that held her, growing suddenly claustrophobic against the confinement. The only result was the noisy ring of steel against iron, and a stab of pain in her abused wrist.

"Chloe—relax."

"Relax?" She stared at his impassive face in disbelief. "How am I supposed to relax under these circumstances?"

"We haven't been harmed. We're being left alone. There's no reason to panic."

"Yet," she muttered grimly.

"Don't let your imagination run away with you. No threats have been made against us. These are just common thugs looking to make some quick money. Criminal types aren't overly bright, and they almost always make stupid mistakes. We'll wait until they make one with us, and then we'll take advantage of it."

"You make it sound so simple. How do you know they *will* make a mistake? How do you know they aren't planning to take the money and then kill us? They let me see their faces." She hated the tremor in her voice, the fear she couldn't hide. Especially since Donovan seemed so unnaturally calm and controlled.

But when she looked into his eyes, she saw that he wasn't as controlled as she had believed. His usually cool green eyes were a dark emerald now, gleaming with an anger so hot she could almost feel the warmth. She'd thought his face was expressionless; now, she saw that the muscles beneath his taut skin were tensed into a steely mask. No, most definitely, he was *not* calm.

"They aren't going to hurt you," he vowed, his voice a low growl.

She sat back on her heels for a moment to study him. Beneath her hand, his heart continued to beat steadily, but the pounding seemed a bit faster now. Stronger. "Tell me what you want me to do," she said simply, literally placing her life in his hands.

"Just stay calm and let me handle things now. I'll keep you safe."

Her gaze still locked with his, she moistened her lips and nodded. "Thank you."

He was the one who looked away first. "Bryan's counting on me to watch out for you," he said gruffly.

She swallowed and took her hand off his chest. "This is more than you signed on for when you agreed to 'babysit' for a few hours, isn't it?"

"As I said—I didn't expect this at all. If I had, I wouldn't have been caught off guard, not even for a moment. As for the babysitting crack—well, don't take that personally."

Studying his uncomfortable position, and the dark circles under his eyes that were so noticeable, she knew she couldn't hold a grudge now. "Don't worry about it," she said. "I'm sure you were frustrated because you were being kept from your work for so long."

"That's one explanation," he muttered.

Before she could ask for clarification, the doorknob turned and the door opened. Instinctively, Chloe moved closer to Donovan—though she couldn't have said whether it was to seek protection or to offer it.

The man who walked in was the smallest of the three who had blindsided them. Dark-haired, dark-eyed, his narrow face half covered with a sparse, patchy beard, he walked with a hunch-shouldered shuffle and spoke with a smoker's raspiness. "Y'all need some water or something?"

"We need the keys to these cuffs," Donovan retorted, rattling his restraints.

Their captor gave him a remonstrative look. "Let's not waste time with irrelevancies."

"I would say letting us go is very relevant to your welfare."

Though it was exactly what she had expected, Chloe wished Donovan wouldn't challenge the other man quite so aggressively. It wasn't as if he could defend himself in his current position. Fortunately— at least in her opinion—the other man didn't allow himself to be baited. He looked instead at Chloe, pointedly ignoring Donovan. "Are you comfortable? Is there anything you need?"

"Comfortable?" She looked at the handcuffs. "Hardly."

"Sorry about the restraints. I'm sure you can understand the need for them."

Donovan made a sound of disgust. The other man flicked him a look and then turned back to Chloe. "I can bring you some water, if you like."

"No." She almost added an automatic thank you, stopping herself just in time. She wasn't about to thank her kidnapper for anything short of letting her go.

He nodded. "Call out if you need anything."

With that, he turned and left the room, closing the door firmly behind him.

Donovan muttered an expletive beneath his breath, bring her attention back to him.

"I'm surprised you didn't ask him any questions," she commented. "Like what they want, how long they plan to keep us, what their next step is."

"Questions weren't necessary," he murmured, his gaze still fixed on the door. "I know exactly what's going on."

She frowned. "You learned something from him just now?"

He nodded.

After a moment, she prodded. "Well?"

"Find that hairpin for me, will you?" he requested, instead of explaining.

"Donovan…"

"Let's save the conversation for later."

Something about his tone gave her a renewed sense of urgency. Biting her lower lip, she ran her left hand through his hair until she found the hairpin he'd hidden. He winced a little when she pulled it out. "I'm sorry. Did I pull your hair?"

"Doesn't matter. Put the pin in my right hand."

She did so, then sat back again while he fumbled with the pin and the cuffs. He dropped the hairpin once, which caused him to curse and her almost to panic until she was able to find the pin on the mattress beneath his hands. They both breathed sighs of relief when she gave it back to him.

"If I could just see what I'm doing," he grumbled, starting again.

"Have you done this before? Picked a lock with a hairpin, I mean."

"Once or twice," he answered distractedly, his concentration focused on what he was doing above his head.

Chloe had a feeling there were some interesting stories behind that reply, but this, of course, wasn't the time to ask. For one thing, she didn't want to distract him, possibly causing him to drop the hairpin again.

She didn't know how much time passed while she sat there watching him, listening to him mutter beneath his breath in frustration. Once they heard something crash in another part of the cabin, and they both froze, their heads whipping in the direction of the door. After a moment, Donovan went back to work on the lock.

It was getting darker outside, and their captor hadn't turned on the overhead light when he'd left them. Long shadows filled the room now. The fierce determination in Donovan's eyes made them seem to gleam like a cat's eyes in the gloom.

The lock opened with a muted click. Such a quiet and anticlimactic sound that Chloe almost didn't realize its import. When she did, she caught her breath. "You got it?"

He freed his left hand, lowering it to his side and flexing it to restore the circulation. His right wrist was still shackled, but he unhooked the cuffs from the headboard and levered himself into a sitting position. He swayed. Chloe reached out with her left hand to steady him. For just a moment, he leaned against her for support.

"The sedative must still be affecting you," she murmured, her free arm around him. "Are you okay?"

"A little nauseous, but it's passing."

Drawing a deep breath, he straightened and reached for her cuffed wrist. "Let me see if I can get this open."

Another distant sound made her heart beat faster. "What are you going to do if he catches you doing this?"

"My hands are free now. I won't be taken without a fight this time."

"He's the one who had the gun earlier. What if he still has it on him?"

Instead of answering, Donovan bent his head closer

to her wrist. Even with his hands free—though the cuff still dangled from his right wrist—and with her in front of him, he couldn't immediately free her. Chloe was beginning to worry that this was taking too long, that the dark man would return and catch them.

She kept picturing him holding that gun to Donovan's head while Donovan had been unconscious and vulnerable. She'd had no doubt then that he would pull the trigger if she refused to cooperate, just as she had little doubt that he would shoot them now if he caught them trying to escape—no matter how solicitous of her welfare he'd pretended to be earlier.

Of the three men who had ambushed them, she'd gotten the impression that the small, dark man hadn't been in charge, but he'd been the most dangerous.

"Maybe you had better go without me," she urged in a whisper, as if their captor had his ear pressed to the other side of the door. "You can bring the police back…"

"I'm not going anywhere without you." Donovan's tone was pure steel, making it clear that he expected no argument.

She might have argued anyway, had the lock not given way at that moment. Relief flooded through her when he removed the cuff from her wrist. She shook her hand vigorously. The bracelet hadn't been overly tight, but just being restrained had made it feel as though it were squeezing her.

"Okay?" Donovan asked.

"Yes. Thank you. What do we do now?"

Donovan slid off the bed, his movements steady now, and reached a hand out to Chloe. "We get the hell out of here."

His fingers closed firmly around Chloe's when she took his hand and climbed as silently as possible off the bed. The bed frame creaked when she moved off it, causing her heart to stop for a moment, but Donovan was already moving toward the window. Their stockinged feet made no sound on the wooden floor.

"Damn it."

Chloe had been looking anxiously over her shoulder toward the door. Donovan's mutter brought her head back around. "What? Is the window locked?"

"Nailed shut. There's no way I'll get it open without being heard."

She bit her lip, swallowed, then asked quietly, "Now what?"

In a seemingly automatic gesture, he reached out to run the knuckles of his left hand along her jaw line. "I'm still going to get you out of here."

The brief but oddly intimate contact caught her off guard, causing her to freeze for a moment. Motioning her to stay where she was, Donovan moved silently across the room to the door. With his left hand resting on the doorknob, he listened through the wood for a moment, then tried the knob. It wasn't locked.

"They weren't expecting us to get free," he murmured.

"So what do we do?" Her voice was barely loud enough to reach her own ears.

Holding up his left hand in a silencing gesture, he opened the door a bit wider and peeked carefully out. The handcuff still dangled from his right wrist, but he tried to keep it quiet.

Holding her breath, Chloe tiptoed a bit closer to him, peering over his shoulder into the short, dark hallway outside the room. A gleam of light at the far end indicated where their captor waited. She heard the faint strains of music coming from that direction. A radio, perhaps?

She imagined him sitting in the main room, reading and listening, patiently killing time until his cohorts rejoined him. And then what?

Donovan must have heard something she didn't. He eased the door closed again and put a hand on her forearm. "Back to the bed," he murmured. "Get in the same position you were in before."

"But..."

"Hurry." He almost pushed her back to the bed. Once she was kneeling there, he handed her the closed cuff he had removed from her right wrist. "Hold this at your side," he ordered. "Keep your arm down, as if you're still wearing the cuff."

He was already stretching into the position he'd been in earlier, flat on his back, hands above his head, gripping the empty end of his own cuffs so that it wasn't immediately apparent that he wasn't restrained.

Chloe heard footsteps coming down the hallway now. "What do you want me to do?" she whispered, her heart in her throat.

"Just stay out of my way."

The door opened as the words left Donovan's mouth. The dark man entered, carrying two small plastic cups of water in his left hand. He looked distracted, which Chloe hoped was a good sign. "I brought water," he said. "You'll get something to eat later, when my partners return."

Chloe didn't want to think about his partners returning just yet.

Donovan glared at him. "I hope you're planning

to unlock these cuffs. I can't drink lying flat on my back.''

''Yeah, nice try, Chance. But don't worry, I won't let you drown.''

The dark man walked closer to the bed, extending one of the cups toward Chloe. Suddenly terrified that he would notice the empty bracelet in her hand, she looked quickly at Donovan.

A muscle flexed in his cheek. It was the only warning of his intentions. A heartbeat later, he made his move, coming off the mattress in one smooth, powerful motion. The dangling handcuff clattered against the iron headboard, and the bed frame squeaked loudly. The two cups of water flew, splashing all of them.

Caught completely off guard, the dark man was engaged in a fight almost before he realized what was happening. He stumbled and went down, hitting the wooden floor with a crack.

The scuffle didn't last long. Using his fists and the heavy handcuff bracelet, Donovan efficiently rendered the other man unconscious. Even though she acknowledged the necessity for it, Chloe was a bit taken aback by the cold, controlled violence of Donovan's actions.

She'd thought once before that he looked dangerous dressed in black. Now she knew that he *was* dangerous—no matter what he wore.

He stood and wiped a trickle of blood from the corner of his mouth with the back of his left hand. Apparently, his opponent had gotten in a few defensive blows. ''You said you saw this man with a gun?''

Chloe took a tentative step forward. ''Yes. He was the only one I saw with one earlier.''

"He doesn't have one on him now. It must be in the other room."

A flash of light through the window made Chloe gasp. "That's a car. The others are coming back."

"We'll go out the back. Come on."

He caught her hand, almost pulling her with him as he moved rapidly toward the door. She didn't take time to look around the shabby cabin as they rushed through it. She just wanted out.

A swinging door at the back of the sparsely furnished main room led to a cramped kitchen. Still half-dragging Chloe behind him, Donovan turned the doorknob, shoved the door open and barreled through it.

The cabin was obviously remote. There were no lights to guide their way across the small clearing that lay behind it. They stumbled several times before plunging into the dense forest that crowded around the clearing.

Trying to force her eyes to adjust to the darkness, Chloe looked up at the sky. Tree limbs just leafing out for summer partially blocked the pale moon from her sight. The faint illumination it provided gave them little assistance in making their way across the rocky, uneven ground. Donovan's black clothes made him blend perfectly into the darkness. She was painfully aware that her light khaki pants, denim shirt and coral T-shirt were all too visible.

Already, her thin socks were torn, and she was sure there was a fairly deep cut on her right foot. Afraid that their captors could be right behind them—with shoes, flashlights and guns—she tried to ignore her discomfort and keep moving forward, but she couldn't help stumbling several times. She might have fallen more than once if Donovan had not provided support.

She couldn't help wondering why it seemed easier for him. Was he more accustomed to walking almost barefoot across rocky ground?

"Do you think they're chasing us?" she asked breathlessly.

He helped her over a fallen log. "They won't just let us go. We have to keep moving."

"Can we—" She winced when her foot fell on a spiny pinecone. "Can we get to the road?"

He didn't slow down as he answered in a low voice, "They'll be patrolling the road. Our best bet now is to get as far away from them as possible. They can't know which direction we've gone, so it won't be easy for them to follow."

"But—"

"Chloe." He put a hand at the small of her back, the gesture both supporting her and urging her forward. "Don't talk. Move."

Biting her lip, she made a grim effort to comply.

It was a nightmarish journey. Rocks, fallen branches, pinecones and other debris stabbed into the soles of her feet. Tree branches slashed at her face. Deep holes and sheer limestone bluffs made their passage even more treacherous.

Staying very close to Donovan, Chloe locked her jaws and pressed onward. She was winded, exhausted and in pain, but she refused to given in to her weaknesses in front of Donovan. She would keep going as long as he did—or die trying.

The latter seemed more likely, she thought, a ragged gasp escaping from her when her ankle twisted excruciatingly on a rough patch of ground. She limped after that, but she didn't stop.

By the time Donovan tugged her to a stop, she had entered a zone—moving without thinking, without feeling, without looking from side to side. Swaying on her feet, she blinked at him, barely able to focus on his deeply shadowed features. She concentrated on his eyes, which reflected the faint glow of the moon as he studied her intently.

"Are you all right?" His voice sounded odd—muffled, hollow, distant.

"I'm fine," she answered automatically, her own voice sounding like a stranger's.

"You have to rest. I think it's safe to do so now."

"I can keep going," she insisted, exerting an effort to lift her chin.

"Then *I* need a rest." Still holding her arm, he looked around for a moment, then nudged her toward a large tree. "We'll sit here for a while."

They settled carefully on the ground beneath the tree. The rock-, leaf- and twig-covered ground didn't make a particularly comfortable seat, but it was such a relief to be off her feet that Chloe didn't even think about complaining. She leaned back against the rough bark of the tree with a weary sigh.

The sigh changed almost immediately to a gasp of pain.

Donovan turned quickly toward her. "What's wrong?"

"My feet," she gasped. Spears of pain stabbed upward from the soles of her feet through her legs, up her back, all the way to the base of her neck. There wasn't an inch of her that didn't hurt, but the pain was especially concentrated in her abused feet.

Donovan scooted around to take her right foot in his hands. He had no light to examine her closely, but he ran his fingertips lightly over the bottoms of her torn and filthy socks. As light as his touch was, she winced when she brushed a deep cut. He set her right foot down very gently, then repeated the motions with her left.

"You're bleeding from several cuts. They probably have dirt, maybe even tiny pieces of gravel embedded in them. You've also got some bad bruises and scrapes. It's no wonder you're hurting."

"Aren't *you?* You aren't wearing shoes, either."

"I have a few cuts, but not as many. The bottoms of my feet are more callused than yours."

Of course they were. Her head back against the tree, Chloe closed her eyes and swallowed a moan. She hated looking so weak in front of this tough, strong and very self-sufficient male, but she had just about reached her limit.

"Anybody ever tell you that you're tougher than you look?" Donovan asked as he set her feet carefully on the ground.

A single tear escaped from her right eye. "There's no need to try to flatter me now."

"I don't flatter. I just state facts." He scooted around until he was sitting beside her again and then he pulled her against his shoulder. "Get some rest," he said gruffly. "We're safe for now."

Safe? They were sitting in an unknown forest in pitch darkness while three armed kidnappers searched for them. They had no lights, no food or water, no way to call for help—not even any shoes. They were hardly safe.

And yet she found herself relaxing against Donovan's side, her breath escaping in a long, tired sigh. Allowing herself to float on waves of pain, she closed her eyes and tried to turn off her thoughts.

She would be strong again later. For now, she simply had to rest.

Chapter Six

Donovan didn't know if Chloe was sleeping or just drifting. Her breathing was deep and even, her body warm and limp against his. Remembering the condition of her feet—at least from what he could tell in the dark—he wouldn't blame her if she were whimpering at this point.

Definitely tougher than she looked.

Sitting very still so he wouldn't disturb her, he took a quick assessment of his own physical condition. His face was a little sore from close contact with the other guy's fist. The heavy, skin-chafing handcuff was still clasped around his right wrist, the closed left bracelet still dangling. He'd lost the hairpin back at the cabin, but the annoying weight around his wrist was the least of his problems at the moment.

Chloe sighed and shifted against him. Suspecting that her discomfort was keeping her from resting well, he wrapped his left arm around her and pulled her more snugly into his shoulder. She murmured something unintelligible and nestled into him, hiding her face in his throat as if to hide from everything that threatened them.

No one was getting to her without going through him first, he vowed. And then he loosened his hold on her a bit as he remembered that it was his job to protect her. For Bryan.

Not that he expected Bryan to appreciate his efforts so far. He'd antagonized Chloe's sister, bored Chloe into closing herself in her room with a stack of paperwork, and then carelessly let them get taken captive. He hadn't been careful enough, hadn't been vigilant enough—even though he'd sensed that something was wrong.

He should have listened to his instincts, kept his guard up. Instead, he'd let himself get distracted by…well, by things he'd had no business noticing.

A strand of Chloe's hair tickled his cheek. Without thinking, he reached up with his right hand to brush it away, nearly conking her with the swinging handcuff bracelet. He caught it just in time, then spent several minutes berating himself for almost causing her more pain.

He'd tried to tell her he was no bodyguard. Not anymore, anyway.

He'd say their present circumstances provided ample proof of that.

It was still dark when Donovan roused Chloe. "We should probably move on," he said.

"How long have we been resting here?" she asked groggily, lifting her head from his shoulder.

"I'm guessing about an hour. I haven't heard any sounds of pursuit, but I know they're looking for us somewhere. We can't just sit here and wait for them to find us."

She drew a deep breath and pushed herself upright. The very thought of standing made her want to groan, but she clenched her teeth and accepted Donovan's hand when he rose and extended it to her. The groan almost escaped when her battered feet immediately protested her weight, but she bit it back and took a few halting practice steps. The pain was intense, but she could handle it because she had no other choice. "Which direction?" she asked.

Donovan ran a hand lightly over her tumbled hair in what seemed like a gesture of approval. "Do you want to hold my arm for support?"

"I'll probably have to do that later," she admitted. "But I'll try to make it on my own for a while."

His nod was just visible in the gloom. "Then let's go."

Maybe she took some small comfort in noticing that Donovan was limping, too. While it was reassuring to believe that Donovan was totally in control of this situation, it was also a little nice to know he wasn't completely immune to the mortal weaknesses that were affecting her.

She forged on, following him deeper into the forest, trusting him to make decisions on her behalf. For now.

She started counting her steps. One, two, three, four...the silent cadence was the only thing that kept her moving forward. She told herself that if she could just take ten more steps...and then ten more...she would survive.

They made it over the rocks and fallen limbs that blocked their way, through the heavy brush that appeared in clusters to tangle their feet, along the edge of the many bluffs that filled the mountainous region. "Do you know where we are?" she asked Donovan at one point. "Do you know how to get to a road or a phone?"

"No," he answered simply. "At this point, I couldn't even say what state we're in, though I assume it's either Missouri or Arkansas."

So they were lost. But at least they weren't handcuffed to an iron bed frame at the mercy of three kidnappers. Ten more steps, she told herself, pressing forward. Ten more steps…and then ten more…

Again, it was Donovan who brought them to a halt beside a small, running stream they could easily step over. He knelt beside it and scooped a handful of water into his mouth.

"It isn't safe to drink water from a stream like that," Chloe pointed out automatically.

"I don't happen to have any purification tablets on me. Do you?"

Because she knew the question was rhetorical, she didn't answer.

"Have a drink," he urged. "Just a small amount. You don't want to dehydrate."

Images of microbes and pollution flitted through her mind, but she was thirsty. Just the sound of the trickling water made her mouth feel dry. She knelt beside him.

The water shimmered black in the moonlight. It felt cold when she dipped her hands into it. The night air was cool against her overheated face. She might have felt cold had they not been exerting themselves so much.

The water tasted just a little metallic, but it felt good as it slid down her throat. An owl hooted above her as she swallowed another handful. She had been only marginally aware of the nightlife that shared the forest with them. The occasional rustling in the leaves, or flutter of wings, or distant cry—she'd heard them all, but hadn't paid much attention. Nor had she worried about any wild animals they might encounter.

The predators that frightened her most tonight walked on two legs, not four.

Donovan helped her back to her feet. "You need to rest again," he said, his hands on her shoulders.

"Is it safe?"

"I think so. We've put a lot of distance behind us, and I've been changing direction frequently. It won't be easy for them to track us."

She hadn't even noticed that he'd changed directions. "Can we hide somewhere to rest?"

She didn't like the thought of dozing out in the open again where anyone could stumble onto them.

"Exactly what I had in mind."

He helped her over the stream, then led her a short distance farther to a bluff that rose straight above them. Surely he wasn't expecting her to climb now.

Instead, he pushed a low-hanging branch out of the way to reveal a darker area on the shadowed face of the bluff. "A cave," he said. "I spotted it when I bent down to drink."

Apparently his night vision was better than hers—which shouldn't surprise her. She eyed the dark hole warily. "What if there's a bear or a mountain lion or a family of snakes in there?"

"I'll check." He bent to pick up a good-sized branch at his feet, then moved forward. "Wait here."

Chewing her lower lip, she watched as he bent to poke cautiously around in the hole. She held her breath when he moved farther into the opening. She didn't like having him out of her sight even for that short time, and she was relieved when he reappeared in front of her.

"It looks clean," he said. "And it's well hidden. We'll be safe in there for a while."

When she hesitated, he flashed her a smile, his teeth gleaming for a moment in the darkness. "Have I led you wrong so far?"

It was the first time she actually remembered seeing him smile—and he'd picked a hell of a time for it, she thought with a shake of her head. And yet it disarmed her enough that she moved with him toward the cave.

Cave was a generous description, she discovered when she ducked into the opening with him. *Hole* was more fitting. Indentation, maybe. There was just enough room for the two of them to sit side by side with their legs stretched in front of them. The back of the cave was a bit damp and slimy. For all she knew it could be covered with creepy-crawlies.

She didn't care. She leaned gratefully back, her body going limp against the rock. Shoulder to shoulder, she and Donovan sat in silence while they let their breathing and heartbeats slow from the strenuous hike.

She couldn't see him at all now. No light penetrated the opening. She was glad their shoulders were touching—just for the reassurance of contact, she told herself, closing her eyes. No other reason, of course.

* * *

When she opened her eyes again, the gray light of a cloudy dawn was filtering into the cave and she was lying curled on her side with her head on Donovan's thigh.

With a slight gasp, she lifted her head.

"It's okay." Donovan sounded completely alert, making her doubt that he'd slept at all. "We're safe."

Had he sat there guarding her all this time? She cleared her throat as she righted herself, pushing a hand through her tangled hair. "I'm sorry. I don't know how I ended up in that position—"

"I put you there." He shifted his weight, indicating that he'd gotten a bit cramped serving as her pillow. "You fell asleep. You looked uncomfortable, so I shifted you a little."

She tried to put the feel of his solid thigh out of her mind. "Did you get any rest?"

He shrugged. "Just sitting still felt good."

Maybe their arduous trek had been more difficult for him than he had allowed her to see.

Now that she had a little light, Chloe decided to risk a look at her feet. Sitting cross-legged, she turned her soles toward her. The sight made her grimace.

The bottoms of her once-white socks were now black with dirt and dried blood, with gaping holes revealing the bruised and shredded skin beneath. She didn't even want to think about removing the socks yet. When that time came, they would have to be peeled away—and that was going to hurt.

Still leaning back against the cave wall, Donovan watched her. "You haven't walked barefoot much, have you?"

"Not much," she admitted. "When I was young,

I stepped on a nail once. It tore into my skin and I had to have a tetanus shot. I was so traumatized by that experience that I refused to go barefoot for years. I never got into the habit. Even at home I always wear slippers.''

"That explains your delicate feet. The walk last night must have been hell for you.''

"It wasn't easy. What about you? Are you in the habit of going barefoot outdoors?''

Again, his shoulders moved in a shrug. "I almost never wore shoes when I was a kid. Typical Arkansas redneck kid—wild and barefoot.''

She found it hard to reconcile the composed and sophisticated man who had arrived at her doorstep— the man who had just returned from Venice, who moved among politicians and captains of industry, Bryan Falcon's best friend and trusted confidant— with his description of a wild, barefoot ''redneck kid.''

"So, did you spend much time in the woods?'' she asked lightly.

"A fair bit. Why?''

She placed a hand on her hollow-feeling stomach. "I was sort of hoping you'd know how to scavenge breakfast.''

"I usually carried a bag of supplies with me when I spent a day in the woods.''

She sighed wryly. "Oh, well. I suppose it won't hurt me to diet for a couple of days.''

He gave her a leisurely once-over. "You hardly need to diet.''

She looked quickly toward the cave opening to hide an unexpected and unwelcome blush. "I'm very thirsty again. Maybe I'll risk another drink of that stream water before we move on.''

Donovan's reply was lost in a loud crash of thunder. Chloe started, proving that she was still very much on edge no matter how calm they were both pretending to be. ''It sounds like it's going to rain,'' she said, trying to cover her jumpiness with nonchalance.

The sound of a hard rain filled the cave almost before she'd completed the sentence. A gust of wind pushed a fine mist inside, chilling the cool air even more.

''Yeah, I think it might rain,'' Donovan murmured.

''Great.''

''That's not such a bad thing. Any tracks we might have made last night will be eradicated by a downpour this heavy.''

She knew he was trying to put a positive spin on their circumstances for her sake. She appreciated the effort. ''What's our agenda now?''

''We can wait out the rain here for a while. There's no need to go out in it.''

''And when the rain stops?''

Looping his arms around his upraised knees, he looked toward the opening. ''We move on.''

She kept her own legs outstretched, keeping her poor feet as still as possible. The thought of hiking several more miles was hardly pleasant. The cave was dry and well-hidden—both of which made her reluctant to leave—but they couldn't wait here for rescue. For one thing, no one was looking for them—except their kidnappers.

''Do you think we'll be able to find our way out of the forest before…well, before anyone finds *us?*''

"We're going to be very careful about who finds us. Our biggest problem right now is figuring out which direction to go when we leave the cave. We're probably in the middle of several thousand uninhabited acres. If we go deeper—farther from civilization—it could be days before we stumble across anyone. I hate to risk going that long without food."

"But if we go back the way we came, we could run into the kidnappers."

"Exactly. I'm sure they're still looking for us—and they might well have brought back-up."

"So?"

"We do our best," he replied. "I'll make some educated guesses—and we'll hope for some luck."

"Are you usually lucky?"

It was nothing more than a quip, intended to keep the conversation light. But instead of smiling, Donovan frowned and let the question pass unanswered.

After an awkward moment, Chloe tried again to keep him talking. The weather was always a nice, neutral subject, she figured. "It sounds as though the rain has settled in for a while."

He nodded. "It's coming down hard."

She pulled the denim shirt more snugly around her. "It's getting colder."

"Not much. It's just that the air blowing in is damp, which makes it feel cooler."

"At least the cave is a bit elevated, so the water isn't running in."

She didn't even get a monosyllabic reply that time—just a grunt. They might as well have been back in the car again—only this time she didn't even have passing scenery to entertain her.

It could turn out to be a very long morning, she

thought, leaning back against the cave wall. But at least they were dry, and safe for the moment. She would concentrate on those positive points for now.

She had never been very good at estimating passing time. She'd been sitting close to the cave opening, watching the rain fall in the woods outside, for what seemed like a very long time when she broke the silence to ask, "I wonder what time it is."

Donovan roused from his deep introspection to reply, "Just guessing, I'd say mid-morning. Maybe ten, ten-thirty."

"I hope Grace hasn't heard we're missing yet," she said, vocalizing a concern that had been nagging at her all morning. "She'll be frantic."

"I suppose that depends on whether Bryan chose to contact her—and my prediction is that he won't until he has more information."

"So you think Bryan has been contacted by the kidnappers?"

"Probably. I expect that's what the other two were doing while they were gone."

"You've known Bryan a lot longer than I have. What do you think he's doing now? Has he contacted the police? Called my sister?"

Donovan gave it a moment's thought before he answered. "He hasn't called the police. And he won't take any chance of a media leak, so he probably hasn't told your sister, either."

"So what *is* he doing?"

"He's looking for us. He has contacts. They'll be on our trail quicker than any official agency would be."

"What was it you learned when that man offered

us water yesterday? When he left the room, you said you knew then what was going on.''

Donovan's response caught her by surprise. ''I recognized him.''

Wide-eyed, she scooted around to face him more fully. ''You know him? Who is he?''

''I didn't say I know him. I said I recognized him. I don't think he realized it.''

''So you've seen him before, but you were never introduced?''

''Right. I saw him leaving an office that I was about to enter. It was a couple of weeks ago in New York. The guy probably never saw me—and if he did, he probably doesn't suspect that I recognized him.''

''How *did* you recognize him?''

One of his typical shrugs was followed by, ''I have a good memory for faces.''

''You're sure it was the same man?''

''Yes.''

''So he was in New York. Do you know who he works for—or do you think he and his two cronies cooked this scheme up on their own?''

Donovan shook his head. ''I'd put my money on the CEO of the company Bryan's been trying to take over during the past couple of weeks. It's a hostile takeover, but everything was in place, all the details ironed out. That's why Bryan and I were surprised by the last-minute glitches that cropped up to detain him in New York. They're annoying and time-consuming, but they wouldn't have stopped the takeover.''

''You think Bryan was deliberately detained so we could be taken?''

''Seems too coincidental not to consider that possibility.''

"So you think the condition of our release is for Bryan to stop his takeover attempt?"

"No, nothing that obvious. I'd imagine it's a straightforward demand for ransom. Childers has been complaining that he didn't get enough for his company shares, even though he got all he deserved, probably a bit more than he deserved. Looks like he decided to make a little extra on the side."

"Childers—that's the CEO you mentioned?"

Donovan nodded.

"And he's the type who would do something like this?"

"The guy's a crook. He basically got his company by swindling someone else out of it. He'd almost drained it dry by the time Bryan moved in to take it over. Childers's name has been connected with several crimes—mail fraud, embezzlement, that sort of thing—but there's never been enough evidence to bring him up on charges. Yeah, he's the type who would do this."

"Do you—?"

He looked at her when he faltered. "Do I what?"

"Do you think they ever intended to let us go?"

Donovan's eyes held hers for a moment, and then he looked away.

He had never lied to her, Chloe mused. He simply chose not to answer some of her questions. And maybe that was just as well.

Still, she felt the need to ask just one more question. "Do you think Bryan will find us?"

He answered that one without hesitation. "He'll find us."

"You seem to have a lot of confidence in him."

"I do," he answered simply.

"I hope you're right."

After a few more minutes of listening to the rain fall, Donovan stirred. "How are your feet?"

"Numb. I can't really feel them right now."

"Still thirsty?"

"Not enough to go out in the rain," she answered with a faint smile.

"I'd go get you some water, but I don't have anything to carry it in."

He was so determined to take care of her. A bit wistfully, she found herself wondering if it was only because it was his job to do so. "That's okay."

"I wish I had something for you to eat. I guess we could chew on some acorns or something."

That made her laugh. "No, thanks. I'm not quite that hungry yet."

"You have a nice laugh," he murmured, his gaze on her smiling mouth.

Her smile immediately froze.

Donovan looked away. "Uh—Bryan thinks so, too. He mentioned it when he first told me about you."

Bryan. The name slid between them like an invisible wall.

Funny. Chloe could hardly bring Bryan's face to her mind at the moment.

The rain eventually slowed and then stopped. Chloe inched to the cave opening to peer out again. Water dripped steadily off the leaves of the branches that nearly obscured their hideaway. Swollen by the downpour, the stream ran more swiftly than before. A deer and her fawn drank downstream, then turned and disappeared gracefully into the trees. The sky was still low and gray, but the rain seemed to have ended for a while.

Under any other circumstances, Chloe might have been enjoying this encounter with unspoiled nature.

She wasn't surprised when Donovan said, "We should get moving. Before it starts raining again."

Though it wasn't easy, she nodded. "I'm ready."

"You're sure you can walk?"

That brought her chin up. "I can walk."

"It's going to be wet. Slippery in places."

"I'll be careful."

He placed a hand on her arm when she started to rise. "Chloe—I'm sorry this happened to you. You don't deserve this."

"Neither do you. So let's get going."

His mouth quirked. "Right behind you, General."

His rare flashes of humor always caught her off guard. With a chuckle, she let him help her to her feet. Resisting an impulse to curse against the pain that shot up from her feet, she fell into step behind Donovan.

Ten steps at a time, she told herself. She would make this journey ten steps at a time.

Chapter Seven

Cold waves of anger poured off the black-haired man behind the desk, seemingly lowering the temperature in the room a good ten degrees. Bryan Falcon didn't lose his temper very often—but when he did, the people around him usually ducked for cover.

Jason Colby didn't duck, but he kept his voice as soothing as possible as he completed the report. "We had a possible sighting last night of the van the witness at the diner reported seeing at the same time Donovan and Chloe disappeared. It was reported speeding in north-central Arkansas by a state trooper who lost sight of it after it took a series of sharp turns on twisting side roads. That's also the general area to which we traced the ransom call. There are dozens of hunting cabins and isolated rural buildings where they could be hiding. If they haven't moved on, of course.''

Falcon studied his security officer through narrowed, midnight-blue eyes. "We'll assume for now that they have not. It wouldn't be easy to take Donovan in the first place, much less to keep moving him around, so we'll concentrate the search in that area."

"The St. Francis National Forest covers about a million acres, but I think we can narrow it down more than that. I've marked off several search grids, and the teams have already been set into motion."

"I want them found, Jason."

"Yes, sir."

"In the meantime, I'll keep stalling the callers. They're supposed to contact me again tomorrow. I asked for twenty-four hours to get the ransom together without arousing media suspicion."

Jason frowned. "They didn't argue with you?"

"The guy made a show of blustering and threatening me, but yeah, they gave it to me."

"Interesting."

"Exactly what I thought. Why do you think the guy would sound almost relieved about a delay?"

"Problems on their end."

"Maybe."

Jason cleared his throat and phrased his next question very carefully. "Is it possible that they're willing to stall—because something has happened to their hostages?"

The only change in his boss's expression was the muscle that jumped in his clenched jaw. "Just keep looking for them."

Because Jason had known Bryan long enough to recognize the genuine pain behind the stern control, he nodded and rose quickly to his feet. "We'll find them, Bryan."

Bryan stared at him without really seeing him. "Yes, we'll find them."

He would accept no other possibility.

The rain didn't hold off for long. Donovan and Chloe had been walking maybe an hour when it started again. They ducked under a jutting bluff for cover, but it provided little protection, and both of them got pretty wet. Chloe tried to hide her shivering from Donovan, but she suspected he knew she was cold. He just didn't mention it because there was nothing he could do about it except keep her moving, which he did as soon as the rain stopped a second time.

She was thirsty again, and so hungry that her stomach rumbled and her head ached. She wanted a cold glass of water; a nice, long shower; a hot meal and a soft bed—in that order. And a toothbrush, she added, running her tongue over her teeth. She'd done her best to rinse her mouth and finger-scrub her teeth at the stream they were following through the forest, but she wanted a toothbrush and her favorite mint-flavored toothpaste.

In a futile attempt to distract herself from her discomfort, she made an effort to concentrate on the beauty of nature—which meant trying to ignore the heavy gray sky crowding down on them. Had there been sunshine, the spring leaves would have been a soft, fresh green. The hills and steep valleys were dotted with dogwoods and redbuds in full bloom. She saw an occasional bird or squirrel, but most of the wildlife seemed to be holed up from the dismal weather.

She'd taken her eyes off her feet while she surveyed the area. She tripped over a thick vine, and for once Donovan wasn't fast enough to catch her. She went down hard, landing on her hands and knees.

He was beside her instantly. "Are you all right?"

Embarrassed, she straightened, brushing mud and wet leaves off her hands. "I'm fine."

"Let me see." He took her hands in his, turning her palms up so he could examine them. Fortunately, the ground was still soft from the rain and only her pride had been injured in the fall. The knees of her khaki slacks were damp and filthy now, but the fabric had protected her skin.

Still cradling her hands in his, Donovan frowned down at her. "Can you walk?"

"Of course I can walk." She rolled her eyes. "I just stumbled, Donovan. I'm fine, really."

His face had settled into the rock-hard mask he used to conceal his emotions, but she recognized the glint of anger in his eyes. Though he was still a mystery to her in many ways, she was getting to know him better now. Well enough to know that he was blaming himself for letting her fall. Typical of him.

"You shouldn't have to be going through this," he muttered. "When we get out of here and I get my hands on the people behind this...."

She squeezed his hands gently with her muddied ones. "We'll get out," she said confidently. "And then you can take steps to get justice for what we've been through—legally, of course."

She didn't quite catch his growl of response, but she had a feeling he wasn't too concerned about the legality of the revenge he was plotting.

"Let's keep walking," she suggested. "I'll be more careful."

They moved onward, but this time Donovan was never more than an arm's length away from her. Chloe was both annoyed and reluctantly amused by his obvious assumption that she could hardly take care of herself. She noted that his steps were slowing, too, and that he was limping almost as badly as she was. She took no pleasure in his discomfort, but she focused on it occasionally to remind herself that if he could keep going, she could, too.

She glanced up at the sky, noting that it looked as though the rain could start again at any minute. As if to confirm her prediction, a single fat drop landed on her cheek, sliding off her chin. "How long do you think it's been since we left the cave?"

"I don't know. Maybe four hours. We've got a few more hours until dark."

"We've walked so far. It seems like we'd have come across some sign of civilization."

"Didn't you read about that little girl who was lost in a forest in north Arkansas a year or so ago? She simply slipped away from her grandparents during an outing, and it took hundreds of searchers three or four days to find her. Even then it took the men who found her nearly six hours to return her to her family—and they were riding mules. The forest is big and dense, and the terrain so uneven that it's easy to get lost here and hard to be found."

She swallowed. For once, Donovan had told her more than she wanted to know. She took some comfort in remembering that the child had been unharmed when she was found, even after several nights and days with no food.

She tucked her head and kept moving, looking only at her feet now. She wouldn't risk falling again—and there was nothing ahead except more trees and bluffs. Occasionally, Donovan helped her up a steep incline or over a log or across a large, mossy boulder that blocked their way, but for the most part they traveled in silence.

They were walking along a ridge of rock so narrow that they had to go single-file when Donovan came to a stop so abruptly that she nearly barreled into him. ''What is it?'' she asked, craning to see around him.

''A cabin. More of a lean-to, actually.''

She was looking in the same direction he was, toward a heavy tangle of brush on the other side of a deep, erosion-carved crevasse. Water ran through the crevasse—the same stream they'd been more or less following all day. She didn't see any sign of a building. ''Where?''

''There.'' He nodded toward the heaviest section of brush. ''It's almost covered with vines, but it's there.''

She thought she saw it now, a rickety structure made of boards and metal. ''Abandoned,'' she said with a sigh. No help there.

''Maybe.'' His whole body alert, Donovan seemed to be studying the area intently. Warily.

She lifted her eyebrows. ''What are you looking for?''

''That shelter probably belongs to someone who grows illegal crops in the nearest clearing. It's fairly common in areas this isolated.''

''Marijuana?'' Chloe whispered, her eyes wide.

He nodded.

''Do you think they're still here?'' Shrinking back into the shadow of a tree behind her, she looked around for crazed drug growers with shotguns.

She was relieved when Donovan shook his head. "I think the shelter's been abandoned. I don't see any signs of recent activity. It's still too cool outside for agricultural activities, anyway."

A sudden, exciting thought occurred to her, making her clutch Donovan's arm. "There must be a road that leads to civilization from here. Whoever built this shelter had to have a way to get here."

"There's probably an old logging road or a rough trail of some sort nearby," he agreed, looking as though he'd already considered that possibility.

"We can follow it out."

"We'll have to be careful, but that's exactly what we'll do."

He moved toward the shelter and she started to follow, but he motioned for her to remain where she was. "I want to check the place out. You wait here until I'm sure it's safe."

"What are you expecting to find?"

He shrugged. "If we're lucky—nothing. But there could be animals. Or booby traps."

She moistened her lips. "Booby traps?"

"Drug farmers are notoriously paranoid about being raided by the feds. It's not at all uncommon for them to rig primitive but effective security systems."

"But what if you—"

"I know what to look for," he interrupted, speaking over his shoulder. "Stay put. This won't take long."

Chewing her lip, she sank to the ground beneath the big tree, knowing she was fairly well hidden in the shadows. It felt good to sit again, but she couldn't relax because she worried about Donovan blundering into a dangerous situation.

Not that Donovan ever seemed to "blunder," she mentally amended. She'd never met anyone who seemed more competent, more fully in control. Though she hadn't truly felt safe since they'd been kidnapped in that parking lot—was it really just over twenty-four hours ago?—she'd trusted Donovan to take care of her, and he had. Their captors had greatly underestimated him. She didn't make that mistake.

What had he done, she wondered, to make him an expert on primitive booby traps? Or opening handcuffs with hairpins? Or hand-to-hand combat?

He had told her he entered the military straight out of high school, and there had been a gap between his leaving the military and going to work for Bryan. He'd been evasive about what he'd done during those years. Chloe couldn't help but be curious now.

Donovan wasn't out of her sight for long. Emerging from the brush-covered lean-to, he strode toward the shallow ravine that separated them. He looked satisfied, she decided. Apparently his search had revealed no dangers.

"It's clear," he said, still several yards away from her. "And even better—I found food."

"Food?" She pushed herself to her feet, her stomach growling in anticipation. "Did you say food?"

Still making his way toward her, he nodded. "Some canned fruit, a few canned vegetables. The cans are dusty, but intact. They haven't been here too long—probably since last summer. It should be safe to—"

The words were cut off when he stepped unsuspectingly into a deep hole just before he reached the crevasse. His right leg disappeared to the knee, and he went down hard. His choked cry of pain brought her heart into her throat as she ran toward him, her socks sliding on the damp ground. "Donovan? Are you all right?"

"It's my leg," he answered through clenched teeth, holding his right leg with both hands.

"Your leg?" She knelt beside him, one hand on his back. "Do you think it's broken?"

"I think there's a good chance. *Damn* it."

Apparently he'd stepped into a sinkhole created by soft dirt being washed away from an area of rocks and tree limbs. The heavy rain that morning had softened the ground around the hole, letting it give way when he'd set his foot down. A sharp-edged rock had sliced into his pants leg, and blood made a large, dark splotch on the fabric.

"Oh, my God." She helped him stretch the injured leg in front of him, and then knelt beside it to examine the damage. Pulling the torn fabric out of the way, she was relieved to determine that the cut wasn't deep, though it was bleeding steadily. Nor had broken bone punctured the skin. She couldn't feel a break when she ran her fingertips lightly over his shin, but that didn't mean the bone wasn't cracked. Without an X-ray, there was no way to tell for certain.

"We need to stop this bleeding first." She pulled off her denim shirt, then reached for the hem of her coral T-shirt. "Turn your head."

Though his face was pale and his mouth set in a tight line of pain, Donovan still managed a quizzical look at her. "I beg your pardon?"

"We need fabric for a bandage. I have an extra shirt, so turn your head." No way was she stripping to her undies with him looking. He wasn't hurt *that* badly.

When she was sure he was looking away, she pulled the T-shirt over her head. The cool, damp air swept her skin, tightening her nipples beneath her thin cotton bra and making goose bumps parade down her arms. She snatched up her denim shirt and shoved her arms into the sleeves, drawing it snugly around her. She'd lost a button at some point, but she fastened the ones that remained.

She took the T-shirt in both hands and pulled, trying to rip it. She discovered a moment later that she had invested in a very high-quality fabric. Though it stretched, it wouldn't tear. She muttered a mild curse and tried again.

Donovan reached out to take the shirt from her hands. A few efficient pulls and he had the shirt in shreds.

She sighed and accepted the coral strips from him. "Thank you."

Fortunately, his black pants fit loosely, so she was able to push the right leg up and out of the way. The cut looked clean, and the edges even, so she wrapped one strip of fabric around his leg and tied it securely.

"That should keep the cut clean, anyway," she murmured. "Now what are we going to do about the break?"

He'd made a visible effort to force his pain aside and speak without any show of emotion. "We'll splint it. I saw some short boards lying next to the cabin—probably left over from when it was built. We can use a couple of those to brace my leg and keep the bone from moving if it is broken. We'll secure them with strips of cloth. It won't be ideal, but maybe it'll brace my leg when I walk. I'll rig up some crutches or something to help bear my weight."

She frowned at him. "You're not planning to start walking again?"

"We aren't going to fly out of here."

"Donovan, you can't hike when your leg could be broken."

"Chloe, I have no choice."

"That's crazy."

"Just find some narrow boards to use for the splint, will you?"

Muttering deprecations about foolishly macho men, Chloe searched the small pile of rotting wood for usable boards. She found two that were roughly two feet long and four inches wide, each about an inch thick. Definitely not ideal—but all she had at the moment. Stumbling over the occasional rock or twig—and promising herself she would never step foot outside without her shoes again—she carried them back to where he waited.

With Donovan's help, she splinted his lower leg tightly. Already it was beginning to swell, and she worried that they could be causing more damage than they were preventing, but he refused to listen to her concerns. He fully intended to keep walking as soon as he was upright again, and there didn't seem to be anything she could do to talk him out of it.

"At least rest a few minutes before we start again. You said there was some food in the cabin. We should eat something if it looks safe. And besides," she added as thunder made itself heard in the distance, "it's going to rain again soon."

He nodded. "Help me up."

Wedging her shoulder under his arm, she supported him as he rose, keeping his weight on his left foot. She served as his crutch while they made their way to the shelter. The swinging handcuff bracelet bumped her upper arm, but she ignored it. He was heavy, but he spared her his full weight, hopping on his good foot until they reached the building—which really was more lean-to than cabin.

They ducked through the small door that dangled precariously on its hinges. The inside of the tiny building was dark and dusty, little light filtering in through the one small glass pane set into the back wall. The only furnishings were a couple of rickety chairs, a dust-covered table, and what appeared to be a wood-framed bed covered with a heavy tarp. Against one wall was a rough countertop littered with abandoned supplies—a broken lantern, several stacks of cans, and a box filled with assorted tools and utensils.

Chloe helped Donovan into one of the chairs, caught her breath for a moment, then moved toward the counter. There was no sink for washing any of the dirty items. Nor was there a stove of any sort. ''How do you suppose he cooked?''

''Probably on a portable camp stove—maybe a campfire, though he wouldn't risk much smoke in case of DEA planes flying over.''

She found a battered metal saucepan, the bottom scorched black with soot, sitting upside down on the counter. ''I'll bring water in from the stream to wash a couple of utensils so we can eat.''

''Be careful.''

''I will.'' Carrying the saucepan, she went back outside to the stream. Kneeling beside the stream, she dipped the pan into the water, then drew a deep breath and closed her eyes for a moment, her shoulders sagging.

She hadn't wanted to fall apart in front of Donovan, but she was beginning to despair that they would ever be rescued. They were stranded in a remote cabin probably owned by drug dealers, miles from anywhere, with three armed men on their trail. Donovan's leg could be broken, and she suspected that her bloodied feet were becoming infected. Even if Bryan had been contacted by their kidnappers, he had no way to know where they were now, couldn't possibly be looking for them here.

Maybe they should have stayed where they were. Who was to say that they wouldn't have been released, unharmed, after Bryan paid the ransom? What made Donovan so certain their safety had depended on escape?

She drew a deep breath and forced her shoulders straight. They *had* escaped, and now Donovan was hurt, waiting inside for her to return. He'd been so conscientious about taking care of her; the least she could do was return the favor now.

She scrubbed the pan as best she could with sand, gravel and stream water. When it was as clean as she could manage, she filled it with water and carried it back to the cabin. There was a pinhole leak in the bottom of the pan. Drops of water oozed out of it, but slowly enough that it didn't concern her much.

Donovan was still in the chair, his head back, his eyes closed, his shackled right hand resting on the thigh of his outstretched, injured leg. It was the second time since she'd met him that he looked even slightly vulnerable. The first had been when he'd lain unconscious in that van, his head resting on her lap.

She ran a hand through her damp hair and cleared her throat. "I brought water."

He opened his eyes and straightened, apparently embarrassed to be caught giving in to his weakness for even a moment. "No problems?"

"None. Would you like to lie down on the cot? I can help you—"

"I'd like to eat," he cut in gruffly. "Do you see a can opener over there?"

He was making it quite clear that he didn't want her hovering over him. She carried the box full of tools and utensils to the table and rummaged through it until she found an old-fashioned can opener—along with a few other things that would definitely come in handy. Two partially-burned candles and a box of matches were an especially welcome sight, since it was growing darker every minute in the cabin as the dark clouds gathered again outside. The sight of an unopened bar of soap still in its original wrapper was almost as welcome a discovery as the food.

Dipping the can opener in the pan of water to clean it as best as she could, she turned to the half-dozen cans stacked in one corner of the counter. A fat beetle waddled across the counter top when she poked at the cans, and there was a rustling in the far corner of the cabin that could only be mice—but she put squeamishness out of her mind and concentrated on the food. A large, undented can of fruit cocktail, the label faded but clearly readable, seemed the best bet.

There were no plates, but she scrubbed a couple of dented forks, then set the opened can of fruit in front of Donovan. "You're sure it's safe to eat this?"

He studied the contents, sniffed them, then nodded. "As long as the can was intact, there should be no problem. Trust me, I've eaten worse."

"If you say so."

He offered her the can again. "Go ahead. Have what you want and I'll finish the rest."

"You eat first," she said, turning toward the soap. "I'm going out to the stream to wash up a bit."

"That sounds good. Maybe I'll hobble out to the stream after I've eaten."

"Why don't I bring water back in here, instead?" she countered, picking up the saucepan she'd used earlier, and adding it to the soap and extra strip of T-shirt fabric she already held. "I'd like you to stay off that leg for a little while."

He shrugged. "The longer I wait to get back on my feet, the harder it's going to be when we have to start moving again."

"Still, it won't hurt you to rest some first." She opened the creaky cabin door. "I won't be long."

"Just be careful."

Nodding, she slipped outside.

The sky was so overcast that it looked like twilight, even though she knew nighttime was still officially a couple hours away. Hoping the rain would hold off just a little longer, she set the pan, the scrap of fabric and the soap beside the stream and unbuttoned her shirt.

She wasn't one to strip outside, but she absolutely had to wash. And it wasn't as if there was anyone around to see her, anyway. She only wished she had clean clothes to put on when she finished.

Wearing nothing but her ragged socks, she waded into the shallow, fast-running stream, being very careful not to lose her balance. Kneeling, she used the soap and cloth to scrub herself. She used the pan to scoop water over her hair, which she washed as best she could with the hard bar of soap. She was freezing—her teeth chattering, her skin covered with goose bumps—but she was determined to be as clean as she could get under the circumstances.

She put her clothes back on over wet skin—not a particularly pleasant feeling, but at least they helped warm her a little. Turning the pan upside down, she used it as a little stool so she wouldn't have to sit directly in the mud while she turned her attention to her feet. The wet, shredded socks were somewhat cleaner now and she was able to peel them away from her scabbed feet with only a little hissing and cursing.

Her feet looked awful—bruised, torn, scraped, swollen—but she reminded herself that Donovan was hurt worse. She washed them gently, trying to ignore the pain, concentrating on how good it felt just to be clean.

She didn't really want to put the wet socks back on, but she didn't want to walk barefoot to the cabin, either. She turned the socks upside down so that the relatively undamaged parts were on the bottom to provide some protection for the soles of her feet. Wrinkling her nose at the squishy, soggy feel of wet socks against damp ground, she filled the pan with water and headed back to the cabin.

She was wet, cold, hungry and tired—but Donovan needed her.

Chapter Eight

From his chair at the table, Donovan looked up when Chloe reentered the cabin. He decided right then it was a good thing their unwitting landlord wasn't vain enough to keep a mirror in the cabin. Because he had already discovered that Chloe was fastidious when it came to her cleanliness and appearance, he knew she would be appalled if she could see herself at that moment.

Her hair was wet and slicked close to her head, her denim shirt was wrinkled, dirty and missing a button in the middle, her khaki slacks were liberally splashed with mud and grass-stained at the knees. Her lips were a bit blue from the cold, and there were dark smudges beneath her eyes. She still limped with every step. But he was pleased to note that she didn't look quite as pale and worn-out as she had earlier.

"Your bath must have revived you a bit," he commented.

"It feels so much better to be clean—at least cleaner than I was," she amended, approaching the table.

Her eyes widened when she saw the handcuffs lying next to the half-full can of fruit. The silver metal gleamed in the dim, flickering light of the candle Donovan had set in the middle of the table. "You got the cuffs off."

He nodded and unconsciously rubbed his right wrist. "I found a few usable tools in the box of junk."

"You had to walk over to the counter to get the candle and the matches. Honestly, Donovan, you could have fallen again or reinjured your leg. Why didn't you wait for me?"

"Because it was getting too dark to see in here. And I needed to find out if I could walk on my own."

He thought it best not to mention that he'd also peeked out the door, just to make sure she was all right. He hadn't liked having her out of his sight for that long. What he'd seen had caused him to spend the short time that had passed since getting his stubborn and uncooperative body back under control.

He couldn't recall ever seeing anything more beautiful than Chloe standing unselfconsciously nude in that stream, a gracefully feminine cameo against the heavy gray clouds. It was a vision he would remember for a long time, one he expected to see quite often in his dreams.

Pushing the appealing image out of his mind for the moment, he nudged the can of fruit toward her. "You must be hungry now. Have the rest of this fruit."

Still shaking her head in disapproval at his stubborn refusal to baby his leg, she moved to the other chair. She sank into it slowly, then nearly pitched sideways out of it when the chair wobbled sharply on uneven legs. She steadied herself quickly.

He'd started to move to catch her, but relaxed again when it was obvious that she didn't need his assistance. "Okay?"

She bent to peer beneath the seat of her chair. "Looks like you're not the only one in this room with a broken leg," she murmured, then seemed to immediately regret the flippant words, judging by her self-recriminating expression.

He chuckled, wryly amused rather than offended. They might as well try to find some humor about their situation. It sure beat whining and griping, which wouldn't have benefited either of them. And he was greatly relieved that Chloe hadn't yet succumbed to tears. There was nothing that discomfited him more than a crying woman.

"Eat," he said. "The fruit tastes pretty good."

She picked up a fork with a weary smile. "I'm sure it does. But I'm almost too tired to chew."

But she ate, anyway, and seemed to enjoy the simple fare. She had to have been as hungry as he'd been earlier.

She hadn't even finished eating before the sky opened up again. Rain hammered noisily against the metal room. There were leaks, of course, but nothing too problematic.

In resignation, Donovan figured they might as well spend the rest of the night here and head out again at dawn. They would follow what little excuse for a road they could find, and hope that they found help before anyone dangerous found them.

He was certainly in no shape to defend himself and Chloe against at least three adversaries now.

Except for the sound of the rain, it was quiet in the cabin. Donovan couldn't think of much to say as he rubbed his still-chafed right wrist and glared at his injured leg. It still throbbed from his activity earlier, and he could see that there was some swelling beneath the makeshift splint, but he didn't think the break was too bad if it was broken. Cracked, maybe.

At least the bone didn't seem to have shattered, and hadn't punctured the skin. He'd broken bones before, and he knew this injury was more worrisome than dangerous, but he was still furious with himself for allowing it to happen.

How many more stupid mistakes could he make in front of Chloe? He'd been screwing up since she'd first gotten into his car, finally resulting in her being in this dismal position. He'd bet she never wanted to see him again once they got out of this mess. And he *would* get her out. Or die trying.

It had been well over twenty-four hours since they'd been taken. Donovan had no doubt that Bryan had already mobilized an extensive search, which would begin at the diner where they'd abandoned the car. Jason Colby, Falcon's head of security, would be leading the search—and he was the best. If there had been any witnesses—anyone at all who'd seen the van near his car—Jason and Bryan would find them.

Because he knew them both so well, and because they'd trained and prepared for eventualities like this one, Donovan knew exactly what procedures Jason and Bryan would be following now. The entire area within driving distance of the diner would be marked into sections and teams dispatched to each. Bryan would spare no money or resources for the search— and he had plenty of each. He would be furious—and he wouldn't rest until he knew Donovan and Chloe were safe.

Chloe set the empty can aside, the movement drawing his attention back to her. He was beginning to strongly doubt now that Bryan's selection of a potential mate had been as calculated and cold-hearted as he'd led Donovan to believe.

Bryan had insisted that he'd chosen Chloe because of her qualifications as a potential wife and mother, and Donovan acknowledged those traits now. She was intelligent, competent, composed, resourceful—and stronger than she looked. She'd kept her head during this crisis; he knew plenty of women—and a few men—who would be in hysterics by now. Not once had she complained during the long, difficult night, even though her tender feet had been shredded by the nearly barefoot hike.

But there was more to admire about Chloe, he had to acknowledge. The way her hazel eyes reflected her emotions. The tiny dimples that flirted around the corners of her mouth when she smiled. The graceful sway of her hips when she walked. The silkiness of her hair, the softness of her skin. Her slender waist that emphasized the nice curves of her breasts and hips. Her long, shapely legs.

Since his friend was neither blind nor stupid, Donovan had no doubt that Bryan was aware of those physical attributes.

Donovan was becoming entirely too aware of them himself.

He watched as she smothered a yawn behind her hand. He started to rise, using a heavy stick he'd found propped in a corner for a cane.

Chloe moved to stop him. "What are you doing? If you need something, I'll get it for you."

"I'm just checking out the bed. Maybe it's reasonably clean since it's been covered with a tarp."

"The mattress is probably disgusting."

But they discovered when he pulled off the dirty tarp that there *was* no mattress. The homemade, full-bed-sized cot was made army style, consisting of a heavy wooden frame over which had been stretched a strong green canvas hammock. The canvas was faded and slightly frayed in spots, but looked relatively clean and sturdy.

"It's not too bad," he said, studying the primitive structure. "Certainly as clean as the cave we slept in last night. Why don't you try to get some rest?"

She eyed the bed warily. "You're the one who needs to lie down," she replied. "You shouldn't be standing on that leg. You must be in so much pain."

"It's not too bad," he lied.

It was obvious that she didn't believe him. She glanced toward the cluttered countertop. "I wonder if there's any chance of finding a painkiller among that mess."

Donovan chuckled. "I don't believe I want any of the drugs you'd find in here, thanks."

She wrinkled her nose at him, an expression he found particularly enticing. "I meant an aspirin. Or some other over-the-counter medication, obviously."

Still smiling a little, he shook his head. "I'll be okay."

She looked again at the bed. "I doubt that this cot

is going to be particularly comfortable for you. But then, neither was that cave, I suppose—especially since you had to sit upright all night.''

"I've slept in worse positions."

Moving toward the cot, she cocked an eyebrow at him. "Someday I'd like to hear more about your past adventures."

That comment made his slight smile fade. Though he knew she was mostly teasing, he couldn't respond in the same light tone. There were still too many raw wounds from his adventurous past that were barely scabbed over. He'd rather deal with a broken leg any day rather than have those old emotional wounds examined.

Apparently, she had learned not to expect a response to everything she said to him. Without waiting for him to speak, she motioned toward the bed. "You first. I want you off that leg."

"Actually, I'd like to wash up first. You seemed to feel a lot better after your bath, and I'm pretty grubby myself."

That argument obviously made sense to her. "Of course you want to wash. It really does feel better to be clean."

She hesitated a moment, then sat on the edge of the cot. "I'll turn my back. Unless you need my help, of course."

He felt his mouth kick into another slight smile, though the thought of having Chloe help him bathe was anything but humorous to him. "I can handle it. And I'm not really modest."

It was hard to tell in the deep shadows, but he thought her cheeks went pink before she lay on the cot and turned her back to him. "*I* am," she muttered.

Definitely a good thing he hadn't mentioned checking on her while she was bathing, he decided wryly, tugging his grubby black shirt over his head. He had to drag his gaze away from the sight of Chloe's nicely rounded bottom as he turned to pick up the soap.

She never glanced around as he washed as best he could under the circumstances, using the leaking pan of cold water, the hard bar of soap, and the last dry scrap from the T-shirt. When he was finished and fully dressed again, he pulled the two chairs close together.

"What are you doing now?" she asked, turning around when she heard the chairs scraping against the wooden floor.

He had come to the conclusion that it would be much better if he didn't climb into a bed—not even this sorry excuse for one—with Chloe. "The cot's not really big enough to hold both of us comfortably. I'll sit in one chair and prop my legs on the other. You get some sleep, I'll be fine."

Frowning, she wriggled into a sitting position on the cot. "There's no way I can rest on our only bed while you're sitting in that awful chair with a broken leg. You, I mean, not the chair. Well, both you *and* the chair. Oh, you know what I mean."

He couldn't help smiling again at her disjointed tirade. Funny how often she made him smile, even under these circumstances. "I told you, I'm—"

"Look, this cot is bigger than it looks. There's room for both of us to get some sleep if we're still."

The only way they would fit was to lie pressed together. And that position would most likely drive him insane by daylight. "I don't think we should—"

She didn't let him finish. "Come on, I slept with my head in your lap last night. It's no big deal."

Because he could still very clearly remember the feel of her head on his thigh, her cheek resting close to a very sensitive area—not to mention the sight of her bathing in that stream—he was even more certain he should stay right where he was. "I—uh—"

She stood. After waiting for a rolling grumble of thunder to end, she said firmly, "This storm could go on all night. There's no chance we'll be able to leave before daylight, and little chance that anyone will find us here. If you're really crazy enough to try hiking again tomorrow, you're going to have to get some rest first. And I can't sleep unless I know you do."

She had a stubborn set to her mouth that told him she wasn't going to listen to argument. She was fully prepared to sit up all night if he did argue.

The thought of climbing onto that narrow bed with her was unsettling—but he *was* tired. And, hell, with his leg in a splint, there wasn't much he could do with her in that bed, anyway...not that she'd had anything like that in mind when she'd invited him over, of course.

Since she needed rest and swore she couldn't until he did, he would practically be doing her a favor to get into bed with her.

Satisfied with his logic, he nodded and reached for the stick again.

She sprang to his side. "Let me help you."

It had become apparent to him that Chloe was more comfortable taking care of someone else than she was being cared for. He paused to blow out the candle, plunging the room into near-darkness, then allowed her to assist him to the bed. He motioned for her to take the inside, next to the wall. And then he sat on the edge and lifted his legs carefully onto the cot, his right leg on the outside edge.

It was a close fit, as he had expected, but not much tighter than the cave had been the night before. There were no pillows, of course, so he was lying flat on his back, as was Chloe. Pressed side to side, they lay so still and stiff they could have been plastic mannequins.

This was ridiculous, he thought. Neither of them would get any sleep this way.

"Relax," he advised her. "You won't bother me if you move."

"Donovan?" Her voice was very quiet in the darkness.

He bent his right arm under his head, staring up at the rain-hammered metal roof. "Mm?"

"How far do you think we are from civilization?"

"Don't know. I figure it's quite a way, since the guy who built this place obviously didn't care for company. It's probably an all-day drive with a four-wheel-drive vehicle."

"And how long walking?"

"More than a day." Especially with his leg broken, he added silently.

"How *much* more?"

"I don't know."

After a brief silence, she asked in a small voice, "Are you ever afraid that we *won't* get out?"

For the first time since they'd gotten away from their kidnappers, Chloe sounded scared. Vulnerable. She needed comforting—and while he wasn't very good at that sort of thing, he would do his best.

He shifted his weight, then slid his left arm beneath

her and pulled her onto his shoulder. "We'll get out," he said gruffly. "It's just a matter of not giving up."

Her hand on his chest, she burrowed into his shoulder as if grateful for the contact. But her voice was steady when she said, "I'm not giving up. I just wondered if you ever have any doubts."

"I'm only human, Chloe." Human enough to have a decidedly physical reaction to her nestling against him—but he pushed that awareness to the back of his mind and continued, "I can't help wondering if something else will go wrong. Believe me, I've thought of every bad scenario that could happen to us—from wild animal attacks to a fall from one of those bluffs. But we can't let fear paralyze us if we're going to survive."

He was half afraid his impulsive admission of weakness might increase her anxiety. Instead, she said, "It's kind of nice to know you're worried about those things, too. It makes me feel a little less cowardly."

"Cowardly?" He shook his head against the canvas beneath him. "Chloe, you're one of the least cowardly people I've ever met, man or woman. After all we've been through, I wouldn't blame you if you were a basket case by now, but you've handled everything that's come our way without complaining once."

He wasn't usually one to lavish praise, but he thought she should know he admired her courage and resilience.

There were a lot of things he admired about Chloe Pennington.

"Has anyone ever told you that you can be very sweet?" she asked after a rather lengthy pause.

He couldn't see her face in the darkness, of course, but he knew she was smiling up at him. "*Sweet* isn't a description I've heard very often," he muttered wryly, though he was pleased to note that she sounded more at ease now.

"That's because you come across so tough. But I want you to know how much I appreciate the way you've taken such good care of me throughout this ordeal." Stretching upward, she brushed a light kiss against his jaw.

The contact jolted him like an electric shock, coursing through his veins and spilling into his groin. His arm tightened reflexively around her, but he forced himself to loosen his grip.

It was only gratitude, he reminded himself. And gratitude was all he had a right to accept from her.

"Go to sleep," he said, his voice more curt than he had intended. "We've got a long day ahead tomorrow."

He might have expected her to be rebuffed by his tone—or at least a tad annoyed. Instead, she laughed softly and burrowed more cozily into his shoulder. "G'night, Donovan."

Grunting a response, he stared up at the rain-pounded metal roof and prepared for another near-sleepless night.

It was early Wednesday—before 8:00 a.m.—when Bryan Falcon knocked on Grace Pennington's door. He'd called first, so he knew she would be expecting him. But he was still a bit startled by how quickly she threw open the door.

"Good morn—" he began.

"Where's my sister?" she cut in, glaring at him.

It always amazed him that Chloe and Grace were identical in appearance, yet so different in personality. Chloe was calm, courteous and serene, while Grace was impatient, impulsive and quick-tempered.

He wasn't looking forward to the next few minutes. "May I come in?"

She moved aside, then barely allowed him time to step into the converted warehouse, loft-style apartment before she asked again, "Where's my sister?"

He motioned toward the colorful, contemporary furniture arranged invitingly around the big, airy room. "Maybe we should sit down."

"You're avoiding my question." She planted her feet and fisted her hands on her hips. "I'm starting to lose patience with you."

Patience? He wasn't aware that she possessed any.

As wary as he was of her temper, he softened when he saw the genuine fear reflected in her hazel eyes. She was doing her best to bluster and intimidate him, but, truth was, she knew something was wrong with Chloe—and she was terrified.

Because he could understand those feelings, and because he shared them, he was able to keep his expression pleasant. "We need to talk, Grace."

Her throat moved with a hard swallow. "Just tell me," she whispered. "Is she all right?"

He set his hands on her shoulders and turned her gently toward a bright purple couch.

"Sit," he said, speaking more firmly now to penetrate the fog of fear that seemed to grip her. "I'll tell you everything I know at this point."

Donovan must have been more tired than he had realized. Though he hadn't expected to sleep, he did. Heavily.

The dirty porthole of a window allowed enough sun to seep through that he could tell it was midmorning when he finally opened his eyes. Nine, maybe even ten o'clock, he surmised, startled by the realization. He never slept that late, no matter how tired he was.

It must have been a combination of exhaustion, pain and the dim light in the cabin that had lulled him into sleeping for so long—not to mention the pleasure of having a warm, soft body snuggled against his, he thought, turning his attention to Chloe. He felt her stir, and sensed with a touch of regret that she was waking. They would have to start hiking again soon. Who would have thought he would find himself reluctant to leave this shabby excuse for a cabin?

She opened her eyes and blinked up at him, taking a moment to orient herself. And then she gave him a sleepy smile that brought out the little dimples at the corners of her mouth. "Good morning."

Her voice was sleep-husky, her tone intimate. The sound of it did things to him that he was best not thinking of at the moment. He shifted his hips a bit, pulling away from her just far enough that she wouldn't become aware of just how pleasant he found it to awaken with her.

"Good morning," he said, making an effort to keep his own voice brusque. "Sleep well?"

"Mm-hmm." Still obviously half-asleep, she stretched like a lazy cat, the movement brushing her against him again.

Much more of this, he decided, and he was going to explode. He turned away from her, reaching for the stick he'd left on the floor beside the bed. "I'll see what sort of fruit we're having for breakfast."

"Don't suppose you can stir up some coffee while you're at it?" she asked around a yawn as she, too, rose to a sitting position.

"I wish." He'd just about break his other leg for a steaming mug of coffee, but since that wasn't an option at the moment, he put it out of his mind and limped to the counter.

His leg was bruised and swollen, so sore it required effort not to wince with every step. He knew there was a risk of infection with every break, even simple ones, but he hoped an infection would at least hold off until he and Chloe could walk to safety.

Hearing Chloe moving around behind him, he stood at the counter mentally preparing for the next stage of their journey. His gaze fell on the box of matches they'd left lying on the counter the night before. He slipped that and a small knife into one deep trouser pocket.

He wouldn't be able to carry much and still keep his weight off his leg, but he'd take what he could. They would rig up something in which to carry the remaining few cans of fruit. He figured they had a couple of days of hiking ahead of them—if they were lucky and he led them in the right direction—and they needed all the supplies they could safely carry.

Opening a can of peaches, he set it on the table. "Dig in," he said, handing her one of the forks and taking the other for himself.

The impending walk on both their minds, they ate the fruit quickly and without much conversation. "You're sure you'll be able to walk today?" Chloe asked, nodding toward his leg with a frown.

"I'm sure I have no choice," he answered with a shrug. "The longer we wait here, the more chance both of us have of being hurt again or coming down with infections from the injuries we've already sustained."

She sighed almost imperceptibly, but nodded with characteristic acceptance of logic. "I would like to wash up before we start out."

"So would I. Tell you what, why don't I go first just to make sure it's all clear outside. I won't be long. While I'm gone, see if you can figure out a way to carry cans of fruit that won't weigh either of us down too badly."

"I'll see what I can find. But are you sure you don't want me to walk out with you? I'm afraid you're going to fall again."

He leaned on the heavy stick, demonstrating how sturdy it was. "I'll be fine. I'm able to keep most of my weight off the bad leg."

"Just be careful," she warned him.

"I will."

Trying to minimize his limp for her sake, he made his way to the door and opened it, wincing at the shrill creak of rusty hinges. Someone needed to—

The sight of the scruffy man standing on the other side of the door, holding a shotgun leveled directly at him, made Donovan forget all about the creaky hinges.

Chapter Nine

"What the hell are you doing in my cabin?" the armed man, whom Donovan judged to be in his late fifties, demanded in a harsh voice.

Chloe's gasp from behind Donovan indicated that she had seen the gun. He motioned with his left hand for her to be calm, even as he held the man's gaze with his own.

"I'm sorry for trespassing on your property," he said, keeping his tone placating. "We got lost in the forest and we—"

His faded blue eyes glittering in a weathered, whiskery face, the armed man cut in, "Who do you work for? IRS? CIA?"

Donovan recognized that there would be no negotiating with this guy. He shook his head. "You've got it all wrong. We're on the run. See those cuffs on your table?"

The other man looked away just long enough to spot the handcuffs. Still pointed directly at Donovan's heart, the shotgun never wavered.

Without waiting for a response, Donovan added, ''I took those off last night. The feds are out there looking for us now. They hear a gunshot, they'll come down on this place before you can blink twice.''

The other man frowned, then made a motion with the gun. ''Get out. And then keep going.''

''We're going,'' Donovan said, motioning for Chloe to join him. He wanted to get her out of here before the guy changed his mind about sending them away.

''But my friend is hurt,'' Chloe protested, looking at the angry man in disbelief. ''His leg could be broken. And we don't know which direction to go for help. Couldn't you at least—''

The shotgun leveled directly at Donovan's chest again. ''Out,'' its owner growled. ''I ain't giving you another warning.''

''We're going,'' Donovan assured him again, leaning on the stick as he took a careful step forward.

''And leave that here! That's my good stick.''

Donovan quickly set the stick aside, then held up both hands to show that they were empty. ''No problem. My friend here will help me, won't you, Chloe?''

She still seemed to find it impossible to believe that this man wasn't going to offer them assistance. ''But couldn't we at least—''

His eyes on that steady shotgun, Donovan spoke sharply this time. ''*Now,* Chloe.''

Subsiding into a bewildered silence, she moved beside him and offered him her shoulder for support.

Donovan made sure to exaggerate his limp as they made their way slowly out the door—not that he had to play it up much, since his leg really did hurt like the devil. He wanted to appear as non-threatening as possible to the other man.

The scruffy man watched them suspiciously, staying on guard against any sudden moves. When they were outside, he stepped into his doorway as if to prevent them from going back inside. "Don't come back here," he warned. "You won't be leaving again if you do."

"You won't see us again," Donovan replied.

The door slammed shut. Then immediately opened again. "Get moving!" he shouted. "And stay off my road. I'll be watching it. You know what will happen if I find you again."

"We're leaving." Donovan nudged Chloe toward the woods. "And don't worry, we never saw you."

They made their way as swiftly as possible into the shelter of the trees. Donovan's back itched with the awareness that there was a shotgun aimed right at the center of it.

He heaved a slight sigh of relief when they reached the tree line and slipped into it, letting themselves be swallowed by the shadows. Only then did they hear the crash of the cabin door closing again.

Releasing his grip on Chloe's shoulder, Donovan reached out to prop himself with one hand against the trunk of a large tree, needing a moment to get his equilibrium. He might have seemed calm, but his heart was pounding like a jackhammer against his ribs. He'd been scared that he would do or say something wrong and put Chloe in further jeopardy.

Realizing that Chloe was frowning at him in heavy silence, he lifted his eyebrows at her. "What?"

"You could have at least tried to reason with him."

"I could have," he agreed equably. "But I really wasn't in the mood to get shot today."

"You really think he would have shot us? Even if we had taken the time to make him understand that we—?"

"Chloe," he interrupted her gently. "Do you know what that guy is probably doing right this minute?"

She blinked a minute, then shook her head. "No."

"He's probably searching every inch of that cabin for the listening devices he's certain we've placed there. He's convinced himself by now that I was lying to him, that we're really government agents who were spying on his activities. He doesn't believe I have a broken leg, or that we have no idea where we are. The only reason he didn't shoot us is because he was afraid the sound of shots would make our army of jackbooted partners rush in to rescue us. If we'd waited much longer, he would have taken the chance and shot us, anyway."

"But—"

"He's not sane, Chloe. He's scared and confused and paranoid. There was no chance of negotiating with him without putting both our lives at risk. And besides, there's not that much he could have done to help us, anyway."

Biting her lip, she looked back toward the cabin. "I was just surprised that you cooperated so easily with him."

"What would you have had me do? Tell him he had no right to throw us out of his own cabin? If I *had* tried to fight him, and by some miracle I had overpowered him without getting shot, would you have had me beat him up for protecting his few belongings?''

She sighed. ''Not when you put it that way.''

''If you'd ever stumbled into a bear's den, you'd know how dangerous it is to surprise a wild creature in its lair. That's pretty much what we just did.''

''I take it you've stumbled into a bear's den before?''

''Yeah.'' He glanced back toward the cabin, and pushed away from the tree. ''And we'd better get moving before this particular bear decides to come out and make sure we're gone.''

She hurried to support him. ''I didn't see a car anywhere around the cabin when we left. How do you suppose he got there?''

''He could have been on foot, maybe camping out all night. He obviously hadn't been to the cabin in a while, so maybe he has other hidey holes and switches around between them—to make himself harder to find, of course. If he has a vehicle of some sort, it's probably an old junker to haul a few supplies in.''

''Maybe we could find it. You could hot-wire it, and we could, well, borrow it to get to safety and then make sure he gets it back when we're rescued. Or return an even nicer one, maybe, to compensate him for the inconvenience.''

Donovan cocked an eyebrow at her without pausing in his walking. ''What makes you think I know how to hot-wire a car?''

She responded with a delicate snort. ''Anyone who knows how to open handcuffs with a hairpin would surely know how to hot-wire a car. You do, don't you?''

''Yes,'' he answered with a shrug. ''But it doesn't matter. Even if he's got a vehicle, I'm sure he has it hidden so well that he would find us again before we came across it. It's not worth it, Chloe. We'd be better off walking until we find someone more willing to help us.''

''*If* we find anyone willing to help us.''

''We will,'' he assured her. ''Just remember what you promised me last night. Don't give up.''

He watched her draw her shoulders straighter, her chin rising to a stubborn tilt. ''I'm not giving up. I can keep going if you can.''

''Good. See that big, forked branch over there? It looks to be about the size I need for a walking stick. Want to fetch it for me?''

Stepping carefully over rocks and pinecones, Chloe made her way to the stick and then returned it to him. As he'd hoped, it made a pretty decent crutch.

''It doesn't look exactly comfortable,'' Chloe commented, eyeing him doubtfully as he supported his weight on the sturdy branch.

He shrugged. ''It's okay.''

''You've had worse, right?''

He had to smile a little at her ironic tone. ''Right.''

Muttering beneath her breath, she fell into pace with his slow but steady steps. He wasn't sure what she said, but it sounded like, ''Ten steps at a time.''

Hell of a way to start the new day, he thought again. But at least it had stopped raining. For now.

The befuddled man with the shotgun didn't have to worry about finding them on ''his'' road, Chloe thought later. She and Donovan had been slowly making their way for hours, and had yet to come across anything that actually resembled a road.

Donovan's theory was that the hermit hid his vehicle some distance from the cabin and hiked the rest of the way, either to avoid leading anyone to the place or because the terrain directly around the cabin was too rough to traverse in whatever vehicle he possessed. Apparently, he and Chloe had blundered off in the wrong direction when they'd made their hasty exit from the cabin.

For all he knew, they could be walking deeper into the forest rather than out of it.

"What about supplies? How does he get them to his cabin? There certainly wasn't enough there for him to survive on for more than a day or two." Chloe tried to keep one eye on their path and the other on Donovan as she spoke. She worried about him falling again, or somehow re-injuring his leg. It was insane that he was attempting this walk with a broken bone, but it wasn't as if they really had any other choice, either.

"He probably stashes supplies nearby. Cases of canned food and bottled water, that sort of thing."

Chloe thought of the way Donovan had spoken of the armed man with something close to compassion. "He really is a strange, sad man, isn't he?"

"Yeah. One of those unfortunate cases that slipped through the cracks of the veterans' system."

"You think he's a veteran?"

"You didn't notice the fatigue jacket or the boots?"

"All I saw was the gun," she admitted a bit sheepishly.

He nodded. ''I focused fairly intently on that shotgun, myself.''

He paused, leaning heavily on his improvised crutch, and studied the area ahead. Stopping beside him, Chloe, too, looked forward. The sight was enough to make her gulp. They'd hit rough patches before during the hours they'd spent in this forest, but this time they'd reached a particularly difficult area.

Erosion from an ancient, fast-flowing river had carved a deep furrow into the rocky ground. Still wet from the heavy rains yesterday, the ground around the ravine looked slippery and treacherous. Heavy underbrush lined the narrow clearing they'd been following, and a steep limestone bluff rose on their right, preventing them from going that direction without climbing. Behind them, of course, was a crazy man with a shotgun—and possibly three armed kidnappers.

She felt her shoulders sag. She wasn't giving up, she assured herself. But she was so tired of having one obstacle after another thrown their way. It felt sometimes as if the whole universe was conspiring against them—and yet they'd survived it so far, she reminded herself. Battered, but unbroken. At least for now.

''I don't know about you, but I'm ready for a break,'' Donovan said, making her wonder if he found the scene ahead as daunting as she did.

''Definitely,'' she agreed.

They found a mossy patch of ground in the shade of a twisted old hickory tree. Chloe helped Donovan lower himself to sit, then sat beside him.

It felt good to be off her feet again. It was warmer today than it had been, the sun shining straight down through the holes in the clouds that still covered most of the sky. She wouldn't have preferred the rains of yesterday, but she hoped it didn't get too hot as the afternoon wore on.

Bolstering her courage, she decided to examine her feet. She noted in resignation that her socks were now torn on both sides. Several new scrapes decorated her feet, but she supposed she'd grown accustomed to the constant, nagging throbbing. It was like a dull tooth-ache—unpleasant, relentless, but tolerable for now.

"How are your feet?" Donovan asked, just as she noticed an area of exposed skin on the ball of her right foot that was beginning to look particularly in-flamed and nasty.

Infection, she thought, turning the foot so he couldn't see it as she replied, "They're okay. How's your leg?"

"Hardly bothers me at all."

They were both lying, of course, and they both knew it. But neither felt the need to examine those lies at the moment.

Sitting side by side, their legs stretched in front of them, they sat in silence for a while, resting and con-templating their situation.

Chloe was the one who broke the silence, as usual. "Donovan?"

"Mm?"

"What time do you think it is?"

It didn't surprise her when he glanced up at the sky and answered matter-of-factly, "Around two o'clock. Maybe two-thirty."

She touched her empty stomach. "Too bad we don't have a can of fruit cocktail lying around, isn't it?"

"Mm. Want to try an acorn?"

"Thanks, but I'll hold out for a nice, fresh salad when we get rescued. With lots of crunchy veggies and breadsticks on the side."

He grunted. "You can have the rabbit food. I want meat. Red. Medium-rare. Maybe a baked potato with some butter and sour cream."

"And what would you have for dessert? Personally, I'd like a bowl of sherbet. Pineapple—maybe orange."

"Coconut pie topped with a couple inches of meringue," Donovan countered without even stopping to think about it.

"Your favorite from the diner," she remembered with a smile.

It was obvious that he didn't like to be reminded of the diner where they had been taken. He nodded shortly, his expression grim.

She hurried to keep the conversation moving. "Did your mother make pies like that?"

"My mother didn't do much baking. She sometimes made fried pies for a treat. They were good—especially peach."

He'd mentioned the first day they met that he had no family. "When did you lose her?" she asked quietly.

"I was eleven. She died of an infection that set in after a relatively minor surgery."

Neither his voice nor his expression had changed when he answered her question. She took a chance and asked another. "And your father?"

"Took off when I was six. I never saw him again, and my mother never remarried."

"No brothers or sisters?"

"No."

She bit her lip, then asked, "Who raised you after your mother died?"

"Assorted distant relatives. By the time I was fourteen, I was pretty much on my own."

She remembered his description of himself as a "wild, redneck kid." No wonder he'd been wild.

Her heart went out to the lonely little boy he must have been. And she couldn't help admiring the capable, influential man he had become.

Apparently deciding he'd talked enough about his past, Donovan changed the subject. "I figure we were grabbed about forty-three, maybe forty-four hours ago. Wonder how much progress Bryan's made in tracking us down?"

"He wouldn't have already paid a ransom, would he? Not without proof that we're safe?"

"No." He spoke confidently. "He wouldn't do that unless he knew without doubt that he could grab them while they were trying to collect."

"Do you think the kidnappers are still looking for us?"

"It's a good bet that they are. We're their only bargaining chip. I'm sure they'll try bluffing, try to convince Bryan that they have us and that he'd better pay up quickly or they'll kill us. But Bryan isn't easy to fool. They'll want to find us before we get to a phone. They'd have been watching for news that we've been rescued. Since there has been no such report, they'll likely figure out the truth—that we're still wandering in the forest. They know how treacherous the terrain can be, and it was dark when we headed out. They might even figure we've fallen off a bluff, or have been hurt in some other way."

She touched one of the slats that made up the leg splint they had rigged for him. "They wouldn't be entirely wrong—but I doubt that they could imagine how far we've walked, considering everything."

He let that comment go without answer, which worried her a little. Maybe he thought the kidnappers were closer on their trail than Chloe realized. She spoke quickly to push that worrisome thought out of her mind. "Do you think Bryan has any idea who took us, or why?"

"I wouldn't be surprised if he's coming close to answers, if he hasn't already figured them out. Those last-minute distractions were a foolish mistake on Childers's part. He might as well have given notice that he was trying to detain Bryan in New York for as long as possible."

"If Bryan's reasoned that much out, will he confront Childers?"

"Oh, yeah. If he can find him. And if he does, I'd hate to be in Childers's shoes," Donovan replied with grim satisfaction.

"Then maybe Bryan has tracked us to that cabin. And if he's gotten that far, maybe he knows we're out here. Maybe he's got search-and-rescue teams looking for us even now."

Donovan made an obvious effort not to dampen her optimism. "Maybe so."

She looked up. A few faint trails of high-flying airplanes traced across the spring-blue sky as scattered clouds floated lazily overhead. But she'd seen no small planes or helicopters or anything that implied a search in progress. Whatever Bryan was doing on his end, it was still up to her and Donovan to make as much headway as possible on their own.

She turned to face him, scooting down to his injured leg. "I want to check these bindings."

Keeping her touch as gentle as possible, she adjusted the wooden slats they had used for splint material and made sure the stretchy T-shirt fabric was holding them in place as snugly as possible. She had no idea whether this contraption they'd rigged was protecting the bone from further damage, but she didn't know what else they could do under the circumstances.

She looked up at him. He had bent his head to watch what she was doing, so their faces were very close together now.

"Look like it's going to hold?" he asked without pulling back.

"I hope so. I just don't know if it's doing any good," she admitted.

He shrugged. "It's the best we can do for the moment."

"That's pretty much what I've concluded. Are you in much pain? And tell me the truth, don't be all macho and brush me off."

"It hurts," he answered candidly. "Sometimes more than other times. Just like you must hurt with every step you take. But since the only way we're getting out of here is to keep walking, it does no good to concentrate on the pain."

"I suppose you've hiked on a broken leg before?"

His mouth quirked into that semi-smile that she was finding more appealing all the time. "Something like that."

"I thought so. I just hope your leg holds out until we get ourselves rescued."

Suddenly aware of how close they were sitting, she

told herself she should move away. Their gazes were locked, their mouths only inches apart. She glanced downward, noting that his mouth wasn't curved into a smile now—but it still looked entirely too appealing.

She couldn't help wondering if Donovan Chance kissed as competently and skillfully as he seemed to do everything else.

''We'd better find out.''

His words made her blink. Surely he didn't mean…

''We'd better get going,'' he added, as if he wasn't quite sure she'd heard him.

She must have looked like an idiot, scrambling to her feet with her cheeks on fire, but she needed a little distance from him just then. She barely gave him time to struggle to his feet before she pressed on, making her way very carefully across the treacherous ground—and feeling as though she had just missed stepping onto a path that could prove every bit as dangerous as this one.

They sat in another dark cave, this one a mere indentation in a limestone wall. Donovan's outstretched legs barely fit inside; had they been an inch longer they'd have been sticking out. There wasn't room for either of them to stand up, but it provided a cozy shelter in which to rest for the night.

The sun had been setting when Donovan spotted the cave, and it had been he who'd suggested they stop here for the night. It hadn't been too soon to call it a day as far as Chloe was concerned.

As the hours had worn on, the terrain had become even more perilous. Their progress had been painfully slow and tedious as they had made their way around heavy brush, large boulders, fallen trees, gaping holes and slippery patches of mud left from yesterday's heavy rains. There had been times when it had seemed they were making no headway, when it would have been easier to simply sit down and cry.

She'd kept going because she had no choice—but she had stopped counting her steps. They'd moved at such a snail's pace that it had been too depressing to count that slowly.

"*How* long was that little girl lost in the forest?" she asked after she and Donovan had been resting in the cave for a while in silence.

He must have sensed that she was growing discouraged. "A few days. I can't remember, exactly. It happens often, actually. Hikers are always getting lost, falling off bluffs and whatever, and it sometimes takes days to find them, even with whole teams of searchers."

"It just seems like we would have seen some sign of civilization by now. Something besides that poor, strange man's cabin."

"If we're where I think we are, this is a million-acre forest. Federally protected wilderness, no development encouraged. We're bound to come across someone before too much longer, but it's not so strange that we've been able to wander around for two days without finding our way out."

"What if we're wandering in circles? Maybe heading away from people instead of toward them."

"We're not traveling in circles. Zigzagging a bit, but not circles."

"You're sure?"

"Positive."

Either he really was certain—or he lied as well as he did everything else.

"I'm not giving up," she said wearily.

"I know you're not. But I can't blame you for being discouraged. You're exhausted."

"You must be, too."

"I'm tired, but I slept well last night."

So had she, actually. She'd roused only a couple of times to strange sounds, and both times she'd drifted straight back into sleep, safe and warm in Donovan's arms.

Her growing attachment to him—dependence upon him?—was beginning to worry her. She'd been fascinated by him since the moment she'd met him, but it seemed to be developing into something more than that. Was it only proximity? Only the fact that her safety—perhaps her very life—depended on him now?

Or was it more than that?

She'd long since given up on finding a real hero—a true soul mate. The kind of man she'd fantasized about meeting when she'd been younger and more idealistic. She'd convinced herself that she was willing to settle for a compatible partner—someone she liked very much, with whom she had a great deal in common. Someone like Bryan.

She was beginning to understand how close she was coming to making a huge mistake.

"You're being very quiet all of a sudden," Donovan murmured. "Blaming me for getting you into this mess?"

"I'm trusting you to get me out of it," she replied more lightly than she felt.

"I hope I can justify your faith in me."

"Something tells me you will."

Though it was too dark to see his face clearly, she sensed his frown. "I'll do my best. But, Chloe—I've made mistakes in the past. And people have been hurt because of them."

"We've all unintentionally hurt people."

Shaking his head, he muttered, "That's not what I meant."

She laid a hand on his arm, feeling the tenseness of his muscles. "I know you've led a...colorful past. And I won't deny I'm curious, which is only natural considering how much time we've spent together. But whatever mistakes you've made, I can't imagine any-one more capable or resourceful or tenacious than you've been since those men grabbed us."

She couldn't see his face in the darkness, but he covered her hand with his and spoke quietly, "I'll get you out of this, Chloe."

"We'll get each other out," she replied, leaning her head against his shoulder. "We just need some rest tonight. Tomorrow we'll find civilization."

"And then you can have that salad you've been fantasizing about."

In response to the mention of food, her stomach growled softly. "Actually, that red meat you men-tioned is starting to sound pretty good."

"Then I'll buy you a steak as soon as we find a restaurant," he promised rashly. "With a salad on the side. Followed by sherbet—pineapple or orange, right?"

"You're starting to know me well," she teased.

When he spoke again, his mouth was very close to her ear. "Maybe I am."

All she had to do was turn her head and their lips

would touch. Her curiosity about kissing him would finally be satisfied.

Only a few days ago, Chloe wouldn't have had the courage to move. But the last forty-eight hours had changed her. She had learned to take advantage of every opportunity that presented itself to her.

She turned her head.

Chapter Ten

Chloe's lips brushed Donovan's jaw, just as they had the night before when she'd given him that impulsive good-night kiss. And then she adjusted her aim so that their lips met.

For only one tantalizing moment he responded. His lips moved against hers, warm and firm and skilled. It was wonderful—but unsatisfying. She wanted more.

She could almost feel his urge to take her into his arms and deepen the embrace. A short, hard tremor seemed to course through him at the same time a jolt of pleasure shook her—and then, abruptly, he drew away.

"I'll consider that a very nice thank you," he said, and though he tried to speak lightly, his voice was rough-edged.

She moistened her lips, which still tingled in reaction to that brief contact and ached with a hunger for more. "Donovan—"

"Bryan will be glad to see you if—when—we do find our way back," he added, drawing even farther away from her physically so that they were barely touching now. "Your sister, too, of course. I just hope she doesn't blame all this on Bryan, since she seemed so eager to find fault with him, anyway."

He'd used Bryan's name like a shield—and she realized now it wasn't the first time he had done so.

Leaning back against the cool rock wall, she told herself she shouldn't take his withdrawal as a personal rejection. Under the circumstances, he was being prudent to hold back. After all, he worked for the man with whom she'd been discussing marriage. And he probably wondered—as she did—if their emotions were being heightened by the drama of their situation. If there was a natural tendency to turn to each other because they had no one else to turn to.

"Grace won't blame Bryan for this," she said, deciding to follow his example. "At least…I don't think she will," she added a bit less confidently.

"If she does, she'll just have to get over it. This wasn't Bryan's fault."

"I've already assured you that I know that. And Grace will understand once she hears all the facts."

Donovan grunted. "Yeah. Then she'll probably blame *me*."

"She'll blame the people who are responsible. Just as I do. And you aren't one of them."

After a short pause, Donovan asked, "You and your sister are very close, aren't you?"

"Of course. We're twins. And best friends. I know your first impression of her wasn't good, but she's really a lot of fun. She's big-hearted and generous and has a great sense of humor."

"And a temper."

"And a temper," Chloe agreed wryly.

"Did she get it all? Or have you been known to blow your top occasionally?"

"Oh, I have a temper. It just takes longer to set mine off than it does Grace's."

There was another pause, and then Donovan spoke again. "Do you think your sister will accept your decision to marry Bryan? It would be difficult for you if your twin couldn't get along with your husband."

He'd spoken without any particular emotion, but the word *husband* seemed to reverberate for a moment in the shallow cave.

Chloe swallowed, then replied, "I've told you repeatedly, Donovan, I have not agreed to marry Bryan."

"He's asked you, hasn't he?"

"He suggested it might be an advantageous arrangement for both of us," she replied carefully. "I told him I would consider his proposition."

"You decided to accept, didn't you? You wouldn't have agreed to spend this week with him if you hadn't pretty well made up your mind already."

He *was* getting to know her well. And, truth was, she had almost made up her mind to marry Bryan when she'd agreed to join him here. But things had changed since then.

Was Donovan trying in his not-so-subtle way to find out her true feelings for Bryan? Was he interested only as Bryan's friend—or for more personal reasons?

She decided to answer him candidly. "I had almost convinced myself that I would never have a better offer. Bryan is an extraordinary man and I've grown quite fond of him during the past few weeks. I want a family—children—and I'm not getting any younger. I thought I would be foolish not to at least give his flattering offer careful consideration. But that was before—''

''Before?''

Before I met you. She hadn't grown quite brave enough to let those words escape.

''Before I decided that my sister was right about one thing,'' she answered instead. ''I don't want to marry anyone because it seems like the logical and practical thing to do at the time. I want it to mean more than that.''

''You, uh, really shouldn't be making *any* decisions under these circumstances,'' Donovan said somewhat awkwardly. ''You're exhausted and scared, and you can't think clearly like that. Things that you feel out here—well, you can't trust that they're real.''

So Donovan *was* worried that their emotions were being influenced by their situation. Maybe he was warning himself as much as her. And while she acknowledged the validity of his concerns, she didn't really believe she was letting herself be overly influenced by circumstances.

True, the past forty-eight hours had thrown them together so that they'd had no choice but to get to know each other, to lean on each other and depend on each other. But there had to be more to it than that.

What she was starting to feel for Donovan was too powerful to be mere infatuation, too compelling to be simple attraction. She had never been the sort of woman who fell in love easily—and she wasn't quite ready yet to say she was in love with Donovan—but it was more than circumstantial.

Because she wasn't at all sure of his feelings for *her,* she said simply, "I'm not making any big decisions tonight."

That seemed to satisfy him—at least enough that he let the subject drop. "You'd better get some sleep. We'll start early in the morning."

An outcropping of rock jutted from the cave wall beside her. Using her arm for a pillow, she laid her head on it and closed her eyes while Donovan leaned against the opposite wall. The only sound in the cave came from the wildlife outside.

They wouldn't be nestling together tonight. Donovan had deliberately withdrawn from her since he'd brought up Bryan's name.

He was absolutely right to do so, of course, she reflected as she pretended to sleep. As he'd said, this was no time to make important decisions. Or to take rash actions. After that, she needed to have a long talk with Bryan. And after that...

She couldn't say now whether she and Donovan would ever spend time together after they were rescued. But she suspected that it wouldn't be her decision if they did not.

Grace had worried about her being hurt during this vacation. Chloe had wondered if there was a chance she could fall in love this week.

She spent a long time reflecting on the ironic aspects of those uncanny predictions. It gave her something to do besides think about how very close Donovan sat to her—and how nice it would have felt to be lying in his arms rather than against a cold, hard rock.

* * *

A wireless telephone in his hand, Bryan Falcon sat in the den of his Ozarks vacation home and gazed somberly at the woman sleeping restlessly on the couch across the room. He'd draped an afghan over her earlier and she had stirred, but, to his relief, she hadn't awakened. He'd needed a break from her pacing and questioning.

He'd tried to talk her into taking one of the bedrooms for the night, but she'd refused. She wouldn't sleep, she had vowed, until Donovan and Chloe were safe.

She'd lasted until nearly 2:00 a.m. before sleep had claimed her. Bryan couldn't remember the last time he'd slept, but he couldn't rest yet.

She looked so much like Chloe, he thought, studying Grace's face in the soft glow of the only lamp he'd left on in the room. And yet they were so different. When he was with Chloe, he always felt comfortable. Peaceful.

Peaceful was not the first word that came to mind when he thought of Grace. Neither was *comfortable.* He felt as though there were several large strips of his skin missing after spending the past several hours with her. She most definitely blamed him for the danger her sister was in now.

He'd held on to his patience only because he understood how greatly she had suffered today as the hours had crept by with no word of Chloe. He'd talked her out of calling her parents, but there'd been no way he could make her stay home and leave everything to him. She had insisted on joining him here, on knowing every detail of what he was doing to find Chloe.

There had been no further ransom calls, and that was starting to make him even more nervous.

The kidnappers should be pushing him, demanding that he hand over the money immediately. Even if— and he had to swallow at the thought—even if Chloe and Donovan were dead, the kidnappers should be bluffing, working to convince Bryan that they were unharmed and would stay that way if he paid the ransom.

But something was very wrong on that other end. He knew it…and so did Grace.

Rubbing his forehead, he wondered how he could live with himself if anything had happened to Chloe because of him. And losing Donovan was something he couldn't even think about right now.

Grace shifted on the couch, opened her eyes, then sat straight upright. "How long have I been asleep?"

"A little over an hour."

She looked at the phone in his hand. "Have you…?"

"There's been no word yet. I had the phone set to vibrate so it wouldn't startle you if it rang."

She shoved the afghan away. "What time is it?"

"Just after 3:00 a.m. Are you sure you won't lie down upstairs for awhile? I promise I'll wake you if I hear anything at all."

Wearing the stubborn look he'd come to expect from her, she shook her head. "I couldn't sleep in that room with Chloe's things all around me."

"You could take one of the other rooms."

"I don't want to sleep. I want to find my sister."

"We're doing everything we can, Grace."

"Then do more."

"I know it looks as though I'm not doing enough,

but believe me, I am. I'm just trying to keep it quiet. I want to keep the media away from this as long as possible. It hasn't been easy doing so this long, and we won't be able to hide it much longer, but if the press gets wind of what's happened, we'll have a circus on our hands. That could be dangerous for Chloe and Donovan.''

He'd explained that to her before, but he figured it was worth reiterating. Grace had never experienced the press in full feeding frenzy. He had.

She started to say something else, but was interrupted when Jason Colby walked into the room, a look of grim satisfaction on his face.

Bryan jumped to his feet. Across the room, Grace did the same.

''I've got news,'' Jason announced.

As if she needed reassurance—even if it came from him—Grace moved closer to Bryan. ''Tell us,'' she said, her voice strained. ''Where is my sister?''

With Chloe cradled in his arms, Donovan watched the gray light of another cloudy dawn creep slowly into the shallow cave. The temperature had dropped during the night, and he'd sensed Chloe shivering in her sleep.

He still had the old vet's matches in his pocket, and he had considered building a small fire. But since the cave wasn't ventilated and he was more likely to asphyxiate them than warm them, he'd turned to the only other source of warmth he'd had to offer—body heat.

Chloe hadn't roused when he'd pulled her into his arms, which only proved the extent of her exhaustion.

He decided the cool nights were much preferable

to what they'd have been suffering if they'd been stranded in the forest in August rather than April. Dangerous heat, burning sun, higher risk of dehydration, more problems with insects and snakes…he supposed if they had to be lost in the woods this was the best time for it to happen. The biggest problem with spring was the threat of severe weather—and he'd been hearing thunder rolling in the distance for about an hour now.

Though Chloe still shivered occasionally, her face felt warm when he laid the back of his hand against her cheek. He hoped she wasn't getting sick, though he wouldn't be surprised if she was.

He honestly didn't know how she kept going. Little sleep, less food, only occasional sips of water from the stream, the bottoms of her feet shredded. He was hardly in top shape, himself, but he'd had more experience with this sort of thing—from boot camp to Saudi Arabia and assorted other demanding locales.

As he'd thought several times before, Chloe was definitely tougher than she looked.

He could still almost taste her lips on his. Could still feel their texture, their warmth, their softness. And it took very little stretch of his imagination to fantasize about taking the kiss further and making love with her—in a bed or here in this wannabe cave. Those fantasies had kept him awake all night.

Being neither stupid nor oblivious, he was well aware that Chloe had developed an attraction for him. As mutual as those feelings might be, he was making a massive effort not to let them get out of hand.

He had seen his share of what he'd always thought of as ''battle-zone romances''—relationships that developed rapidly under intense conditions, then fizzled just as swiftly when life returned to normal. He wouldn't risk anything of that sort with Chloe.

For another thing, he would be betraying Bryan—something he'd long ago vowed never to do.

Even if Chloe was starting to have doubts about her future with Bryan, Donovan had no intention of taking advantage of those misgivings. Despite her repeated assertions that she didn't blame Bryan for this situation, he wasn't sure that she wasn't secretly harboring some resentment. The very natural anger she surely felt had to find an outlet. After the kidnappers themselves, she probably directed at least part of it toward Bryan.

Considering Bryan's renowned charm, Donovan didn't think it would take his friend long to get past that repressed resentment once Chloe was safely back with him.

But it wasn't just loyalty alone that was making Donovan hold Chloe at emotional arm's length, though that would have been enough in itself. There was also the niggling suspicion that his own emotions were being unduly influenced by their circumstances. It seemed uncharacteristic of him, but how else could he explain his growing fascination with her?

Sure, she was pretty. And intelligent. Resilient. And brave. Everything he admired most in a woman. But it seemed like more than that this time.

He couldn't stop thinking about her. Couldn't stop watching her. Couldn't help wanting to take care of her, even though she'd proven quite capable of taking care of herself. He'd never been particularly susceptible to battle-zone romance, but he supposed there was a first time for everything.

Since Chloe was going to be a significant part of

his life if Bryan convinced her to marry him—and Bryan's powers of persuasion were legendary—Donovan didn't want to do anything that would create more awkwardness between them than would already exist now. Any lingering feelings he had for her when this was over—well, he would deal with them then.

In the meantime, he would keep things between them friendly, cordial, as pleasant as possible under the circumstances. But not too personal. He had to keep emotion out of it, and rely on logic instead.

She stirred against him, the movement brushing her soft breasts against his chest. And then she opened her eyes and gave him a sleepy smile. "Is it morning already?"

He had to clear his throat hard before he could speak. "Yeah."

Keeping his emotions under control for however long it took to get them out of this forest wasn't going to be at all easy. It was going to be a continuous battle between logic and emotion—and, to his surprise, he couldn't be certain of which would eventually win out.

Definitely a new experience for him.

They had planned to start walking at first light. It was a little after that time when they finally made their way out of the cave, tried to stretch out the stiffness and soreness from their cramped sleeping quarters, and then agreed which direction to head in first.

Thinking she looked pale, Donovan asked Chloe several times if she wanted to wait a while longer before getting started, but she assured him she was ready. The sky was growing darker by the moment, which indicated another impending rainstorm. They needed to make as much progress as possible before it began, she pointed out.

She made it less than three yards before she collapsed.

Donovan caught her just before she hit the ground. The impact knocked the makeshift crutch from his hand, forcing him to stagger, his weight coming down on his injured leg. A sharp hiss escaped between his teeth, and they fell together, but somehow he managed to cushion their landing.

Pushing the awareness of his own pain to the back of his mind, he struggled to sit up. Once he'd accomplished that feat, he bent over Chloe, who lay on her back beside him, her breath escaping in soft moans. "Chloe?"

Her eyelids fluttered. Her voice was very weak. "I—I'm sorry. I think I...fainted."

He touched her cheek. Her face felt hotter now than it had before. Her eyes were glazed and there were dark circles beneath them, in stark contrast to her face, which was pale except for two vivid patches of red on her cheeks.

"You haven't eaten," he murmured, stroking a damp strand of hair away from her face. "And you have a slight fever."

"Slight" was an understatement, of course. She was burning up. But he saw no need to go into technicalities at the moment. "I'll get you some water. Wait here."

"I can walk," she said, but she didn't move.

"Just lie still. I'll be right back."

He groped for his crutch, then used both hands to drag himself upright with it. The stream was nearby, but he had nothing to carry water in. The knife and matches he'd filched from the cabin were still in his pocket, but they did him no good at the moment. He settled for tossing the crutch aside and cupping his hands.

His right foot dragging behind him, he made his way painfully back to Chloe's side. Kneeling beside her sent fiery spears of pain stabbing through his leg; he ignored them as he held his hands to her lips. Water trickled down her chin, but he was satisfied that she drank a little. He fervently hoped it wasn't stream water making her sick—but he suspected the infection in her feet was spreading.

Just the thought of spreading infection made his heart beat faster in fear. He couldn't help remembering that an infection had killed his mother. He had to push those old memories ruthlessly aside to keep his hands steady for Chloe.

When his hands were empty again, he made his way slowly back to the stream, where he removed one of the strips of cloth from his splint and soaked it in the cold water. And then, setting his teeth against the pain, he returned to her.

She was trying to rouse herself, having worked her way up to one elbow. Donovan pressed a hand gently against her shoulder. "Lie back down. You'll get dizzy again."

"I can walk."

"Chloe. Lie down." He laid the cool fabric against her face when she reluctantly complied. "It's still very early. We've got time for you to recuperate awhile before we start moving again."

She closed her eyes, looking suddenly frail and vulnerable. But her chin was firm when she murmured, "I'm not giving up."

An odd pang shot through his chest. His reply was gruff. ''I know you aren't. You never give up, do you, General?''

She didn't smile at the nickname as she had the last time he'd teased her with it. Instead, she whispered, ''Sometimes I do.''

He stroked the cloth against her fever-reddened cheeks. ''Not this time.''

''No. Not this time.'' Drawing a deep breath, she opened her eyes again. ''I'm sorry. I keep holding us up.''

''Hey, I'm the one with the gimpy leg, remember? I'm hardly moving at top speed these days.''

She tried to laugh, a rather pathetic attempt. ''We're both in pretty sorry shape, aren't we?''

''I won't give up if you won't.''

She reached up to push the cool cloth away from her face. ''Then let's get moving, shall we?''

He tried to talk her into resting a little longer, but she was determined to prove that she could keep walking if he could. She swayed just a bit when he helped her to her feet, but she quickly steadied herself, spreading her feet and squaring her shoulders as she pushed her hair out of her face and started walking.

He followed close at her heels, ready to catch her if she staggered again.

Damn, but it was getting harder every minute to keep himself from falling for her. It had to be circumstantial, he assured himself. His feelings would pass when they returned to their own world.

But his feelings sure as hell felt real now.

To Chloe's chagrin, they hadn't walked very far before her vision started to blur again. Her ears buzzed and perspiration beaded above her lip. She tried to clench her teeth and forge on, but everything began to go gray around her. She knew she had to stop before she passed out again. "Donovan?"

He put a hand beneath her elbow. "Dizzy?"

"A little. You think we could rest for a minute?"

"As long as you need. Sit down. Put your head between your legs."

She followed his instructions, and was relieved when the world finally stopped spinning. "I'm sorry. I—"

"Would you stop apologizing? I need a rest, too. My leg hurts like hell."

That brought her head back up. "Do you think you've re-injured it? Is there anything I can do?"

He placed a hand on her shoulder. "You worry about your health and I'll worry about mine, okay?"

Though the words were brusque, his gentle tone belied them. She knew full well that he was more worried about her than he was about himself. "Right," she answered lightly. "I'll be completely selfish. Doesn't matter to me if your leg falls right off."

"That's the spirit," he replied with a hint of a smile.

Her own smile faded as another wave of weakness coursed through her. She put her head down again.

Donovan's hand tightened on her shoulder. "Want me to get you some water?"

"No, thank you. Maybe I'll just lie down for a few minutes."

He urged her to lie with her head on his left thigh rather than on the rocky ground. She felt his fingers in her hair as he brushed it away from her fever-dampened face.

"It seems warmer today," she murmured, her eyes closed, her head pillowed comfortably on his firm thigh.

"Maybe a little. I'm afraid we're facing another thunderstorm. Those clouds don't look promising."

She spoke without opening her eyes. "I've been hearing a lot of thunder. Seems like it's getting closer. How far do you think we've walked since we left the cave?"

He hesitated a moment, then said, "Maybe a mile. A mile and a half at the most."

She frowned. "That's all? But we've been walking for hours."

"A couple of hours. We just haven't been moving very quickly."

"Have you seen any signs of civilization?"

"A few."

That made her eyes open. "Are you serious or just trying to make me feel better?"

"I'm serious. There have been hikers through here in the past few weeks, probably following the stream as we have been. This could even be an established hiking trail, though I doubt there are many hikers out with this weather threatening. We're probably no more than ten miles from a road of some sort."

"Ten miles?"

"Just a guess, of course."

"Your guesses have been on target so far. We should be able to walk ten miles today, shouldn't we?"

Again, that telltale hesitation before he answered. "Under normal circumstances, sure. With the shape we're both in, maybe. If the rain starts again as heavily as I think it's going to, we'll have to find shelter again. Spring storms can be dangerous, especially around this stream.''

''Do you think there's *any* chance there are rescuers looking for us in this area?'' she asked with a wistful note she couldn't quite conceal.

''There's always a chance.''

She couldn't take much encouragement from his tone. She closed her eyes and tried to gather strength to start walking again. Her head pounded and every inch of her body ached. It was so tempting to just let herself slide into sleep and stay there. Oblivion was sounding better all the time.

She felt Donovan stroke her hair again. She felt the tension in his leg, and knew she was causing him concern again. She was sorry about that, but she just couldn't put on a strong front at the moment. She hoped to be able to do so again after a brief rest.

She had just convinced herself to open her eyes again when the first raindrop hit her cheek. It was followed by more, becoming a light rain punctuated with increasingly loud claps of thunder.

''We have to find shelter,'' Donovan urged. ''We can't risk being out in the open or beneath a tree in case of lightning. There's a rock overhang a few yards away. We'll huddle under that until the storm passes, okay?''

Had it just been herself, she might well have lain right there and dared the lightning to hit her. The thought of forcing herself to her feet was almost enough to make her wish it would. But Donovan's safety was at risk, too, she reminded herself.

She pushed herself upright. "I'll help you up," she said, forcibly ignoring the dizziness.

His attempt to smile came across more like a grimace. "We'll help each other."

Doing so had gotten them this far, she reminded herself. No matter how tempting the thought might be, she couldn't give up as long as Donovan still depended on her.

Chapter Eleven

Wallace Childers's florid face was covered in a film of sweat, his muddy brown eyes were bulging with panic. An outside observer might think he was in fear for his life, though the two well-dressed men who faced him had been almost excessively polite when they had invited him to sit and "chat" with them.

Several suitcases were stacked behind him, testifying to his activity just before his uninvited guests had arrived so dramatically. Twenty minutes later and they would have missed him altogether.

"You've got this all wrong, Falcon," he blustered, speaking to the man he considered to be the most dangerous. "I had nothing to do with the disappearance of your—"

"Childers," Bryan cut in, his voice very soft but quite clear. "I think you should reconsider the rest of that sentence. You see, Jason and I aren't debating about whether to have you arrested for arranging a kidnapping.''

Standing behind his seated employer, his arms crossed over his chest, his face totally impassive, Jason Colby shook his head.

''You aren't?''

''No. We've actually been discussing whether we should let you live.''

Childers jerked as if he'd been shocked by an electric current. ''You can't just burst into my apartment and threaten my life!'' he shouted, waving a trembling hand at the door that still hung precariously from its broken hinges.

''You're absolutely right,'' Bryan agreed pleasantly. ''Why don't you call the police?''

There was a lengthy silence in the room. No one moved.

Childers's eyes jumped from the telephone to the two deceptively relaxed-looking men waiting for him to make a move. Standing just inside the open doorway, almost quivering with the suppressed urge to speak, stood a young woman with brown hair and furious hazel eyes. A woman who looked so much like Chloe Pennington that Childers had nearly fainted when he'd first seen her.

He swallowed hard. ''I told you, already. I don't know where your friends are.''

''Perhaps you should think a bit harder,'' Bryan prodded.

From the doorway, the woman spoke impatiently. ''He's not going to help us. Just kill him, Colby.''

Childers could almost feel the blood drain from his face as Jason Colby looked fully prepared to follow the woman's suggestion.

Though Bryan's mouth twitched with what might have been a hint of a smile, he held up a hand without looking around at his companions. "Grace—you promised not to speak," he reminded her, causing her to subside into resentful silence again. "And Jason follows my instructions alone. Now, Mr. Childers— perhaps you'd like to start over? *Where are my friends?*"

The narrow rock ledge above them provided little protection from the driving rain, but maybe it gave them some shelter from the lightning that ripped across the charcoal-colored sky above them. At least, Donovan hoped he hadn't made another mistake by stuffing them into this hollow.

Holding Chloe in his arms, he had his back turned as much as possible to the outside, trying to shield her from the rain that blew in on them. His back was soaked, his hair dripping. Chloe wasn't much drier, but at least he seemed to be taking the brunt of it.

As often as he had urged her not to give up during the past three days, he found himself teetering on the verge of doing so now. Maybe he'd been in worse situations—he couldn't remember at the moment— but it was Chloe's suffering that was ripping his heart out.

She'd tried so hard, but she had just about reached her limits. And he hadn't been a hell of a lot of help to her—first letting her get kidnapped, then leading her into the forest, idiotically hurting his leg, bringing her into the sights of a crazy man's shotgun, and now sitting with her in the middle of a damned lightning storm.

Bryan wouldn't have to fire him when this was

over, he decided. He was going to quit. He didn't deserve to keep a position of responsibility and trust.

Maybe he could build himself a lean-to in another deserted forest somewhere.

The air crackled around him as a bolt of lightning sliced through the forest nearby. The crash of thunder competed with the sound of splitting wood and hammering rain. Donovan could smell the ozone in the air and feel the hairs standing up on his arms and the back of his neck. He could only hope again that the ledge would protect them.

The way his luck had been running, it would more likely fall on them, he thought glumly.

Cradled against his shoulder, Chloe moaned a little, then stirred, interrupting his private orgy of self-recrimination.

"I must have fallen asleep," she said, her voice thick.

"Only for a few minutes. Go ahead and rest. There's nothing else to do until this storm breaks."

"I've been thinking about that," she said. "At least, I *was* thinking about it before I fell asleep."

"Thinking about what?"

"When the storm is over. Even with your injured leg, you've been making better time than I have today, since this stupid fever keeps making me so dizzy. If you leave me here, maybe you can—"

"I'm not leaving you."

Though his sharp tone had been intended to stop any argument, she persisted anyway. "Think about it before you say no, Donovan. You said yourself we're probably close to a road."

"I could be wrong. It was a total guess."

"I know, but you could be right. If we wait much

longer, we're both going to be too weak and too sick to walk at all. God knows how, considering your leg and all, but you're still holding up pretty well. You're the logical one to go for help."

"Chloe, I am not leaving you in the forest alone with a high fever. End of discussion."

She sighed. "All right. I'll try to keep walking as soon as the storm is over."

"I know it won't be easy, but you have to try. We have to get you to help as quickly as possible. Infections can be…well, they can be dangerous."

She bit her lip, probably remembering what he'd told her about his mother. "It's probably just a passing fever. Or weakness from not eating. I'm sure I'll be able to go on after resting for a while. I just thought it would be quicker if you—"

"If I have to carry you on my back, I'm not leaving you here alone."

She didn't speak again for a while. They listened to the storm, shivered when cold rain blew in on them, and dealt silently with their individual mental and physical discomforts. Donovan was just about to start another silent litany of his failings when Chloe broke the silence between them again with a request that caught him completely by surprise. "Tell me why you hate to be called a bodyguard."

"What?"

"I need to talk to take my mind off my problems."

"So you want to talk about my problems instead?"

"Is being called a bodyguard a problem for you?"

"It's just inaccurate. Bryan didn't ask me to serve as your bodyguard when I picked you up the other day. I was simply supposed to drive you to his house and wait with you there until he arrived."

"I know. You've explained all that. But you still haven't explained why you get all tense when I use the word. Have you worked as a bodyguard before?"

"Briefly." He looked out at the rain and hoped his short reply would discourage her from asking more.

It didn't, of course.

"What went wrong?"

"The person I was guarding got killed. I ignored my instincts, and went along with him when he insisted that I leave him alone with his girlfriend for a few hours. He was tired of being guarded all the time, thought he would be safe for a while in the hideaway we had selected for him, and he convinced me that he would be safe there—but he wasn't."

"You were working for the man who was killed?" she asked, trying to follow the terse story.

"Yes."

"And he asked you to leave him alone for a few hours?"

"I shouldn't have listened. I should have insisted I stay with him."

"Donovan, you can't blame yourself for following your employer's orders. It sounds as though he made the mistake, not you."

Staring blindly into the rain, he shook his head. "I was hired to protect him. I failed. He died. I'm not the only one who blamed me for that failure."

"The only person who should be blamed is the killer. Was he ever caught?"

"Yeah. Lot of good that did my client."

"Who was your client? A friend?"

"No. A man who'd made some powerful enemies on his way to fame. You would probably know the name if I mentioned it, but it doesn't matter now. That ended my bodyguard career.''

"Was that when you went to work for Bryan?''

He shrugged. "I bummed around for a few years after that, taking some assignments I'd just as soon not discuss now for some people who operated just barely within the range of the law. My reputation was going downhill fast when Bryan tracked me down and convinced me to join him.''

He hadn't planned to tell her all that. But maybe now she could understand the intensity of his loyalty to Bryan. Why he wouldn't do anything to jeopardize that relationship.

Maybe she could also understand that he wasn't exactly what anyone would consider a hero—just in case she had made the mistake of thinking of him in that light during the past few days.

"No more talk," he said abruptly, twisting to arrange his injured leg in a slightly more comfortable position—which meant sticking it straight out into the rain. "Get some rest. You're going to need it.''

Donovan waited until he was sure the rain had stopped for a while before he suggested they move on. It took all the strength Chloe had to make herself climb to her feet and start walking beside him. He hovered nearby to give her support, though he leaned so heavily on his walking stick that he looked as though he needed a great deal of support himself.

They made a pathetic sight, she couldn't help thinking as they pushed on one halting step at a time. She didn't want to think about what she must look like with her stringy hair, assorted bruises and clothes that would go straight into a trash can if she made it out of here. Donovan was unshaven, his hair limp and damp from the rain, his black clothing dirty and torn, his leg bound in boards and scraps of coral-colored cloth. Beneath his whiskers, she could see a dark bruise on his left cheek from his fight with the kidnapper.

Yet as battered as he looked at the moment, she had a feeling there wasn't a woman alive who would dismiss him without a second glance. He was bruised and weary, but competence and power still seemed to surround him like an invisible mantle. A battle-scarred warrior, she mused. Battered, but unbroken.

And then she made a face and shook her head in response to her fanciful mental ramblings. Maybe her fever was climbing again.

"Is something funny?" Donovan asked, proving how closely he'd been watching her.

"Look at us," she retorted. "Don't you find us a funny sight?"

He glanced down at himself, then at her. His mouth twitched in that little smile she found herself watching for so often. "Not many women would find anything about this picture amusing."

"I've decided to attribute my amusement to fever. I seem to be suffering delusions."

"Don't suppose you could hallucinate us a cup of coffee?"

"I'll try. Having a caffeine attack?"

He reached out to push the low-hanging limbs of a tree out of their way. "There are a lot of things I'd like to have right now, but a cup of coffee definitely tops the—"

His words ended abruptly. From behind him, Chloe studied his suddenly still back. "What is it?"

"A road."

"A road?" She hurried to catch up with him, hardly even wincing when she stepped on a rock. "Where?"

He nodded ahead. "An old logging road, from the look of it. But it's been used recently. Four-wheelers, at a guess. ATVs."

She stared in some dismay at the rutted dirt track Donovan had generously called a road. "How do we know which way to follow it?"

Limping forward, he studied the tracks, then pointed. "That way. South."

Frowning, she looked in that direction. Trees, hills, and more trees lay ahead—both directions. "Why south?"

"It leads out."

She looked again at the track. "And you know this how?"

He shrugged.

She studied his impassive face for a moment before asking, "Do you really have a reason to choose that direction, or are you just making a guess?"

"Look at it this way. I have a fifty-fifty chance of being right."

After a moment, she nodded. "Okay. We'll go south."

Making a gallant motion with his left hand, he said, "After you."

She drew a deep breath as she stepped onto one hard-packed track and turned to follow it. It was a road, she reminded herself. It had to lead somewhere.

It was no easier making their way along the old road than it had been across the forest floor. Thick mud made walking slippery and brush and vines tangled around their ankles.

Chloe was hit with several more dizzy spells, forcing her to stop and rest several times. Donovan stumbled twice, almost falling, and scaring her half to death. She was so afraid he was going to further hurt his leg, shatter the cracked bone so that it pierced the skin or caused him some permanent disability. Both times he managed to catch himself with his crutch.

Her steps slowed to a near-crawl, and she suspected she couldn't walk a straight line in a sobriety test. The world was doing funny things around her, the lines waving, merging, creating a surreal landscape straight out of a Dali painting. She wasn't hallucinating—exactly—but she wasn't exactly coherent, either. She hoped it was a good sign that she was aware of her condition.

"We're going to have to stop," Donovan said, sliding his left arm around her. "You can't go any farther."

"I can keep going," she said, staring fiercely at the road ahead.

"Not without collapsing. Come on, we can sit beneath that big tree if it isn't too muddy."

She shook her head, irrationally afraid that if she sat down she wouldn't get up again. "We have to keep walking or we won't get out."

"We'll get out, Chloe." His voice was unusually gentle. "You just need to rest a little while. And so do I, okay?"

"What time is it?" she asked as he led her toward the tree he'd indicated.

"I don't know. It's so cloudy it's hard to tell. It was about seven when we started walking, and the rainstorm lasted maybe an hour—it's probably around noon.''

''It feels later. Do you think it's going to rain again?''

He glanced at the sky before turning to help her sit down on the damp moss beneath the tree. ''Probably. There were predictions for a lot of rain this week.''

''I know. Grace pointed it out to me several times, asking me how much fun I thought it would be to spend a week of vacation watching rain fall.''

''I'm sure you'd have found something more interesting to do than that.''

He'd kept his voice uninflected, but she bristled a little, anyway. Or she would have, if she hadn't been so tired and so sick. ''Bryan and I were going to talk,'' she murmured, leaning her head back against the tree. ''Just get to know each other better. That's all there was to it.''

''You'd have had a nice time. Bryan can be very good company.''

Donovan's bland tone was starting to annoy her. She decided to let the conversation end before exhaustion and fever made her say something she might regret later.

He didn't seem to be listening to her anyway.

After their awkward conversation, Donovan seemed impatient to start hiking again. He allowed only a short rest before he asked Chloe if she felt like moving on again. She didn't, of course, but she struggled to her feet. Donovan believed they were close to rescue, and she had learned to trust his instincts.

The walk seemed to get harder as they pressed on. The ground grew progressively muddier and slipperier as the grass on the packed-dirt trail became sparser. Chloe hoped that meant the road had been used more in that area recently, which could mean they were getting closer to a populated area.

And then the rain began again, this time a slow, misty drizzle that was just heavy enough to make them soggy, chilled and uncomfortable.

Chloe had walked almost as far as she physically could when she heard Donovan growl something incomprehensible—something she was probably better off not asking him to clarify, judging by his tone. Looking forward, she saw what had upset him.

The torrential rains of the past two days had flooded a fast-running section of the stream, causing the roiling, tumbling water to completely cover the road ahead of them. The road had fallen off into a deep ditch dug by previous floods. In late summer, the stream was probably quite shallow here, just enough to give the ATV riders a good splash. Now it might as well have been a river blocking them from the other side of the road.

For several long, silent moments, Donovan stood unmoving, staring at the rushing water as if he could hardly believe he was really seeing it. And then he erupted in fury, slamming his walking stick to the ground and letting loose a string of colorful curses that made Chloe's eyebrows rise.

So Donovan could lose his composure occasionally. She'd wondered about that. This latest setback was apparently the last straw for him.

She stepped in to soothe him before he hurt himself. ''We'll find a way around it,'' she said, laying a hand on his arm.

''There is no way around it. Look at the bluffs we'd have to climb if we go upstream. Or the steep slopes we'd have to descend downstream. Why do you think this road runs where it does? It's the only relatively level path.''

He'd spoken through clenched teeth, obviously trying to get himself back under control. ''Then we'll wade through it,'' she suggested. ''We'll help each other across. It couldn't be that deep.''

''It isn't how deep it is, it's how fast it's moving. One misstep and we'd be swept downstream.''

''We could wait here, find a place to take shelter until the stream goes down some.''

He looked up at the sky. The drizzle was becoming heavier now, and showed no signs of ending soon. ''That could be a while. Days, maybe.''

''We don't seem to have a whole lot of choices.''

''That thought has occurred to me.''

She stepped to the edge of the erosion-carved ravine and looked down, watching the increasingly heavy rain merging into the surging flood waters. The temperature was falling again; or maybe it just felt that way because she was so wet and tired. She shivered and wrapped her arms around herself in a futile attempt at warmth.

Donovan stepped beside her, placing a hand on her shoulder. ''I'm sorry,'' he said, his voice calmer now. ''I shouldn't have snapped at you just because I'm frustrated.''

She offered him a tentative smile. ''You deserve to blow off steam sometimes.''

''Still, I shouldn't have—''

Their combined weight must have been too much for the waterlogged ground at the edge of the gully. Before Donovan could finish his sentence, the earth gave way beneath their feet.

Chapter Twelve

Maybe they could have caught themselves if they hadn't already been in such weakened condition. Or maybe not. The ground literally fell from under them, tumbling into the hungry stream which took them with it.

Chloe went into the water on her back. She was immediately swept downstream, crashing against rocks and the dirt sides, struggling to get her face above the surface. Her first gasp for breath ended with a mouthful of water. Choking and gagging, she went under again.

The water was no more than four feet deep but running so fast she couldn't keep her feet beneath her when she tried to stand. She slammed hard into another large rock, tried to grab it, but had her grip torn away by the force of the water. The current was too strong, the ground too uneven and slippery to give her a grip. All she could do was go with the flow and try to gulp air whenever her face broke the water.

Something snagged her shirt, jerking her to a stop. She scrabbled to catch hold of it, her hands closing around something hard and slick. Tree roots, she realized as she gulped air, trying to focus through water, rain and tears. The flood had washed the dirt away from the bottom of a large tree, leaving long, bare roots extending out into the water.

It took all her strength to cling to the roots and keep herself from being swept away again. She didn't know how far she had been carried by the floodwaters, or how long she'd been battling them. The heavy gray sky pressed down above her and rain fell in windswept sheets around her. All she could see was the forest and the bluffs rising around her.

She couldn't see Donovan.

Whipping her head from one side to the other, she searched desperately for any sign of him. "Donovan?"

She could barely hear her own voice over the sounds of the rain and rushing water. She called louder, "Donovan!"

She couldn't help thinking of his injured leg. What if he'd been pushed under the water when they were first swept in? Even now he could be trapped, struggling to get his head above water, slowly losing consciousness…

"Donovan!"

She tried dragging herself out of the water, but her hands kept sliding on the slick roots. She lodged herself firmly into a notch among them and rested a moment, panting.

Her head was spinning now, and she felt as though

she could very easily faint again, but she fought off the dizziness. She had to find Donovan.

She tried calling him again. "Donovan!"

"Chloe?"

She jerked her head around so quickly that dizziness almost overwhelmed her again, loosening her grip on the roots. She scrambled to regain her hold, clinging so tightly her hands ached.

"Donovan?" Had she only imagined she'd heard him? Was it only desperate, wishful thinking?

"Chloe—where are you?"

It was definitely his voice, she thought with a choked cry of relief. He was all right. Somehow he'd gotten out of the water.

She tried again to pull herself out, but she was unsuccessful. She called out to him again and waited, hanging on while Donovan made his way to her. She could hear him now, crashing through the brush, his occasional muted curses drifting to her on wet gusts of wind.

It took him a while to reach her. When she finally saw him, she understood why.

The left side of his face was covered with rain-streaked blood from a cut at his temple. His right leg dragged so badly that he was almost hopping on his left. He looked as though he was in terrible pain, but he also looked as close to frantic as she had seen him to this point.

He didn't see her at first. "Chloe?"

"I'm here."

He limped toward her. She called out again.

Finally spotting her, he stopped, his shoulders seeming to sag in relief for a moment. "Are you all right?"

"I think so. But I can't get out."

"Hang on." He made his way carefully toward her. Stopping on the bank, he rested a hand on the trunk of the tree and looked down at her. "I'm going to try to pull you out. You'll have to hold very tightly to make sure you aren't swept away again."

"How did you get out?"

"I hit a shallow area, grabbed a tree branch." His foot slipped on a patch of mud, but he caught himself quickly. He steadied himself with one hand wrapped around a sturdy limb and leaned toward her, his other hand outstretched. "Brace your foot against the root and push toward me. Catch my hand and don't let go."

The position he was in had his weight almost fully on his right leg, which had to be causing him agony. Yet she knew he wouldn't falter as he helped her out, no matter how bad the pain. Once again, she trusted him with her life.

He hadn't let her down so far.

Somehow, she managed to place her hand in his. Somehow, he found the strength to drag her out of the water.

They stumbled away from the crumbling edge. And then they fell limply to a wet, grassy patch of ground, both too tired to stand, clinging to each other as though they were afraid to let go again. Lying there in the rain, Donovan buried his face in her dripping hair, while she burrowed into the wet curve of his throat. She felt heavy tremors running through him. She didn't know whether to attribute them to cold, pain, exhaustion, reaction or—as in her case—a combination of all those things.

He drew back far enough to cup her face in his

hands, studying her with anxious eyes. "You're sure you're all right?"

"I'm fine." She reached up to touch her fingertips to the deep cut on his forehead. "How did this happen?"

His shrug was impatient, dismissing his latest injury as unimportant. "I saw you go under. I never saw you come back up."

"It took me a while. The force of the water kept shoving me back down."

"You could have drowned." His voice was suddenly bleak. "I was afraid you had."

"I thought the same about you," she whispered. "I was so afraid for you."

"We're okay now. It's over."

"Yes." She tried to give him a smile. She couldn't quite manage it.

A new look of panic flitted across his face as he leaned over her. "Don't cry, Chloe. We're safe."

"I'm not crying," she insisted. She was sure the moisture on her cheeks were raindrops, not tears. Until her breath caught in a sob. And then another.

Donovan groaned. "Damn it, Chloe."

He touched his lips to one of her rain-and-tear-streaked cheeks, and then the other. His mouth felt so warm against her icy skin—and yet she shivered in reaction to his touch.

When his lips settled on hers, she forgot all about the rain and the cold, her aches and pains, and their bleak situation. She simply wrapped her arms around his neck and allowed herself to get lost again. This time she didn't even try to find her way to safety.

Their lips had touched before, but this was the first

time he had really kissed her. And it answered one question once and for all—

Donovan really did kiss as skillfully as he did everything else.

His lips were hard. Hungry. Either his emotions were being influenced by the dramatic near-miss they had just survived or this kiss had been building for a long time. She knew which one was the case for her.

Four days ago, this man had been a complete stranger to her. Sometime between that day and now, she had managed to fall in love with him.

She had waited so long for it to happen to her. She had almost given up hoping that it ever would. How could she have known that love would find her so soon after she'd finally stopped searching for it?

He lifted his head only a fraction of an inch and started to speak. Chloe wasn't quite ready to hear what he might have said. She drew him back down to her.

He kissed her again, but something had changed this time. She sensed him trying to gather himself, trying to get his needs under control. Donovan wasn't a man to let himself get swept away for very long, if ever.

She didn't try to stop him when he pulled away this time. He rolled to his back, letting the rain pelt his face for a moment before he shoved himself upright.

"We should walk as far as we can before dark," he said, his voice impassive, his face expressionless. "We're both too wet to worry about the rain now, anyway, so finding shelter wouldn't do us much good. And you're shivering. You'll probably warm up quicker if we're moving than if we sit still."

She knew he must be fully aware that her trembling had little to do with being cold, but he seemed to be pretending nothing earth-shattering had just happened between them. "Donovan?"

"At least we're on the other side of the stream," he said, half turning to look back at the water. "Not exactly the way I would have preferred to cross, of course."

"Donovan, I—"

Still without meeting her eyes, he offered her a hand. "Here. Let me help you up."

He wasn't going to talk about it. Not now, anyway. She took his hand, but was careful to support her own weight as she rose slowly. "Do you know how to get back to the road?"

"Yes. You really weren't carried very far by the water. Not as far as it probably seemed to you."

"The rain seems to be letting up a little."

He moved a spreading bush aside and held it until she moved past. "Yeah. I think it's about to stop. It's about time we had a little luck. Watch your feet. It looks slippery ahead."

It was ridiculous that they were discussing the weather, she thought as she glared fiercely at the ground ahead. How could he kiss her the way he had and then start talking about the chances of rain?

He was right, of course, to change the subject. This was hardly the time to discuss the future—at least any future beyond getting out of these woods.

And still she heard herself saying, "I'm not going to marry Bryan."

Donovan hesitated a few moments, then stumbled on. "That's between you and Bryan. But I still don't think you should make a decision of that magnitude under these conditions.''

''I'm not being impulsive. My decision would have been no different even if we hadn't been kidnapped.''

He stepped carefully over a fallen tree trunk, grimacing when he was forced to put his weight down on his right leg. ''Let's just concentrate on getting out of here, shall we?''

He moved ahead of her, and she looked at his back. His shoulders were squared, his spine very straight, even though his steps were slow and halting. He had withdrawn from her mentally, emotionally *and* physically.

Her instincts warned her not to push him. He was the one who obviously needed time to process what had happened between them. Maybe it wasn't as easy for him to identify his emotions as it had been for her when she'd been struck with that stunning revelation that she was in love with him.

Remembering the unguarded look on his face when he had first seen her after fearing that she'd drowned, she told herself that he had to feel something. Replaying those passionate kisses in her mind, she wanted to believe that his feelings were as strong as her own. It was the possibility that she was wrong— that she had only read into the kisses what she wanted to find there—that kept her quiet now.

As badly as she wanted to be rescued, she couldn't help wondering if leaving this forest would also mean saying goodbye to Donovan.

After finding the dirt road again, they struggled along without giving each other much assistance, since neither of them was in much better shape than the other. It had stopped raining again, though the air was still so heavy and damp that it was almost like breathing water.

Wet and cold, miserable and edgy, Chloe winced in pain with every step. She knew Donovan was hurting every bit as badly—if not more so—though he didn't complain. He didn't say *anything,* actually. He just limped on, his face grim, his movements determined.

He'd become the uncommunicative stranger again. Only this time she sensed that he was having to make an effort to remain that way. Now that he had reached out to her, she thought he would have liked to do so again. She could only speculate about his reasons for withdrawing so abruptly—loyalty to Bryan, uncertainty of her feelings, fear of the future or baggage from his past. All of the above.

"It's getting so dark," she gasped after stumbling into a rut and nearly falling on her face. "I can't see where we're going. Shouldn't we find another cave or someplace to spend the night?"

"Try to make it just a little farther."

Was he uncomfortable with the idea of spending another night in a cave with her? They'd spent three nights in each other's arms now, their feelings escalating each night—was he afraid of what might happen if they spent another night that way?

Personally, she didn't think he had much to worry about. She was so tired she suspected she might become comatose the moment she stopped moving.

She started to tell him so, but he reached out suddenly to grab her arm. "What—?"

"Look—over that way."

Frowning in bewilderment, she followed the direction of his pointing finger. "I don't—oh, my God. Is that—?"

"Yes. Come on."

He hadn't let go of her arm. Half supporting her, half dragging her, he led them off the road and across a rocky clearing toward the small, battered-looking mobile home they had spotted.

Her heart pounded against her chest, and her breath caught in excited half gasps, half sobs. *Rescue,* she thought. Only now did she admit that she had begun to wonder if it would ever happen.

It took them a good fifteen minutes to make their way across the rough clearing to the trailer. There were no lights on in the windows, and Chloe had the distinct feeling that no one was inside. The feeling was confirmed when Donovan pounded on the front door and no one answered.

"Now what?" she asked wearily.

"We break in," he answered, as if it should have been obvious to her.

"Just—break in?"

"Under the circumstances, I don't think anyone would blame us. And if I cause any damage, I'll pay for it. I just hope there's a phone in there. At the very least, we can get dry and warm."

Because dry and warm sounded so appealing at the moment—not to mention the prospect of a telephone—she stood aside without further comment and watched him efficiently break into the locked trailer.

She no longer even questioned where he'd learned the skills he'd displayed during the past few days. She was just glad he'd picked them up somewhere in his undoubtedly colorful adventures.

Motioning for her to wait a minute, Donovan stepped inside first. "Hello?" he called out.

Silence was his only answer. He groped at the wall near the door, and a moment later light flooded the main room of the trailer. "We have electricity," he announced with satisfaction.

Her knees almost went weak in relief. She moved in behind him. The room was furnished in a style she could only think of as "early garage sale"—but it *was* warm and dry.

"I would speculate that this is someone's hunting and fishing retreat," Donovan said, glancing around the sparsely decorated trailer. "We must be close to a river—probably the one that stream empties into. And I'd guess we aren't very far from other people."

"Thank God. Is there a phone?"

"Not that I've seen yet. I'll check the back rooms, you look in the kitchen."

"I'm dripping all over the carpet."

Donovan glanced down at the ragged green shag carpeting beneath their feet. "I'm sure it's not the first time it's been dripped on. Don't worry about it."

"I know. You'll buy him new carpet, right?"

"Hell, I'll buy him a new trailer," he answered rashly. "Check the kitchen."

It felt so good to flip a switch and have lights come on as a result. She didn't see a telephone, but there was a sink, an old electric range and a small refrigerator/freezer combination. The fridge hummed; she opened the door and cool air brushed her wet skin, making her shiver and smile at the same time.

Closing the refrigerator door, she moved to the sink and twisted the left knob. After a moment, warm water cascaded over her hand. She could have a hot bath, she realized in delight. The prospect made her almost giddy.

A thick quilt was draped suddenly over her shoulders. Clutching it around her, she turned to find Donovan standing behind her. "Did you find a phone?"

"No. But there are some men's clothes in one of the bedrooms. Jeans, flannel shirts, a couple pair of shoes. No shower, but a bathtub with hot water. And I found a real treasure under the sink—bars of soap, packages of disposable razors, several new toothbrushes still in the packaging. Why don't you take a hot bath and put on some dry clothes while I look around for clues about where we are."

Toothbrushes. If her feet hadn't hurt so badly, she might have bounced in anticipation. She settled for a smile. "I feel a little odd about raiding someone's closet without permission—but I'm sure you'll buy him a whole new wardrobe when we get back to civilization."

He almost smiled. "Absolutely."

"Then I'll ignore my scruples and take you up on that suggestion." She smiled in anticipation as she hobbled past him.

"Chloe." Donovan caught her arm when she would have passed him.

She looked up at him. He pressed a hand to her forehead, testing for fever. Their faces were very close together and for a moment she saw real emotion in his bright-green eyes. A quiver of response ran through her. But then he masked whatever he was feeling, released her, and stepped back. "You're still running a fever. I didn't see any aspirin in the bathroom, but I'll look around in the rest of the trailer, see what I can find while you're taking your bath."

She nodded and left the room as quickly as her battered feet would allow.

Donovan was waiting outside the bathroom door when Chloe finally emerged. He'd begun to worry that she'd been in there too long. For all he knew, she could have passed out in the tub or something. He was too tired and stressed to consider how unlikely it was that, having survived a flooded stream, she would drown in a bathtub.

Her hair was wet again, but looked squeaky clean this time. Her fresh-scrubbed skin was starkly pale, except for the purple smudges beneath her eyes. She wore a big flannel shirt that almost swallowed her, falling all the way to her knees. Her poor battered feet were bare, revealing all the abuse they had taken in those woods.

The big shirt made her look small in comparison. Delicate. Almost fragile. He knew first-hand how deceptive that impression could be.

He remembered the first day he'd met her, when he'd thought of her as more pretty than beautiful. Funny how that impression had changed during the past few days. Now he was convinced that he'd never seen a more attractive woman.

"I found coffee in the kitchen, and I brewed a pot," he said, his voice a bit brusque. "And I heated some canned soup. I also found a first-aid kit stuffed in one of the kitchen cabinets. I set out a bottle of acetaminophen. Take a couple to reduce your fever and then you can eat while I bathe. After that, we'll see about treating some of your wounds."

She nodded in response to his list of directions. "Soup and coffee sound good," she admitted. "The hot bath warmed my outside, but I still feel cold inside.''

He smiled a little, as she had hoped he would, but it was hard for him to find any humor in what she had been through. ''The food is in the kitchen. Have all you want, I've already eaten. I'll hurry with my bath and join you in a few minutes.''

''Don't hurry. Trust me, it feels too good to be clean again to rush through it.''

''I'll keep that in mind.''

He watched her walk away, taking a moment to appreciate the graceful sway of her hips. Even walking on shredded feet, she carried herself like a princess, he thought—then scowled at his uncharacteristic fancifulness as he turned to lock himself in the bathroom.

A short while later, bathed, clean-shaven, dressed in a flannel shirt that was too short in the sleeves and jeans that were too big in the waist, Donovan ran his tongue over his brushed teeth and reminded himself to reward the owner of this trailer generously.

He'd removed the waterlogged, rigged-up splint before his bath. His leg was about three different shades of purple, but the painkillers he'd taken while he was making the coffee had eased the throbbing somewhat. He didn't know if his leg was broken, cracked or bruised to the bone, but he figured it wouldn't fall off before he could have it treated.

The cut at his temple had stopped bleeding, but that was a new lump and bruise to add to his collection. In his ongoing battle with nature, the other side was definitely a few licks ahead, he thought in resignation.

He found Chloe in the living room, sitting on the couch cross-legged with the first-aid kit beside her.

She was making some rather odd contortions in an attempt to see the bottom of her feet.

"I told you I would help you with that," he said, moving toward her as quickly as his own injuries would allow.

She must not have heard him approaching. Hurriedly making sure the big flannel shirt covered her adequately, she tucked an almost-dry strand of hair behind her ear and asked, "Why did you take off your splint?"

"I couldn't take a bath in it."

"I'll help you get it back on."

"Never mind. I'm not sure it was helping much, anyway."

"But—"

"Forget it, Chloe. Let's see about your feet." He sat beside her and reached for the first-aid kit. "Did you have enough to eat?"

"Yes, plenty, thank you. The soup was wonderful."

"Straight out of a can. You were just hungry enough for anything to taste good."

"You're probably right."

"Give me your feet."

"That sounds a bit odd," she murmured, even as she turned sideways on the couch and complied.

Donovan ordered himself to keep a tight lid on his emotions as he reached for her right foot and rested it on his knee. Even making a fierce effort to be completely objective and impersonal, he couldn't help noticing that her feet were small, high-arched and perfectly formed.

And so bruised and torn that the sight of them made his chest ache. "Damn, these must have hurt," he muttered, running a fingertip very lightly over her scarred and peeling sole.

She squirmed and laughed softly. "That tickled."

"Sorry," he said, but he had liked hearing her laugh. He would bet she did so often under the right circumstances—and in more entertaining company.

Frowning, he set to work with antibiotic ointment and bandages, covering the worst of the cuts. Two cuts looked badly infected; he suspected they would have to be treated by medical professionals. "I hope you're current on your tetanus shots."

"I am."

"Good." He reached for her left foot. To his relief, it didn't seem to be as badly damaged, though there were several deep scratches around her ankle. Looked as though she'd tangled with a thorny vine. He spread ointment on those wounds, as well, still trying to keep his mind off the intimacy of their position.

Not to mention the fact that she was wearing nothing but a large flannel shirt.

Either his awkwardness was affecting her or she, too, was trying to divert herself when she asked, "Why do you suppose the electricity is turned on in this trailer? D'you think the owner leaves it on all the time, even when he isn't here?"

"He's probably been here recently—maybe even last weekend. Probably fishes nearby."

"If he comes often, then he probably doesn't live very far away. We must be getting closer to civilization."

"I think you're right." Satisfied that he'd treated every visible cut, he looked up from her feet. "Any other injuries you need me to treat?"

Her smile was suddenly wicked. Before he could

predict what she was going to do, she leaned forward and wrapped her arms around his neck. "Just one," she murmured against his lips. And then kissed him.

Oh, hell. He was only human. Dragging her against him, he slanted his mouth to a better angle and took her up on what she was offering.

Chapter Thirteen

Chloe's lips had been ice-cold when Donovan had pulled her from that stream. Now they were warm enough to sear a brand on his soul…if he wasn't careful. But maybe it was too late for caution.

She murmured her pleasure with his response and snuggled closer, so that it was too damned obvious she wasn't wearing a bra beneath the shirt. Or anything else, most likely. His hands wandered almost without volition, stroking her smooth thighs, her softly curved hips and slender waist. Her breasts were on the small side, but firm and high—just the right size to fill his hands when he smoothed them slowly upward.

Pressing herself into his touch, Chloe locked her hands in his damp hair, and kissed him as though she had been starved more for him than for food.

Being wanted so badly was intoxicating. Made him

feel special. Almost like a man who deserved a woman like Chloe.

He started to pull back. She tightened her grip and parted her lips for him. There was no way he could resist the temptation to deepen the kiss. Just for a moment, he promised himself.

One taste and he was lost.

The too-loose borrowed jeans grew significantly tighter as his tongue plunged repeatedly into her mouth to mate with hers. Her hands were suddenly all over him, stroking, exploring, testing his strength. She seemed to take as much pleasure from touching him as he did her—and that, too, was a heady sensation.

He tried to remind himself that she was endowing him with qualities he didn't possess. That she was turning him into some sort of hero because they had grown so dependent on each other during their ordeal. Yet when she kissed him like this, he found it all too easy to believe she wanted him for exactly who he was. Flaws, baggage and all.

That sort of self-deception was dangerous. Addictive. He'd never even been tempted to indulge in it before.

Everything was different with Chloe. She tempted him in ways he'd never been tempted before.

She almost tempted him to forget she was the woman his best friend planned to marry.

The thought of Bryan gave him the willpower to rip his mouth from Chloe's. "We can't do this."

She blinked and moistened her lips with the tip of her tongue—a gesture that almost shattered his sanity again. "Are you in pain?" she asked, her voice bedroom-husky.

"Oh, yeah," he groaned, pushing himself away from her. How had they ended up sprawled in this position, with her on her back and him draped over her? He didn't even remember moving.

Rising to her elbows, she studied him anxiously. "Is it your leg? Have you twisted it?"

"My leg is fine." It hurt like hell, of course, now that his attention had been called to it, but he welcomed the pain. It gave him something to concentrate on besides the throbbing ache in his groin.

She reached out to brush her fingertips through the lock of hair that habitually tumbled onto his forehead, being careful to avoid the swollen bump at his temple. "You're being macho again, aren't you? I know your leg is hurting."

He pulled away from her gentle touch, sliding to the other end of the couch. He wasn't quite ready to stand. "I'll take some more painkillers. Why don't you go lie down for a while? I want to look around for a way to get us out of here."

"And after we get out?" she asked, keeping her gaze locked on his face.

After that, he thought, they would go their separate ways. She would get over this danger-induced crush she seemed to have developed for him, and she would probably marry Bryan. And he would have to figure out how to spend the rest of his life avoiding his best friend's wife. The woman who was everything he could have wanted—had things been different. Had *he* been different.

"Get some rest, Chloe," he said again, refusing to meet her eyes. "By tomorrow you'll be home."

"Home," she murmured. "Where is home for you, Donovan? I don't even know."

''I don't have a home.'' He had an apartment, of course, but he thought of it as a place to sleep, a place to store his stuff. Not home. ''I haven't wanted one.''

''Everyone wants a home.''

''Not everyone.'' He finally stood, balancing his weight carefully on his left leg. ''Go to bed. We're both tired and keyed up. Things will look different tomorrow.''

''Not that different. Not to me. You don't give me much credit, do you?''

He heard the irritation in her voice as she also rose. He knew she didn't like his repeated assurances that her feelings for him were being unduly influenced by what they had been through together—but eventually she would realize that he was right.

He was afraid she was going to argue more. But it seemed even Chloe's impressive courage had limits. ''I'll lie down for a while in the small bedroom,'' she said, turning toward the door. ''Let me know if you find anything interesting.''

''I will.''

He watched her leave. There was wounded pride in the angle of her shoulders when she stepped into the hallway. Maybe she was already getting over her crush, he mused. Maybe she was beginning to re-member now why she hadn't much liked him before they'd been forced to spend so much time together.

Picturing the condition of her feet, he grimaced, almost feeling the pain she must have endured. She hadn't deserved any of what she had been through the past few days. He was convinced that Bryan would do everything he could to make certain she would never have to suffer fear or pain again. Chloe de-served to live in luxury.

Donovan still believed Bryan would charm her into marrying him. Bryan had recognized immediately what a special woman she was—perhaps even more quickly than Donovan had. A fitting match for an extraordinary man like Bryan Falcon.

As for himself—well, he was merely ordinary. From his dysfunctional childhood to his occasionally disreputable adulthood, he'd been nobody until Bryan had given him a job—and, more than that, a future.

A future that included her only as his best friend's wife.

He closed his eyes and gave himself a moment to deal with that pain. And then he shoved his feelings aside and turned away from the hallway into which she had disappeared. He had to figure out a way to get them out of here. The sooner, the better.

Chloe was tired, but not sleepy. Lying on top of the quilt that served as a spread on the twin bed in the smaller of the trailer's two bedrooms, she stared at the ceiling and wondered what the next day would bring—as she had been doing for the past half hour or so since she had left Donovan in the living room.

By this time tomorrow, if not before, she could well be back in her own apartment, reunited with her sister, back to her ''normal'' life. Perhaps trying desperately to pretend that she was still the same person she had been before three greedy and unscrupulous men had ordered her into a van just four days earlier.

She had a bad feeling about the way Donovan had just shut her out after kissing her until she hadn't been able to think of anything but him. About how badly she wanted him. And how hard she had fallen for him.

She knew he still didn't trust their feelings, still felt

torn by his loyalty to Bryan, but she was afraid if they didn't talk while they had the chance, they never would. She would break things off with Bryan, and then Donovan would disappear from her life forever.

She couldn't allow that to happen without even making an effort to stop it. If there was one thing she had learned from this ordeal, it was that sometimes she had to forge ahead despite fear, despite risk, despite the possibility of pain.

She was trying to decide how to confront him about his feelings for her when she heard the outside door to the trailer open and close rather forcefully. Donovan?

She rolled off the bed and hurried toward the main room again.

Donovan was standing just inside the front door to the trailer. His hair was wind-tossed, he was still wearing the ill-fitting flannel shirt and jeans, and he'd found a pair of slip-on canvas shoes that looked a good two sizes too big for him. Anyone else might have looked a bit silly in that garb, she mused, taking a moment to study him. Donovan looked devastatingly sexy—but then, she'd thought the same when he'd been unshaven and dirty and dressed in his ripped black clothes.

His eyebrows lifted when he saw her standing in the doorway. "I'm sorry, did I wake you?"

"I wasn't asleep. What were you doing outside?"

"Just looking around."

"You shouldn't be walking around on that leg. Are you trying to do as much damage to it as possible?"

"I'm trying to get you back to your family," he retorted. "And I found our way out."

Her heart jumped into her throat. "You did? What? How?"

"An ATV. One of the big two-passenger four-wheelers hunters use. It's stored in a small shed out back."

"A locked shed, I presume?"

"It was."

She shook her head. "Did you find a key to the ATV?"

"No. But we won't need one. As soon as you're ready, we'll get on the road."

"You're going to hot-wire it?"

He nodded, apparently having no concern about his ability to do just that.

"We, um, won't be in danger of being arrested for breaking and entering or theft as soon as we reach a town?"

"We aren't stealing anything. We're borrowing— and the owner will be reimbursed for his trouble."

She looked around the trailer, suddenly, unaccountably nervous about leaving it. "What should I do to get ready?"

"Let's try to find you some pants and socks, maybe a pair of shoes. They'll all be too big, of course, but it'll be better than trying to ride on the back of an ATV wearing nothing more than a shirt."

She nodded and turned back toward the bedrooms.

They found her a pair of black sweatpants with a drawstring waist and some thick white tube socks that covered her all the way to her knees. Shoes were more of a problem. They finally uncovered a pair of rubberized lace-up boots that were ridiculously large, but she was able to keep them on by lacing them tightly around her ankles.

"I look ridiculous," she said ruefully, glancing down at her outfit.

As if by impulse, Donovan reached out to smooth a strand of hair away from her face. "You look fine."

Something in his voice made her reach out to him. "Donovan—"

He turned away. "We'd better get going. It's almost 4:00 p.m. now, and we don't know how far we are from a town."

"I know we have to concentrate on getting rescued now," she said evenly, though his rebuff had stung. "But when we get back, we need to talk."

"When we get back, we're both going to be very busy," he replied. "First thing we do is make sure the guys who grabbed us are identified and brought to justice. After that, I've got a week's worth of work to catch up on. I'm going to be tied up for quite a while—as I'm sure you will be."

"And what about us?"

He shrugged, refusing to meet her eyes. "I doubt that we'll see each other much. Except for your connection to Bryan, you and I don't exactly move in the same circles. If you break things off with him, as you say you're thinking about doing, there will be no reason for us to see each other at all."

She bit her lip. He couldn't make his message much clearer. He had every intention of taking her back to civilization and then walking away from her.

"I'll miss you," she said quietly.

His cheek muscles flexed. "You'll get over it."

"I don't think so."

He took a step toward the doorway. "I'll go start the ATV, and bring it around to the front."

"Donovan." It took more courage for her to speak

then than it had to plunge into that forest on the first night, or to face any of the obstacles they had shared since. "What *do* you feel about me?"

He stopped with his back to her, his shoulders tense. "What I feel at this moment isn't really relevant. It's what's waiting for us in our real lives that matters. You have your shop, your sister, your parents—you can have Bryan, if you want him. I have my work. You want to get married, have kids, paint your picket fences. I don't even want a houseplant. Too much responsibility. The thing would die of neglect."

Was it that he didn't want responsibility—or was he afraid of it? He'd survived a father who had walked out on him, a mother who had died of a neglected infection, relatives who apparently hadn't wanted him or cared enough about him, a stint in the military, a bodyguarding assignment that had ended badly. The only stability he'd known in his life had apparently come from his friendship with Bryan.

Understanding his fears didn't help her figure out how to get through them.

Maybe she was reading too much into a few kisses. But she didn't think so. She believed Donovan cared for her. He'd shown her so in too many ways to discount. Now if only she could get him to admit it— first to himself, and then to her.

He didn't give her a chance to argue any further. "I'll bring the ATV around to the front. Meet me there when you're ready to go."

He walked out of the room without looking back.

Pushing away a weary urge to cry, Chloe ran a hand through her hair and tried, in vain, to be more excited about the prospect of rescue.

* * *

"Chloe!"

Looking around in response to her name, Chloe didn't even have a chance to speak before she was engulfed in a hug that nearly cut off her air supply. Instead of protesting, she returned the embrace, as happy as Grace was to be reunited with her twin. The IV line in her right arm got in the way, but they ignored it as they rejoiced in being back together.

Wearing a thin hospital gown to replace the clothes she'd borrowed from the trailer, she was lying in a narrow bed in a northwest Arkansas hospital. She could hardly remember how she'd gotten here. After a teeth-jarring, bone-jolting hour on the back of the noisy ATV, she had been dazed, feverish and exhausted when Donovan had driven them into a small town. The town's tiny police station was one of the first buildings they had spotted. Donovan had driven her straight to the front door.

The next couple of hours had been a blur of activity. Explanations, telephone calls, people hovering over her, bringing her blankets and warm drinks, and finally a long ambulance ride to this hospital, where she and Donovan had been separated immediately. She'd wanted to cling to him, but she'd managed to resist, knowing that he needed medical attention as badly as she did.

It bothered her that he had hardly looked at her as they'd wheeled him away.

She hadn't been in this room long before Grace and Bryan had rushed in. Sitting on the bed beside her, Grace finally pushed back far enough to study her. "Oh, my God, you look awful. Are you all right?"

"The doctor treated some wounds on my feet and

prescribed some strong antibiotics to ward off infection. I was mildly dehydrated, so they hooked up the IV. I'm tired, of course, but I'll be fine.''

"You scared me half to death," Grace scolded, lines of strain still visible around her eyes and mouth. "I didn't know if you were alive or hurt or…well, you know.''

"I know. I'm sorry for what you went through.'' Chloe could only imagine how she would have felt if the situation had been reversed.

Having held back until after the sisters' reunion, Bryan approached then, his blue eyes dark with concern. "I'm so sorry about this, Chloe. If I'd had any idea something like this would happen—''

Managing to give him a weary smile, she shook her head against the thin hospital pillow. "It wasn't your fault. Donovan was certain some man named Childers was behind the kidnapping.''

"Donovan was right—as he usually is. Childers hired the men who grabbed you.'' Though he kept his expression pleasant enough, there was a hardness in Bryan's voice that she hadn't heard before.

"And the other three? The men he hired?''

"We have two of them. The other's still at large— but we'll get him.'' His eyes were as hard as his voice now, glittering like polished blue metal.

This was the Bryan Falcon she'd heard about but had never personally encountered, she realized. The ruthless businessman who was as cool as ice in the toughest business crisis, utterly merciless when he was double-crossed. He wore his power like an invisible cloak—not a soldier, but a general who surrounded himself with a small, carefully selected and highly skilled ring of followers.

And yet it was his second-in-command who occupied Chloe's thoughts. Who had captured her heart.

"How is Donovan?" Bryan asked, looking toward the open doorway of her room. "I haven't seen him yet."

She roused herself to answer briskly. "He's having his right leg X-rayed. I'm pretty sure he broke a bone in a fall a couple of days ago. He's been walking on it ever since, so I'm worried that he's done some damage to it."

"What have you been through since Monday evening?" Grace murmured, brushing a strand of hair from Chloe's cheek.

Chloe sighed. "It's a long story."

Bryan pulled up a chair on her other side and took her hand, which had been lying limply next to her. "Is there anything I can do for you now? Anything you want?"

She wanted Donovan. She wanted to be back there with him right now, finding out how he was, holding his hand instead of Bryan's. She couldn't say any of those things, of course. She settled for a wan smile. "I'm okay now. But thank you."

Bryan frowned a little, as if he sensed that something had changed between them. He probably thought she blamed him for what she had been through. She would have to convince him that she didn't blame him in any way, even as she tried to come up with a way to let him know that there was no future for them now.

Some instinct made her look toward the doorway. Braced by a set of metal crutches, Donovan stood there with no expression at all on his face as he looked at her lying there between Grace and Bryan—with Bryan holding her hand.

She pulled her hand quickly from Bryan's. Bryan didn't seem to notice as he stood and moved quickly toward his friend.

"How are you, Donovan?" he asked, and his voice was much warmer now than it had been when he'd spoken of the kidnappers.

"Can't complain," Donovan drawled in response.

Even Chloe had to smile at that. If anyone had a right to complain, it was Donovan. His face was hollow and pale, bruised at the temple and the corner of his mouth. The clothes he'd found at the trailer had been replaced by a set of pale green hospital scrubs, and assorted scrapes and bruises were visible in the V-neckline and beneath the short sleeves. His right leg was encased in a temporary cast from the knee down.

She hadn't seen much of his sense of humor during the past few days, though she'd known from things Bryan had said about him that he had one. According to Bryan, a dry and clever one. She wished she could have gotten to know that side of him better. Not that it would have made her love him any more than she already did. She simply wanted to know every aspect of Donovan.

"They didn't want to hook you up to any tubes and pumps?" Bryan asked him.

Donovan shrugged. "They wanted to. I didn't want them to. I won."

"Big surprise."

Chloe couldn't believe he was just planning to walk out of the hospital—even on crutches. "Aren't you even going to stay overnight?" she fretted. "Surely you need more treatment than a brace and a pair of crutches. Is your leg broken?''

The faint smile he'd worn for Bryan disappeared when he glanced her way. ''They gave me some shots. Some pills to take for a few days. I've cracked a bone in my leg, as we suspected. The local doc patched it up until I can get to an orthopedic specialist.''

Bryan nodded. ''You'll have the best, of course, as soon as we get you back home.''

Chloe remembered Donovan's assertion that he didn't have a home. She hadn't believed him then, nor did she now. He had ties he simply didn't choose to acknowledge. She wondered again if it was apprehension or preference that kept him from doing so.

''You're sure you don't want to spend the night here?'' Bryan asked Donovan. ''It wouldn't hurt you to let someone else take care of you for a few hours.''

Donovan shook his head fiercely. ''I've already had this argument with a couple dozen hospital personnel. I'm not staying. I have things to do. I'll see a doctor in Little Rock tomorrow about the leg.''

''Thick-headed,'' Grace murmured.

Chloe shot her sister a frown. ''Don't start, Grace. Donovan saved my life more times than I can count during the past few days. You should be thanking him.''

Grace studied Chloe's face for a moment, then glanced at Donovan, whose frown had only deepened in response to Chloe's defense. ''In that case, I *will* thank you. With all my heart.''

''Not necessary,'' he said gruffly. ''Just doing my job.''

If he'd been trying to hurt her, he couldn't have done it any better, Chloe thought.

Bryan shook his head. "I'd say you definitely went beyond the call of duty this time, pal. And now you're exhausted. We'd better get on our way. Jason's waiting in the lobby. Grace…?"

"I'd like to stay here with Chloe tonight," Grace answered quickly. "I'll sleep in that recliner."

"That isn't necessary, Grace," Chloe assured her.

Her twin shook her head. "I'm not letting you out of my sight for a couple of days. Besides, you know I don't trust hospitals. Someone has to stay here to make sure you get the proper care."

Chloe was sure the hospital staff would not appreciate Grace's close supervision. Still, she was glad her sister was staying. She didn't want to be left alone with her thoughts tonight.

"We need to get you off your feet," Bryan said to Donovan. "You look like you could fall over in a strong wind."

He approached the bed again and leaned over to press a kiss to Chloe's forehead. "I'll see you in the morning. Have Grace call me if you need anything at all, okay?"

She forced another smile for him. "I will. Thank you, Bryan."

He studied her for another moment, his expression a bit quizzical. And then he turned back to his friend. "Let's go, D.C. You can tell me all about your adventures in the car."

Chloe looked quickly toward Donovan, growing a little panicky at the thought of him walking out that door. She had grown so accustomed to being with him. Their eyes met—and, for only a moment, she thought she saw a similar emotion there, a reluctance to leave her.

And then he turned his head away, speaking to Bryan in a low voice that she couldn't quite hear as they moved out into the hallway together.

He hadn't said goodbye, but Chloe heard it, anyway. As far as Donovan was concerned, it was over between them.

Chapter Fourteen

Surrounded by mirrors of every shape and style, Chloe tried not to pay much attention to her reflection. Her short, artfully choppy hairstyle was flattering, but she'd worn the longer bob so long it still startled her occasionally to catch a glimpse of the new cut. It made her seem like a different person than she had been four weeks ago—but then, she *was* a different person. She'd figured she might as well look it.

Noting that it was ten minutes after closing time, she politely ushered the last browser out of her shop and locked the door behind her. It had been a long, busy day. Good for business, but it had left her tired.

But, then, she was tired a lot these days. She'd found it very difficult to shake the depression that had gripped her since Donovan had walked out of her hospital room.

She had neither seen him nor heard from him since.

Carrying a box of bubble-wrapped pottery candle-sticks, Grace entered from the storeroom and crossed to the shelf where they would be displayed. "Did Mrs. Purvis finally leave?"

"Yeah. I sort of herded her out."

"For someone who spends so much time in here, you would think she'd buy something occasionally."

"She bought that bag of potpourri last month," Chloe reminded her ironically.

"Oh, right. We've made a whole fifty cents off her."

"She's a sweet lady. Just lonely. She likes us, and she loves our mirrors. She just can't bring herself to spend the money for one."

Grace muttered something beneath her breath and set a candlestick on the shelf with a thump.

If Chloe had been depressed during the past month, Grace had been more temperamental than usual. Chloe had chalked it up to lingering anxiety; Grace tended to get snappy when she was stressed or worried, and she had been worried sick about Chloe. But now she was beginning to wonder if there was more to it than that. After all, Chloe had been safe for weeks.

Nor should Grace have to fret any longer about the possibility of Chloe entering an amiable marriage of convenience with Bryan. That was over. Chloe had politely informed Bryan only days after she was rescued that she'd given his offer a great deal of thought and had decided to decline. She had assured him that he shouldn't take the rejection personally; she was very fond of him and thought he would make a wonderful husband and father. Just not with her.

He'd taken the news well, without any sign of disappointment. Either he'd been prepared for her decision or he'd come to the same conclusion. Assuring her that they would remain friends, he had made a polite exit. He'd called two or three times since to check on her and Grace, but their conversations were growing shorter each time.

She didn't think she would be seeing either Bryan or Donovan again.

She had not mentioned her feelings for Donovan to Bryan. Hadn't mentioned Donovan at all, actually, except to politely inquire about his leg, which she had been told was healing satisfactorily. She wouldn't risk causing any problems between Bryan and Donovan, especially since she didn't know whether Donovan had even given her a second thought since he'd brought her out of those woods.

She'd thought he would have at least called her.

"So are you going to stand there gazing out the door the rest of the night, or are you going to help me set out this new shipment?"

Grace's acerbic question brought her attention back to the present. "Sorry. I was distracted."

"You're always distracted these days," Grace muttered.

"And you're always grumpy," Chloe retorted.

Rather than snapping back at her, Grace knelt in front of the display shelf in silence for several long moments, and then she looked up at Chloe with a grimace. "I am, aren't I? I'm sorry."

Chloe could rarely hold a grudge against her twin. "It's okay. I know you've been through a lot lately."

Grace groaned. "That's hardly an excuse, especially since you went through so much more. I just—well, I've been worried about you."

"About me?" Chloe set a yellow-and-blue-patterned candlestick on a shelf, then fussed with its placement for a moment. "There's no need. Bryan has repeatedly promised us that the kidnapping threat is over."

"From what I saw of the weasel Childers, I agree. I thought he was going to faint when Bryan and Jason faced him down in his apartment."

Chloe nodded. "Anyway, now that the publicity has died down and the press has turned its attention to other things, other misfortunate people, I can fade quietly and safely back into obscurity. I'm fine."

Her sister moved to stand beside her, studying her profile. "You're unhappy."

Chloe didn't meet her twin's eyes as she shifted a marble egg into a more conspicuous position. "Of course I'm not un—"

"Chloe." Grace sounded irritated again now. "Please don't try bluffing with me. You know you've never been able to fool me."

Chloe sighed heavily. "You're right. I don't know what's been wrong with me lately. A mild case of post-traumatic stress syndrome, maybe. I'm sure I'll get over it soon."

"I feel like it's my fault."

That comment startled her into turning to stare at Grace. "Your fault? Why on earth would you think that?"

Hanging her head a little, Grace replied, "I think you broke up with Bryan because I made such a fuss about it at the beginning. You had decided you wanted to marry a decent guy and have a family, and I had no right to interfere. I would still rather see you marry for love, but if friendship is more important to you, then that should be all that matters. Bryan's a decent guy. I'm sure he would beef up his security for you if you start seeing him again, so you'd probably be safer than you are just driving to work in the morning now."

She shook her head impatiently, drew a deep breath and blurted, "What I'm trying to say is, I think you and Bryan should get back together if it would make you happy again. You should marry him and have those kids you both want so badly. I'll support your decision whole-heartedly."

For the life of her, Chloe couldn't have explained why tears suddenly gathered in her eyes. "That's very considerate of you, Grace, but I don't *want* to marry Bryan. As you have pointed out on numerous occasions, I don't love him. I never will."

Grace looked startled. "You said yourself that you're very fond of him."

"I am. Very. But that isn't enough."

"Since when?"

Since she had fallen passionately and permanently in love with another man, Chloe thought in despair. "I just changed my mind."

Grace studied her for a long time, then pushed a hand through her hair. "Sorry. I would have sworn you've been behaving like a woman with a broken heart."

Unable to come up with a good response, Chloe turned away.

They worked in silence for a few minutes, with Chloe hoping Grace would change the subject, and Grace apparently lost in her thoughts. It was Grace who broke the silence again. "When did you talk to Bryan last?"

"He called earlier this afternoon. He said to tell you hello, by the way."

Grace cleared her throat, then asked, "Did he mention how Donovan's doing?"

Just the sound of his name made her chest ache. "He's fine. He's off the crutches, but still in a walking cast."

"Donovan's never called you himself?"

"No."

"That seems a bit odd, doesn't it?"

"I'm sure he knows Bryan is keeping me updated."

"Mm. So I guess you and Donovan didn't become fast friends during your ordeal?"

"No, I suppose we didn't." Because this conversation was entirely too painful, she turned abruptly away. "You can finish this. I'll go close out the register."

Lost in her own thoughts again, Grace didn't reply.

Donovan and Bryan were walking through the lobby of a St. Louis hotel when Donovan was nearly slammed to the floor. It was only Bryan's lightning reflexes that save him from an ignominious fall.

"Whoa, there, buddy." Bryan scooped the runaway three-year-old into his arms only a moment before the child barreled into Donovan's bum leg.

Grateful for the quick save, Donovan glanced around for the kid's parents. There were a lot of people around, but he didn't see anyone who seemed to be looking for the boy.

"Where's your mom?" Bryan asked the child as he set him back on his feet.

The red-haired tot waved an arm vaguely in the direction of the gift shop. "Over there."

"Let's go find her, shall we?"

The boy took Bryan's outstretched hand and nodded obligingly. "'Kay."

It always amazed Donovan how quickly children took to Bryan. That notorious charm of his was as effective with the kids as it was with the ladies.

"I'll be right back if you want to wait here," Bryan said over his shoulder as the boy led him away.

Donovan nodded and moved to one of the deep sofas arranged invitingly around the big, airy lobby. He was sitting there when Bryan rejoined him a few minutes later.

Bryan was still smiling. "Cute kid," he said, taking a chair near Donovan's sofa. "His mother was going nuts looking for him in the gift shop. She says he's worse than Houdini when it comes to making dramatic escapes."

"She needs to put a leash on him. Anyone could have snatched him." The thought of his own recent encounter with kidnappers was enough to make Donovan scowl.

"She said she would watch him more carefully from now on. She seemed like a good mother. She just got distracted for a minute."

Donovan watched as Bryan looked toward the gift shop again, and something in his friend's eyes made him ask, "You still want kids, don't you?"

Bryan seemed startled by the question—which, admittedly, *was* more personal than Donovan usually got—but he answered candidly, "Yeah. I've always thought I'd make a pretty good father, even though my own was hardly a role model."

"I think you would, too."

"Thanks for the vote of confidence."

Donovan waited as long as he could before saying reluctantly, "Chloe would make a good mother."

Again, Bryan's eyebrows shot up in an expression of surprise, probably because Donovan had hardly mentioned Chloe's name in the past month. "Yes, I thought she would, too. That was one of the reasons why I decided she and I would make a good match. Obviously, I was wrong about that part."

"You didn't fight for her very hard. When she broke it off, you just let her go."

"And what was I supposed to do?" Bryan asked dryly. "Lock her up?"

"You should have been patient. You knew she was still suffering from shock when we came out of those woods, but you let her break it off only a few days later. If you'd hung in there, been there for her, comforted her, tried to make it all up to her, she would have come around."

"I don't think so."

Donovan didn't know why he was pushing this—hell, he should be glad he wouldn't have to deal with watching Bryan and Chloe together—but for some reason he felt he had to say it.

He was very fond of both Bryan and Chloe, he told himself, feeling a bit noble for his unselfishness. He didn't like the thought of either of them being alone, unsatisfied. "Maybe you should give it another try."

Bryan sighed. "To be honest, I'm not sure I want to give it another try. I like and admire Chloe a great deal. I think she's amazing—brave, resourceful, intelligent. I just don't think I want to marry her."

Donovan couldn't believe what he was hearing. "Why the hell not?"

"I don't know," Bryan answered, a bit defensively now. "Maybe Grace was right. I was thinking about marrying Chloe for the wrong reasons. Respect and admiration aren't synonymous with love."

Shaking his head in disgust, Donovan muttered, "Grace is hardly one to be giving romantic advice. From what I saw, she's a spitfire."

"Grace isn't so bad. She just genuinely wants what's best for Chloe. And so do I. Chloe deserves to find someone who'll love her and treat her right."

"I can't imagine she would find anyone who would treat her better than you would."

"I'm touched."

"I'm beginning to believe that you are," Donovan muttered. "Look all you want for the perfect match, but you aren't going to find anyone better than Chloe."

Bryan chuckled. "Hell, D.C., if you feel that way about her, why don't *you* marry her?"

To his chagrin, Donovan felt a wave of heat rise from the collar of his crisp white shirt. He looked away quickly, pretending interest in a silicone-busted blonde who was mincing past them, making an obvious play to get their attention. "As you said," he muttered, "Chloe deserves the best."

He was aware that Bryan was watching him closely, but he refused to look around. "We'd better get moving again," he said, pushing himself off the sofa. "We don't want to be late for the meeting."

Feeling like a complete idiot, he headed toward the elevators.

This was what he got for trying to do something

nice for two people he cared about, he thought irritably. He'd made such a botch of it that he had been left looking like a fool. God only knew what Bryan was thinking right now. He should have just stayed out of it—but he'd had an irrational hope that getting Bryan and Chloe back together might help him get her out of his mind. Out of his dreams.

Out of his heart, damn it.

He should have known better.

Bryan was sitting in his Little Rock office a couple of days later when the intercom on his desk buzzed. "Mr. Falcon? Ms. Pennington is on line two. Are you available to take her call?"

He looked up from the paperwork in front of him. "Yes, thanks, Marta."

He picked up the receiver. "Good morning, Chloe. Is everything all right?"

"It isn't Chloe, it's Grace."

That made him sit back in his chair, his eyebrows rising sharply. "Grace? What is it? What's happened?"

He couldn't imagine that Chloe's sister would be calling him unless something was terribly wrong.

"No, everything's okay. I just need to ask you a question."

He relaxed—a little. A call from Grace Pennington was still fraught with peril. "What question do you want to ask me?"

"How's Donovan?"

This call was becoming more intriguing all the time, Bryan thought, settling more comfortably into his chair. Perhaps he and Grace had been on the same wavelength recently—definitely an astonishing thought. "Why do you ask?"

"I still don't know why you were so insistent that we needed to spend the day at the river house," Chloe announced as she sat in her sister's car one Wednesday morning in early June, watching Grace drive. "I really had quite a few things to do today."

"I told you," Grace replied, "I just needed to get away for a day and I didn't want to come by myself."

Grace *had* been working awfully hard lately, Chloe conceded. And she did seem in need of a vacation; she had been so tense and stressed.

"I'm surprised Mom and Dad didn't want to come, too. They love to spend the day with us at the river."

"Mom had that garden club thing this afternoon," Grace reminded her.

Chloe sat back in the leather bucket seat of Grace's two-seater, which bumped a bit roughly over the rural roads that led to their parents' vacation cabin on the Little Red River. It had been quite a while since she'd made this trip. She'd been too busy before the kidnapping, and since then she'd been avoiding any reminders of vacation homes and woods and lakes and rivers—anything that made her think of the time she had spent with Donovan.

But she couldn't spend the rest of her days hiding from her memories. She had to get on with her life—and she supposed this was as good a time as any to get started.

It was obvious that their parents had been to the river house recently, she noted when Grace drove onto the long gravel driveway. Their mother's flower beds had been watered and weeded, and the many windows in the two-story log cabin had been washed until they sparkled in the bright sunlight. A large porch lined with swings and rockers and cooled by old-fashioned ceiling fans hinted of lazy summer days spent relaxing and watching the river roll by.

She smiled at the memory of cookouts with her family, trout-fishing with her dad and sleepovers with her sister and their friends in the loft bedroom. She'd spent a lot of happy times here; why had she been so reluctant to come today?

"Maybe this *was* a good idea," she admitted.

Grace flashed her a smile. "Didn't I tell you so? It's our slowest day at work, so Bob and Justin can handle everything there. You and I can just chill out."

"I can't wait to get into my waders. It's been so long since I've had a fly rod in my hands I've probably forgotten how to cast."

"Oh, I doubt that. I have a feeling you'll definitely catch something today."

Chloe had to smile at Grace's wording. "A cold, probably."

"Cute." Grace parked the car and opened her door. "Grab the groceries, will you? I'll carry the drinks."

They had come prepared to grill hamburgers later. Grace had brought so much food that Chloe had accused her of buying enough for half a dozen people instead of just two. Grace had merely shrugged and claimed she'd gotten carried away.

The inside of the house had not changed since Chloe had last visited. They entered into a two-story-high main room with a large rock fireplace and a ceiling fan with a light fixture overhead. To the back of the main room, separated by a low dining bar, was the kitchen and dining room combination. The master bedroom opened off the other side of the living room, beneath the stairs. Upstairs, a loft sitting room overlooked the living room, and two small bedrooms shared another bath. One entire side of the house consisted of large windows that overlooked the river.

The log walls were hung with duck prints and primitive art, the furnishing were worn and comfortable, the wooden floors warmed by thick braided rugs. Chloe always thought of her parents' weekend hideaway as a nap waiting to happen.

She carried the groceries into the kitchen and deposited them on a tile countertop, stowing perishables in the refrigerator. Returning to the main room, she found Grace peering out a window toward the driveway. "Expecting someone?"

Grace jumped, looking almost comically guilty. "Of course not," she said, her voice oddly breathless. "Why do you ask?"

Eyeing her twin curiously, Chloe shook her head. "You *do* need a day off, don't you? You're as jumpy as a cat."

"I told you, I've been working too hard."

"Apparently. So, what do you want to do first? It's too early to start the grill. We could fish."

"You know, I think I'd rather just rest for a while. I brought a new mystery, so I think I'll curl up in a rocker and read for a couple hours."

"Okay. I'll go fish by myself. You always scare the trout away, anyway."

"I don't always scare them away. I just get mad sometimes when I hook one and then lose it."

Chloe grinned as she pictured Grace stamping her feet in the water and throwing rocks at the fish that got away. She never actually hit one of them, of course, but she guaranteed that no one else would catch any, either. "Enjoy your book. I'll see you later."

"Mm," Grace murmured behind her. "Much later."

Deciding she would never figure out her twin's odd mood, Chloe headed out to the storeroom where her father kept the fishing gear.

"Tell me again why you want to buy another vacation cabin?" Donovan asked Bryan quizzically, watching cornfields, cow pastures and mobile homes pass by outside the passenger window of Bryan's car.

Sitting behind the wheel, Bryan glanced away from the road ahead to reply, "I've gotten tired of the place in Missouri. Bad memories there now. I'd like to find someplace smaller and easier to get to. The cabin you and I are visiting sounds ideal."

"So why do you need me here? You don't require my approval to buy anything."

"I just wanted company, okay? And I do value your opinion."

Donovan shrugged. "Then I'm happy to oblige."

A small red sports car passed them going the opposite direction. It was driven by a woman in large sunglasses and a floppy hat, both of which concealed her face. Donovan told himself it was a depressing clue to his state of mind that the woman still looked like Chloe to him.

Sometimes he saw her everywhere he looked.

Bryan's cell phone buzzed. He sighed heavily, reached into his pocket, and held the small device to his ear. "Falcon."

Donovan gazed out the window as Bryan carried

on a brief, monosyllabic conversation. And then Bryan disconnected the call and brought Donovan out of his morose musings with an exclamation of satisfaction. "Ah. This is the cabin, I think. Nice, isn't it?"

Donovan studied the neat log cabin in front of them. A pleasant place—well-tended flower beds, a big, inviting porch, nice river view—but it was hardly as luxurious as Bryan's vacation home in Missouri. That one obviously belonged to a very wealthy man; this one looked like a middle-class weekend cottage. There wasn't even a security system, as far as he could tell.

"It has potential, I guess," he said to Bryan. "You could probably put a gate at the end of this driveway, maybe fence the boundaries of the lot."

"Turn this pretty place into a fortress? That would be a shame, don't you think?"

"I think a man in your position has to be more concerned about security than the average fisherman—as you should know very well by now," Donovan retorted.

"Ever since Childers went nuts and implemented that crazy kidnapping plan, you've been more protective than an old nanny," Bryan scolded indulgently. "Might I remind you that Jason is my security chief, not you?"

"So why isn't he with you today?"

"Because I want the opinion of a friend, not a paid advisor."

Though this whole plan still seemed impulsive and illogical to Donovan, he decided to humor his friend for now. "Okay, let's go check the place out. You have a key?"

"Of course."

As Donovan followed Bryan into the cabin, he was reminded again of middle-income suburbia. No professional decorator had stepped foot through these doors. The furnishings and decor looked as though they'd been assembled during years of family vacations and long weekends. Some of his and Bryan's wealthy friends would have turned up their noses in scorn at what they would have considered such primitive accommodations—but Donovan rather liked it. It was…comfortable. Inviting. Homey.

Bryan rubbed the back of his neck as he looked around. "Nice," he murmured, "but I don't know if it's exactly what I have in mind."

If Bryan decided he didn't want the place, Donovan thought he might consider buying it himself. He didn't have to worry about security as much as Bryan—not usually, anyway. And while he hadn't been in the habit of taking leisurely weekends away from work before now, he'd been considering making some changes in his routines. A man needed something besides work in his life, he had recently concluded. Maybe he should take up fishing.

He wandered to the far side of the room, looking out through the wall of glass there. "There's a rock walkway that leads down to the river."

"Why don't you check it out while I look around a bit more in here?" Bryan suggested. "I'll join you down by the river shortly."

Bryan must have sensed that he was feeling drawn to the river. He nodded and reached for the handle of the French doors that led out onto a big wooden deck.

"Donovan."

He paused and looked over his shoulder. "Yes?"

"Sometimes decisions have to be made with the heart, not the head, to be right. Keep that in mind, will you?"

Frowning, Donovan blurted, "What the hell are you talking about?"

"Just remember what I said." Bryan's smile looked a little smug and just a bit wistful. "Go on down to the river. I'll see you later."

Closing the door behind him, Donovan shook his head as he carefully descended the steps to the rock walkway. He still wore a walking cast, but it was hidden beneath his loose slacks and he'd gotten used to getting around in it.

As he walked, he wondered if Bryan could be going through some sort of midlife crisis, though thirty-eight seemed a bit early for midlife. He had done and said some strange things lately, leaving Donovan struggling to keep up. What was that stuff about making decisions with the heart? Was he talking about this place? Pointing out that sometimes a decision felt right even when it didn't seem logical? If Bryan wanted to buy this cabin despite the drawbacks, Donovan certainly wouldn't try to stop him.

Someone was standing beside the river on the other side of a stand of trees that had blocked the view from the cabin. It was a woman, dressed in a pink tank top beneath suspendered fishing waders, standing with her back to him. A floppy hat covered her short hair, and a fly rod lay on the ground beside her, although she wasn't fishing at the moment. She was just standing there, looking out at the water, seemingly lost in her thoughts.

She, too, looked like Chloe, he thought with a scowl. He really was seeing her everywhere.

He was just about to turn around and leave her to her privacy when she suddenly knelt down, picked up a stone and threw it at the water. It was an obvious attempt to skip the rock across the water—but the angle was all wrong. The rock sank with a splash.

The woman's exasperated mutter carried on a soft breeze to where he stood.

His hands clenched into fists at his sides. ''Chloe,'' he said, hardly aware that he'd said her name aloud.

She froze, then jerked around to face him, her eyes wide beneath the brim of her floppy fishing hat. ''Donovan! What are you doing here?''

Chapter Fifteen

Chloe couldn't believe Donovan was standing there on her parents' walkway, looking at her as though she had materialized from thin air in front of him. Her first instinct was to run toward him, to throw herself into his arms. But he looked so stern and stiff that she wasn't entirely sure he would catch her if she did.

"What are you doing here?" she asked again when he didn't answer the first time.

"I was just about to ask you the same question."

She tilted her head curiously. "You didn't know I was here?"

"I had no idea."

He looked wonderful, she couldn't help noticing as she tried to process his words. His hair looked freshly cut—though that recalcitrant lock still fell forward on his forehead—and the dark hollows of pain were gone from his clean-shaven face. His left foot was encased in a leather slip-on shoe, and his right foot was wrapped in a cast designed for walking. He wore a designer shirt and crisply tailored chinos, but he had looked just as good to her in the ill-fitting garments he'd borrowed from that trailer. "I still don't understand why you're here."

"I came with Bryan. He's thinking about buying this place."

That made her frown deepen. "This place isn't for sale. It belongs to my parents."

"Your parents?" Donovan looked as confused as she was now. "Are you sure they don't want to sell it?"

"I'm positive. They would have told me if they were. They knew Grace and I were coming here today—they certainly would have mentioned if it was for sale."

"Grace is here, too?" Donovan looked around as if he expected to see her twin lurking behind a tree nearby.

"She's in the house. Didn't you see her?"

"No. Bryan and I were just in the house. Bryan let us in with a key. No one was there."

"Bryan has a key to my parents' vacation house?" This situation was getting stranger by the minute. "I think we'd better go find out what's going on."

Donovan nodded. "I think you're right."

She bent to pick up her fly rod. She hadn't been in the mood to fish, anyway. She'd spent the time since she'd walked down here gazing at the water and thinking about Donovan. And then to turn and see him standing there—as if her thoughts had conjured him—well, she was still half in shock.

He waited for her to pass him. She noticed as he

followed her that he was walking well, hardly limping at all despite the cast. She couldn't stop looking at him, though she tried to be subtle about it. Yet every time she shot a glance at him, she found him looking back at her as if he was also having trouble looking away.

Reaching the back deck of the house, she propped her rod against the railing, then unlaced and removed her waterproof boots. She unbuckled the belt and suspenders of her stocking-foot waders, and peeled off the shapeless garment to reveal the pink tank top and denim shorts. She was entirely too aware of Donovan watching her every move. She felt as self-conscious as if she were doing a striptease for him, though fishing waders and denim shorts hardly qualified as sexy clothing.

She'd left a pair of pink flip-flops lying beside a chair on the deck; she slipped her feet into them and opened the French doors that led into the house. "Grace?" she called out as she entered with Donovan on her heels.

The house was eerily quiet. Obviously empty. She frowned. "That's odd. Maybe they're on the front porch."

She crossed the main room rapidly and opened the front door. Not only were there no people on the porch, but there were no cars in the driveway. No sign of Grace's two-seater. "Where in the world—?"

"Does Grace drive a red sports car, by any chance?" Donovan asked as she slowly closed the front door and turned to face him.

"Yes. Why?"

"Damn. That's who called him."

"Called who?"

"Bryan." Placing a hand to the back of his neck, he rested his other hand on his hip and gave her a faint, wry smile. "I hate to tell you this, Chloe, but I think we've been kidnapped again."

She gaped at him for a moment, then ran a hand through her disheveled hair, dislodging the fishing hat she was still wearing. She hardly even noticed as it fell to the floor at her feet. "Either my brain isn't working very well today, or everyone is behaving very strangely. I don't understand what's going on."

"You've cut your hair."

She dropped her hand in response to his unexpected comment. "Yes. Grace says I chopped it off."

"I like it."

"Thank you." She motioned toward the couches arranged for conversation around the fireplace. "Sit down. See if you can explain to me what's going on. I assume you've figured it out?"

"I think so."

He waited for her to be seated, and then he sat on the same couch, though at the other end. He turned to face her. "I didn't realize Grace and Bryan had stayed in touch since you and I got back."

"As far as I know, they haven't. I've spoken with Bryan a few times, but the only time he mentioned Grace was when he would tell me to say hi to her for him. And I certainly can't imagine that she would have conspired with him for anything like this."

"Obviously, she did. Uh, Bryan can be impulsive sometimes. Especially when something amuses him."

"So can Grace. It's never easy to predict what she's going to do. But this…"

Because it still made no sense to her, Chloe's thoughts drifted from Grace's strange behavior. She studied Donovan's face, thinking there was some slight difference in his expression, and trying to decide what it was. "I thought you might call me after we returned to our homes. I was disappointed that you didn't," she admitted.

His mouth pulled a bit at one corner. "I didn't want to intrude on your life. And I wasn't sure you'd want to be reminded of what you went through with me."

She shook her head. "That wouldn't have been a problem. I haven't been able to stop thinking about those days we spent together."

"Neither have I."

His low admission gave her the courage to say, "I've missed you, Donovan."

He looked down at his hands. "You certainly didn't waste any time breaking things off with Bryan. I would have thought you'd have given it a little more time."

"I didn't need any more time. I knew there was no future between us. I told you so in that forest, though you didn't seem to believe me at the time."

"I believed you. I just thought—"

"I know. You thought I'd been so traumatized by the ordeal that I couldn't think straight. That my poor little nerves had been overwrought."

He gave her a chiding glance in response to her sarcasm—but at least he was looking at her. "I didn't think that, exactly. I just thought you needed more time for Bryan to convince you what a great guy he is."

"I didn't *need* to be convinced of that. Bryan is a terrific guy. A real prince. And he deserves someone better than me."

Donovan scowled. "That's bull. He could never find anyone better than you."

Locking her hands in her lap, Chloe hoped her instincts about Donovan's feelings were right. If not, she was on the verge of making a fool of herself. Not to mention the fact that she was about to risk a very painful rejection.

Despite the enormous stakes, she managed to speak evenly. "You say you want the best for Bryan. Would you honestly want him to marry someone who's desperately in love with his best friend?"

Donovan went so still he could have been carved from marble. She wasn't even sure he breathed for the next minute or two.

Her fingers clenched so tightly the knuckles ached when she spoke again. "You said my feelings would change when we were out of that forest and back in our real lives. You were wrong. I still feel the same way."

His jaw clenched as he slowly shook his head. "I'm not the kind of man you've been looking for. I've never wanted marriage or kids."

"You didn't want them—or you never thought you would have them because of the bad experiences of your past?" she countered.

"Same difference."

"No. Not even similar."

"You deserve better," he muttered, his usually bright-green eyes dark with suppressed emotion.

"I deserve the same thing Bryan does," she whispered. "Someone who loves me."

She watched his throat work with a hard swallow.

"I asked you once how you felt about me," she reminded him again, her tone very gentle now. "You said it wasn't relevant then. I think it *is* relevant now. How do you feel about me, Donovan?''

His voice was so low she could hardly hear him. ''I've never been in love. I'm not even sure I know what the word means. But I know you haven't been out of my thoughts for one minute since I left you. I know I've never met any woman I admired or respected more. I know I want you so badly my teeth ache. I wake up every night in a cold sweat, aching for you. Missing you.''

Tears were running down her cheeks now. Tears of joy. Of relief. Of hope. And of sympathy, because this was obviously so difficult for him. ''That's close enough.''

He held up a hand. ''I also know that it would kill me if I hurt you or let you down. I don't ever want to see you suffer again. I don't ever want to cause you pain. But I'm afraid I will, because I don't know how the hell to go about making a woman happy. I can give you things—my association with Bryan has made me very comfortable financially—but I know that isn't enough for you.''

She dashed a hand against her cheek. ''No. If money and material things were enough to make me happy, I would have married Bryan. But you're right, it takes a lot more than that to make me happy.''

''And you think you can be happy with me?'' He sounded as though that concept was almost impossible for him to believe.

She couldn't resist reaching out to touch his hard cheek. ''I know I will. And I know I can make you happy, too, if you'll let me.''

Catching her hand, he pressed his lips to her palm in a hard caress that made her heart trip. ''There are people who would say you're crazy to choose me over Bryan.''

"I don't care what anyone says. In my opinion, I've chosen the best man. I love you, Donovan.''

He pulled her into his arms, his mouth crushing hers in a kiss that said everything he couldn't put into words. Sheer poetry, she decided, happily losing herself in the embrace.

"How long do you think Bryan and Grace will stay away?'' she murmured against his lips.

"I don't expect to see them for awhile.'' He brushed his fingers experimentally through her short hair, seemed to like the feeling and did it again. "Why—do you want to go fishing?''

She gave him a look. "Now is not the time to start teasing me,'' she informed him, breaking away from his arms to stand and offer him her hand. "You can prove that you really do have a sense of humor after you make love with me.''

"Are you going to be a demanding sort of wife?'' he asked as he rose to stand beside her.

Wife. The word shot through her like an arrow. Was this Donovan's idea of a proposal?

She swallowed before answering lightly, "Yes, I'm going to be very high-maintenance. You're going to have to spend the rest of your life catering to my whims.''

He pretended to give her warning a moment's thought, and then he nodded. "I can live with that.''

Apparently, they were engaged.

So the man she loved wasn't exactly the most romantic or silver-tongued charmer in the world. She didn't care. She adored him exactly the way he was.

Smiling like an idiot, Chloe led him up the stairs

toward the bedroom that had always been hers. He stopped at the top of the stairs to kiss her half sense-less again.

"There's only one problem," he murmured, his hands already exploring her curves. "I didn't come prepared for this. I know you want kids, but…"

She broke away with a shaky laugh, feeling as though her skin was melting everywhere he'd touched. "Wait right here," she ordered, and dashed into Grace's room, where she rummaged through a nightstand drawer, emerging with a couple of plastic packets she had suspected she would find there.

She returned triumphantly to Donovan. "I do want children," she assured him, leading him into the other bedroom. "But not quite yet."

Being the gentleman that he was, he didn't ask any questions about the conveniently appearing condoms. She would tell him another time about Grace's broken engagement, and the weekends Grace had once spent here with the man she had planned to marry—but for now, she concentrated only on her own engagement. One that she was certain would end much more hap-pily than her twin's had.

Finally closed into the small, early-American-furnished bedroom with the slanted roof and day-dream-tempting window seat, Donovan turned to pull her back into his arms. It didn't take him long to rid her of her tank top and shorts, nor the flimsy bra and panties she had worn beneath. He growled approval of the skin he'd revealed, his fingers exploring her so slowly and so skillfully that he soon brought her to shivering incoherence by his touch alone.

She helped him remove his own clothes, though her hands were shaking so hard she fumbled more than she assisted. She had never wanted anyone more than she wanted Donovan now. She had never ached, never burned like this. When he finally stood in front of her, naked except for the short cast below his right knee, she saw to her utter delight that he had a powerful ache for her, too.

She reached for him, drawing him slowly against her. Her breath caught when they finally stood skin-to-skin. He groaned.

His hands cupped her bottom, drew her tightly against his rock-hard arousal. She rubbed against him, knowing she was playing with fire, but loving the tremor that ran through him in response. Donovan's control was so formidable that it gave her a heady sense of feminine power to know she had the ability to break through it.

He tumbled her to the bed, falling with her, his mouth locked with hers. She ran her hands over as much of him as she could reach, loving the hard, hot, pulsing strength of him. He didn't wait for her assistance with the protection she'd found for him. He donned it swiftly and with a skill that bespoke experience she wouldn't think about right now.

And then he made her incapable of thinking at all by thrusting so deeply into her that she fancied they would never be completely separate again. He'd made them one—physically, emotionally, permanently.

"I love you, Donovan," she whispered, wrapping herself around him.

"I love you, too," he murmured, his mouth against hers. "This has to be love. It's too much to be anything else."

That made her cry. And then he made her soar.

She'd known since those days in the forest that

they were a perfect match. Together, there were no obstacles they could not overcome.

She'd been looking for a partner. She had found a mate. Now she understood the difference.

They had been recuperating in each other's arms for a long time when they were disturbed by the buzz of Donovan's cell phone, which he'd set on the nightstand when he'd removed the clip from his belt.

"Ignore it," he said when Chloe reached for it.

She shook her head and handed him the small plastic phone, her smile so drowsily satisfied that he almost threw the phone aside and fell onto her again. "It's probably Bryan. You really should talk to him."

Though he sighed, he held the phone to his ear. "What?"

"I was just wondering if you need a ride any time soon," Bryan said without bothering to identify himself. "Or if you're still speaking to me."

"I won't be needing a ride for a while. And I'll have plenty to say to you later," Donovan growled in response.

"How's Chloe?"

"Chloe is fine," Donovan replied, nuzzling against her temple, enjoying the way her newly short hair tickled his cheek. She murmured her pleasure and pressed a kiss to his throat.

"Grace and I thought the two of you needed to talk. Knowing how stubborn you can be, I thought this might be the only way to convince you."

"Mm. From now on, let me make my own moves." He shifted against the sheets as Chloe's hand wandered over his stomach and then dipped downward.

"I'll do that. So, um, things are working out between the two of you?"

"Let's just put it this way. Chloe took your advice about making a choice with her heart instead of her head."

"I always said Chloe was a remarkable woman."

Donovan cleared his throat, trying to read the underlying expression in his friend's voice. "Uh—Bryan…"

"If ever I've seen two people who were more right for each other, it's you and Chloe. It just took us all a while to realize it. Do yourself a favor, D.C. Let yourself be happy for a change."

Bryan disconnected the call before Donovan could come up with a response.

"Bryan and Grace as matchmakers," Chloe murmured, shaking her head. "It's very bizarre."

Donovan was rather dazed by the image, as well. "What I can't figure out is how they knew the way we feel about each other. Unless you said something…?"

"I didn't say anything," she assured him. "And since I sincerely doubt that you did, either, we must have been more transparent to the people who care most about us than we thought."

"Apparently." He hesitated a moment, then asked slowly, "You, uh, are still going to marry me, aren't you?"

She looked at him quizzically. "Did you think I would suddenly change my mind?"

"Well…"

She sighed. "I can tell it's going to take me a while to convince you that I'm very certain of what I'm doing this time. I've reminded you on numerous occasions that I never told Bryan I would marry him, because I sensed that it wasn't right. And I never even pretended to love him. This time I have no doubts. I love *you*.''

Donovan told himself he was going to have to start believing her sometime—even though it still seemed incredible to him that Chloe had chosen him over Bryan. And he did believe her…but he figured a little more convincing wouldn't hurt.

''Since we're stranded here for a while longer,'' he murmured, gathering her close again.

''We might as well make good use of our time,'' she finished for him, lifting her mouth to his.

''Exactly what I was thinking.''

''See?'' she asked, just before they both lost the ability to speak. ''We're the perfect match, after all.''

* * * * *

Good Husband Material

SUSAN MALLERY

SUSAN MALLERY

is the bestselling author of nearly fifty books. She makes her home in the Pacific Northwest with her handsome prince of a husband and her two adorable-but-not-so-bright cats.

Chapter One

Kari Asbury fully expected to have trouble cashing her out-of-state check, she just didn't think she would have to put her life on the line to do it.

It wasn't just that the check was drawn from a bank in big, bad New York City; it was that her driver's license was also from that East Coast state. Ida Mae Montel would want to know why a girl born and raised in Possum Landing, Texas, would willingly run off to a place like that…a place with *Yankees*. And if a girl had to do such a thing, why on earth would she give up her Texas driver's license? Didn't everyone want to be from the Lone Star State?

No doubt Sue Ellen Boudine, the bank manager, would mosey on over to examine the check, all the while holding it like it was attached to a poisonous snake. They'd make a few calls (probably to friends, letting them know that Kari was back in town and with a New York driver's license, of all things), they'd hem and haw, and sigh heavily. Then they'd give Kari the money. Oh, but first they'd try to talk her into opening an account right there at the First Bank of Possum Landing.

Kari hesitated in front of the double glass doors, trying to figure out if she really needed the cash that badly. Maybe it would be better to pay the service fee and get the money out of the ATM machine. Then she reminded herself that the quicker everyone realized she'd returned to town for a very *temporary* visit, the quicker all the questions would be asked and answered. Then maybe she could have a little peace. Maybe.

There was the added thrill of finding out if Ida Mae still wore her hair in a beehive. How much hair spray did that upswept style require? Kari knew for a fact that Ida Mae only had her hair done once a week, yet it looked exactly the same on day seven as it did on day one.

Still smiling at the memory of Ida Mae's coiffure, she pulled open the door and stepped inside. She paused just past the threshold and waited for the shrieks of welcome and the group hug that would follow.

Nothing happened.

Kari frowned. She glanced around at the bank—established in 1892—taking in the tall, narrow windows, the real wood counters and stylish paneling. Ida Mae was in her regular spot—the first position on the left—as befitted the head teller. But the older woman wasn't talking. She wasn't even smiling. Her small eyes widened with something that looked like panic, and she made an odd gesture with her hand.

Before Kari could figure out what it meant, something hard and cold pressed against her cheek.

"Well, lookee here. We got us another customer, boys. At least this one's young and pretty. What my mama used to call a tall drink of water. That's something."

Kari's heart stopped. It might be nearly ninety in the shade outside, but here in the bank it felt closer to absolute zero.

Slowly, very slowly, she turned toward the man, who was holding a gun. He was short, stocky and wearing a ski mask. What on earth was going on?

"We're robbin' the bank," the man said, as if he could read her mind.

His astuteness startled her, until she realized his deduction wasn't much of a stretch.

She quickly glanced around. There were four of them, counting the man holding a gun on her. Two kept all the customers and most of the employees together at the far end of the bank, while the last one was behind the counter, putting money that Ida Mae handed him into a bag.

"You go ahead and set your purse on the floor," the man in front of her said. "Then start walking toward the other ladies. Do what you're told and no one will get hurt."

Kari flexed her hands slightly. Her chest tightened,

and it was nearly impossible to speak. "I, uh, I don't have a purse."

She didn't. She'd come into the bank with a check and her driver's license. Both were in the back pocket of her shorts.

The robber stared at her for a couple of seconds, then nodded. "Seems you don't. Now head on over there."

This couldn't be happening, Kari thought, even as she headed for the cluster of other customers huddled by the far end of the counter.

She was halfway to the safety of that crowd when the rear door of the bank opened.

"Well, hell," a low voice drawled. "One of us has bad timing, boys. You think it's you or me?"

Several women screamed. One of the masked men by the crowd grabbed an older woman and held the gun to her head. "Stay back," he yelled. "Stay back or the old lady dies."

Kari didn't have time to react. The man who had first held a gun to her jerked her arm to drag her back to him. She felt the pressure of the pistol against her cheek again. He wrapped one wiry arm around her neck, keeping her securely in place.

"Seems to me we've got a problem," the man holding her said. "So, Sheriff, why don't you just back out real slow and no one will get hurt."

The sheriff in question gave a sigh of the long-suffering. "I wish I could do that. But I can't. Want to know why?"

Kari felt as if she'd slipped into an alternative universe. This couldn't be happening to her. One second she'd been too scared to breathe, and the next, Gage Reynolds had walked back into her life. Right in the middle of a holdup.

Eight years ago he'd been a young deputy, tall and handsome in his khaki uniform. He was still good-looking enough to make an angel want to sin. He was also the sheriff, if the gleaming badge on his shirt pocket was to be believed. But for a man of the law, he didn't seem all that interested in the robbery going on right in front of him.

He took off his dust-colored cowboy hat and slapped it against his thigh. His dark hair gleamed, as did the interest in his eyes.

"Don't make me kill her," the gunman said, his tone low and controlled.

"You know who you've got there, son?" Gage asked casually, almost as if he hadn't figured out what was going on in the bank. "That's Kari Asbury."

"Back off, Sheriff."

The robber pressed the gun in a little deeper. Kari winced. Gage didn't seem to notice.

"She's the one who got away."

Kari could smell the criminal's sweat. She was willing to bet he hadn't planned on a hostage situation, and the fact he might be in over his head didn't make her breathe any easier. What on earth was Gage going on about?

"That's right," Gage continued, setting his hat on a table and stretching. "Eight years ago, that pretty lady there left me standing at the altar."

Despite the gun jammed into her cheek, Kari spluttered with indignation. "I did *not* leave you standing at the altar. We weren't even engaged."

"Maybe. But you knew I was gonna ask, and you took off. That's practically the same thing. Don't you think?"

He asked the last question of the robber, who actually considered before replying.

"If you hadn't really proposed, then she didn't leave you at the altar."

"Fair enough, but she *did* stand me up for the prom."

Kari couldn't believe it. Except for her grandmother's funeral seven years ago, she hadn't seen Gage since the afternoon of her high school prom. While she'd known that Possum Landing was small enough that they would eventually run into each other again, this wasn't exactly what she'd had in mind.

"It was complicated," she said, unable to believe she was being forced to defend herself in front of bank robbers.

"Did you or did you not skip town without warning? You left nothing but a note, Kari. You played with my heart like it was a football."

The bank robber glared at her. "That wasn't very nice."

She glared right back. "I was eighteen years old, okay? I apologized in the note."

"I've never gotten over it," Gage said, emotional pain oozing from every pore. He reached into his breast pocket and pulled out a package of gum. "You see before you a broken man."

Kari resisted the urge to roll her eyes. She didn't

know what Gage's game was, but she wished he would play it with someone else.

Her confusion turned to outrage when Gage took a stick of gum for himself, then offered the pack to the bank robber. Next they would be going out for a beer together.

Gage watched the anger flash in Kari's eyes. If she could have spit fire, he would be a scorched stick figure right about now. In different circumstances, Gage might have worried the issue, but not now.

The gunman shook off the gum, but that wasn't important. The gesture had been made and well received. Gage had established rapport.

"She went on up to New York City," Gage continued, tucking the gum package back into his breast pocket. "Wanted to be a fashion model."

The robber studied Kari, then shrugged. "She's pretty enough, but if she's back, then she didn't make it."

Gage sighed heavily again. "I guess not. All that pain and suffering for nothing."

Kari stiffened at his words, but didn't try to break away. Gage willed her to cooperate for just a few more seconds. While every instinct in his body screamed at him to jerk her free of the gunman, he forced himself to stay relaxed and focused. There were more people to protect than just Kari. Between the bank employees and the customers there were fifteen innocent citizens within the old walls. Fifteen unprepared folk and four men with guns. Gage didn't like the odds.

Using his peripheral vision, he checked on the

progress of the tactical team circling around the building. Just another minute or two and they would be in place.

"You want me to shoot her?" the gunman asked.

Kari gasped. Her big blue eyes widened even more, and the color drained from her face.

Gage chewed his gum for a second, then shrugged. "You know, that's mighty neighborly of you, but I think I'd rather deal with her in my own way, in my own time."

The team was nearly in place. Gage's heart was about to jump out of his chest, but he gave no outward sign. Another few seconds, he thought. Another—

"Hey, look!"

One of the robbers near the back turned suddenly. Everyone looked. A tactical team member dropped out of sight a moment too late. The gunman holding Kari snarled in rage.

"Dammit all to hell and back."

But that's all he got to say.

Gage lunged forward. He jerked Kari free, yelled at her to get down on the floor, then planted a booted foot firmly in the robber's midsection.

The bad guy gave a yelp of dismay as all the air rushed out of his lungs and he fell flat on his ass. He scooted a couple of feet backward, but by the time he sucked in a breath, two armed tactical team members had guns on him.

But they weren't as quick to capture the man by Ida Mae. A gunshot exploded.

Gage reacted without thinking. He turned and threw himself over Kari, covering her body with his.

A half-dozen or so rounds were fired. He pulled out his sidearm, looking for targets, and kept his free arm over Kari's face.

"Don't move," he growled in her ear.

"I can't," she gasped back.

After what felt like a lifetime, but was probably just seconds, a man called out. "I give, I give. You shot me."

There were muffled sounds, then a steady voice yelled, "Clear."

Five more "clear"s followed. Gage rolled off Kari and glanced around to check on the town folk. Everyone was fine—even Ida Mae, who had kicked the wounded gunman after she climbed to her feet. The leader of the tactical team walked over and stared down at Gage. He was covered in black from head to toe, with a visor over his face and enough firepower to take Cuba.

"I can't figure out if you were a damn fool or especially brave for walking in on a bank robbery in progress," the man said.

Gage sat up and grinned. "Someone had to do it, and I figured none of your boys was going to volunteer. Plus we know these were small-town criminals. They're used to seeing someone like me around. One of you all dressed in the Darth Vader clothes would have scared 'em into acting like fools. Someone could have gotten killed."

The man nodded. "If you ever get tired of small-town life, you'd be a fine addition to our team."

Gage didn't even consider his offer. "I'm flat-

tered,'' he said easily, ''but I'm right where I want
to be.''

The man nodded and walked off.

''You knew they were there.''

He turned and saw Kari staring at him. She still lay
on the ground. Her once long blond hair had been cut
short and stylish. Makeup accentuated her already
big, beautiful blue eyes. Time had sculpted her face
into something even more lovely than he remembered.

''The tactical team?'' he asked. ''Sure. They were
circling the building.''

''So I wasn't in danger?''

''Kari, a criminal was holding a gun to your head.
I wouldn't say that ever qualifies as safe.''

She smiled then. A slow, sexy smile that he still
remembered. Lordy but she'd been a looker back
then. Time hadn't changed that.

He suddenly became aware of the adrenaline pour-
ing through his body. And the fact that he hadn't had
sex in far too long. Eight years ago, he and Kari had
never gotten around to that particular pleasure. He
wondered if she would be more open to the experience now.

He got to his feet. If she was back in Possum Landing for any length of time, he would be sure to find
out.

''Welcome back,'' he said, and held out his hand
to help her up.

She placed her fingers against his palm. ''Jeez,
Gage, if you wanted to find a unique way to welcome
me home, couldn't you just have held a parade?''

* * *

"You can go now, Ms. Asbury," the wiry detective said nearly four hours later.

Kari sighed in relief. She'd given her statement, been questioned, been fed and watered, and now she was finally free to head home. As far as she could tell, there were only a couple of problems. The first was that her heart refused to return to normal. Every time she thought about what had happened in the bank, her chest felt as if it were filled with thundering horse hooves. The second problem was that she had walked to the bank, a scant mile or so from her house, but the sheriff's station was clear on the other side of town. It was summer in the middle of Texas, which meant billion-degree heat and humidity to match.

"Do you think I could have a ride home?" she asked. "Or is Willy still running a cab around these parts?"

The detective gave her a once-over, then grinned. "Wish I could take you home myself. Unfortunately I have more work to do. I'll get one of the deputies to take you."

Kari smiled her thanks. When she was alone, she glanced out of the glass-enclosed office. Just looking around, she told herself. She wasn't actually looking for someone specific. Certainly not Gage.

But like a bee heading for the sweetest flower, she found herself settling her gaze on him. He was across the large office, still in a glass room of his own, chatting with some members of the federal tactical team. Were they trying to talk him into leaving Possum Landing to join them? Kari shook her head. She might have been gone for eight years, but some things never changed. Gage Reynolds would no more leave Possum Landing than NASA would send Ida Mae up in the next space shuttle.

She watched as Gage spoke and the other men laughed. Time had honed him into a hard man, she thought. Hard in a good way—with thick muscles and a steady set to his face. Despite the fact that she'd been there when it happened, she couldn't believe that he'd actually walked into a bank robbery. On purpose! He'd been calm and cool and he'd about made her crazy.

The detective strolled back into the office. "Ms. Asbury, if you'll wait by the front desk, the deputy will be with you in a couple of minutes."

She smiled her thanks and followed him out to the waiting area. Ida Mae sat there, her hands folded primly on her lap. When she saw Kari, her wrinkled face broke out into a welcoming smile.

"Kari."

The older woman rose and held out her arms. Kari moved forward and accepted the hug. Everything about it was familiar—Ida Mae's bony arms, her bee-hive hairdo with not a hair out of place, the scent of the gardenia perfume she always wore.

"You're looking fine, child," Ida Mae said as she released Kari and sank back onto the bench.

Kari settled next to her. "You haven't changed a bit," she said, then patted her hand. "Are you all right?"

Ida Mae touched her chest. "I thought I was gonna have a heart attack right there in the middle of the bank. I couldn't believe my own eyes when those boys pulled guns on us. Then you walked in and it was like seeing a ghost. And then Gage strolled in. Wasn't he brave?''

''Absolutely,'' Kari agreed. She wasn't sure she could have knowingly walked in on a bank robbery, regardless of who was at risk. But Gage had always believed in doing what was right.

Ida Mae gave her a knowing look. ''He's still a handsome devil, too, don't you think? Is he taller than when you left?''

Kari wanted to roll her eyes, but figured she was getting a little old for that particular response. Fortunately, Ida Mae was on a tear and didn't require an answer.

''No one knew you were coming back,'' the older woman said. ''Of course, we knew you'd have to eventually, what with you still owning your grandma's house and all. I can tell you, tongues wagged when you left town all those years ago. Poor Gage. You about broke his heart. Of course, you were young and you had to follow your dreams. It's just too bad that your dreams didn't include him.''

Kari didn't know what to say. Her heart had been broken, too, but she didn't want to get into that. The past was the past. At least, that's what she told herself, even though she didn't actually believe it.

Ida Mae smiled. ''It's good that you're back.''

Kari sighed softly. ''Ida Mae, I'm not back. I'm just here for the summer.'' Then she was going to shake the dust from this small town off her shoes and never look back.

"Uh-huh." Ida Mae didn't look convinced.

Fortunately the deputy arrived just then. Kari asked Ida Mae if she needed a ride home, as well.

"No, no. My Nelson is probably waiting out front for me. I called him just before you walked out."

Led by the deputy, they headed out the front door and down the three steps to the sidewalk. By the time she saw that Nelson was indeed waiting for his wife, Kari had broken out into a sweat and was having trouble breathing in the heat.

"Little Kari Asbury," Nelson said as he approached. He grinned at her as he mopped his forehead with a handkerchief. "You're all grown up."

Kari smiled.

"Didn't she turn out pretty?" Ida Mae said fondly. "But then, you were always a lovely girl. You should have entered the Miss Texas pageant. You could have gone far with a title like that."

Kari smiled weakly. "It was very nice to see you both," she said politely, then headed toward the squad car that the deputy had pulled around.

"Gage has had a couple of close calls," Nelson called after her, "but no one's gotten him down the aisle."

Kari waved by way of response. She wasn't going to touch that particular topic.

"Good to have you back," Nelson yelled louder.

This one Kari couldn't resist. She turned toward the older man and shook her head. "I'm not back."

Nelson only waved.

"Just perfect," she muttered as she climbed into the car with the deputy. He'd told her his name, but she'd already forgotten it. Probably because he looked so impossibly young. She was only twenty-six, but next to this guy she felt ancient.

She gave him her address and leaned back against the seat, breathing in the air-conditioned coolness. There were a thousand and one details to occupy her mind, yet instead of dealing with them, she found herself remembering the first time she'd met Gage. She'd been all of seventeen and he'd been twenty-three. At the time, he'd seemed so much older and more mature.

"I know this is a crazy question," she said, glancing at the young man next to her. "But how old are you?"

He was blond, with blue eyes and pale cheeks. He gave her a startled glance. "Twenty-three."

"Oh."

The same age Gage had been eight years ago. That didn't seem possible. If Gage had been as young as this guy, Kari shouldn't have had any trouble standing up to him. Why had she found it so incredibly difficult to share her feelings while they'd been dating? Why had the thought of telling him the truth terrified her?

There wasn't an easy answer to the question, and before she could come up with a hard one, they arrived at her house.

Kari thanked the deputy and stepped out into the late afternoon. In front of her stood the old house where she'd grown up. It had been built in the forties, and had a wide porch and gabled windows. Different colored versions of the same house sat all along the street, including the home next door. She glanced at it, wondering when she would have her next run-in with her neighbor. As if returning to Possum Landing for the summer wasn't complicated enough, Gage Reynolds now lived next door.

Kari walked inside her grandmother's house and stood in the main parlor. Never a living room, she thought with a smile. It was a parlor, where people "set" when it wasn't nice enough to settle on the front porch. She remembered countless hours spent listening to her grandmother's friends talking about everything from who was pregnant to who was cheating on whom.

She'd arrived after dark last night. She hadn't turned on many lights after she'd come in, and somehow she'd convinced herself that the house was different. Only now, she saw it wasn't.

The old sofas were the same, as was the horsehair chair her grandmother had inherited from *her* grandmother. Kari had always hated that piece—it was both slick and uncomfortable. Now she touched the antique and felt the memories wash over her.

Maybe it was the result of all the emotions from the robbery, maybe it was just the reality of being home. Either way, she suddenly sensed the ghosts in the house. At least they were friendly, she told herself as she moved into the old kitchen. Her grandmother had always loved her.

Kari looked at the pecan cabinets and the stove and oven unit that had to be at least thirty years old. If she expected to get a decent price for the old place, she would have to do some serious updating. That was the reason she'd come home for the summer, after all.

A restlessness filled her. She hurried upstairs and changed out of her clothes. After showering, she slipped on a cotton dress and padded back downstairs barefoot. She toured the house, almost as if she were waiting for something to happen.

And then it did.

There was a knock on the door. She didn't have to answer it to know who had come calling. Her stomach lurched and her heart took up that thundering hoof dance again. She drew in a deep breath and reached for the handle.

Chapter Two

Gage stood on Kari's front porch. She didn't bother pretending to be surprised. Her time with him in the bank had been too rushed and too emotionally charged for her to notice much about his appearance...and how he might have changed. But now that they were in a more normal situation, she could take the time to appreciate how he'd filled out in the years she'd been away.

He looked taller than she remembered. Or maybe he was just bigger. Regardless, he was very much a man now. Still too good-looking for her peace of mind. He appealed to her, but, then, he always had.

"If you're inviting me to attend another bank robbery," she said with a smile, "I'm going to have to pass."

Gage grinned and held up both hands. "No more crime…not if I can prevent it." He leaned against the door frame. "The reason I stopped by was to make sure that you were all right after all the excitement today. Plus, I knew you'd want to thank me for saving your life by inviting me to dinner."

She tilted her head as she considered him. "What if my husband objects?"

He didn't even have the grace to look the least bit worried. "You're not married. Ida Mae keeps track of these things, and she would have told me."

"Figures." She stepped back to allow him inside. Gage moved into the front room while she closed the door behind him. "What makes you think I've had time to go to the grocery store?" she asked.

"If you haven't, I have a couple of steaks in the freezer. I could get those out."

She shook her head. "Actually, I did my shopping this morning. That's the reason I ran out of cash and had to go get more at the bank." She frowned. "Come to think of it, I never did cash that check."

"You can do it tomorrow."

"I guess I'll have to."

She led the way into the kitchen. Having him here was strange, she thought. An odd blending of past and present. How many times had he come over for dinner eight years ago? Her grandmother had always welcomed him at their table. Kari had been so in love that she'd been thrilled he'd wanted to spend mealtimes with her. Of course, she'd been young enough to be excited even if all he wanted was for her to keep him company while he washed his car. All she'd needed to be happy was a few hours in Gage's presence. Life had been a whole lot simpler in those days.

He leaned against a counter and sniffed. ''That smells mighty good. And familiar.''

''Grandmother's sauce recipe. I put it in the slow cooker this morning, right after I got back from the grocery store. I also got out the old bread maker, but as it's been gathering dust forever, I can't promise it'll all work.''

His dark gaze settled on her. ''It works just fine.''

His words made her break out in goose bumps, which was crazy. He was a smooth-talking good-ol' boy from Possum Landing. She lived in New York City. No way Gage Reynolds should be able to get to her. And he didn't. Not really.

''Did you get all the paperwork wrapped up, or whatever it was you had to do after the robbery?'' she asked as she checked on the pasta sauce.

''Everything is tied up in a neat package.'' He crossed to the kitchen table and picked up the bottle of wine she'd left there.

''Kari Asbury, is this liquor? Have you brought the devil's brew into our saintly dry county?''

She glanced up and chuckled. ''You know it. I remembered there weren't any liquor sales allowed around here and figured I had better bring my own. I stopped on my way over from the airport.''

''I'm shocked. Completely shocked.''

She grinned. ''So you probably don't want to know that there's beer in the refrigerator.''

''Not at all.'' He opened the door and pulled out a bottle. When he offered it to her, she shook her head.

"I'll wait for wine with dinner."

He opened the drawer with the bottle opener in it on the first try. Gage moved around with the ease of someone familiar with the place. But then, he *had* been. He'd moved in next door, the spring before her senior year. She remembered watching him carry in boxes and pieces of furniture. Her grandmother had told her who he was—the new deputy. Gage Reynolds. He'd been in the army and had traveled the world. To her seventeen-year-old eyes, a young man of twenty-three had seemed impossibly grown-up and mature. When they'd started dating that fall, he'd seemed a man of the world and she'd been—

"Are we still neighbors?" she asked, turning back to face him.

"I'm still next door."

She thought of Ida Mae's comment that Gage had never made it to the altar. Somehow he'd managed to not get caught. Looking at him now, his khaki uniform emphasizing the breadth of his shoulders and the muscles in his legs, she wondered how the lovely ladies of Possum Landing had managed to keep from trapping him.

Not her business, she reminded herself. She checked the timer on the bread machine and saw there was still fifteen minutes to go, plus cooling time.

"Let's go into the parlor," she said. "We'll be more comfortable."

He nodded and led the way.

As she followed him, she found her gaze drifting lower, to his rear. She nearly stumbled in shock. What on earth was wrong with her? She didn't ever stare at men's butts. Nothing about them had ever seemed overly interesting. Until now.

She sighed. Obviously, living next door to Gage was going to be more complicated than she'd realized.

He settled into a wing chair, while she took the sofa. Gage drank some of his beer, then put the bottle on a crocheted coaster and leaned back. He should have looked awkward and out of place in this fussy, feminine room, but he didn't. Perhaps because he'd always been comfortable anywhere.

"What are you thinking?" he asked.

"That you look at home in my grandmother's house."

"I spent a lot of time here," he reminded her. "Even after you left, she and I stayed close."

She didn't want to think about that...about the confidences that might have been shared.

Gage studied her face. "You've changed."

She wasn't sure if he meant the comment in a good way or a bad way. "It's been a long time."

"I never thought you'd come back."

It was the second time in less than three hours that someone had mentioned her being back. "I'm not back," she clarified. "At least, not for anything permanent."

Gage didn't look surprised by her statement, nor did he seem to take issue with her defensive tone. "So why are you suddenly here? It's been seven years since your grandmother died."

Her temper faded as quickly as it had flared. She

sighed. "I want to fix up the house so I can sell it. I'm just here for the summer while I do that."

He nodded without saying anything. She had the uncomfortable sense of having been judged and found wanting. Which wasn't fair. Gage wasn't the type of man to judge people without just cause. So her need to squirm in her seat had nothing to do with him and everything to do with her own state of mind.

Rather than deal with personal inadequacies that were probably better left unexplored in public, she changed the subject. "I can't believe there was a bank robbery right here in Possum Landing. It's going to be the talk of the town for weeks."

"Probably. But it wasn't that much of a surprise."

"I can't believe that. Things couldn't have changed that much."

He nodded. "We're still just a bump in the road, with plenty of small-town problems, but nothing even close to big-city crime. These boys were working their way across the state, robbing hometown banks. I'd been keeping track of their progress, figuring they'd get here sooner or later. Four days ago, the feds came calling. They wanted to set up a sting. I didn't have a problem with that. We talked to everyone at the bank, marked a drawer full of money, then waited for the hit to take place."

Kari couldn't believe it. "All that excitement right here, and I was in the thick of it."

Gage narrowed his eyes. "As you saw, things got out of hand. I don't know if those robbers got lazy or cocky, but this time, they decided to hold up the bank while there were still customers inside. Previously they'd waited until just before the doors were locked for the day, to go in.''

"So you weren't expecting to deal with a hostage situation?''

"No one was. The feds wanted to wait it out, but those were my people inside. Someone had to do something.''

She turned that thought over in her mind. "So you just waltzed inside to distract them?''

"It seemed like the easiest way to get the job done. Plus, I wanted to be there to make sure no one went crazy and got shot. At least, no one from here. I don't much care about the criminals.''

Of course. In Gage's mind, they had brought the situation upon themselves. He wouldn't take responsibility for their coming to Possum Landing to hold up a bank in the first place.

"I have to agree with the federal officer," she said. "I don't know if you were brave or stupid.''

He smiled. "You could probably make a case for either point of view.'' He took another drink of his beer. "You know that I wasn't really mad at you. I was trying to distract that one guy so he didn't take you hostage.''

She shivered at the memory of the gun held to her head. "It took me a few minutes to catch on to what you were doing.''

But that didn't stop her from wondering how much of what he had said was true. Did Gage really think she was the one who got away?

Did she want to be?

Once she easily would have said yes. Back before

she'd left town, Gage had been her entire world. She would have thrown herself in front of a moving train if he'd asked. She'd loved him with all the crazy devotion a teenager was capable of. That had been the trouble—she'd loved him too much. When she'd figured out there were problems, she hadn't known how to deal with them. So she'd run. When he hadn't come after her, he'd confirmed her greatest fear in the world…that he hadn't loved her at all.

They spent all of dinner talking about mutual friends. Gage brought her up to date on various weddings, divorces and births.

"I can't believe Sally has twins," Kari said, as they moved to the porch and sat on the wooden swing.

"Two girls. I told Bob he has his work cut out for him once they become teenagers."

"Fortunately that's a long way off."

Kari set her glass of wine on the dusty, peeling table beside the swing and leaned back to look up at the sky. It might be after dark, but it was still plenty hot and humid. She could feel her dress sticking to her skin. Her head felt funny—fuzzy, heavy and more than a little out of sync. No doubt it was due to the combination of the fear she'd experienced earlier in the day and a little too much wine with dinner. She didn't normally allow herself more than half a glass on special occasions, but tonight she and Gage had nearly split the bottle.

Gage stretched out his long legs. He didn't seem bothered by the wine. No doubt his additional body mass helped, not to mention the fact that he wouldn't have spent the past several years trying to maintain an unnaturally thin body.

"Tell me about life in New York," he said.

"There isn't much to tell," she admitted, wondering if she should be pleased or worried that he'd finally asked her a vaguely personal question. "When I arrived, I found out that small-town girls who had been told they were pretty enough to be a model were spilling out of every modeling agency within a thirty-mile radius. The competition was tough and the odds of making it into the big time were close to zero."

"You did okay."

She glanced at him, not sure if he was assuming or if he actually knew. "After the first year or so, I got work. Eventually I made enough to support myself and pay for college. As of last month, I have teaching credentials, which is what I always wanted."

Gage glanced at her. "You're still too skinny to be a PE teacher."

She laughed. "I know. I sure won't miss all those years of dieting. I'm proud to tell you that I've worked my way up from a size two to a six. My goal is to be a size ten and even eat chocolate now and then."

He swept his gaze over her. She half expected a comment on her body, but instead he only asked, "So what kind of teacher are you?"

"Math at the middle-school level," she said.

"A lot of those boys are going to have a crush on you."

"They'll get over it."

"I don't know. I still get a hankering for Ms. Rosens. She taught eighth grade social studies. I don't think I'd bothered to notice girls before. Then she walked into the room and I was a goner. She married the high school football coach. It took me a year to get over it.''

She laughed.

They rocked in silence for a few minutes. Life was so normal here, Kari thought, enjoying the quiet of the evening. Instead of sirens and tire screeches, there were only the calls of the night critters. All around Possum Landing people would be out on their porches, enjoying the stars and visiting with neighbors. No one would worry about half a glass of wine causing facial puffiness, or being too bloated for a lingerie shoot. No one would lose a job for gaining three pounds.

This was normal, she reminded herself. She'd nearly been gone long enough to forget what that was like.

''Why teaching?'' Gage asked unexpectedly.

''It's what I always wanted.''

''After the modeling.''

''Right.''

She didn't want to go there—not now. Maybe later they would rehash their past and hurl accusations at each other, but not tonight.

''Where are you applying?''

''To schools around Texas. There are a couple of openings in the Dallas area and in Abilene. I have some interviews scheduled. That's why this seemed like the perfect time to come back and fix up the house. Then I can move on.''

She paused, expecting him to respond. But he didn't.

Which was just as well, because she suddenly found that sitting next to him on the old swing where he'd kissed her for the first time was more difficult than she would have thought. Her chest felt tight and her skin tingled all over.

It was just the wine, she told herself. Or it was the old memories, swimming around them like so many ghosts. The past was a powerful influence. No doubt she would need a little time to get used to being back in Possum Landing.

"Did you apply locally?" Gage asked.

"No."

She waited, but he didn't ask why.

"Enough about me," she said, shifting in her seat and angling toward him. "What about your life? Last I heard, you were still a deputy. When did you run for sheriff?"

"Last year. I wasn't sure I'd make it my first time out, but I did."

She wasn't surprised. Gage had always been good at his job and well liked by the community. "So you got what you always wanted."

"Uh-huh." He glanced at her. "I was always real clear about my goals. I grew up here. I'm a fifth-generation resident of Possum Landing. I knew I wanted to see the world, then come back home and make my life here. So I did."

She admired his ability to know what he wanted and go after it. She had never been quite that focused.

There had been the occasional powerful distraction. One of them was sitting right next to her.

"I'm glad you're where you want to be," she said. Then, because she wasn't always as bright as she looked, she said, "But you never married."

Gage smiled. "There have been a few close calls."

"You always were a favorite with the ladies."

His smile faded. "I never gave you cause to worry when we were together. I didn't fool around on you, Kari."

"I never thought you did." She shrugged. "But there were plenty of women eager to see if they could capture your attention. The fact that you and I were going out didn't seem to impress them."

"It impressed me."

His voice seemed to scrape along her skin like a rough caress. She shivered slightly.

"Yes, well, I…" Her voice trailed off. So much for being sophisticated, she thought wryly. Yup, her time in the big city had sure polished her.

"It's getting late," Gage said.

He rose, and she wasn't sure if she was sad or relieved that he was going. Part of her didn't want the evening to end, but another part of her was grateful that she wouldn't have another chance to say something stupid. As much as she'd grown and matured, she'd never quite been able to kick that particular habit.

She stood as well, noticing again how tall he was. Especially in his worn cowboy boots. Barefoot, he only had four inches on her. Now she had to tilt her head slightly to meet his gaze.

The look in his eyes nearly took her breath away. There was a combination of confidence and fire that made her insides sort of melt and her breathing turn ragged.

What on earth was wrong with her? She couldn't possibly be feeling anything like anticipation. That would be crazy. That would be—

"You're still the prettiest girl in Possum Landing," he said as he took a step toward her.

She suddenly felt overwhelmed by the Texas heat. "I, um, I'm not really a girl anymore."

He smiled a slow, easy, "I'm in charge here and don't you forget it" kind of smile that didn't do anything positive for her equilibrium. She seemed to have forgotten how to breathe.

"I know," he murmured as he put his hand on the back of her neck and drew her close. "Did I mention I like your hair short?"

She opened her mouth to answer. Big mistake. Or not, depending on one's point of view.

Because just at that moment, he lowered his mouth to hers. She didn't have time to prepare…which was probably a good thing. Because the second his lips touched hers, protesting seemed like a really silly idea—when Gage could kiss this good.

Kari wasn't exactly sure what he was doing that was so special. Sure there was soft, firm pressure and plenty of passion. As if the night wasn't warm enough, they were generating enough heat between them to boil water on contact. But there was something else, some chemistry that left her desperate and longing. Something that urged her to wrap her arms around him so that when he pulled her close, they were touching everywhere it mattered.

He moved his mouth against hers, then lightly licked her lower lip. Pleasure shot through her like lightning. She clutched at his strong shoulders, savoring the hardness of his body against hers, liking the feel of his hands on her hips and his chest flattening her breasts.

Her head tilted slightly, as did his, in preparation for the kiss to deepen. Because there wasn't a doubt in her mind that they were taking this to the next level.

So when he stroked her lower lip again, she parted her mouth for him. And when he slowly eased his tongue inside, she was ready and very willing to dance this particular dance.

He tasted sweet and sexy. He was a man who enjoyed women and knew enough to make sure they enjoyed him. Kari had a hazy recollection of her first kiss with Gage, when he'd been so sure and she'd felt like a dolt. Right up until he'd touched his tongue to hers and she'd melted like butter on a hot griddle.

Now that same trickling sensation started deep inside. Her body was more than ready for a trip down memory lane. She wasn't so sure the rest of her could play catch-up that fast…even if the passion threatened to overwhelm her.

He moved his hand up from her hips to her sides, then around to her back, moving higher and higher until he cupped her head. He slid his fingers into her short hair and softly whispered her name.

She continued to hold on to him because the alternative was to fall on her rear end right there on the porch. When he broke the kiss and began to nibble along the line of her jaw, she didn't care where she fell as long as he caught her. And when he sucked on her earlobe, every cell in her body screamed out that sex with Gage Reynolds would be a perfect homecoming.

Fortunately, the choice wasn't hers. Just when she was starting to think they were wearing too many layers, he stepped back. His eyes were bright, his mouth damp with their kisses. She was pleased to see that his breathing was a tad too fast and that parts of him were not as…modest as they had been a few moments before.

They stared at each other. Kari didn't know what to say. Finding out that Gage kissed better than she remembered meant one of three things: her memory was faulty, he'd been practicing while she'd been gone, or the chemistry between them was more powerful than it had been eight years ago. She wasn't sure which she wanted it to be.

He didn't speak, either. Instead, he leaned close, gave her one last hot, hard kiss, and walked down the porch steps, into the night.

Kari was left staring after him. Restlessness seized her, making her want to follow him and…and…

She sucked in a breath before slowly turning and heading back into the house. Obviously, coming back to Possum Landing was going to be a whole lot more complicated than she'd first realized.

Chapter Three

Gage ambled toward the offices of the *Possum Landing Gazette* the following morning. Under normal circumstances, he would have put off this meeting for as long as possible. But ever since the previous evening, he hadn't been able to concentrate on his work, so he figured this was a better use of his time than staring out the window and remembering.

He'd always known that Kari would come back to Possum Landing one day. He'd felt it in his bones. From time to time he'd considered what his reaction to that event would be, assuming he would be little more than mildly interested in how she'd changed and only slightly curious as to her future plans. He hadn't thought there would still be any chemistry between them. He wasn't sure if that made him a fool, or an optimist.

The chemistry was there in spades. As were a lot of old feelings he didn't want to acknowledge. Being around her made him remember what it was like to want her…and not just in bed. There had been a time when he'd longed to spend his whole life with her, making babies and creating a past they could both be proud of. Instead, she'd gone away and he'd found contentment in his present life. While the kiss the previous evening had shown him that parts of him were still very interested in the woman she'd become, the rest of him couldn't afford to be.

Kari was a beautiful woman. Wanting her in bed made sense. Expecting anything else would take him down a road he refused to travel. He'd been there once and he hadn't liked the destination.

So, for however long she stayed in Possum Landing, he would be a good neighbor and enjoy her company. If that led to something between the sheets, that was just fine with him. He hadn't had much interest in the fairer sex these past few months. Instead, a restlessness had seized him, making him want something he couldn't define. If nothing else, Kari could prove to be a welcome distraction.

Gage entered the newspaper office and nodded at the receptionist. "I know my way," he called as he headed down a long corridor. "I'd be obliged if you'd tell Daisy I'm here."

The woman picked up the phone to call back to the reporter. Gage pulled off his cowboy hat and slapped it against his thigh.

He didn't much want to be here, but experience had taught him that it was safer to show up for interviews than to allow Daisy to come to him. This way, he was in charge and could head out when he felt the need to escape. He'd figured out that by leaning against the conference room chairs just so, he could activate the test button on his pager. It went off, and he could glance down at the screen and pretend something had come up, forcing him to leave. He was also sure to seem real regretful about having to head out unexpectedly. He was just as sure to ignore Daisy's not-so-subtle hints that they should get together sometime soon.

Daisy was a fine figure of a woman. A petite redhead with big green eyes and a mouth that promised three kinds of heaven if a man were only to ask. They'd been in the same class in high school but had never dated. Newly divorced, Daisy was more than willing to reacquaint herself with Gage. He appreciated the compliment and couldn't for the life of him figure out why he wasn't interested. But he wasn't. As he'd yet to decide on an easy way to let her down, he did the next best thing and avoided anything personal.

He wove his way through the half dozen or so desks in the main room of the newspaper office. Daisy was in the back, by a window. She looked up and smiled as Gage approached. Her long, red hair had been piled on her head in a mass of sexy curls. The sleeveless blouse she wore dipped low enough to prove that her cleavage was God-given and not the result of padding. Her smile more than welcomed…it offered. Gage smiled in return, all the while monitoring parts south. Over the years he'd found that part of him was a fairly good judge of his interest in a woman. As had occurred every other time he'd been in Daisy's company, there wasn't even a hint of a stirring. No matter how much Daisy might wish the contrary, as far as he was concerned, there wasn't any future for them.

"Gage," she murmured as he approached. "You're looking fine this morning. Being a hero seems to agree with you."

"Daisy," he said with a smile. "If you're going to write anything about me being a hero in your article, I'm not going to cooperate. I was doing my job— nothing more."

She sighed and tilted her head. "Brave *and* modest. Two of my favorite qualities in a man." She batted her long lashes at him. "I have a call to make. Why don't you wait for me in the conference room, and I'll join you there."

"Sure thing."

He spoke easily, even though the last place he wanted Daisy to send him was that back room with no windows and only one door. Yesterday, facing four armed bank robbers hadn't done much but increase his heart rate. But the thought of being trapped in a small place with Daisy on the hunt made his insides shrivel up and play dead.

Still, there was no escaping the inevitable. And he always had his handy-dandy test button escape route.

He walked down the hallway that led to the conference room and stepped inside. But instead of finding it empty, he saw someone else waiting. A tall, slender someone with short blond hair and the prettiest blue eyes this side of the Mississippi.

"Morning, Kari," he said as he stepped into the room.

She glanced up from the list she'd been making, frowned in confusion, then smiled. "Gage. What are you doing here?"

"Waiting on Daisy. She's going to interview me about yesterday's bank robbery." He hesitated before taking a seat.

Some decisions were harder than others and this was one of them. Did he want to sit next to her so he could catch the occasional whiff of her soft perfume, or sit across from her so he could look at her lovely face? He decided to enjoy the view, and pulled out the chair directly opposite hers.

"What brings you to the newspaper this morning?" he asked as he set his hat on the table.

Kari's mouth twisted slightly. "Daisy called and asked to interview me about the bank robbery. I wonder why she wanted us to come at the same time."

Gage had a couple of ideas, but figured this wasn't the time to go into them. Instead he studied Kari, who seemed to be trying *not* to look at him. Was that because of last night? Their kiss? The heat they'd ignited had kept him up half the night. He might not have much of a reaction to Daisy, but being around Kari proved that he could be intrigued in about a tenth of a second under the right circumstances.

This morning she wore a white summery dress that emphasized her slender shape. He eyed her short hair, which fluttered around her ears.

"What?" she said, watching him watch her. She touched her hair. "I know—it's short."

"I said I liked it."

"I wasn't sure if you were lying," she admitted with a smile. "I always figured you were more of a long hair kind of a guy."

He leaned back in his chair. "Actually, I try to be flexible. If it looks nice, I like it."

He continued to take in her features, noting changes and similarities.

"What are you thinking?" she asked.

He grinned. He was thinking that he would very much like to take her to bed. Once they'd shared several hours of one of life's greatest pleasures, he would like to get to know the woman she'd become while she'd been gone. Not that he was going to say that to her. From time to time, circumstances forced a man to tell little white lies.

"I was wondering how much work you're planning on doing at your grandmother's house."

Kari blinked at Gage. She'd expected him to say a lot of things, but not that. He'd been looking at her as if he were the big bad wolf and she were lunch. But in the kind of way that made her body heat up and her heart rate slip into overdrive.

So, she'd been thinking about last night's kiss and he'd been mulling over paint chips and siding. Obviously her ability to read Gage and handle herself with grace and style hadn't improved at all in the time she'd been gone.

"I'm still figuring that out," she said. "The biweekly cleaning service kept the house livable, but it's still old and out of date. I could redo the whole place, but that doesn't make sense. I have a limit to both my time and money, so I'm going to have to prioritize.''

He nodded thoughtfully.

My, oh my, but he still looked good, she thought, as she had yesterday. And the pleasure she took in seeing him hadn't worn off yet. She wondered if it would. By the end of summer, would he be little more than just some good-looking guy who happened to live next door? Could she possibly get that lucky?

Before she could answer her own question, Daisy breezed into the conference room. From her low-cut blouse to the red lipstick emphasizing her full lips, she was a walking, breathing pinup girl. Kari felt bony and string-bean–like in comparison.

''Thanks so much for coming,'' she said as she closed the door, then took the seat next to Gage. ''I'm writing a follow-up article for the paper and I thought it would be fun to interview you both together. I hope you don't mind.''

Kari shook her head and tried not to notice how close Daisy sat to Gage. The other woman brushed her arm against his and smiled at him in a way that had Kari thinking they were way more than friends.

But that didn't make sense. Gage wasn't the kind of man to be involved with one woman and kiss another. Which meant Gage and Daisy had once been a couple or that they were still in the flirting stage. Either concept gave her the willies.

Daisy set her notebook on the table in front of her but didn't open it. She leaned toward Kari. ''Wasn't that something? I mean, a bank robbery right here in PL.''

Kari blinked. ''PL?''

''Possum Landing. Nothing exciting ever happens here.'' She smiled at Gage. ''At least, nothing in public. I thought it was so amazing. And, Gage, throwing yourself in front of the bullets. That was amazing, too. And brave.''

He grunted.

With a speed that left Kari scrambling, Daisy turned to her and changed the subject. ''So, you're back. After all those years in New York. What was it like there?''

''Interesting,'' Kari said cautiously, not sure what this had to do with the holdup the previous day. ''Different from here.''

''Isn't everywhere,'' Daisy said with a laugh. ''I've spent time in the city, but I have to tell you, I'm a small-town girl at heart. PL is an amazing place and has everything I could ever want.''

She spoke earnestly, focusing all her attention on Gage for several seconds before swinging it back on Kari.

''What's it like seeing Gage again after all these years?''

Kari blinked. ''I'm, uh, not sure what that has to do with the bank robbery.''

''I would have thought it was obvious. Your former fiancé risks his life for you. He protects you from the hail of gunfire. You can't tell me you didn't think it was romantic. Don't you think it was the perfect homecoming? I mean, now that you're back.''

Kari risked a glance at Gage, but he looked as confused as she felt. What on earth was Daisy's point with all this? As Kari didn't want anything she said taken out of context and printed for the whole town to see, she tried to think before she spoke.

"First of all," she said slowly, "Gage and I were never engaged. We dated. Second, I'm not back. Not permanently."

"Uh-huh." Daisy opened her notebook and scribbled a few lines. "Gage, what were you thinking when you walked into the bank?"

"That I should have followed my mama's advice and studied to be an engineer."

Kari smiled slightly and felt herself relax. Trust Gage to ease the tension in the room. But before she could savor her newfound peace, Daisy broke into peals of laughter, tossing her pen on the table and clutching Gage's arm.

"Aren't you a hoot?" she said, beaming at him. "I've always enjoyed your humor."

The expression on her face said she had enjoyed other things, as well, but Kari didn't want to dwell on that. She tried to ignore the couple across the table. Daisy wasn't having any of that. She turned her attention back to Kari and gave her a look of friendly concern.

"I'm so pleased to hear you say that you're not staying for the long haul. You and Gage had something special once, but I've found that old flames never light up as brightly the second time around. They seem to fizzle and just fade away."

Kari smiled through clenched teeth. "Well, bless your heart for being so concerned."

Daisy beamed back.

They completed the interview fairly quickly, now that Daisy had gotten her message across. Obviously she'd called Kari and Gage in together to see them in the same room, and to warn Kari off. Like Kari was interested in starting up something with an ex-boyfriend.

Small-town life, Kari thought grimly. How could she have forgotten the downside of everyone knowing everyone else?

Daisy continued to coo over Gage and he continued to ignore her advances. Despite being incredibly uncomfortable, Kari couldn't help wondering about the state of their real relationship and vowed to ask Gage the next time she felt brave. In the meantime, she would do her best to avoid Daisy.

People in big cities thought nothing happened in small towns, she thought as she finally made her escape. People in big cities were wrong.

"You spoil me, Mama," Gage said a few nights later as he cleared the table at his mother's house.

Edie Reynolds, an attractive, dark-haired woman in her late fifties, smiled. "I'm not sure cooking dinner for you once a week constitutes spoiling, Gage. Besides, I need to be sure you're getting a balanced meal at least once in a while."

He began scraping plates and loading the dishwasher. "I'm a little too old to be eating pizza every night," he teased. "Just last week I had a vegetable with my steak."

"Good for you."

He winked at her as he worked. His mother shook her head, then picked up her glass of wine. "I'm still very angry with you. What were you thinking when you burst in on those bank robbers?" She held up her free hand. "Don't bother telling me you weren't thinking. I've already figured that out."

"I was doing my job. Several citizens were in danger and I had to protect them."

She set her glass down, her mouth twisting. "I guess this means your father and I did too good a job teaching you about responsibility."

"You wouldn't have it any other way."

"Probably not," she admitted.

The phone rang. His mother sighed. "Betty Sue from the hospital auxiliary has been calling me every twenty minutes about our fund-raiser. I'm amazed we got through dinner without her interrupting. This will just take a second." She picked up the receiver on the counter and spoke in a cheerful tone.

"Hello? Why, Betty Sue, what a surprise. No, no, we'd just finished eating. Uh-huh. Sure."

Edie headed for the living room. "If you want to rearrange the placement of the booths, you're going to have to clear it with the committee. I know they told you to run things, but…"

Gage grinned as he tuned out the conversation. His mother's charity work was as much a part of her as her White Diamonds perfume.

He finished with the dishes and rinsed the dishcloth

before wiping down the counters. Every now and then his mother protested that he didn't need to help after dinner, but he never listened. He figured she'd done more than her share of work while he and his brother Quinn were growing up. Loading the dishwasher hardly began to pay her back.

He finished with his chores and leaned against the counter, waiting for her to finish her conversation with Betty Sue. The kitchen had been remodeled about seven years ago, but the basic structure was still the same. The old house was crammed full of memories. Gage had lived here from the time he was born until he'd left to join the army.

Of course, every part of Possum Landing had memories. It was one of the things he liked about the town—he belonged here. He could trace his family back five generations on his father's side. There were dozens of old pictures in the main hallway—photos of Reynolds at the turn of the previous century, when Possum Landing had been just a brash, new cow town.

His mother returned to the kitchen and set the phone back on its base. "That woman is doing her best to make me insane. I can't tell you how sorry I am that I actually voted for her to run the fund-raiser. I must have been experiencing a black out or something."

He laughed. "You'll survive. How's the bathroom sink?"

"The leak is fixed. Don't fret, Gage. There aren't any chores for you this week."

She led the way back into the living room, where

they sat on opposite ends of the recovered sofa. Edie had replaced the ugly floral pattern with narrow-striped fabric.

"I don't invite you over just to get free labor," she said.

"I know, Mama, but I'm happy to help."

She nodded. "Will you be all right when John takes over that sort of chore?"

His mother had never been one to walk around a problem—if she saw trouble, she headed right for it. He leaned forward and lightly touched the back of her hand.

"I've told you before, I'm pleased about John. Daddy's been gone five years. You're getting a second chance to be happy."

She didn't look convinced.

"I'm telling the truth."

He was. The loss of his father had been a blow to both of them. Edie had spent the first year in a daze. Finally she'd pulled herself together and had tried to get on with her life. A part-time job she'd taken for something to do rather than because she needed the money had helped. As had her friends. Nearly a year before, she'd met John, a retired contractor.

Gage was willing to admit that he'd been a bit put off by the thought of his mother dating, but he'd quickly come around. John was a solid man who treated Edie as if she were a princess. Gage couldn't have picked better for his mother himself.

"You'll still come to dinner, won't you? Once we're married?"

"I promise."

He'd been coming to dinner once a week ever since he'd returned to Possum Landing after being in the army. Like many things in his life, it was a tradition.

His mother's dark gaze sharpened a little and he braced himself. Sure enough, she went right for the most interesting topic.

"I heard Kari Asbury is back in town."

"Subtle, Mama." He grinned. "According to Kari, she's not back, she's here for a short period of time while she fixes up her grandmother's house and sells it."

Edie frowned. "And then what? Is she going back to New York? She's a lovely girl, but isn't she getting a little old to be a fashion model?"

"She's going to be a teacher. She has her credentials and is applying for jobs in different parts of Texas."

"Not Possum Landing?"

"Not as far as I can tell."

"Are you all right with that?"

"Sure."

"If you're lying to me, I'm not averse to getting out the old switch."

He grinned. "You'd have to catch me first. I'm still a fast runner, Mama."

Her face softened with affection. "Just be careful, Gage. There was a time when she broke your heart. I would hate to see that happen again."

"It won't," he said confidently. A man was allowed to be a fool for a woman once in a lifetime, but not twice. "We'll always be friends. We have too much past between us to avoid that. We're neighbors, so I'll be seeing her, but it won't amount to anything significant.''

It was only a white lie, he thought cheerfully. Because getting Kari into bed was definitely his goal. And if things were as hot between them as he guessed they would be, the event would certainly qualify as ''significant.'' But that wasn't something he wanted to share with his mother.

''You heard from Quinn lately?'' he asked, changing the subject.

''Not since that one letter a month ago.'' She sighed. ''I worry about that boy.''

Gage didn't think there was any point in mentioning that Quinn was thirty and a trained military operative. ''Boy'' hadn't described him in years.

''He should be getting leave in the next few months.''

''I'm hoping he'll make time to come to the wedding. I don't know if he will, though.''

Gage wasn't sure, either. He and Quinn had once been close, but time and circumstances had changed things. They'd both headed into the military after high school, but unlike Gage, Quinn had stayed in. He'd gone into Special Forces, then joined a secret group that worked around the world wherever there was trouble.

Despite being from the same family as Gage, Quinn had never fit in. Mostly because their father had made his life a living hell.

As always, the thought made Gage uncomfortable. He'd never understood why he'd been the golden boy of the family and Quinn had been the unwelcome stranger. He also didn't know why he was thinking so much about the past lately.

Maybe it was Kari returning and stirring it up. Maybe now was a good time to ask a question that should have been asked long ago.

"Why didn't Daddy like Quinn?"

Edie stiffened slightly. "What are you saying, Gage? Your father loved you two boys equally. He was a good father."

Gage stared at her, wondering why she was lying. Why avoid the obvious?

"The old farmer's market opened last week. I'm going to head over there this weekend and see if I can get some berries. Maybe I'll bake a pie for next time."

The change of subject was both obvious and awkward. Gage hesitated a second before giving in and saying that he always enjoyed her pies.

But as they chatted about the summer heat and who was vacationing where, he couldn't shake the feeling that there were secrets hiding just below the surface. Had they always been there and he had never noticed?

Twenty minutes later, he hugged his mother goodbye, then picked up the trash bag from the kitchen and carried it out as he did every time he left. He put it in the large container by the garage and waved before stepping into his truck.

His mother waved back, then returned to the house.

Gage watched the closed back door for a while before starting the truck and heading home. What had happened tonight? Was something different, or was he making something out of nothing?

He slowly drove the familiar streets of Possum Landing. The signal by the railroad tracks had already started its slow flashing for the night. Those downtown would stay on until midnight, but on the outskirts of town they went to flashing at eight.

Unease settled at the base of his spine, making him want to turn around and demand answers from his mother. The problem was, he wasn't sure what the questions were supposed to be.

Maybe instead of answers, he needed a woman. It had been a long time and his need hadn't gone away. There were, he supposed, several women he could call on. They would invite him inside for dessert…and breakfast. He paused at the stop sign. No doubt Daisy would do the happy dance if he turned his attention in her direction. Of course, she would want a whole lot more than breakfast. Daisy was a woman in search of a happy ending. Gage was sure it was possible—just not with him.

He drummed his fingers on the steering wheel, then swore and headed home. None of those welcoming beds appealed to him tonight. They hadn't in a long time. He'd reached that place in his life where the idea of variety only made him tired. He wanted the familiar. He wanted to settle down, get married and have a half-dozen kids. So why couldn't he make it happen? Why hadn't he fallen in love and popped the question? Why hadn't he—

He turned into his driveway, his headlights sweeping the front of the house next door. Someone sat on the top step, shielding her eyes from the flash of light.

A familiar someone who made parts of him stand up at attention without even trying.

Been there, done that, he told himself as he killed the engine and stepped out into the quiet of the night. But that didn't stop him from heading toward her, crossing his lawn and then hers.

Anticipation filled him. He wondered how she liked her eggs.

Chapter Four

Kari watched as Gage approached. He moved with the liquid grace of a man comfortable in his own skin. He was what people called "a man's man," which made the most female part of her flutter. How ironic. She'd spent nearly eight years surrounded by some of the most handsome, appealing male models New York had to offer—a good percentage of whom had *not* been gay—and she'd never once felt herself melt just by watching them move. What was it about Gage that got to her? Was she just a sucker for a man in uniform, or was it something specific about him?

"So, how was your date?" she asked to distract herself from the liquid heat easing through her belly. "You're back early, so I'm going to guess the ever-delightful Daisy is playing hard to get."

She thought about mentioning her surprise that Daisy would let Gage leave without visiting the promised land, but was afraid the comment would come out sounding catty.

He settled next to her on the front step and rested his forearms on his knees. "You always were a nosy thing back when you were in high school. I see that hasn't changed."

"Not for a second." She grinned.

He glanced at her and gave her an answering smile that made her heart do a triple flip.

"I had dinner with my mother," he said. "I do it every week."

"Oh."

She tried to think of a witty comeback but couldn't. The admission didn't surprise her. Gage had always been good to the women in his life…his mother, her grandmother. She remembered reading an article somewhere, something about paying attention to how a man treats his mother because it's a good indication of how he'll treat his wife. Not that she was planning on marrying Gage Reynolds. Still, it was nice to re-confirm that he was one of the good guys.

"How *is* your mom?" she asked.

"Good. She had a rough time after my dad died. They'd been together for so long, I'm not sure she thought she could make it without him. Eventually she got it together. Last year she started dating again. She met a guy named John. They're engaged."

Kari straightened. "Wow. That's great." Then she remembered how close Gage had been to his father. "Are you okay with it?"

He nodded. "Sure. John is one of the good guys."

Takes one to know one, Kari thought. "When's the wedding?"

"This fall. He's a retired contractor. He has a lot of family up in Dallas. That's where he is this week. One of his granddaughters is having a birthday, and he wanted to be there for the party."

"They say people who have one successful marriage can have another."

Gage stared up at the night. "I believe that's true. My folks loved each other. There were plenty of fights and difficult times, but on the whole, they were in love. From what John has said about his late wife, they had a strong marriage, too. I figure the two of them are going to do just fine."

"I'd like to see your mother again. I always liked her."

"She's working up at the hardware store. It's a part-time job to get her out of the house. You should head on up and say hi."

"I will."

When Kari and Gage had been dating, Edie had welcomed her with open arms. Kari didn't know if the woman had done that with all Gage's girlfriends, but she liked to think she and Edie had been especially close. Of course, Edie wouldn't have been thrilled about her dumping Gage via a note and running away.

"Is she still mad at me for what I did?"

He glanced at her, laughter lurking in his dark eyes. "She seems to have recovered."

"Okay. Then, I'll pop over and congratulate her on

the upcoming nuptials. I think it's great that she's found someone. No one should be alone.''

As soon as the words fell from her mouth, she wanted to call them back. Obviously, both she and Gage were alone. She knew her circumstances—but what were his? He was the kind of man who had always attracted women, so the choice to be single must have been his. Why?

She was about to ask, when he beat her to the punch.

"So, why aren't you married, Kari?''

Before she could answer, he shrugged. "Never mind. I forgot. You weren't interested in home and hearth. You had things to do and places to be.''

She bristled. "That's not true. Of course I want to get married and have kids. I've always wanted that.''

"Just not with me?''

He didn't look at her as he spoke, and she didn't know what he was thinking.

"Just not on your timetable,'' she told him. She sighed. "Eight years ago, you were right on track with your life. You had seen the world and were ready to settle down. I was a senior in high school with a lot of unrealized dreams. I was young and hopeful, and as much as I cared about you, I was terrified by your life plan. You seemed so much older—so sure of yourself. Everything you said was reasonable, yet it felt wrong for me at the time. I didn't want to be like my mother and grandmother, marrying out of high school, having kids right away. I wanted *my* chance to see the world and live my dreams.''

"I thought I was one of your dreams.''

"You were. Just not right then. When I heard you were going to propose, I panicked, which is why I ran away. I thought..." She hesitated. "You were so clear on the way everything would be. I was afraid I'd get lost in that."

He sat close enough for her to feel the heat of his body and inhale the scent of him. She was torn between wanting to lean against him and heading for the hills. Confessions in the night were frequently dangerous. What would be the outcome of this one?

Gage surprised her by saying "You're right."

She blinked at him. "I didn't expect that."

He shrugged. "I thought I knew everything back then. You were what I wanted in a wife, we were in love—why wouldn't we get married and settle down? You talked about going to New York and being a model, but I didn't think you were serious." He glanced at her and shrugged again. "That was pretty arrogant of me. I'm sorry, Kari. I should have listened to you. Instead I focused on what I wanted and tried to steamroll my way to the finish line."

His confession caught her off guard. "Thanks," she murmured. "I wish we'd had this conversation eight years ago."

"Me, too. Maybe we would have found a way to make it work."

She nodded but didn't say anything. Privately, she doubted that would have happened. Even after all this time, the truth still hurt her. Gage might have wanted to marry her, but he hadn't loved her enough to come after her and ask her to return home with him. He hadn't loved her enough to get in touch with her and say he would wait while she followed her dreams. She took off, and he seemed to simply get on with his life.

"So I went into the army when I wanted to see the world and you went off to New York," he said lightly, as if trying to shift the tone of their conversation. "I'm guessing you had a better time."

She tamped her sadness and laughed. "Oh, I don't know. At least you got regular meals."

"Was money that tight?"

"A little. At first. But I got some part-time jobs and eventually modeling work. The food thing is more about being the American ideal of a working model. I didn't eat because I had to lose weight. I was young and determined, which meant I wasn't sensible. It wasn't a very healthy lifestyle."

"Aside from the lack of food, is it what you thought it would be?"

"I don't know. I think young women want to be models because it's glamorous. Where else can an eighteen-year-old girl make that kind of money and travel all over the world? There are lots of invitations. Men want to date models. Being a model is an instant identity."

She pulled her knees close to her chest and wrapped her arms around her legs. "But the reality can be difficult. Thousands of girls come to New York, and only a tiny percentage make it to supermodel status. A few more are successful. I was a little below that—a working model who earned enough to pay the bills and put myself through college, with a bit of a nest egg left over. The truth is, I never fit in.

I found some of the parties were scary places. I wasn't allowed to eat, I never was one to drink. And men who only date models have expectations I wasn't comfortable with.''

She smiled at him. "I guess you can take the girl out of Possum Landing, but you can't take Possum Landing out of the girl."

"I'm glad."

As he studied her, she wondered what he was thinking. Had her experiences shocked him? Compared with most of her friends, she'd practically been a nun, but she wasn't going to tell Gage that. It would sound too much like making excuses.

"You were talking about finding a teaching job near Dallas," he said. "Will you miss New York?"

"Some things, but I'm ready for a change. I was born and bred in Texas. This is where I belong."

He rubbed the cracked paint on the handrail. "What are your plans for the old house?"

Kari considered the question. "I'm still debating." She suddenly remembered. "Oh, I went around and did an inventory of furniture...mostly the antiques."

Gage looked interested but didn't say anything.

She sighed. "I loved my grandmother, but she was a bit of a pack rat. Anyway, I have a list. There are some I want to keep for myself...mostly those with sentimental value. I checked and my parents don't want anything. So I'm going to sell the others, except for the ones you'd like."

He raised his eyebrows. "What do you mean?"

"I didn't know if you were interested in antiques.

If you are, I'd like you to have first pick at what she had.''

"Why?''

Wasn't it obvious? "Come on, Gage, we both know how much you helped her. You were always willing to run over and fix whatever was broken. After I left, you kept her company and helped her out, even though you had to have been really angry with me.''

"I wouldn't have let that affect my relationship with her.''

She noticed he didn't deny the anger, which made her uncomfortable. Funny how after all this time Gage's disapproval still had the power to make her cringe.

"That's my point,'' she said, staying on topic. "You could have been difficult and you weren't. After she died, you contacted the real estate management company whenever there was a problem with the house. I owe you. I figured you'd be deeply insulted if I offered money, so this seemed like a good compromise.''

He stared at her. Despite the fact that the sun had gone down a while ago, the Texas summer night was still warm. As his intense gaze settled on her face, she had the feeling that the temperature had climbed a couple of degrees. Despite the fact that she was wearing shorts and a cotton sleeveless shirt, she felt confined...restricted...and far too *dressed*.

Kari couldn't help smiling. Boy, he was good. If he could make her writhe just by looking at her, what would happen if he ever kissed her again?

Too late, she remembered she'd promised herself she wasn't going to think of the kiss again. Not when she'd spent most of two days reliving it. She'd firmly put it out of her mind…almost.

"All right," he said slowly. "I'll consider taking one of the antiques as payment. If you haven't kept it for yourself, I wouldn't say no to the sideboard in the dining room."

It took her a second to figure out what on earth he was talking about. As far as her mind was concerned, the previous conversation hadn't even taken place. Then all her synapses clicked into place.

"No, I haven't claimed that one. Consider it yours."

"I'm much obliged."

His eyes held hers for a couple more heartbeats, then he finally looked away. She felt as if she'd been released from a force field. If she hadn't been sitting already, she would have collapsed.

She struggled to pick up the thread of their conversation. Oh, yeah. They'd been talking about her fixing up the house. "I'm going to paint the whole place," she said. "Inside and out. I'm doing the inside myself and hiring someone to do the outside."

Gage glanced up at the tall eaves and nodded. "Good idea. I'd hate to see you falling off a ladder."

"Me, too." She stretched out her legs in front of her. "There are a couple of windows that need replacing, and the whole kitchen is a 1950s disaster. I'll strip the cabinets and refinish them. I've already ordered new appliances and carpeting. I think that's about it."

"Sounds like you'll be busy."

"That's the plan. I'm going to start slow with the painting. Just do one room at a time. Everything needs a primer coat—it's been years between paint jobs."

He seemed to consider the night sky, then he turned to her. "I have a couple of days off coming up. I could offer you some brawn for moving things around and reaching the high places."

She shivered slightly at the thought of his "brawn." "I'm five-ten—I can reach the high places on my own. But I will say yes to whatever help you're willing to offer."

"Then, I'll be here."

She found herself leaning toward him as he spoke, as if what he said had great significance and she wanted to be close enough to breathe in every word. She sighed. Whatever was wrong with her was more serious than she'd thought. After all this time, she couldn't possibly still be crazy about Gage. Not when they'd both gone in such different directions.

He rose suddenly. "It's getting late," he said, moving off the stairs. "I should be getting back home."

She waited—more breathless than she wanted to admit—until he gave her a slight nod and headed toward his place.

"'Night, Gage," she called after him, as if his leaving was a good thing. As if she wasn't thinking about what it would be like if he kissed her again. Not that he was going to, obviously. Apparently, that one kiss had been enough for him. It had been enough for her, too. More than enough. In fact, she was really glad that he didn't plan to try anything. She would have to say no and it would get really embarrassing for both of them.

She *hated* that he hadn't kissed her.

By the next afternoon, Kari still hadn't figured out why. Why he hadn't and why it bugged her. Didn't Gage find her attractive? Hadn't he enjoyed their previous kiss? She *really* hated that his not kissing her had kept her up in the night nearly as much as his kissing her had.

It was the past, she told herself as she stood in her grandmother's bedroom and slowly opened dresser drawers. But after all this time, she was finding herself being sucked back into what had once been.

Kari shook her head to chase away the ghosts, then plopped on the floor to study the contents of the bottom drawer. There were several sweaters wrapped in lengths of cotton and protected by cedar chips. She held up a pale blue sweater, admiring the workmanship and the old-fashioned style. This particular sweater had been a favorite. Kari could see her grandmother in it as clearly as if the woman stood in front of her.

"Oh, Grammy, I miss you," she whispered into the silence of the morning. "I know you've been gone a long time, but I still think about you every day. And I love you."

Kari paused, then smiled slightly as she imagined her grandmother whispering back that she loved her favorite girl, too. More than ever. Despite everything, her grandmother had been the one constant in her life.

Kari slowly put the sweater back. She realized she needed a few boxes so she could sort those items that were going with her from those that were not. She touched the sweater before closing the drawer. That she would keep. It would be a talisman—her way to connect to some of her happiest memories.

The middle drawer yielded scarves and gloves, while the top drawer held her grandmother's costume jewelry. There were plenty of real pieces, Kari remembered as she touched a pin in the shape of a dragonfly. They were in a jewelry chest on the top of the dresser. A string of pearls and matching earrings, a few gold chains. Perhaps her grandmother had worn them, too, but all of Kari's memories of the woman who had raised her were much more connected with the costume pieces.

There were the gaudy necklaces that Kari had dressed up in when she was little and the fake pearl choker her grandmother had worn to church every Sunday. The bangle bracelets and the butterfly earrings and the tiny enameled rose pin Kari had been allowed to wear on her first date with Gage.

She shifted on the floor so that she leaned against the old bed. The rose pin didn't look the worse for wear. She rubbed her fingers across the smooth petals, remembering how her grandmother had pinned it on Kari's blouse five minutes before Gage had arrived to pick her up.

"For luck," her grandmother had said with a smile.

Kari smiled, too, now, even as she fought tears. Back then she'd wanted every bit of luck available. She hadn't been able to believe that someone as grown up and handsome as Gage Reynolds had asked her out. When he'd issued the invitation, it had been all she could do not to ask him why he'd bothered.

But she hadn't. And when she'd gotten nervous on that date, she'd touched the rose pin for luck. It had happened so many times, Gage had finally commented on the tiny piece of jewelry.

They'd been walking out back, Kari remembered, her mouth trembling slightly as she battled with tears. After a dinner at which she'd barely managed to swallow two bites, he'd taken her for a walk in the pecan grove.

She could still smell the earth and hear the crunch of the fallen pecans under their feet. She'd thought then that he might kiss her, but he hadn't. Instead, he'd taken her hand in his. She'd almost died right there on the spot.

It wasn't that no one had held her hand before. Other boys had. But that was the difference...they were boys. Gage was a man. Still, despite the age difference and her complete lack of subtlety, he'd laced his fingers with hers as they'd walked along. Kari had relived the moment for days.

They'd been out exactly five times before he finally kissed her. She touched the pin again, smiling as she remembered pinning it on her sweater that October evening. Once again, Gage had taken her to dinner and she'd only managed to eat a third of her entrée. She hadn't been dieting—that didn't come until her move to New York. Instead, she'd been too nervous to eat. Too worried about putting a foot wrong or appearing immature. After only five dates, she was well on her way to being in love with Gage. Her fate had been sealed that evening, as she leaned against the pecan tree, her heart beating so fast it practically took flight.

She closed her eyes, still able to feel the tree pressing into her back. She'd been scared and hopeful and apprehensive and excited, all at the same time. Gage had been talking and talking and she'd been wishing he would just *do it*. But what if he didn't want to kiss her? What if…

And then he had. He'd lightly touched the pin, telling her how pretty it was. But not as pretty as her. Then, while she was still swooning over the compliment, he'd bent low and brushed his mouth to hers.

Kari sighed softly. As first-kiss memories went, she would bet that hers was one of the best. Before then, she'd dated some, and kissed some, but never anyone like him. In fact, she couldn't remember any of her first kisses with other boys. But she remembered Gage. Everything from the way he'd put his hand on her shoulder to how he'd stroked her cheek with his warm fingers.

A shiver caught her unaware as it lazily drifted down her back. The restless feeling returned, and with it all the questions as to why he hadn't bothered to kiss her again the previous night.

Impulsively, she fastened the rose pin to her T-shirt. Maybe she was still floundering around in her love life, but she had some fabulous memories. However it might have ended, Gage had treated her incredibly well when they were together. There weren't many men like him.

She had the brief thought that it would be wonderful to be meeting him now, for the first time. She had a feeling that without all their past baggage to trip over, they could make something wonderful happen between them.

The daydream sustained her for a second or two, until she reminded herself that it didn't matter what would or would not be happening if she and Gage had just met. Possum Landing was his world, and she was most definitely not back to stay.

Chapter Five

After walking through the upstairs and deciding on paint colors, Kari made a list and headed for the hardware store. Since she'd last been in Possum Landing, one of those new home improvement superstores had opened up on the main highway about ten miles away. She was sure their selection was bigger, their prices were lower and that she probably wouldn't run into one person she knew. But starting a refurbishing project without stopping by Greene's Hardware Center would probably cause someone from the city council to stop by with a written complaint. Her grandmother had always taught her the importance of supporting the local community. And old Ed Greene had owned the store since before Kari was born.

New York was a big city made up of small neighborhoods. Over time, Kari had come to know the people who worked at the Chinese place where she ate once a week, and she and the lady at the dry cleaner had been on speaking terms. But those relationships hadn't had the same history that existed here in Possum Landing.

So she drove across town to Greene's, then pulled into the parking lot that had last been repaved in the 1980s. The metal sign was still there, as was an old advertisement for a certain brand of exterior paint. Advertising slogans, long out of date, covered most of the front windows.

Kari smiled in anticipation, knowing there would be a jumble of merchandise inside. If she wasn't careful she would come out with more than just paint. She still remembered the old rooster weather vane her grandmother had come home with one afternoon. For the life of her, she couldn't figure out how Ed had talked her into buying it.

Kari pulled her list out of her purse, determined to be strong. She walked up the creaking steps of the building's front porch and stepped into the past.

Old file cabinets stood by the front door. They contained everything from stencils to paint chips, instruction on lawn care and packets of exotic grass seeds. To the right was a long wooden counter with Peg-Board behind it. Dozens of small tools hung in a seemingly unorganized array. The place smelled of dust and cut wood and varnish. For a moment Kari felt as if she were eight again. She could almost hear her grandmother calling for her to stay out of trouble.

"Kari?"

The female voice was familiar. Kari turned and saw Edie Reynolds walking in from the back room. Gage's mother was a tall, dark-haired woman, still attractive and vibrant. She smiled broadly as she approached and pulled Kari into a welcoming hug.

"I'd heard you were back in town," Edie said when she released her. "How are you? You look great."

"You, too," Kari managed to say, too surprised by the friendly greeting to protest that she wasn't back for any length of time. She knew that Gage's mother would have known about her son's plans to propose and that she, Kari, had broken off the relationship in a less than honorable way. Apparently, Edie had decided to forgive and forget.

Edie pulled out one of the stools in front of the counter and took a seat, then motioned for Kari to do the same.

"Tell me everything," the older woman said. "You're staying at your grandmother's house, right?" She smiled. "Actually, I suppose it's your house now."

"I still think of it as hers," Kari admitted. "I want to fix it up and sell it. That's why I'm here. I need supplies."

"We have plenty." Edie laughed. "So you were in New York. Did you like it? Gage showed me some of your pictures. You were in some pretty big magazines."

"I managed to make a living. But it wasn't the career I thought I wanted. I went to college and just received my teaching credentials."

"Good for you." Edie glanced around the store. "As you can see, nothing's changed."

Kari didn't know if she agreed or not. Some things seemed different, while others—like her reaction to Gage—didn't seem to have evolved at all.

"You working here is different," Kari said. "I only remember seeing Ed behind the counter."

"That old coot," Edie said affectionately. "I took a part-time job a year or so after Ralph died. I didn't need the money, but I desperately needed to get out of the house. The walls were starting to close in on me."

"I'm sorry about Ralph," Kari said.

Edie sighed. "He was a good man. One of the best. I still miss him, of course. I'll always miss him." She smiled again. "Which probably makes the news of my engagement a little hard to understand."

"Not at all. I think it's wonderful you found someone."

"We met right here," Edie said, her eyes twinkling. "He's retired now, but he was still working then. A contractor on a job. He ran out of nails and popped in to buy some. It was just one of those things. I had started dating a few months before and really hated the whole process, but with John... everything felt right. Somehow I knew."

Kari envied Edie her certainty. She'd dated from time to time, and no man had ever felt right. Well, Gage had, but that had been years ago.

"When's the wedding?" Kari asked.

"This fall. We're still planning the honeymoon. I can't wait."

"It sounds wonderful."

"I'm hoping it will be. Now, enough about me, tell me about yourself. I'll bet you never expected a bank robbery to welcome you back."

Kari nodded. "I managed to avoid crime the whole time I was in New York, but after less than twenty-four hours in Possum Landing I had a man holding a gun to my head." She touched Edie's arm. "Gage was very brave."

"I know. I hate that he put himself in danger, but as he pointed out to me, it's his job. I tell myself that the good news is he doesn't have to do it very often. Possum Landing is hardly a center of criminal activity."

They chatted for a few more minutes, then Edie helped Kari buy primer and paint, brushes, rollers, tarps and all the other supplies she would need for her painting project.

She left the hardware store with her trunk full and her spirits light. There was something to be said for a place where everyone knew her name.

"You'd better be awake or there's going to be hell to pay," Gage called as he strolled in through the back door without knocking.

Kari didn't bother looking up at him. Instead, she grabbed another mug from the cupboard and filled it with hot coffee.

"Good morning to you, too," she said, turning to face him as she handed him the mug.

Whatever else she'd started to say fled her brain as she took in the worn jeans and tattered T-shirt he wore. She'd only seen him in his uniform since she'd returned to Possum Landing, and while the khaki shirt and pants emphasized the strength of his body, they had nothing on worn denim.

What was it about a sexy man in blue jeans? Kari wondered as her chest tightened slightly. Was it the movement of strong thigh muscles under fabric made soft by dozens of washings? The slight fading by the crotch, or the low-slung settling on narrow hips? She barely noticed the cooler he set on her kitchen table.

"I have a list of demands," he said after taking a sip.

She blinked. "Demands for what?"

"Work. I might work for free, but I don't come cheap. I expect a break every two hours and I expect to be well fed. Before we start, I want to know what's for breakfast and lunch."

She burst out laughing, but Gage didn't even crack a smile.

"Okay, big guy," she said. "Here's the deal. Take a break whenever you want—I don't care how often or how long. Seeing as I'm not paying you, I can't really complain. There's cold cereal for breakfast and I have sandwich fixings for lunch. Oh, and you'll be making your own sandwich."

Gage muttered something about Kari not being a Southern flower of motherhood, then started opening cupboards. "Cereal," he complained. "Aren't you even going to offer me pancakes?"

"Nope."

He muttered some more. "I'm just glad I stopped by my mama's place. She made potato salad and macaroni salad. I'll share, but that means you have to make my sandwich.''

"Blackmail."

"Whatever works."

She poured herself more coffee and sighed. "All right. It's a deal."

He poked through her cereal collection, which consisted of several single-serving boxes.

"You turned into a Yankee while you were gone. I'll bet you can't even make grits anymore."

"I couldn't make them when I lived here, so you're right. I can't make them now."

He pretended outrage. "I could arrest you for that, you know. This is Possum Landing. We have standards."

She topped off his coffee mug, then started for the stairs. "If you're done complaining, let's get to work."

"Oh, great. No pancakes, you won't make my sandwich and now you're turning into a slave driver. Don't that just beat all?"

Kari chuckled as she reached the second floor. Gage's teasing had managed to divert her attention from his jeans and what they did to her imagination…not to mention her libido. Far better to play word games than dream about other kinds of games. That would only get her into trouble.

"I thought we'd start in here," she said, walking into one of the small spare bedrooms. "I haven't painted in years and I doubt I did a very good job when I was twelve. So I'm trying to gear up."

He looked around. She'd taken out the smaller

pieces of furniture and had pushed the rest into the center of the room.

After setting his mug on a windowsill, Gage grabbed a four-drawer dresser and picked it up. "Let's get rid of a little more so we have room to work," he said. "Where can I put this?"

She stared at him. Last night she'd practically pulled a muscle just trying to move the dresser across the floor. Gage picked it up as if it weighed as much as a cat. Figures.

"In my grandmother's room."

He followed her down the hall. "Are you sleeping in there? Isn't it the biggest bedroom?"

"No and yes. I'm in my old room. I just felt better being in there."

He put down the dresser and turned. "She wouldn't mind," he said seriously. "She loved you."

"I know. I just…" How to explain? "I want to keep the memories as they are."

"Okay."

He put his arm around her as they walked back to the spare room. Kari tried not to react. Gage's gesture was friendly, nothing more. Nothing romantic…or sexual. Her imagination was working overtime and she was going to make it stop right this minute.

So why did she feel each of his fingertips where they touched her bare arm? And why did the hairs on the back of her neck suddenly stand at attention?

"I, uh, did some patching yesterday," she said, slipping free of his embrace. Casual or not, his touch made her breathing ragged. "There were some nail holes and a few cracks. I guess we sand it next."

He stepped around her and studied her supplies. "I'll sand. It's man's work."

"*Man's* work?"

"Sure."

"What will I be doing while you're dragging home the woolly mammoth?"

"You can clean up your putty knife and take off the baseboards."

She eyed the strips of wood encircling the room just above the carpeting. "Why isn't that man's work?"

He sighed. "If I have to explain everything, we'll never get the painting started, let alone finished."

"Uh-huh. Why do I know this is more about you doing what you want to do than defining tasks by gender?"

Gage looked up blankly. "I'm sorry. Did you say something?"

Kari thought about throwing something at him, but laughed, instead. While he went to work with sandpaper, she knelt on the opposite side of the room and gently began to pull the baseboards free of the wall.

They worked in silence for nearly half an hour.

"You do good work," Gage said finally.

"Thanks. I can read directions. Plus, I've learned to be good at odd jobs."

"Why is that?"

"The need to eat and pay rent," she said easily. "I told you, I didn't get any modeling work for over a year. New York isn't exactly cheap. So I worked different places to support myself. Some months it was tough."

He finished sanding and picked up a screwdriver. In a matter of seconds, he'd popped the pins out of the hinges and removed the door.

"You didn't call home and ask for money."

It was a statement, not a question. Obviously, he and Grammy had talked about her after she'd left.

"Nope. It had been my decision to leave, so it was my responsibility to make it on my own. I didn't want to get complacent, thinking that I always had someone waiting to send me money. The only thing I allowed myself was the promise my grandmother had made to send me a ticket home should I ever want it."

"Were you tempted?"

"A couple of times. But I held on and then things began to turn around. I got my first well-paying modeling job right before she died. She didn't get to see the magazine spread, but she knew about it, so that was something."

Kari pulled off the last piece of baseboard and dragged it out into the hallway.

Gage reached for the can of primer. "You know she was proud of you," he said.

She nodded. "I know. She never made me feel bad for leaving, and she always said I was going to make it."

"And you did."

"Sort of. But in the meantime, there were all those other lovely jobs."

He poured primer into two small buckets, then took a brush and handed her another. "Any painting?" he asked.

"No. I think there's a union. I did more conventional things. Worked in retail, walked dogs, delivered packages."

"Waited on tables?"

She shook her head. "I didn't eat much, and being around food was torture. I tried to avoid restaurants whenever possible. My favorite gig was house-sitting. I stayed in some amazing places. Great views, soft beds, and not a cockroach in sight."

"Were you ever scared?" Gage asked.

"Sometimes. At first. I'd never been on my own. It was a trial by fire."

While Gage enjoyed hearing about her previous life, he didn't ask the one question he wanted to. Had she missed him? Had she thought about him after she left, or had she shaken off his memory like so much unwanted dust?

"It was quiet after you left," he said instead as he brushed primer on the wall by the window.

Kari crouched by the door frame. She half turned and glanced at him over her shoulder. "I'm sorry if…" Her voice trailed off. "I never asked because I was afraid of what I'd hear. I'm sorry if it was bad for you after…"

He knew what she meant. After she left. After she stood him up and walked out of his life. Word spreads fast in a small town and by prom night nearly everyone knew that he'd bought an engagement ring for Kari. It was months before well-meaning folk stopped asking "No, how are you *really?*"

"It wasn't so bad," he said, because it was true. The blow to his pride was nothing compared with the pain in his heart. He'd never been in love before. Having Kari walk away so easily had taught him a hard lesson—that being in love didn't guarantee being loved in return.

Until Kari had left him, he'd assumed they would spend the rest of their lives together. He'd planned a future that had included only one woman. Finding out she didn't share his dreams...or want to marry him...had shattered his hopes and broken his heart.

"I used to look for your pictures in women's magazines," he admitted.

She stood up and laughed. "I can't believe you bought them."

"Some. I went to the next town, though."

"I should hope so. We can't have one of Possum Landing's finest checking out fashion magazines." Her laughter faded. "I'm guessing you gave up long before you found me on one of the pages."

"Nope. I told you I saw that hair ad."

There had been others. It was nearly five years before he'd been able to let Kari go.

"That was my first big break," she said.

"I liked the lingerie spread," he teased. "You looked good in the black stuff, but the teal was my favorite."

The brush fell out of Kari's hand. Fortunately it tumbled onto the tarp rather than the carpet. She blinked at him as a flush climbed up her cheeks.

"You saw that?" she asked in a strangled voice.

"Uh-huh."

She cleared her throat, then realized she'd dropped her brush and picked it up. "Yes, well, I don't know how the regular lingerie models stand it. I hated wearing so little and how everyone stared at me. Plus, I was starving. I hadn't eaten for three days beforehand so I wouldn't be bloated. I started to get light-headed, so I worried that I was going to have a really spacey expression on my face and the client wouldn't like it.'' She shivered slightly. ''I never looked at those pictures when they came out. They were a part of my portfolio, but I avoided them.''

''You were beautiful,'' he said sincerely. ''I had no idea what was under all those clothes you used to wear.''

''Just the usual body parts.''

''It's all in the details, darlin'.''

Kari laughed.

They worked in silence for a few minutes. Gage didn't mind that they weren't talking. Being around Kari took some getting used to. At one time she'd been everything, then she'd been gone and he'd had to figure out how to make her not matter. Having her back confused him. While his body was very clear on what it wanted from her, the rest of him wasn't so sure.

Not that it was going to be an issue. She was moving on. Which meant anything other than sex would make him a fool for love twice. No way was he going to let that happen.

''I always wanted to thank you,'' Kari said as she poured primer into roller trays.

He noticed she was careful not to look at him.

''For what you did…or didn't do, when we were going out.''

He had no idea what she was talking about. "What didn't I do?"

She shrugged. "You know."

"Actually, I don't."

She turned to him. "You never pushed me. Now the age difference between us is nothing, but back then it was a big deal. You had been in the military and traveled the world. You'd seen and done things and you never..." Her voice trailed off.

Gage stared at her. "Are you talking about sex?"

For the second time in a half hour, she blushed. "Yes. You never pushed me. I didn't think it was a big deal back then, but now, I know that it was. You wanted things from me, but you never made me feel that I had to give in to keep you."

"You didn't. Kari, I wanted to marry you. I wasn't going to dump you because you were young and innocent."

"I know. I just want to thank you for that."

He wondered what kind of guys she'd met that would make her think his behavior was anything but normal.

She picked up a roller. "I thought you were a knight in shining armor that first night we met."

He frowned. "I was doing my job and you were damn lucky I came along."

"I know." She smiled sadly. "I was so excited to be invited to that party with real college boys. I'd never been to one before. One of my friends, Sally, had beer at her seventeenth birthday party, but that was a girls-only sleepover, and while it was exciting for us, it didn't have the same thrill as a boy–girl party with hard liquor.''

He shook his head. ''Unless you've changed, you're not much of a drinker at all.''

She laughed. ''Oh, I didn't want to drink any, I just wanted to be in with the cool kids. I never was all that popular.''

That surprised Gage. He remembered her having lots of friends in high school. But he knew that she'd never belonged to any one social group. Part of the reason was that Kari hadn't fit any label, part of it was that she had been so pretty. She'd intimidated the boys and alienated the girls.

''I was so scared,'' she said with a sigh. ''Walking down that back road by myself.''

''You should have been scared.''

He remembered their first official meeting. He'd moved back to Possum Landing after getting out of the service and had taken a job as a deputy. He'd bought his house a year later, right beside Kari's grandmother's place. While in the process of moving in, he'd noticed the pretty young woman next door. He hadn't thought anything of her at the time. Not until he'd been called out to a loud party on the edge of town.

Gage had given a warning and had known he would be called back in less than an hour. The second time he would get tough, but he always figured everyone deserved one chance to screw up. On his way back to the station he'd seen an old Caddy crawling along at about five miles an hour. The top was down and there were four very drunk college guys in the vehicle. Gage had hit his lights. A flash of movement on the side of the road had caught his attention. It was only then that he saw a teenage girl looking scared and out of place.

He'd sized up the situation in less than a minute. Girl goes to wild party, tries to escape and has no ride home, so she walks. Drunk boys follow, looking for trouble. He told her to climb into his squad car before telling the guys to walk back to the party or risk being arrested for drunk driving. They'd protested, but finally agreed. Gage had taken the keys, saying they could get them back the following day...as long as they were accompanied by a parent. Then he'd returned to his car to find a trembling teenager fighting tears.

He'd prayed she wouldn't break down before he got her home. It was only when she whispered her address that he realized she was his neighbor.

Now, all these years later, he remembered how concerned he'd felt. Kari was only a kid. But kid or not, she'd been drinking.

"You nearly threw up in my car," he complained, speaking his thoughts out loud.

Kari glared at him. "I did not. I got out of the car before I threw up."

"You looked awful."

"Gee, thanks. I felt awful. But you were really nice. You gave me your handkerchief afterward."

"You notice I didn't ask for it back."

She laughed. "Yes, I did notice that." She rolled on more primer. "I haven't thought about that night for a long time. I was in over my head. Everyone at the party was drunk. I drank some, but not enough to forget myself. Some of the boys wanted to have sex and I didn't.''

''So you started walking home.''

''And you saved me.''

''I gave you a ride.''

''Yes, and then you lectured me on being stupid.''

Gage remembered that. He hadn't let her out of the car until he'd given her a stern talking to. Her blue eyes had widened as he talked about the dangers of parties that could get out of hand.

He'd given the lecture several times before, but never had he been distracted by a passenger. He found himself having thoughts that didn't go with the job.

''Then you asked me how old I was,'' Kari continued. ''I couldn't figure out why. I thought maybe it had something to do with arresting me.''

''Not exactly.''

''I know that, now.''

''You'd been eighteen for two days,'' he said in disgust. ''I was twenty-three, almost twenty-four. Six years seemed like a big gap back then.''

''But you asked me out, anyway.''

''I couldn't help myself.''

He was telling the truth. Gage had tried to talk himself out of his attraction for nearly a month. Finally he'd gone to Kari's grandmother and sought her opinion.

''Grammy said it was fine,'' Kari said softly. ''I think she really hoped I would marry you and live next door.''

She turned away suddenly, but not before Gage thought he saw tears in her eyes.

"She would have liked that," he said quietly, "but more than anything, she wanted your happiness."

"I know," she said with a nod. "It's just..." She glanced around the room. "Being back here makes me miss her. Silly, huh?"

"No. You loved her. That's never silly."

She gave him a grateful smile. He felt a tightening low in his gut. Being back might make her miss her grandmother, but it made Gage miss other things. Oddly enough, they were things that had never happened. He didn't have memories of making love with Kari, yet he knew exactly what the experience would be. He knew the taste of her and how she would feel. He knew the sounds she would make and the magic that would flare between them. Despite the years and the miles, he still wanted her.

"You always understand," she said.

"Not even close."

"You understood me before and you still understand me."

"Maybe you're just simple."

She chuckled. "That must be it."

He didn't want it to be anything else—he didn't want to have any kind of connection to Kari Asbury. Sex was easy, but anything else would be complicated…and potentially dangerous.

"You're probably just really good with women," she said. "I mean, I was gone on you in thirty seconds, and now Daisy obviously has the hots for you."

"I don't want to talk about either of you."

"You want to talk about me," she teased. "Don't you? Don't you want to take a long walk down memory lane?"

"Isn't that what we've been doing?"

"I guess." She stared at him. "Have you slept with her?"

He stared back. "No."

"You didn't sleep with me, either. You do have sex with some of them, don't you, Gage?"

He saw the twinkle in her eyes. He kept his face sober as he continued to paint. "Sure. But I'm sort of a go-all-night kind of lover and that cuts into my sleep. I can't take on any new women until I get rested again."

She groaned. "Oh, please."

"Right now? You want to do it on the tarp?"

She laughed, then her humor faded. "I'm sorry *you* weren't my first time," she said, not looking at him, then shrugged. "You probably didn't want to know that."

He was stunned by the confession, probably because he had so many regrets about the same thing. "I wanted that, too," he admitted. "I'd thought about it a lot, but I wanted to wait..."

"And then I was gone," she said, finishing the sentence. "I'm sorry. For a lot of things."

"Me, too."

They didn't speak for a while, but he didn't mind the silence. He'd always felt comfortable around Kari. He hadn't thought they needed to make peace with the past, but a little closure never hurt anyone.

Finally he put down his brush and stretched. "Hey,

I've been working way longer than two hours. It's time for a break. I think you should make my sandwich now.''

''Excuse me, I believe I told you I wasn't making anything. That you were on your own.''

She straightened, and he wrapped an arm around her shoulders. ''Naw. You *want* to wait on me. It's a chick thing.''

''I'm tall and wiry, Gage. I could take you right now.''

He grinned. ''Not even on a bet, kid.''

Chapter Six

"What do you mean you're not going to help me clean up?" Kari asked in pretended outrage after they'd finished lunch.

Gage leaned back in his chair, looking full and satisfied and very sexy.

"I made my own sandwich," he said, ticking off items on his fingers. "Despite protests. I brought the potato and macaroni salads."

"But you didn't make them. Your mom did."

"I carried them, and it's damn far from my house to yours." He held up another finger. "I'm providing free labor and charming company, so it seems to me that cleaning would clearly be your responsibility."

She shook her head, more charmed than irritated. "You need to get married so some woman can whip you into shape."

He glanced down at his midsection. "Don't you like my shape? I've never had complaints before."

She didn't want to think about how he looked in his worn jeans and T-shirt. Just a quick glance at his muscles and the way he moved was enough to make her squirm. Not that she was going to admit it.

"You're passable," she said, going for a bored tone.

"You're just used to those sissy boys in New York."

She laughed. "Some of them are pretty nice looking."

"Real men are born in Texas."

"Like you?"

He leaned toward her. "Exactly like me."

They were flirting, she realized. It wasn't something she did very often, mostly because she was afraid of messing up. But with Gage that didn't seem to matter. If she put a step wrong, he wouldn't say anything to make her feel bad. He was, as he had always been, safe.

The thought surprised her. Why would she still think of Gage as safe? What did she know about him? He could have changed. He probably had, she thought, but not in any ways that affected his character.

"Maybe I'll take a nap," he said.

She glared at him. "You will not. I'm practically paying you to help me, so you'll get your butt back upstairs and keep working."

He grinned. "Make me."

Something hot and sensual flared to life inside her.

Something that made her wish for a witty comeback or the physical courage to walk over there and—

The phone rang.

"Talk about being saved by the bell," Kari muttered as she crossed the kitchen.

"I'll go start work," he said, rising. "But don't you take too long. I'm keeping track of hours, and if I work more than you, there will be hell to pay."

She dismissed him with a wave and reached for the phone. "Hello?"

"Hello, darling. How are you doing?"

Her humor faded as if it had never been. Tension instantly filled her. "Hi, Mom. I'm great. What's up with you?" Kari hoped her mother didn't hear the tension in her voice.

"Your father and I are planning a trip soon. You know, the usual."

Kari did know. She hated the fact that twenty-plus years after the fact, the information still had the power to make her feel angry and bitter.

"I received your letter," Aurora Asbury continued. "I never understand why you write instead of calling. Although, I always enjoy hearing from you."

"Thanks," Kari said. She wasn't about to admit that she wrote because it was one-way communication and a whole lot easier than picking up the phone.

"How's the house?" Aurora asked. "It's so old. Are you really going to be able to fix it up?"

"Sure. It won't be too much work, and I'll enjoy the challenge." Kari pressed her lips together. She felt both startled to hear from her mother and guilty about the house. Her grandmother, Aurora's mother, had left it to her, not her mother. Of course, her mother had never been around. She and Kari's father had been traveling the world.

"I think your plan to sell it is a good one," her mother said. "I *had* thought you might want to keep it for old time's sake."

"I don't want to do that." Kari drew in a breath. "So, um, how's Houston?"

"Hot and humid." Aurora sighed. "I can't wait for your father's next assignment. We should be heading overseas soon. I'm hoping for something in the Far East, but you know the company. We never know for sure until he gets his assignment."

There was a pause and then, "Are you sure you'll be all right there in Possum Landing, darling? It's such a small, stifling town. You could always hire someone to update the house, and stay with us for a few weeks."

Kari felt a surge of irritation. The invitation was coming a few years too late. "I'll be fine here," she said. "I'm enjoying reminiscing."

"I don't understand why you would want to stay in Texas after living in New York, but it's your choice." She paused, then said, "I was thinking of coming up for a quick visit in the next few weeks."

Kari stiffened. "Sure. That would be great." What she really wanted to ask was "why?" but she didn't. Aurora had many faults, but since being cruel wasn't one of them, Kari refused to be cruel herself.

"I'm not sure. I'll let you know."

"Okay. Well, I need to get back to work. I'm starting the painting."

"All right, darling. You take care of yourself."

"You, too, Mom."

Kari said goodbye, then hung up. She stood in the kitchen for several minutes, trying to recapture her good mood. When it didn't happen, she figured Gage was the best antidote for a burst emotional bubble and headed up the stairs.

"You're late," he complained, the second she walked into the room. "I'm going to have to—" He broke off and stared at her. "What happened? Bad news?"

"No. Just my mom calling."

"And?"

"And nothing. She might come to visit."

Gage didn't say anything. He clearly remembered that her relationship with Aurora had always been difficult.

She shrugged and moved toward the tray of primer he'd set up for her. "I know I should let it go."

"No one is saying you have to."

"I guess." She walked to the last bare wall. "It's just that I can't get past what she did. I mean, why have a kid if you're just going to abandon it?"

She hunched her shoulders, anticipating that he would defend Aurora's decision, but he didn't.

Kari was grateful. Sometimes she was okay with the past—mostly when she was happy in her life and her mother didn't call. But sometimes she felt the same sense of loss and confusion she had when she was young.

Her parents had married when her mother was barely eighteen. Her father was a petrochemical engineer working for a large oil company. Kari had come along sixteen months after the wedding, and four months later, her father had received his first overseas assignment. Somehow the decision was made to leave Kari with her grandmother. It was supposed to be a temporary arrangement—there had been some concern about taking such a small child so far away. But somehow, Aurora had never returned to claim her daughter.

"I spent my whole life waiting for her to come back for me," Kari said as she rolled primer on the wall. "Don't get me wrong. I loved being with Grammy and, after a while, it would have been weird to leave everything and go live with them. But even though I was happy, it hurt."

Gage lightly touched her arm. She smiled at him gratefully. "The thing is," she continued, "they always used the excuse that they didn't want to take a baby with them overseas. But my brothers were born there and never sent back here."

"It's their loss," he said gently.

She attempted a smile. "I tell myself that, from time to time. Sometimes I even believe it."

She tried to shake off the emotional edginess, along with the pain. Her life was great—she didn't need her family messing things up.

"I'm okay," she said. "Really. Those of us who weren't raised in the perfect family have to learn to adjust."

Gage grinned. "We weren't perfect."

"Sure you were. Parents who loved each other. A

home, a brother you actually got to know and spend time with. What more could you ask for?''

"I guess when you put it like that." He shrugged. "It wasn't always good for Quinn, though. He and Dad never got along."

Kari had never met Gage's younger brother. Quinn had left to join the military before Kari met Gage.

"What was the problem?" Kari asked.

"I never knew. Quinn was a bit of a rebel, but the trouble started long before that. It's almost as if…'' His voice trailed off.

Kari didn't want to pry, so she changed the subject. "What's he doing now?"

"Still in the service."

"Really? Doing what?"

"I have no idea. He's in some special secret group. They travel around the world and take care of…things. Quinn eliminates people."

Kari nearly dropped her roller. "He kills them?"

Gage nodded.

"For a living?"

"Yeah."

She couldn't imagine such a thing. Killing people for any reason was outside of her realm of imagination. She wanted to ask more questions, but had a feeling Gage didn't want to talk about it further.

"Okay, then," she said. "I guess the fact that one of my brothers is an accountant and the other is a zoologist is really boring by comparison."

"It sure is."

She stuck her tongue out at him.

"Childish," he muttered. "I see you haven't changed at all."

"Of course I have. I'm even more charming than when I left."

"That wouldn't have taken much. Besides, I'm the charming one in this relationship."

He grinned as he spoke, and she couldn't help laughing.

"What is it with you?" she asked.

"I think it's something in the water," he said with mock seriousness. "After all, the Reynolds family has been in Possum Landing for five generations. That makes us very special."

"Do you ever wonder what made them stop here in the first place?"

"Good sense."

"Right. Because everyone in America wants to live in a place called Possum Landing."

"You bet."

She continued to paint the wall, while he put a coat of primer on the closet door. They didn't talk for a time. When they finished the room and started to leave, she touched his hand.

"Thanks," she said. "For coming over and making me laugh."

His dark eyes flared slightly. "I'm glad I can help. No matter what, Kari, we were always friends."

Friends. Was that what she wanted, too?

They spent the rest of the afternoon moving furniture out of the second small bedroom, patching the walls and waiting for the primer to dry. By three, they'd put on the first coat of paint.

"It's such a girl color," Gage teased as he rolled yellow paint over the walls.

Kari looked up from the door frame, where she was painting trim. "It is not. Pink is a girl color. Yellow is neutral. I wanted something bright and cheerful that would open up the room."

"What about a skylight?"

She turned away to hide her grin. "I'm ignoring you."

"Your loss. Are you doing all the bedrooms up here in yellow?"

"I haven't decided." There were a total of four on this floor. Hers, her grandmother's and the two they were working on. "I want to do Grammy's room next, which means moving her furniture into here."

"Are you giving it away?"

"I'd like to keep the dresser, but, yes, the rest of it will go." She hesitated, feeling faintly guilty. "I *want* to keep all of it...or even if I don't, I think I should."

"Why?"

"Because it was hers. Because of the memories."

"I doubt she'll mind if you only keep what you like. Her purpose in leaving you the house wasn't to make you unhappy."

"I guess."

Sometimes Gage annoyed her by being sensible, but sometimes he got it just right.

They worked well together, she thought as she moved to paint around the window. The banter made her laugh, the companionship lightened her spirits. Being around Gage made her happy.

She shook her head slightly. *Happy*. When was the last time she'd enjoyed that particular emotion? She'd been content, even pleased with the direction of her life. But happy?

"I'm done in here," he said a few minutes later. "I'm going out back to start cleaning up the brushes and rollers."

"Okay. I'll just be a little longer."

He grabbed the equipment and headed for the stairs. Kari finished painting and followed him. She went out the back door and around to the side of the house—a spray of cold water caught her full in the face.

She screamed. "What on earth—?"

But that's as much as she got out before another blast of freezing water hit her in the chest. She shrieked and jumped back to safety. Okay, she thought as she brushed off her face and arms, if that's how he wanted to play it.

She ran to the other side of the house. Sure enough, she found a coiled hose, which she unscrewed from the tap and dragged around to the back door tap. A few quick twists had it connected. She turned the water on full, then went on the attack.

Gage obviously thought she'd headed into the house, because he stood bent over, cleaning brushes in a bucket and chuckling to himself. She caught him square in the backside.

He jumped and growled, then turned on her. The battle was on.

Kari raced to the safety of the far side of the yard. Her hose stretched that far, but his didn't. While she was able to attack directly, he was forced to arc water toward her. She danced easily out of its reach.

"Big, bad sheriff can't catch me," she teased as she blasted him. "Big, bad sheriff is all wet."

"Dammit, Kari!" He muttered something, then disappeared around the side of the house. Seconds later he appeared without the hose. He walked toward the tap by the back door and turned it off, then put his hands on his wet hips and stared at her. He looked unamused.

She dropped the hose and took off toward the far end of the yard. It had been about nine years since she'd tried to take the fence, but she was willing to give it a try. The alternative was getting caught.

"Don't you dare!" she yelled as she ran, not sure what she was telling him not to do.

"I dare just fine," he said, sounding way too close.

But she was nearly there. Just a few more feet of grass and then she would be—

He caught her around the waist, pulling her hard against him and knocking most of the air out of her. She struggled, gasping and laughing the whole time, but it was pointless. Gage's arm was like a steel band. A very wet, steel band.

"Let go of me," she demanded.

"Not until I teach you a lesson."

"You and what army?"

"I can do it just fine myself, little girl."

"I'm not a little girl."

"No. You're an all grown-up Yankee."

''Who are you calling a Yankee?''

He carried her like a sack to the center of the lawn, then released her. She took off instantly—and didn't get more than one step before he grabbed her again. This time when he pulled her against him, they were facing each other.

Her hair dripped in her face, as did his. They were both breathing hard and very, very close.

''Troublemaker,'' he murmured, staring into her eyes.

His were dark and unreadable, but that was okay. While she couldn't tell what was going on in his brain, there was enough action in his body to keep her occupied. He seemed to be pressing against her in a way that made her think of games more adult than a water fight. The expression of his face had changed as well. His features tightened with something that looked very much like passion. Which was okay with her—sometime in the past three seconds she'd gone from shivering to being filled with anticipation.

''Maybe you need a little trouble in your life,'' she said softly.

''Maybe I do. Maybe you do, too.''

She didn't have an answer for that, which was a good thing, because there wasn't any time to speak. His mouth settled on hers and all rational thought fled.

His lips were still damp from the water, but not the least bit cool. The arm around her waist tightened, pulling her even closer. They connected everywhere that was possible, with her hands touching his shoulders and his tongue brushing against her bottom lip.

She parted for him instantly, wanting, *needing* to taste him. The second he stroked the inside of her lower lip, shivers began low in her belly and radiated out in all directions. Her breasts swelled within the confines of her damp bra. Her thighs pressed together tightly. A light breeze cooled her wet skin, but parts of her were getting plenty hot.

He cupped her face as he deepened the kiss. She clung to him, wanting him to claim her, mark her, do with her whatever he wanted. She longed to be possessed by him.

Her fingers curled into his shoulders. Then she moved her hands to his back where she could feel the hard breadth of his muscles. His tongue circled hers, teasing, touching, seducing. She answered in kind, straining toward him. Every part of her melted against him.

Her breasts ached where they flattened against his hard chest. Her nipples tightened unbearably. When his hands moved to her waist, her breath caught.

His fingers moved higher and hers moved lower. While he inched his way up her damp T-shirt along her rib cage, she slipped down to his waist. Her heart thundered loud and fast until it was all she could hear. Her body trembled. Her thoughts circled, almost frenzied, unable to figure out what to concentrate on. The fabulous kiss? The slow ascent to her chest? The brush of damp jeans against her palms as she moved lower still?

He reached her breasts at the same instant she cupped his tight, high rear. Which was remarkable timing, because when his hands brushed against her, fire ripped through her body, making her gasp and nearly lose her balance. She grabbed on to him and squeezed, which caused him to arch against her. As his thumbs swept over her hypersensitive nipples, his hips bumped hers and she felt his need.

Pleasure shot through her. From their kiss, from the gentle stroking on her sensitive, aroused flesh, from the ridged maleness pressing into her belly. It was too much. It was amazing.

Gage pulled back just enough to put a little space between them. Before she could protest, he cupped her breasts fully, and she saw the wisdom in his actions. He explored her curves, brushing slightly, smoothing and inciting. Want filled her until she couldn't think about anything else…then he broke their kiss and began nibbling along her jaw and by her ear.

His hot breath tickled, his tongue teased, his teeth delighted. She clung to him as her world began to spin. There was only this moment, she thought hazily. The feel of Gage next to her, and what he did to her body.

She gasped when he nipped at her earlobe. Either he'd learned a whole lot while she'd been gone, or he'd been even more gentle back when they'd been going out because she didn't remember anything like this. Not ever. Back then, he'd kissed her and left her breathless, but he'd never—

She gasped as he walked behind her, licking her neck and sucking on her skin. He cupped her breasts at the same time and played with her nipples. Involuntarily, she opened her eyes and saw his large, strong hands moving against her. The combination of feeling and sight nearly made her collapse.

That was why the alarm bell caught her by surprise.

The alarm began as a distant, indistinct noise that grew louder with each beat of her heart, until it filled her head and made it impossible to concentrate on the delights Gage offered. It twisted her mind, clearing the sensual fog that surrounded her and forcing her to think sensibly.

What on earth was she doing? Did she really want to start something now? Like this? What would happen if she and Gage made love? Would it just be a quick trip down memory lane or would it be more? She hated that her brain insisted on being mature right now. Why couldn't she simply give in and then have recriminations later like everyone else?

Unfortunately the mood had been broken. She stepped away and sucked in a deep breath. It took more courage than she would have thought to turn and face him.

"I can't," she said, not quite looking him in the face. "I mean, I've never done the sex only thing. I'm not sure I could start now. So if anything were to happen—physically, I mean—it would lead to trouble. At least, for me."

She risked a glance and saw that he was looking at her with an intensity that made her take another step back. Not that she could read a single thought, which left her in the position of stumbling on with what she was trying to say.

"I'm leaving at the end of the summer. I would like us to be friends, but anything else…" She cleared her throat. "I just don't want to get my heart broken again. I mean, you already did that once."

Gage stared at Kari. He could accept that she wanted to call a temporary halt to their afternoon activities. Even he was willing to admit they'd gone a little too far, too fast. But that she had the guts to stand there and go on about *him* breaking *her* heart? His temper flared.

"What the hell are you talking about?" he demanded.

She blinked. "Excuse me?"

"I didn't break your heart. You're the one who left. You walked away without a backward glance. No warning, nothing. I was going to propose to you, Kari. I had planned to spend the rest of my life with you. You changed your mind and dumped me. So don't go telling me about *your* heart. You trampled mine pretty damn good."

Color rose to her cheeks. "That's not fair. I didn't deliberately set out to be mean. I wanted to talk to you but I couldn't. You didn't want to listen. You only wanted things your way, on your schedule."

He refused to be deflected from the point. "You dumped me without a word."

"I left a note."

He glared at her. "Yeah, a note. That's so great. I was about to propose and you left a lousy note. You're right. That makes everything fine."

"I'm not saying it makes things fine." She planted her hands on her hips. Her wet hair hung in her eyes; her mouth trembled as she spoke. "I couldn't risk speaking with you. I knew you'd do everything you

could to change my mind. You would never understand why I had to leave.''

"I loved you. Of course I wouldn't want you to go
away. Why is that so horrible?''

"It's not.'' She took a deep breath. "You're deliberately misunderstanding me. My point is, I deserved
to have a life, too. I deserved to have my dreams and
the opportunity to make them come true. But you
didn't care about that. You weren't willing to listen.
Besides, it's not as if you even missed me.''

Her words stunned him. He could still remember
what it had been like when he found out she'd left.
It was as if the world would never be right again.

"What the hell are you talking about? I was destroyed.''

"Right. And that's why you raced after me and
begged me to come home. Admit it, Gage. You never
really loved me. You loved the idea of getting married
and starting a family. You certainly never cared
enough to come after me and make sure I was all
right.''

She ducked her head as she spoke, and for a second, he thought he saw tears in her eyes. He swore.

"Is that what this is about?'' he demanded. "Some
stupid teenage girl test? If you really love me, you'll
race after me to the ends of the earth?''

She raised her head. There *were* tears in her eyes,
but he didn't care. He couldn't believe she was making him the bad guy in this.

"Yes, it was a test. And guess what? You failed.''

Fury overwhelmed him. He thought of all that had
happened after she'd disappeared. How he'd raged

and ached and thought he would never get over losing her. He thought about all the times he had gotten in his car to go after her, only to stop himself, because, dammit, letting her go had been the right thing to do. He thought about how he had looked for her in all those magazines, how he'd touched the glossy photo when he'd finally found her picture, still needing her as much as he needed to breathe.

He remembered that despite trying like hell to fall for someone else, he'd never been able to love anyone but Kari.

He thought about telling her all that—but why bother? She believed what she wanted to believe. So without saying anything, he turned on his heel and walked away.

Chapter Seven

"The nerve of that man" and other variations on the theme occupied all Kari's thoughts through the evening and well into the next day. She still couldn't believe what Gage had said to her. And how he'd acted! Like she'd said something so terrible.

Was it wrong of her to want to make decisions about her life? Of course not. But he'd refused to see that, just like he'd refused to understand what she'd been trying to say. Okay, maybe running away from a man she knew wanted to marry her, without explaining why and leaving only a note, wasn't very mature, but she'd been barely eighteen years old. Certainly not old enough to be getting engaged, let alone getting married and having kids! Which was what Gage had wanted. He'd planned it all out, from the date of their wedding to how long they would wait before starting a family to how many children were going to make up that family.

She'd gotten scared. She'd panicked and run.

She flopped down on the sofa in the parlor and stared out the front window. Upstairs there was plenty of work to be done, but she couldn't seem to motivate herself to do it.

Not only was she uncomfortable about arguing with Gage, but she hated all the memories that fight had stirred up. She'd been so in love with him, so crazy for him, that leaving had been incredibly hard. She'd cried the whole way to New York, and then some. She'd wanted to return home, and a thousand times she'd nearly done that. She'd picked up the phone to call him twice that many times. But, in the end, she hadn't. Because she'd known that coming back to Possum Landing would mean giving in to what Gage wanted for her life. It wasn't only the loss of her dreams that she feared…it was the loss of herself.

But he hadn't seen it that way back then, or yesterday. They'd both said things they didn't mean—at least, she hoped they didn't—and now they weren't speaking.

Kari stirred restlessly on the sofa and frowned. She didn't want to be *not* speaking to Gage. He was an important part of her past and about her only real friend in town. He was a good man and she really liked him. Obviously, her body thought he was a deity—but what did her body know? Avoiding each other didn't make any sense.

That decided, she headed for the kitchen where a batch of peanut butter cookies were cooling. After transferring all but a half dozen onto a plate, she went upstairs and changed into a bright blue sleeveless dress and a pair of tan sandals. She fluffed her hair, touched up her lipstick and practiced her best smile.

She would make the first move to show good faith and get things right between them. Once they were speaking again, she would do her best to avoid conversations about the past, because that only seemed to get them in trouble. Oh, and kissing. They would have to avoid that, too, because it led to other kinds of trouble.

She walked downstairs, covered the cookies with plastic wrap, then grabbed her purse and headed for the front door. Seven minutes later she pulled up in front of the sheriff's station. Two minutes after that, she was escorted back to Gage's office.

As she walked down the long corridor, she found her heart fluttering a bit inside her chest. The odd sensation made her feel nervous and just a little out of breath.

Emotional reaction to their fight, she told herself. She was simply nervous that Gage might still be angry with her. She certainly wasn't *anticipating* seeing him again.

He was on the phone when she paused in the doorway to his office. Rather than focus on how good he looked in his khaki uniform, she glanced around at her surroundings.

Gage looked up and saw her. His expression stayed unreadable—something that seemed to happen a lot—

although she thought she might have caught the hint of a smile tugging at the corner of his mouth. He hesitated briefly before motioning her in.

She moved to a straight-backed chair in front of his desk, and perched on the edge. Gage wrapped up his conversation and set down the receiver. She swallowed. Now that she was here, she didn't know exactly what to say. Her situation wasn't helped by the continued fluttering of her heart, not to mention a noticeable weakness in her arms and legs. It was as if she'd just had a very large, very stiff shot of something alcoholic.

What on earth was wrong with her? Then, unbidden, the memory of the passion she and Gage had shared rose in her mind, filling her body with sensations and her imagination with possibilities.

She silently screamed at herself to get down to business. Namely, apologizing. There would be no sexual fantasies about Gage. Not now. Not ever! And she really meant it.

"Kari," he said, his voice low and sexy. *Really* sexy.

She shivered. "I, um, brought a peace offering." She pushed the plate of cookies across the desk toward him. "I figure we both overreacted, but I'm willing to be mature about it."

She was teasing, and hoped he would get the joke. Instead of saying anything, though, he peeled back the plastic wrap and pulled out a cookie. After taking a bite, he chewed.

"I can be mature," he said as he leaned back in his chair and smiled at her. "With motivation."

She relaxed in her seat. "Are these enough motivation?"

"Maybe. It might take another dozen or so."

"I'll see what I can do." The rapid beating of her heart continued, but the tension fled.

"I'm sorry," she said seriously.

"Me, too. Like you said, I overreacted."

"I said a lot of things…" She paused. "I'm sorry about saying I tested you and you failed. I didn't mean it like that. I was a kid back then and completely unprepared for a grown-up relationship. I ran away because I was scared and couldn't face you. I thought you'd be mad and try to get me to change my mind." She shrugged. "Like I said, not really mature. But I didn't plan to hurt you. I thought you'd come after me, and when you didn't, I decided you didn't really love me. I thought I was a placeholder. That any woman would have done as long as she fulfilled your need for a wife and mother for your kids."

Gage picked up a pen and turned it over in his hands. "It wasn't like that, Kari. Any of it. I wanted to go after you. Hell, I thought about it a hundred times a day. I missed you more than I can ever explain, but that didn't mean I couldn't see your side of things. I didn't want to understand why you'd run off, but in my heart I knew. I didn't think I had the right to drag you back. You needed to follow your dreams. I'd just hoped they would be the same as mine."

"They were…just not then. I needed time."

He nodded. They looked at each other, then away.

Kari pressed her lips together. "Maybe we could start over. Be friends?"

"I'd like that. We can hardly be strangers if you're dragging me over to work on your house every other minute."

"I did *not* drag you. You volunteered."

"That's your story."

She smiled. "You make me crazy."

"In the best way possible."

That was true. And speaking of being made crazy... She cleared her throat. "About the kissing."

He waved a hand. "You don't have to thank me. I didn't mind doing it."

"Gee, thanks. Actually, what I was going to say was that I think we need to avoid it. Kissing can lead to other things and those other things would provide a complication neither of us needs."

"Fine by me. I can control myself."

"So can I."

She was almost *sure* she was telling the truth. She should have been able to without a problem. It's just that she sort of wanted to know what it would be like to make love with Gage. In every other area of her life, he'd always been the best man she'd ever known. No doubt he would shine at lovemaking, too.

She knew he would be sensitive and considerate, two things that really mattered to her—what with her never actually having done, well, *that* before. Someone, somewhere was going to have to be her first time, and she'd always thought Gage would be really good at that. Right up until he freaked out when she told him that she was still a virgin.

Rather than tread on dangerous ground, she changed the subject. "I don't remember the sheriff's station being this big."

He grinned. "How many times were you in it before?"

She laughed. "Okay. Never."

"We have a contract to patrol state-owned land. Several of the small towns hire us to take care of them, as well. The department has more than doubled since you left. I have some other plans for expansion. More territory and more officers means a bigger budget. We can qualify for some federal grants and upgrade equipment, stay ahead of the bad guys."

He looked so strong and sure sitting in his chair. A man in charge of his kingdom.

"You're good at what you do, aren't you," she said.

"If I'm not, I won't get reelected."

"I doubt that's going to happen. Something tells me that you'll be sheriff of Possum Landing for a very long time."

"It's what I want."

She envied how he'd always known that. She'd had to search for what she wanted. "Speaking of wants and dreams, I'm heading up to Dallas in the morning. I have an interview."

"Good luck with that."

"Thanks."

She waited, kind of hoping he might express a little regret that she was leaving, but of course he didn't. Which made sense. After all, he knew her stay in town was temporary. He wasn't about to forget that, or start acting surprised when she had interviews in other places. Expecting anything else was really foolish and he knew better than to be that.

"I'll be back on Saturday," she said, rising.

Obviously, with her mental state, she had better head home fast. Before she said or did something she would regret. Like throw herself at him. What if he rejected her? She glanced around at the glass walls and everyone who could see in. Actually she would be in more trouble if he didn't reject her.

"I'll see you then," he said. "You'll dazzle them, Kari."

"Thanks. I'll do my best. 'Bye."

She waved and left his office, then returned to the entrance. The young deputy who had driven her home walked by. He nodded politely and called her ma'am, which made her feel old.

Once outside, she breathed in the afternoon heat and was grateful she'd driven. Any walk longer than ten feet would cause her to sweat through her clothes in about forty seconds. Now, if only she could hire a little elf to go turn on her car and start the air-conditioning. That would be heavenly.

No elf appeared, but just as Kari was about to open her car door, she heard someone call her name. Not Gage, unfortunately. This was a female someone. Kari's body tensed and her shoulders hunched up. Great. Just what she needed.

Still, she forced herself to smile pleasantly as she turned and saw Daisy walking toward her.

The pretty reporter wore a skirt tight enough to cut off the circulation to her shapely legs. An equally snug shirt emphasized large breasts that instantly made Kari feel like a thirteen-year-old still waiting for puberty. Okay, yes, she was tall and slender and she'd been a model, but that didn't change the fact that she was a scant 34B, with hips as wide as a twelve-year-old boy's.

Still, Kari had posture on her side, so she squared her shoulders and forced herself to think tall, elegant, I've-been-in-a-national-magazine type thoughts.

"Hi, Daisy," she said with a big ol' Texas-size smile. "Nice to see you again."

"You, too."

The curvaceous bombshell paused on the sidewalk by the front of Kari's car and gave her a look that could only be called pitying. "This must be so hard for you," she said.

Kari had a feeling Daisy didn't mean the heat, although that was plenty difficult to adjust to. "I'm not sure what you're talking about," she said when she couldn't think of anything else.

Daisy sighed heavily. "Gage, of course. You're still sweet on him. I saw the plate of cookies you took in to the sheriff's office just now. I was across the street getting my nails done."

Kari nodded without turning. She could feel herself flushing, even though she knew she had nothing to be embarrassed about.

Daisy blinked her long lashes. "The thing is, Kari, Gage doesn't go back. He never has. He stays friends with his old girlfriends, but nothing more. And believe you me, more than one girl has tried to get that horse back in the barn." She lowered her voice conspiratorially. "Can you blame them? Gage Reynolds is a catch with a capital *C*. But once things are over, they stay over. What with you being gone and all, I didn't think you knew. I just don't want to see you get hurt."

Kari doubted Daisy's motivation, if not her information. Somehow, she couldn't see the other woman staying up nights worrying about Kari's pain or lack thereof.

"I appreciate the tip," she said, dying to make a move toward her car but not wanting to be rude. She wondered how the very passionate kisses she and Gage had shared fit in with Daisy's revelation. At the same time, she couldn't help smiling at the mental image of him as a runaway horse to be recaptured.

A thought suddenly occurred to her. She glanced at the petite beauty standing on the sidewalk. Something twisted in her stomach and made her swallow hard.

"I didn't know," she said slowly, finally putting all the pieces together.

And she hadn't. Daisy's interest in Gage, her warning Kari away. The fact that Daisy was divorced.

"Didn't know what?" Daisy asked.

Kari felt trapped. "That you're interested in him." What she was thinking was "in love," but she didn't want to say that.

Daisy shrugged. "I am. I won't deny it. He's a good man and there aren't many of those around. I know. I was married to a real jerk, which explains my divorce."

Kari shifted uncomfortably. She didn't want Daisy

saying too much. Somehow it felt wrong. Guilt blossomed inside her. Here she'd been playing fast and loose with an ex-boyfriend, while Daisy had been... What? She didn't know Daisy's position on Gage.

"Are you in love with him?" she asked before she could stop herself.

Oddly enough, Daisy laughed. "Love? I don't think so. I've been in love and it was nothing but trouble. I like Gage a lot. I think we could have a successful marriage, and that's what matters to me. I'm thinking with my head and not any other body part. Not this time. I want a steady man who'll come home when he says and be a decent father to our kids. That man is Gage."

Kari couldn't disagree with her assessment of Gage, but Daisy's plan sounded so cold-blooded, which wasn't Gage's style.

"Does Gage share your feelings on the subject?" she asked.

"No. Like most men, he thinks falling in love makes everything hunky-dory. Which is fine with me. He can love me all he wants. I'll be the sensible one in the relationship." Daisy's eyes narrowed. "So don't for a moment think you can waltz back in here and pick up where you left off."

"It never crossed my mind," Kari said honestly.

"Good. I intend to win him. I just need a little time."

"I'm sure things will work out perfectly." Kari itched to get back in her car and drive away. More than that, she wished this conversation had never taken place.

The other woman sighed. "Don't take this personally, but I wish you'd never come back."

Kari was starting to have the same wish. She wasn't sure if she felt sorry for Gage or not. He was a big, strong guy—he should be able to handle Daisy. She also felt unsettled, but couldn't say why. Nor did she know what to say to end the conversation.

Finally she opened her car door. "For what it's worth," she said, tossing her purse onto the passenger seat, "I'm not back. Not permanently. So you don't have to worry about me."

"Oh, I didn't plan to."

Daisy waggled her fingers, then turned and headed for the sheriff's office. Kari considered calling out "good luck," but she knew in her heart that she would be lying.

"I don't know. Australia." Edie fingered the glossy travel brochure in front of her. "It's very far."

John, her fiancé, smiled indulgently. "Travel does tend to take one away from one's regular world. That's the point."

Edie rolled her eyes. "I know that. I just never thought…" Her voice trailed off. "Australia," she repeated softly.

Gage watched her from his place on the opposite side of the kitchen table. He'd joined his mother and John for dinner. Once the plates had been cleared, John had pulled out several brochures for trips to exotic places. He and Edie had yet to pick a honeymoon destination.

As Gage sipped his coffee, he couldn't help being

pleased with his mother's happiness. His father's death had nearly destroyed her. For a while he'd worried that he was going to lose her, as well. Eventually, she'd started to heal. But she hadn't returned to anything close to normal until she'd met John.

Physically, John wasn't anything like Gage's father, Ralph. The retired contractor was several inches shorter, stocky to Ralph's lean build, and blond with blue eyes to Ralph's dark coloring. But he was a good man with a generous nature and a loving heart. He'd wanted to sweep Edie off her feet and marry her that first month. Instead, he'd courted her slowly, giving her all the time she'd needed. It had taken over a year for her to agree to marry him, but since she'd admitted her feelings, they'd been inseparable.

While their budding romance had been strange to Gage, he'd tried to stay open to the idea. He'd quickly come to see that John wasn't trying to take anyone's place. And his mother deserved a chance at happiness.

"After touring Australia, we board the cruise ship. There are stops in Singapore, Hong Kong and other parts of China before heading to Japan. We'll fly back from there."

Edie shook her head. "Of course it sounds lovely." She glanced at her fiancé and smiled lovingly. "I won't even mention that it will be very expensive."

John gave a playful growl. "Good."

"I've always wanted to see that part of the world," she said wistfully.

"Then, you should say thank you, give your fiancé a big kiss and start making plans," Gage said easily. "Go for it, Mama."

They could both afford the time the long trip would take, and John had retired a millionaire. Even after settling money on his daughters and grandchildren, there was still plenty to keep him and his new wife in style.

Edie glanced from him to John, then nodded tentatively.

John grinned. "Where's that kiss your son suggested you give me?"

She brushed his mouth with hers.

Gage sipped at his coffee again. There had always been good times around this table. Years before, when his father was still alive, they'd often talked long into the night. Ralph had been devoted to his wife in many ways, but he'd been a stubborn man who didn't bend on many things. He hadn't liked to travel, and Edie's pleas to see if not the world, then parts of the country, went ignored.

Ralph had been born and bred in Possum Landing, and as far as he was concerned, a man couldn't do better. Gage knew he had a little of his father in him. He loved the town where he'd been born, and he never wanted to live anywhere else. Unlike his father, though, he hadn't made Possum Landing his whole world. He enjoyed going to different places. He supposed that was because he was also his mother's son.

Edie opened the brochure and spread it over the kitchen table. "I can't believe we're going to do this. Gage, look. We can take a trip to the Australian outback. Oh! There's snorkeling on the Great Barrier Reef."

"Watch out for sharks," he teased.

She gave him a loving smile and returned her attention to the pictures.

While his mother and John planned their trip, Gage stared out the open window into the night. He hadn't been very good company tonight, probably because he felt distracted. He didn't want to admit the cause of the problem, but he knew exactly what it was. Or rather who.

Kari.

She was back from her interview. Her trip had taken her away for three days, but she'd returned that morning. He'd seen her car. While he'd told himself that her comings and goings didn't matter to him, he'd acknowledged an inner relief at knowing she was once again in the house next door.

Trouble, he told himself grimly. Way too much trouble.

He knew at some point he was going to see her. No doubt he would continue to help her with the work she was doing on her grandmother's house. But something had changed between them. He didn't know if it was the fight or what had happened right before the fight. Passion had ignited and they'd both nearly gone up in flames. After all this time, he wouldn't have thought that was possible.

He finished his coffee, then stood and stretched. "It seems to me you lovebirds need to be alone," he teased.

Edie looked up. "Oh, Gage. Don't go. Are we ignoring you?"

He circled around the table, bent down and kissed her cheek. "You're planning your honeymoon,

Mama. I don't think you need your grown son hanging around while you do that.''

He shook John's hand. "Don't let her talk you into a dark cabin in the ship's hold. She'll try."

John grinned. "Don't I know it. But I'm going to insist on a suite."

"Oh, John. That would be *so* expensive."

The men shared a quick look that spoke of their mutual affection for Edie.

Before leaving, Gage headed for the trash container under the sink.

"You don't have to do that," John told him. "I'll take it out later."

Gage shook his head. "Don't sweat it. I have years of practice. Besides, once you two are married, I plan to let you take over all the chores."

"It's a deal."

Gage called out a good-night and walked out the back door. The porch light illuminated his way. He whistled tunelessly as he went to the trash can and pulled off the lid. He was about to set the plastic bag inside when he saw a beautiful cloth box resting on several paper bags. While the floral print made him want to gag, he recognized the container. His mother kept pictures and other treasures inside. She'd had it for as long as he could remember. Why would she be throwing it out now?

Must be a mistake, he thought as he took it out of the trash can and put the kitchen bag in its place. He set the lid down and turned toward the house. But at the bottom porch step, he stumbled slightly. The cloth box went flying out of his hands, hit the next step up and tipped open. Dozens and dozens of pictures spilled out onto the concrete.

Gage swore under his breath. As he bent to retrieve them, he recognized old photos of his mother, back when she was young. So damn beautiful, he thought as he started to pick them up. He saw her with Ralph and with her family. There were several—

Gage frowned as he shuffled through the pictures. There was his mother with a man he didn't recognize. At first he dismissed the pictures as taken before she'd married, but there was a wedding ring on her finger. Yet the man had his arm around her in a way that implied they were more than just friends. The man—

Gage stared at him. He was a stranger, yet there was something familiar about him. Gage picked up more pictures and flipped through them. The man appeared in several different shots. Always close to Gage's mother. Always looking pleased about something.

And then he got it. The man looked like Quinn, Gage's brother. Now that Gage looked closer, he saw a lot of himself in the man, too. So he *must* be a relative. But who?

The back door opened. "I didn't hear your truck start," his mother said. "Is there—" She gasped.

He glanced up and saw the color drain from her face. She pressed a hand to her mouth. Her eyes widened, and for a second he thought she was going to faint.

"Mama?"

She shook her head. "Dear God," she whispered. "I threw those out."

''I know. I saw the box. You always kept your treasures in it. I thought it was a mistake.'' But looking at her stricken expression he realized it hadn't been anything of the sort.

Something went cold inside him. Suddenly he wished he'd never picked up the box. He could be home by now. But instead of backing away, he held up a picture of the stranger with his mother.

''Who is this guy?''

She stared at him as if he held a gun. ''S-someone I used to know.'' Her low voice was barely audible.

Gage had the sensation of walking through a minefield.

''Who is he? He looks a lot like Quinn, and I guess a little like me. Is he a relative? An uncle?''

He kept asking even though she didn't answer. He asked because if he didn't, if he allowed himself to think anything, he might figure out something he didn't want to know.

John stepped outside. He took one look at the pictures, then pulled Edie close. ''It's all right,'' he murmured to her.

Gage's gut tightened. John knew. Whatever the secret was, the other man knew. Suddenly Gage had to know, too.

''Who is he?'' he repeated.

Tears spilled from her eyes. She turned to her fiancé and clung to him, her entire body shaking with her sobs. Gage hadn't felt afraid in a long time, but he felt a cold uncertainty now.

''John?''

"We should all go inside," the older man said quietly. "Let's talk about this inside."

"No. Tell me now."

John stroked Edie's hair. "Gage, there are things…" He broke off and sighed. "Edie, what do you want me to do?"

His mother looked at John. Whatever the man saw in her eyes caused him to nod. He turned to Gage.

"Please come inside, Gage. I don't want to tell you like this."

"I'm not going anywhere until you answer the question. Who is this man?"

John took a deep breath. "He's your father."

Chapter Eight

Kari paced the length of the parlor, pausing every trip to glance out the front window to see if Gage had returned yet. She knew that he was having dinner at his mom's tonight and that she could stop pacing because as long as she stayed at the front of the house, she would hear his truck approach. But logic didn't seem to eliminate her need to keep walking.

She wanted to see him, she admitted to herself. She wanted to talk to him and joke with him and just plain be in the same room with him. She'd only been gone three days, but it felt longer than that. Somehow, reconnecting with Gage would make her homecoming more complete.

Well, not a homecoming, she told herself firmly. This wasn't home and she wasn't back. It's just that she was in Possum Landing temporarily and he was a part of that. Or something.

She crossed to the window again and stared out into the night. She had so much she wanted to tell him. Her interview had gone really well. She'd met with the principal and several of the teachers. The following day she'd met with a small committee from the board of education. On her second interview with the principal, the woman had hinted that an offer more than likely would be forthcoming. So things were going really great. That's why she wanted to see Gage. She wanted him to help her celebrate. Or something.

"Where are you?" she muttered aloud, dropping the curtain and resuming her circuit of the parlor. The restlessness had returned and with it a longing for something she couldn't define or name. It filled her until she wanted to jump out of her skin.

Just when she knew she couldn't stand it one more second, she heard his truck pull into the driveway next door. Kari ran to the front door and pulled it open, then hurried across the porch and down the front steps. Her heart quickened, as did her footsteps.

As he stepped down from the cab, she crossed the last few feet between them. They had agreed to no more kissing, but was it permissible to throw herself in his arms? Because that's what she felt like doing. Just launching herself in his general direction and—

He turned toward her. Light from the house spilled into the night, illuminating a bit of the driveway and part of his face. She came to a stop as if she'd hit a brick wall. Something had happened—she saw it in his eyes. Something bad.

"Gage?"

He stared at her, his expression bleak, his mouth set. Instead of speaking, he shook his head, then walked toward his house.

Kari hesitated, not sure what to do. Finally she followed him up the steps, so much like those at her grandmother's, into a house that mirrored hers.

Same front room, same hallway, same stairs—only reversed and modernized. Several floor lamps provided light. She had a quick impression of hardwood floors, overstuffed furniture and freshly painted walls, before Gage captured her attention by crossing to a cabinet at the end of the parlor. He opened it, pulled out a bottle of scotch and poured himself a drink. He downed it in two gulps, poured another and moved to the sofa, where he sank down.

"Help yourself," he said, his voice low and hoarse.

She watched him take another gulp, then set the half-full glass on the wooden coffee table, leaned back and closed his eyes.

Fear flickered inside her. Instead of claiming the drink he'd offered, she headed for the sofa and settled next to him. She was close enough to study him, but far enough away that she didn't crowd him.

After a few minutes of silence, she lightly touched his arm. "Want to talk about it?"

He shrugged. "I don't know what to say."

"Is everyone all right? Your mom? Quinn? Did you hear from the government?"

He turned toward her and opened his eyes. Anguish

darkened the brown irises. He looked like a man who had been to hell and faced the devil.

"No one's dead," he said flatly. "At least, no one who wasn't dead before."

She didn't know what to say to that. But without knowing the problem, how could she help? Or could she? He hadn't told her to go away, which relieved her, but she had a bad feeling that if he did finally spill the beans, she wasn't going to be any happier for knowing.

He rubbed his temples, then reached for his drink. After finishing it, he set the glass back on the table.

"I've only been really furious once before in my life," he said, his voice still lacking expression or emotion. "I've been mad and angry, just like everyone else. But I'm talking about that inner rage that burns hot and makes a man want to take on the world."

She stared at him. He didn't look angry. He didn't look anything.

"When was that?" she asked.

"When you left."

She winced.

He shrugged. "It's the truth. I read and reread your note about a hundred times, then I went and got skunk drunk. I decided to go after you. It's a little fuzzy now, but I think I had this plan to chase down your bus and drag you off. I was going to tell you exactly what I thought of you. I knew better, but I wanted to do it, anyway. I'd never been so angry in my life."

She swallowed. "What happened?"

"I got lucky. When I crashed, I only hurt myself.

I totaled the car and walked away with a few scars.''
He glanced at her. ''I learned my lesson. I may get
drunk tonight, but I won't be driving.''

''Okay.''

She was no closer than she had been to getting at
the problem. No one was dead and he didn't plan on
getting drunk, then chasing someone down in a car.

''If you're keeping me company, it's going to be a
long night,'' he said. ''You might as well pour me
another and get yourself one, too. You're going to
need it.''

Kari took his advice. She carried his glass back to
the cabinet, got one for herself and poured for both
of them. When she returned to the sofa, she said,
''Tell me what happened.''

Gage stared into his drink. What had happened?
Nothing. Everything. How was he to explain that his
entire world had shifted on its axis? Nothing he knew
as true was as it had been before. Nothing was as it
had been just an hour before. In a heartbeat—with
less than half a dozen words—everything had
changed.

''I was at my mom's for dinner,'' he began slowly,
not looking at her, not wanting her to see inside of
him, not wanting to know what she was thinking.
''When I left, I took the trash out, like I always do.
There was a box in the trash can outside. A cloth-
covered one my mom had kept for years. She always
stored important pictures and stuff in it, so I thought
it must be a mistake. I started to carry it back inside,
but I tripped on the steps and it went flying. Everything fell out. There were pictures inside.''

He fell silent. His brain didn't seem to be working. He could speak the words, but he wasn't thinking them first. They simply came out on their own. He thought about what had happened, but it was as if he were viewing a movie. That man on the stairs wasn't him. The woman wasn't his mother. They hadn't had that conversation.

"A man." He continued before he could stop himself. "My mother with a man."

Kari leaned close and touched his arm again. He liked that. She was warm and steady in his cold, spinning world.

"She had an affair?"

He nodded.

Beside him, Kari sighed. "I know that's a tough one. You have this idea of your parents' marriage and it's one in which they both never mess up. You must have been really shocked."

She didn't understand. Probably because he hadn't told her all of it. The most important part. The part that had torpedoed his past and dropped land mines in his future.

"John knew," he said flatly. "He came out on the porch. She started to cry and couldn't speak, but he told me." Against his will he turned to look at Kari. "The man in the picture is my father."

She stared at him. Her eyes widened, her lips parted and color drained from her face. "Gage," she breathed.

He nodded slightly. "Yeah. I can't believe it, either. It can't be true. My dad—I mean Ralph." He shuddered.

None of this made sense. It would never make sense. Anger filled him again. Anger and pain—a deadly combination. Only, this time he wasn't going to get drunk and go tearing down city streets. This time he was going to sit here and do nothing until it all went away.

"Your father," she said.

"Which one?"

"Your real one. Ralph. I don't understand. Your parents were so in love. Everyone knew it. They spent all their time together. They were always talking and laughing. I know your mom. She's not the kind of woman who would..." Her voice trailed off.

Gage knew what she meant. He would never have guessed his mother was the kind of woman who would have an affair and then pass her bastard off as her husband's kid. And he could never see his father allowing it.

"How did it happen?" she asked.

"I don't know. I didn't stick around long enough to ask questions." Instead, he'd walked out, the sound of his mother's sobs following him to his truck.

"I don't want it to be true," he admitted quietly. "Not any of it. If I'm not my father's son..."

Who was he? Five generations of Reynolds living in Possum Landing. He'd always taken pride in that. He'd made his history a part of who he was. Except, that wasn't his history anymore. He didn't have one— just lies.

Kari shifted close and tucked her arm around his. She leaned her head on his shoulder. "Oh, Gage. I don't know what to say. I have so many questions, but no way to make you feel better. I'm sorry.''

He didn't say anything, nor did he move away. Having Kari next to him felt right. Her touch and her words alone weren't enough to make him feel better, but that didn't mean he wanted her to move away. He needed the connection to her tonight more than he ever had.

They sat in silence for a long time.

''He's Quinn's father, too,'' Gage said finally. ''I could see the resemblance in the pictures.''

Kari raised her head. ''Quinn's father? But then the affair was ongoing. For at least a couple of years. How is that possible?''

''I don't know. While the guy in the picture looked familiar because of Quinn looking so much like him, I've never seen him before. I'm guessing he's not from around here.''

He couldn't comprehend his mother having a brief affair, let alone something that lasted long enough to produce two children. Where the hell had his father, Ralph, been in all this? Gage would have bet his life that his dad— He swore, *not* his father. He didn't know his father. Damn. He would have bet his life that Ralph wouldn't tolerate Edie being unfaithful, no matter how much he loved her. So what had happened?

The phone rang. He didn't move.

Kari turned her head toward the sound. ''Aren't you going to get that?''

''No.''

''It's probably your mom, or maybe John.''

Gage shrugged. He didn't want to talk to either of them.

Kari started to say something, but the start of the message cut her off. The sound of his voice filled the room.

"It's Gage. I'm not in. Leave a message at the tone."

"G-Gage—?" His mother's voice broke. "Are you there? I'm so s-sorry. I know you're upset and—" She began to cry.

Kari got up and walked to the phone. He didn't try to stop her because it didn't matter. She and his mother could talk all night and it wouldn't change anything.

Without Kari beside him, the anger burned hotter and brighter. He didn't like being afraid, so he sank into rage, instead. It was safer, easier. The sense of betrayal nearly overwhelmed him. He knew that whatever his mother had to say, whatever the excuses might be, they weren't going to be enough. He would never forgive her.

When Kari returned, she sat on the coffee table, her knees between his. She leaned toward him and took his hands in hers.

"Your mom wanted to know that you're okay," she told him. "I said you were still in shock."

Her blue eyes were steady as she looked at his face. Despite his pain and confusion, he thought she was one of the most beautiful women he'd ever known. Her wide eyes, her full mouth, her perfect skin.

She squeezed his fingers. "She wants to talk to you."

Rage returned. "No," he said flatly.

"You're going to have to do it sometime."

"Why?"

"To get your questions answered."

"I don't have any."

"Gage, of course you do. Too many questions. Edie said she has to explain. There are things you don't understand."

"You think?" he asked bitterly.

Kari continued to hold his hands. "Your relationship with your mother has always been extremely important to you. After all these years, you're not going to turn your back on her regardless of how angry you are right now."

"Want to bet?"

"Absolutely. I know you. You need to hear her out. You need to know and understand the truth. There are things you have to be told."

He jerked his hands free and glared at her. "Like the fact that the man I thought was my father isn't? I already know that one."

"Biology doesn't change the memories. Your father loved you very much."

"I don't know if my father even knows I'm alive."

"Ralph is your father in every sense of the word."

"Not anymore." Not ever.

Kari glared at Gage. She hated when he got stubborn. He was like a giant steer in the middle of the road. All the prodding in the world wasn't going to get him to move until he decided he was good and ready. Only, being stubborn this time was going to hurt both him and Edie.

Kari didn't know what had happened thirty-plus years ago. Nor had Edie explained how she'd come to be pregnant by a man other than her husband. But Kari knew there had to be a darn good explanation, and if Gage would stop being angry for one second, he would figure it out, too.

But she couldn't bring herself to be upset with him. Not when he looked so broken. The big, strong man she'd always known still sat in front of her, but behind his eyes lurked something dark and lonely. Something that cried out to her.

Impulsively she leaned toward him, sliding to the edge of the coffee table. She could just stretch her hands far enough to reach his shoulders. When she touched the cloth of his shirt, she drew him toward her.

He didn't cooperate, which was just so like him. How difficult could one man be?

"Work with me, here," she said in frustration, then moved to the sofa and knelt beside him.

She rested her hands on his shoulders and brushed his mouth with hers. The kiss came from a need to comfort and connect.

For a second he didn't respond. But just as she was about to move back, his arms came around her waist and he hauled her up against him. Her knee sank in between the cushions, causing her to almost lose her balance. But before she could fall, he turned her slightly, shifting her weight until she sat on his lap, her body angled toward his.

It wasn't exactly what she'd had in mind when she'd first kissed him, but now that she was here, she found that being cradled next to Gage was a really nice way to spend an evening. Especially when he slightly opened his mouth and swept his tongue across her lower lip.

Suddenly the tension in the room shifted. It was no longer about an external situation, but about what was growing between *them*. Hot tension. Sexual tension. Need. Desire.

Her hold on his shoulders changed from gentle to intense. The compassionate ache inside her became a very different kind of ache. She wanted to offer a whole lot more than just comfort.

She parted her lips to admit him, then stroked her tongue against his when he accepted the invitation. He wrapped his arms around her and pulled her even closer to his chest. Then his hands were everywhere—stroking her back, her hips, her legs. In turn she touched his face, feeling rough stubble, then the smooth silk of his hair. She tried to press herself against him, but in their current positions it was impossible.

Still, the deep, powerful, passionate kisses took some of the sting out of that. When he retreated, she followed, only to have him close his mouth around her tongue and suck. Shivers raced through her. Warm, liquid heat stirred between her legs. Her breasts swelled inside her bra as her nipples tightened.

She thought he might have noticed because he moved his hand along the outside of her leg to her hips, then up her waist and rib cage to her breasts. Once there, he settled his palm over her curves. The delightful weight made her squirm. The shivering increased, as did her desire to have him touch her all over...without clothes as a barrier.

The concept should have shocked her, but it didn't. This was Gage—the man she'd always trusted. If he wanted to make love tonight, she would only encourage the idea. She'd never been sure with anyone else, but she was sure with him.

So she arched into his touch and moaned softly when he brushed his thumb against her tight nipple. Against her hip—the one nestling into his groin—she felt something hard pressing into her. She wiggled to get a little closer.

Suddenly he moved her, shifting her so she had to scramble to keep her balance. He set her on her feet, then rose, as well. Questions filled his eyes, but so did need and wanting.

"Kari?"

She leaned in to him and ran her hands up and down his strong chest. It seemed to be the answer he was looking for. He drew her close and kissed her again, this time plunging inside of her and taking what he wanted. She reveled in his desire. Heat filled her, melting her until it was difficult to remain standing.

He cupped her face, then slipped his fingers through her hair. He broke the kiss, started it again, then stopped.

When she looked at him, she saw the darkness was gone. Instead, humor brightened his expression.

"I'm trying to stop long enough to get us upstairs," he said. "I have a very comfortable bed, not to mention protection. But I can't keep my hands off you.''

''Who says you have to?'' she asked as she turned toward the stairs. ''Last one upstairs has to strip for the winner.''

Gage chuckled, then moved after her. Halfway up the stairs, he grabbed her by the waist and drew her to him. They were on different steps, and she shrieked when she almost lost her balance.

''It's okay,'' he whispered, picking her up and turning so that she dangled in front of him while he faced the bottom of the staircase.

''What on earth are you doing?'' she demanded.

''Making sure I get there first.'' He spoke directly into her ear. ''I like to watch.''

She barely had time to absorb his words before he reached the landing.

''I win,'' he said, releasing her so that her feet touched solid flooring again. He clicked on a light.

She sidled away and glanced at him from under her lashes. *I like to watch.* His words made her both excited and a little uncomfortable.

''Gage, I don't know if I can—''

He captured her hand and raised it to his mouth, where he planted tiny, damp kisses on the inside of her wrist. ''I know. It's okay. I was teasing.''

''Are you sure?'' She looked at him anxiously. ''I want to do what—'' She cleared her throat. ''I just couldn't…''

This was probably the time to tell him that she was a virgin, although she had a bad feeling that if she did, he would stop. Which wasn't what she wanted.

And while she fit the technical description of someone who had never had actual penetration, she'd played around some. It's not as if she'd never seen a naked man before. She'd even climaxed once, although that sure hadn't been the experience she'd been hoping for.

"You don't have to strip for me," he said gently as he touched her cheek. "We can save that for next time."

Relief filled her. "I'm not sure I should commit to that, either. Maybe you should strip for me next time."

"It's a deal."

He stared at her, then bent down and kissed her. As his tongue slipped into her mouth, he cupped her breasts, angling his hands so he could rub her tight nipples. The combination of sensations made her knees nearly give way. She had to hold on to him to keep upright.

Then they were moving. As he kissed her and touched her, he urged her backward, heading them toward the large bedroom at the end of the hallway. But before they were halfway there, he broke the kiss long enough to pull off her T-shirt. Then she felt his hands on her breasts with one less layer between them.

His fingers touched the top of her breasts, his thumbs teasing the nipples while his palms supported her curves. He was warm, gentle and very sexy, she thought dreamily as they started to move again.

This time when they stopped, she kicked off her sandals. Gage had something else in mind. He reached for the fastening on her bra and undid it. The wisp of lace seemed to vanish into thin air. Then his hands were back, but on bare flesh this time.

She arched her head as he cupped her, stroked her, teased her. His skin was slightly rough—not enough to hurt her, but just enough to be…delicious. As he played with her breasts, he kissed along her jaw, then licked the sensitive skin just below her ear. She moaned in delight as pleasure swept through her body.

"I want to touch you everywhere," he whispered in her ear. "I want to touch you and taste you and listen to your breathing change. I want to take you to the edge and back, until you don't have any choice but to fall over. Then I want to catch you and make it happen again and again."

She shivered at his words and began to wonder how much farther it was to the bedroom. They began to move. When her bare feet felt the change from hardwood to carpet, she knew they were close. Gage moved away long enough to turn on a lamp on the nightstand and pull back the covers. Then he returned to her side. But he didn't touch her breasts. Instead, he knelt on the floor and went to work on her shorts.

They came off easily, as did her panties. In a matter of seconds, she was naked. Before she could be embarrassed, he pressed a kiss to her belly and began to move lower.

Kari had an idea of his ultimate destination and it worried her. Someone else had done that to her once. All her friends raved about the glories of oral sex, while she had found it embarrassing and more than a little painful. All that sucking and biting had left her bruised and seeking escape. But how to say that without sounding like an idiot?

She put her hand on his head to get his attention, but before she could speak, he reached his goal. He used his fingers to part her slightly, then leaned in close and licked the most sensitive part of her.

Liquid fire shot through her. There was no other way to describe it, she thought, more than a little dazed. The slow, gentle movement of his tongue made her want to moan, or even scream. If he didn't do that again, she wouldn't be able to survive.

Fortunately he did do it again…and again. He licked and pressed and kissed so very lightly. She found herself wanting more. There was also the issue of her standing, which meant she couldn't part her legs enough. But she didn't want him to stop so that she could climb onto the mattress. It was a dilemma unlike any she'd ever faced.

Gage solved it for her by shifting her onto the edge of the bed. She fell back, legs spread shamelessly, her entire body begging him to do more and more until she got so lost in the pleasure that she couldn't find her way out.

He chuckled softly as he moved close, draping her legs over his shoulders. She was exposed and completely at his mercy. She couldn't remember ever being so vulnerable in her life. She felt wonderful.

Then he licked her again, and she felt even better than wonderful. He knew exactly how to touch her, how to make her breathing stop, how to make her scream. He moved faster, then slower, controlling the building passion, making her get so close she couldn't help but release, then he pulled her back at the last second and left her panting.

As he worked his magic between her legs, he reached up and touched her breasts. He cupped the curves and lightly pinched her nipples. The combination of sensations made it impossible for her to catch her breath. Then he was moving faster and faster, and she knew that this time if he stopped she would have a heart attack and die right there in his bed and—

She screamed. Her cry of pleasure filled the room as he took her to the edge and gently pushed her out into the warm, sensual darkness. Shudders raced through her body. Heat filled her as her release went on for a lifetime, rising and falling, but never, ever ending.

It was better than anything she'd ever read about. Obviously she'd been doing something very wrong until this point.

With a sigh of contentment, she floated back to reality and found herself lying on Gage's bed. He'd shifted her fully onto the mattress and was in the process of taking off his clothes. She looked at him as he undressed, taking in the firm muscles and, as he dropped his boxers, the size of him.

Kari searched her feelings and knew this was right for her. There wasn't a doubt in her mind that he would stop if she asked him to. But instead of questions or uncertainty, a little voice inside whispered only one thing—

It's about time!

Gage watched Kari watching him. She seemed lost in thought, then gave a slow smile. "What's so funny?" he asked as he reached for the box of condoms in his nightstand.

"I was just thinking that we've waited a long time to do this. So far, I have to say the experience has been extraordinary."

"I'll do my best to make sure it continues to be so."

"I have every confidence."

He wasn't so sure. Pleasuring her had been easy. He liked everything about her body, from her slender curves to the way she tasted. But once he was on top of her and inside her it was going to be a different story. He had a bad feeling that he wasn't going to last all that long. He felt as if he could explode at any second.

He slipped onto the bed next to her and touched her flat stomach. "So this is where I tell you it's been a really long time since I've been with anyone. Add that to the fact that I used to spend hours fantasizing about making love with you, and we've got trouble. If you're hoping for a stellar performance, you may have to wait for round two."

She leaned on one elbow and kissed him. "You say the sweetest things. Did you really fantasize about me?"

He chuckled. "All those evenings spent kissing in the front seat of my car. Kissing and kissing and very little else. Of course I fantasized. I was so hard, I could barely walk—so what else could I do?"

"Maybe you'd like to take one of those fantasies out for a test drive."

Her words were all the invitation he needed. He slipped on the condom and positioned himself between her legs. He glanced at her perfect body, then shifted his gaze to her face. Her blue eyes stared back just as intently. He began to slip inside her.

She was hot, wet and tight. The combination didn't bode well for his self-control. He gritted his teeth and thought about all the paperwork on his desk. Then he moved on to the city council meeting about adding a traffic light. He was—

He swore silently as he continued to fill her. It was impossible to think of anything but how good she felt. He wanted to lose control. Which would take about two seconds.

No. Better to go slow the first time. He wanted it to be good for her. He—

He stopped suddenly at an unexpected barrier. What…?

But before he could think coherently enough to figure out what was wrong, Kari put her hands on his hips and drew him forward. At the same moment, she arched and made a request using a very bad word.

How was he supposed to refuse?

So he pushed into her, breaking through the barrier. At that second, she stiffened and gave a muffled cry. Only, it wasn't of pleasure. Her eyelids drifted closed. His heart sank.

Dammit all to hell. She'd been a virgin.

Chapter Nine

Gage started to withdraw, but before he could, Kari opened her eyes and clamped her hands on his hips.

"Don't," she whispered fiercely. "There's no reason to stop."

He could think of about fifty...or at least one really good one. But she was moving beneath him, urging him on.

"It's already done," she pointed out. "There's no going back."

Not exactly words he wanted to hear. Unfortunately he'd reached the point of no return, and one way or the other, his body was going to make sure he finished what he'd started. He decided to pull out, to not make things worse, but parts of him had other ideas. He'd barely started his retreat when the powerful rush of his release exploded from him, temporarily making rational thought impossible.

He pushed deep inside her until the last of the shudders faded, then withdrew. As he did, he was damn grateful he'd taken care of birth control.

He rolled off her without saying anything and headed for the bathroom. Once he settled next to her again, he closed his eyes and prayed fervently for no more surprises…at least not for the next twenty-four hours. He didn't think his heart would survive another one. But in the meantime there were the ramifications of the latest newsflash in his life.

He shifted until he could see Kari. She lay on her side of the bed, naked and studying him with a wary expression. As much as he wanted to remind her that she should have told him, that he should have been part of the decision-making process, he didn't want to turn her first time into something ugly. So he banked any lingering temper and remembered what it had felt like to make her climax. He recalled the taste of her skin and the soft sound of her cries. He smiled softly and touched her cheek.

"Want to tell me why?" he asked quietly.

"Why I'm a virgin? Why I chose you? Why now?"

"Any of those would be a good starting point."

Color stained her cheeks, leftover proof of her pleasure. Or maybe she was embarrassed. Her mussed hair framed her face, her mouth was swollen, her eyes were heavy lidded. She looked like a woman who had been well loved. She didn't look anything like a virgin.

She lifted one bare shoulder in a shrug. "I didn't set out to have this happen. I never intended to stay a virgin this long. It's just one of those things."

"Go on," he said, when she stopped talking.

"There's not much to say. I did date while I was in New York, but not all that much. Men who were obsessed with models terrified me, so I avoided anyone who seemed like a groupie. I was selective, cautious, and I moved slow. Most of them gave up on me before I had a chance to give in."

"Their loss."

She smiled slowly. "That's what I always said. I played around some, heavy petting, that sort of thing. But somehow, I never really got around to...you know." She shrugged again.

He wasn't sure what to make of her brief explanation. While he had always regretted not being her first, it had never occurred to him there might be a second chance for them.

"That explains why you were still a virgin," he said slowly. "But why now? Why with me?"

She stared at the bed, tracing a pattern with her finger. "I wanted my first time to be with someone I liked and respected. That's a more difficult combination to find than I would have thought. I didn't come home thinking we'd do what we ended up doing together, but tonight, when I knew you wanted me—" She cleared her throat, then continued. "It just seemed like the right thing to do."

No woman had ever shocked him so much in bed. He still wasn't sure what he felt. No way Kari would have set him up. But he was sure confused.

"I wish you'd told me," he said. "I would have done things differently if I'd known."

"Yeah, you would have run."

He grinned. "Darlin', this is Texas. We don't have any hills."

"What about in the Hill Country?"

"Bumps. They're glorified bumps."

She laughed softly, then her humor faded. "I thought you'd be mad. Or you'd change your mind. Or both."

He considered the possibilities. Had he known, would he have wanted to take on the responsibility of being Kari's first?

"I didn't want to make it a big deal," she said as if she could read his mind. "Are you mad?"

"No. Startled maybe."

Her mouth curved up at the corners. "I'll bet. If you could have seen the look on your face."

He didn't smile back. Instead, he moved close and drew her to him. What was done was done. He might not have controlled how it started, but he would make sure it ended well.

"I'm sorry I hurt you," he said.

"That comes with the territory," she said, snuggling closer still. "The rest of it was great."

"Thank you."

If nothing else, she'd taken his mind off his troubles. Now, in his bed, with both of them naked after just having made love, he refused to think about the other surprise in his life. He focused on the feel of Kari's bare skin and the scent of her body.

"Do you want me to go?" she asked suddenly.

"Go where?"

"Back to my place?"

He rubbed her back, then slipped his hand to her hip. "I would like whatever you would like. Do you want to spend the night?"

"Here?"

"Right here in this bed. Unless you're a cover hog. Then, you'll have to sleep in the guest room."

"I don't really know what I am," she admitted.

"Maybe it's time we found out."

She gave him a smile that could light up the sky. "Maybe it is."

He pulled up the covers and flicked out the light. Kari rested her head on his shoulder.

"Gage?" she said into the darkness.

"Yeah."

"You made my first time terrific. Thank you."

"You're welcome."

He held her tightly against him and listened to the sound of her breathing. If he'd been in possession of all the facts, maybe he wouldn't have chosen to sleep with Kari tonight, but now that it had happened, he couldn't find it in himself to regret it. Not for a minute.

Kari awoke sometime in the middle of the night. A bit of street light filtered in through a crack in the drapes. Gage lay beside her, but she couldn't hear his breathing, so she didn't know if he was awake or not.

Her body both tingled and ached. The remnants of amazing sexual pleasure lingered, but there was a faint soreness between her legs.

She turned toward Gage, studying the barely visible outline of his profile.

He could have been furious with her. After all, she hadn't warned him what he was getting into. In the end, he'd been sweet and funny and he'd made her feel really good. Not just about the sex, but about choosing him.

Her decision hadn't been conscious, she acknowledged. In light of what had been going on, it had seemed to be the logical thing to do. Being with him had felt right. She'd been afraid the actual act of making love would be awkward or embarrassing, but he'd made it all easy and exciting.

"Why aren't you asleep?" he asked unexpectedly.

She blinked. "How do you know I'm not?"

"I can hear you thinking."

She laughed. "Okay. Why aren't you sleeping?"

"Too much on my mind."

"Oh, Gage." She slid closer and placed her arm across his chest. "I wish I could help."

"Me, too. But I have to work things out for myself."

His tone indicated he didn't actually believe that was possible. She thought about telling him there wasn't anything to work out. He had to come to peace with his mother's revelation. However, she doubted he would appreciate the advice.

"Want to talk about it?" she asked.

"No. But thanks for offering."

"Want a massage?"

"No."

"Want me to talk dirty?"

He turned toward her. She thought she caught a glimpse of a smile. "I have another suggestion. Turn over so you're facing the other way."

She did as he requested, shifting until her back was to him. He moved behind her, spooning his body to hers. She felt his strong thighs pressing against hers and his chest heating her back. He wrapped an arm around her waist.

"Go to sleep, Kari," he whispered. "Dream good dreams."

"You, too."

She had more to say, but suddenly it was very difficult to talk. Everything felt heavy, then light, then she didn't remember anything at all.

Kari awoke just after dawn to an empty bed and the smell of coffee. She was also naked and in Gage's bed.

Several thoughts occurred to her at once. First, it was daylight. It was one thing to not mind being naked in a man's bed while it was still night, but in the morning everything looked different. Her second thought was that she'd come over without even closing her front door, let alone locking it. While this was not a big deal in Possum Landing, she'd been in New York long enough to realize she'd behaved like a blockhead. Third…

Gage walked into the bedroom with two cups of coffee, chasing the third thing completely from her mind. Probably because he'd pulled on jeans. Jeans and nothing else.

Kari sat up, pulling the sheet with her, and stared

at his bare chest. Hair dusted the defined muscles, narrowing into a thin line that bisected his belly. He was tanned, strong and so masculine she would swear she could feel a swoon coming on.

The stubble darkening his jaw only added to his appeal. He looked dangerous and sexy, not to mention very yummy.

He smiled at her. "How did you sleep?"

"Good. Better than I would have thought. I was never one for spending the night."

His smile broadened. "That must be a virgin thing."

"Must be."

He handed her a mug of coffee and sat on the edge of the bed. "You okay?"

Suddenly shy, she studied the dark liquid before she sipped it. "Yes. Fine. Great."

"Kari?" His voice was a low growl.

She glanced up at him. "I'm fine," she repeated. "Are you okay with everything?"

"Yeah. Still dealing with the shock, but if you don't have any regrets, I don't either."

Relief filled her. "No regrets. I'll admit I should have told you. But I know you would have completely freaked, so I can't be sorry that I didn't."

"I'll give you that—but no more secrets, okay?"

She smiled. "That was my last big one."

He nodded. "Want to take a shower?"

"Sure." She put her mug on the nightstand. "I'll go first—or do you want to?"

He didn't answer. Instead he simply stared at her.

Kari blinked. Then heat flared on her face. *Shower,*

he'd said. *Do you want to take a shower?* She swallowed.

"Oh," she said in a tiny voice. "You mean together."

"Uh-huh. I have a big old-fashioned tub with a showerhead above it. Plenty of room for two."

"Oh." Oh my!

She had instant visions of them wet and naked and under a stream of hot water. Based on what had happened last night, she was sure whatever she imagined couldn't come close to the glories of reality. Any initial embarrassment would be worth the final result. After all, Gage was very good at what he did.

"Sure," she said, with more bravery than she actually felt. She threw back the covers and headed for the bathroom. "Give me five minutes to, uh, get ready."

"Sure."

She heard him chuckle behind her as she raced into the bathroom and closed the door. One minute to tinkle, one minute and thirty seconds to brush her teeth, one minute to wash the makeup off her face.

She turned on the hot water and let it run. As she'd hoped, Gage took the hint and entered the bathroom…sans clothing. Of course, all he'd had to pull off was jeans, but still, there he was naked and rather ready.

Were they going to— Could they actually do it in the shower? As she fretted logistics, he moved close enough to brush the hair off her forehead, then kissed her.

"You're thinking again. I can hear the gears creaking as they turn faster and faster."

"I can't help it. This is a new experience."

"You'll like it," he promised.

Somehow, she didn't doubt that.

He reached past her and adjusted the water, then stepped into the old-fashioned claw-foot tub. He held the curtain open for her as she stepped in beside him.

The master bath, like much of the house, had been completely refurbished. She wasn't sure, but she thought he might have broken through to the bedroom next door and taken about five feet of floor space. In her grandmother's bathroom, there wasn't this much room.

She was working out the construction details in her mind, when Gage directed her to stand beneath the spray. As warm water ran down the front of her body, he went to work on the other side. He lathered soap in his hands, then rubbed them over her shoulders and down her arms. He lathered her back, her fanny and her legs. Then he turned her toward him so she could rinse off.

While the warm spray sluiced down her skin, he leaned close and kissed her. She parted instantly for him, welcoming him, teasing him, tasting that appealing combination of mint and coffee. As he kissed her, he poured shampoo into his hands, then began to wash her hair. The combination of his tongue in her mouth and his fingers massaging her scalp was a sensual delight. She found herself swaying slightly, needing to rest her hands on his chest to steady herself.

He broke the kiss and had her lean her head back to rinse out the shampoo.

Hands made slick from soap glided over her skin. He circled her breasts, then massaged her nipples until they were hard and she was panting. Desire filled her. When he moved lower, she parted her legs to allow him access.

He soaped her gently, then rubbed lightly, as if aware parts of her were still a little tender. Then he reached above her and unfastened the showerhead. She noticed for the first time that it was on a hose. He lowered it and adjusted the spray to a lighter misting, then applied the warm water to her chest, her breasts, then even lower—between her legs.

She gasped. The pulsing water not only washed away soap, it vibrated against her most sensitive places. Tension swept through her, making her hold on to him with both hands. When he bent down and kissed her mouth, she kissed him back hard.

Their tongues danced together. Between her legs the water flowed just enough to excite, but not enough to take her over the edge. When he finally moved the showerhead back into place, she found herself trembling in anticipation of the next round.

"Your turn," she said, reaching for the soap.

She explored his back, taking her time over rippling muscles and a high, tight rear end that deserved a good nibbling. She made a mental note to take care of that soon. After rinsing him off, she had him turn so she could do the front.

Washing his hair proved something of a challenge as he was several inches taller than her, but she gave it her best shot, and he helped. Then she concentrated on the rest of him.

She massaged his chest, paying attention to his tight nipples. His breath caught when she brushed against them, so she did it several times. She moved lower and lower, dragging her soapy hands to his arousal jutting out toward her. Her fingers encircled him, moving lower, washing between his legs, rubbing back and forth. Just the act of touching him was enough to quicken her breathing. She still ached, but in a completely different way. She wanted him inside her. She wanted to make love with him again. She wanted—

He turned suddenly and rinsed off. ''We'll be running out of hot water soon,'' he said. ''I keep meaning to replace the old water heater, but so far I haven't been motivated. You might change that.''

She stared at his back. That was it? They weren't going to… But he was hard. She was wet. They had time, means, opportunity and plenty of desire.

He turned off the water and she nearly screamed. Then Gage turned back around and caught a glimpse of her face. He chuckled.

''Stop looking so indignant.''

''I'm not,'' she lied.

''Sure you are. But you're wrong.''

With that he bent close, cupped her face and kissed her. She wrapped her arms around him as she surrendered to the need between them. He shifted his weight.

''Step out of the tub, Kari.''

She broke the kiss long enough to see what she

was doing, then did as he requested. When he'd moved out, as well, he dragged a towel off the rack and flung it on the tile counter, then opened a drawer by the sink and pulled out a condom.

Before she knew what was going on, he'd lifted her to the counter, then dropped to his knees between her spread legs. She knew instantly what he was going to do and found herself halfway to paradise before his tongue even touched her there.

Seconds after the first intimate kiss, every muscle in her body tensed. She felt herself spiraling out of control. He brought her close to the edge, but this time instead of letting her down gently, then building her again, he stopped and stood up.

"It'll be okay," he promised, slipping on the condom.

He moved between her legs and began to kiss her neck. Shivers rippled through her as he stroked her breasts and nipples. She felt a hard probing, and instinctively she parted for him, then reached to guide him in.

This time there wasn't any pain. He still stretched her, but it didn't seem as much as it had last night. She was wet and ready, and the combination of his kissing and his fingers on her breasts made it difficult for her to think about anything but surrender.

He began to move in and out of her. With each slow thrust, she felt her body molding itself around him a little more and a little more. When he moved to kiss her mouth, she welcomed him, pulling him close. His hand dropped from her breasts to between her legs, where he rubbed against her most sensitive place, moving in counterpoint to his thrusting, bringing her closer and closer until she had no choice but to scream his name as her release claimed her.

She couldn't believe what was happening. The orgasm filled her inside and out, while he continued to move, drawing out the pleasure until he, too, stiffened and exhaled her name. They climaxed together, her body rippling around him, his surging. As the last tendrils of release drifted away, Gage raised his head and looked into her eyes.

At that moment she could see down to his soul and didn't doubt he could do the same. The profound connection shook her to the core of her being, and she knew then that nothing would ever be the same.

Still tingling from their recent encounter, Kari dressed and followed Gage down to the kitchen for breakfast. Her emotions seemed to have stabilized, but the sensation of having experienced something profound didn't go away. Still, participating in the ordinary helped. He pulled out eggs and bacon, while she grabbed bread from the freezer for toast.

Every inch of her body felt contented. The occasional aftermath of pleasure shot through her, making her catch her breath as she had a sensual flashback. Gage sure knew how to have a good time both in and out of bed, she thought happily.

"Scrambled all right?" he asked, holding up several eggs.

"Perfect. And I like my bacon extra crisp."

"That's my girl."

While she set the table, he started cooking. Soon

the scent of eggs and bacon filled the kitchen. Kari poured them more coffee, then put the toast on a plate she'd warmed in the oven. At the same time he carried two frying pans to the table and set them on the extra place mats.

They sat down across from each other, and Gage offered her the bacon. Kari liked that things were easy between them. No awkward moments, no bumping as they moved. She couldn't imagine the morning after being so comfortable with any of the other men she'd gone out with in the past few years. Of course, she doubted she would have spent the night with them, anyway.

She looked up, prepared to share her observation, when she caught Gage looking past her. The faraway look in his eyes told her that he was thinking about something other than their lovemaking. He'd remembered what he'd learned the night before. Her heart ached for him.

She sighed.

He glanced at her. "What?"

"I just wish I could find something magical to say so you'd feel better."

"Not possible."

"I know."

Everything had changed for him. In a single moment, he'd lost the anchor to his world—his past. He'd always prided himself on being one of the fifth generation of Reynolds to live in Possum Landing. He'd been his father's son. He'd—

She frowned. Why did that have to be different? "Gage, I understand that you no longer have the biological connection to Ralph Reynolds that you had before, but that doesn't mean he's not your father."

He glared at her. "He's not my father."

"That's just biology. What about the heart? He still loved you from the second you were born. He held you and taught you and supported you. He came to every football and baseball game you ever played in. He taught you to fish, and drive. All those dad things."

"How could he have loved me?" he asked bitterly. "His wife had cheated on him. I was another man's bastard."

She didn't have all the answers, but she was very sure about one thing. "No one seeing the two of you together could doubt his feelings for you. I saw it every time we went over there. His love for you lit up his whole face. You can't doubt that."

He shrugged as if he wasn't sure he believed her. Kari didn't know how else to express her feelings. Maybe with time Gage would be able to look at the past and see his father's actions for what they were—a parent's love for his child.

But now wasn't the time to push, so she changed the subject and they discussed renovations on her grandmother's house as they finished breakfast. She'd just poured them a last cup of coffee when there was a knock on the front door.

When Gage didn't budge, she asked, "Want me to get that?"

They both knew who it was. Edie was familiar enough with her son's schedule to know what time he had to leave for work. A quick glance at the clock told Kari there was more than an hour until he had to head out to the station.

She put down the coffeepot and walked to the front door. She had the sudden thought that it didn't look good for her to be here this early. What would Edie think? Then she reminded herself that after what had happened the previous evening, Gage's sleeping arrangements would be the last thing on his mother's mind. She pulled open the door.

"Hi, Edie," she said gently as she took in the other woman's drawn face. Edie looked older than her years, and tired, as if all the life had been sucked out of her.

Edie swallowed, then nodded without speaking. She didn't seem surprised to see Kari as she stepped into the house, but she didn't move past the foyer.

"How is he?"

"Okay, considering. A little confused and angry."

"That makes sense."

Edie wore jeans and a loose T-shirt. The clothes seemed to hang on her. Worry drew her eyebrows together.

"He's in the kitchen," Kari said at last. "I was just about to make more coffee. Do you want some?"

"No coffee for me, thanks."

Edie didn't seem startled to find Kari making coffee in her son's house, either. No doubt she wasn't thinking about something as inconsequential as that.

Impulsively Kari touched her arm. "He'll get over it," she promised. "He needs time."

"I know."

Tears filled Edie's eyes. She blinked them back, then followed Kari to the kitchen.

Gage stood at the sink, scraping dishes and loading the dishwasher. He didn't turn at the sound of their footsteps.

Great. So he was going to make this as difficult as possible for everyone.

"Gage, your mom's here."

"G-Gage?" Edie's voice shook as she spoke.

He put the last plate in the dishwasher and turned to look at her. Kari caught her breath. His face was so set, it could have been carved from stone. He looked angry and unapproachable. She wanted to run for safety, and she wasn't even the one with the recent confession. She could only imagine how Edie felt.

"You two need to talk," she said gently. "As it's a private matter, I'll head home."

Gage spared her a quick glance. "You can stay if you'd like. You already know as much as I do."

Kari shifted uncomfortably. "I know, but your mom would probably be more comfortable to keep it just family."

Edie sighed. "No, Kari. If you're willing to stay, I think you should. Gage may need to have a friend."

Kari hesitated, then nodded slowly. She wasn't sure how she would describe her relationship with Gage. *Friend* was as good a word as any. She motioned to the now cleared table, then crossed to the counter and fixed a fresh pot of coffee. Gage finished with the dishes, then moved to the table. No one spoke until Kari returned to her seat.

Talk about awkward, she thought grimly as they

sat in silence. She glanced from mother to son. Edie had pulled a tissue out of her pocket and was twisting it between her fingers.

"I know what you're thinking," she began, as the coffeemaker began to drip. "That I cheated on your father. I suppose that's technically true, but that's not the whole truth." She glanced up at her son. "I loved your father with all my heart. It started the day I met him and it's never faded. Not even once."

"Then, why the hell am I some other man's bastard?"

She flinched slightly but didn't look away. "The trouble began about a year after we married. We'd wanted a big family and had been trying from the very beginning. When nothing happened, we went to the doctor. We found out we couldn't have children."

Chapter Ten

Couldn't have children? "But you have two," Kari said before she could stop herself. She bit her lower lip. "Sorry."

Gage surprised her by reaching across the table and covering her hand with his. "It's okay."

She smiled gratefully as he turned his attention to his mother. "Are you saying Quinn and I are adopted?"

Edie shook her head. "No. We... It was difficult. Thirty years ago they couldn't do as much to help infertile couples. We each took tests and found out that Ralph was the one who couldn't have children. There was something wrong with his sperm."

"So you went out and had an affair?"

Gage's rage was a tangible presence in the room.

Edie flinched slightly and turned away, but not before Kari saw the tears return to her eyes.

Kari squeezed his fingers. "You have to listen. If you want to be angry when she's done, that's your right, but let her talk."

His jaw tightened, but he didn't release her hand or disagree. He nodded slightly, indicating his mother should go on.

Edie glanced from Kari to Gage, then continued. "As I said, there weren't as many options back then. Your father...Ralph and I didn't have a lot of money. We explored different treatments, discussed adoption. I was comfortable with that, but he didn't want to go through the process. He was concerned that we wouldn't know where the child came from or who its parents were. You know how that sort of thing was important to him."

Gage nodded curtly.

Kari ached for them both. Nothing about this was easy—she could feel their pain, understand the distance between them. Family and heritage *had* been important to Gage's father, and to Gage. So where did that leave him now? Who *were* his people? Where *was* he from?

"He kept saying he wanted me to experience having my own child. We fought and argued and cried together. At one point he threatened to leave me. But I begged him not to go. In the end, he came up with a compromise. That I would find someone who looked like him and get pregnant."

Gage's head snapped up, and he glared at his

mother. "You're telling me this was *his* idea?" His tone clearly stated he didn't believe her.

"I can't prove it," she murmured. "I can only tell you that except for this, I've never lied to you."

Kari held her breath. She believed Edie. There was too much anguish in the other woman's eyes for it to be anything but the truth. Yet Gage hesitated.

Without committing himself to accepting or not, he said, "Go on."

She hesitated a second, then continued. "We fought about that, as well," Edie said. "In the end, I agreed. I went up to Dallas because we didn't want the scandal of me being with someone from around here. Word would get out, and we didn't want anyone to know the truth. There was a convention there. Ralph had read about it and he thought that would be the perfect place. We might not get to know much about the man, but we would know something."

She picked at the place mat in front of her. "They were all in law enforcement. It was some kind of sheriff's convention. Your biological father—Earl Haynes—was a sheriff."

Kari tried to keep her face blank but doubted she succeeded. Involuntarily her gaze flew to the star on Gage's chest. He'd wanted to be a sheriff all his life— at least, that's what he'd always told her.

His fingers tightened on hers.

"So that's where you met him?" he asked coldly.

"Yes. I met him the first day. He was tall and dark haired, and very charming. We got to know each other. At first I didn't think I could go through with it, but I felt I had to. After a few days, I found myself caring for Earl in a way I hadn't thought I would.''

Gage glared at her. ''You fell for him?''

''Maybe. I don't know. I'd never been with anyone but Ralph. Earl was like him, but different, too. Exciting. He'd seen a lot of the world, been with a lot of women. I didn't know how to be intimate without giving away a piece of my heart.''

Tears trickled from the corners of her eyes. She brushed them away. ''I was so confused, and ashamed. I wanted to go home and I didn't. Earl asked me to go back to California with him, but I couldn't. I knew I belonged with Ralph, so I came home.''

Gage tore his hand free of Kari's light hold and sprang to his feet. ''Who the hell are you? How dare you come in here and tell me you didn't just sleep with some man to get pregnant, but that you also fell for him. You said you loved my father. You said you never stopped loving him.''

''I didn't,'' Edie said, pleading with her son. ''I did love him. Earl distracted me from what was important. Do you think I'm proud of what happened or how I felt? I don't want to tell you this, Gage, but I have to. You need to understand the circumstances so you'll know why things were the way they were.''

Gage crossed to the sink, where he stood with his back to the table. When he didn't say anything else, Edie went on.

''I came back home and we found out I was pregnant. Ralph never said anything about what had happened. He never asked or blamed me, and when you were born, he was as proud as any father could have been. He loved you with every fiber of his being.''

Gage visibly stiffened, but didn't speak. Edie looked at Kari, who gave her a reassuring smile.

"You also looked like Ralph, which pleased him," Edie said, then swallowed. "Everything was perfect. We had you, we had each other. But I couldn't forget. What I didn't know then was that my feelings for Earl were just a girlish fantasy—the result of never having been on a date with a man other than Ralph. I mistook infatuation for love, and when you were three months old, I returned to Dallas.''

Gage swore loudly. "You saw him again?"

Edie nodded. "I couldn't help myself. I didn't tell Ralph. I left the baby with my mother and drove to Dallas. I only went for one night." She sighed heavily. "Let's just say, I learned my lesson. I saw the difference between infatuation and real love, and I saw clearly who was the better man. I came home, but it was too late.''

Kari was stunned. Ralph must have been furious with his young wife. The first time they'd agreed on a plan. But to return to Earl Haynes again...

Gage crossed to the table and braced his hands on the back of the chair. "Quinn," he breathed.

Kari stared at him. Of course. His younger brother. How could she have forgotten?

Edie nodded. "Ralph didn't understand. He was furious and so very hurt. We nearly divorced. I still loved him with all my heart and I begged him to forgive me for being such a fool. In the end, he did forgive me. Then we found out I was pregnant. He didn't take it well.''

Gage straightened. ''No wonder,'' he said slowly. ''No wonder he hated Quinn. My brother was a constant reminder of your betrayal.''

Tears filled Edie's eyes again. ''I could never convince him differently. I tried to make things right for Quinn, but I couldn't make up for his father not loving him.''

Gage stared at his mother. She'd been a part of his life for as long as he could remember, but suddenly he didn't know her. It was as if a stranger sat at the table telling him secrets from the past.

He wanted to scream out his anger. He wanted to throw something, break something, hurt something. He wanted to turn back time and forget all he'd been told so he wouldn't have to know. He wanted to put the cloth box back in the trash can and never open it.

''You lied,'' he said wearily. ''Both of you.'' Mother and father. Except Ralph wasn't his father. He was no relation at all.

His mother, who had always known what he was thinking, stared at him. ''Ralph *is* your father in every way that matters. Nothing can change that. You have a past with him and it will always be there.''

Gage shook his head. He'd had enough for one day. ''I need to get to work.''

His mother wiped her face. ''There's more, Gage. More things you need to hear.''

He couldn't imagine what those things might be. Nor did he want to. ''Not now.''

''Then, when?''

"I don't know."

"It has to be soon."

He wanted to ask why. He wanted to refuse her request. Instead, he nodded.

She rose slowly; it seemed she'd become old overnight. After walking to the doorway, she paused as if she would say more. Then she turned and left.

Gage crossed to the window and stared out at the morning. The sky was a clear Texas blue, the temperature already in the eighties. The central air unit he'd replaced three years ago kept the house cool, as did several ceiling fans. He focused on those now, on their whisper-quiet sound and the faint brush of air against the back of his neck. He heard Kari walk up behind him. She placed a hand on the small of his back.

"Gage," she said gently.

He didn't move. "What else could she have to say?" he asked. "Think there's another bombshell?"

"I don't know."

"I don't want to hear anything else. I don't want to talk to her again."

Behind him, Kari sighed. He heard the exhale, felt her disapproval.

"I know this has been a shock, but in time you'll see—"

He spun to face her. "See what? That everything I've believed all my life is a lie? I don't want to see that. I don't want to see that my mother went off to get herself pregnant by a man she'd never met before. Or that she liked doing it with him so much, she went again the following year. I don't want to finally understand why my father always hated my brother. I don't want it to be real and not just something Quinn imagined. I don't have to know any of it.''

She stood her ground. ''There's more to it than that.''

''Is there? Like what? Am I really a part of the Reynolds family? Is Ralph really my father?''

''Of course. Yes, to both. You're furious about something that happened over thirty years ago. You're just learning it now, so it has a big impact on you, but these are not new events. Nothing has changed but your perception. You love your mom— you always have. Despite everything, I know that's not going to change. All I'm saying is that you both need time, and that you have to be careful not to say things you'll regret.''

''She's the one who should have regrets,'' he said bitterly.

''I'm sure she regrets hurting her husband, but I don't believe for a second she regrets either you or Quinn.''

He couldn't disagree with that. However, he was not in the mood to be reasonable. ''Interesting all this advice coming from you,'' he growled. ''Last I heard, you weren't so quick to forgive your family for what they did to you.''

Finally he had gotten what he'd thought he wanted. Kari dropped her gaze and took a step back. But instead of feeling vindicated, he only felt lousy.

''Sorry,'' he said quickly. ''I shouldn't have said that.''

''No, you're right. I want to say that my situation

is different, and of course it is. Every situation is different. But your point is that I'm not in a place to throw stones. I can't argue with that.''

He held out his arms and she stepped into his embrace. ''I hate this,'' he murmured into her hair. ''The information, the questions, how it's all changing.''

''I know.''

''It will never be the same again. I'm not who I was.''

''You're exactly the same man you were at this time yesterday.''

No, he wasn't. She couldn't see the changes, but he knew they were there.

''I don't belong here anymore.''

Kari raised her head and stared at him. ''Possum Landing is still your home. I'm the one who wanted to get away and see the world, but you'd already done that. You wanted to come home.''

''Is it home?'' he asked. ''There aren't five generations anymore. At least, not in my history.''

''I'm sorry,'' she whispered.

''Yeah. Me, too.''

He released her, then glanced at his watch. ''I have to get to the station. Are you going to be around tonight?''

''Sure.''

''Can I come by?''

''Absolutely.''

Gage spent the morning dealing with the crisis of two teenage boys from a neighboring town taking a joyride through a field at four in the morning. They'd been drunk and damn lucky. When they'd plowed through a barbed-wire fence and jerked loose several fence posts, the one that had shot through their front window had missed them both.

The rancher was threatening charges, while one parent thought jail time would teach his wayward son a lesson and the other kept saying "Boys will be boys."

"They'll be dead boys if they keep this up," Gage said flatly to the four adults. "I'm booking them both. They have clean records, so I doubt they'll get more than a warning and some community service. Maybe it will be enough to teach them a lesson, maybe not."

Then he stalked out before any of the parents could speak with him. Normally he didn't mind taking the time to deal individually with kids headed in the wrong direction. He liked to think that he'd steered more than one teenager back onto the straight and narrow. But not today. Today all he could think about was the lie that was his past, and his suddenly unclear future.

He stalked into his office and closed the door. Several staff members looked up at the sound. Gage couldn't remember the last time he'd shut himself off from what was going on in the station. Mostly he liked to be in the thick of things. Hell, maybe he should have just stayed home.

But instead of clocking out for the day, he reached for the phone and dialed a number from memory. He gave the appropriate name, number and password to the computer before a pleasant-sounding woman picked up the phone.

"Bailey," she said crisply.

"I'd like to get a message to my brother," he said.

He heard her typing on a keyboard. "Yes, Sheriff Reynolds. I have authorization right here. What is the message?"

There was the rub, he thought grimly. What to say? "Tell him…" He cleared his throat. "Tell him to call me as soon as he can. It's a family matter. No one's sick or anything," he added quickly.

"Very well, sir. I'll see that he gets the message."

Gage didn't bother asking when that might happen. He'd tried to contact Quinn enough to know it could be weeks before he heard back, maybe even a couple of months. Or it could be tomorrow. There was no way to be sure.

"Thanks," he said, and hung up.

He leaned back in his chair and stared into the office. Instead of seeing people working, talking and carrying files, he saw his past. The idyllic days of growing up in Possum Landing. He'd been so damn sure he belonged. Now he wasn't sure of anything. His identity had been ripped from him.

As far as he could tell, the only good thing to come out of all of this was an explanation for his brother. Not that an answer would be enough to make up for Quinn's particular hell while he'd been growing up.

Gage had never understood the problem between father and son. Gage could do no wrong and Quinn could do no right. Ralph hadn't cared about his younger son's good grades, ability at sports or school awards. The only time he'd bothered to attend a game of Quinn's was when Gage was on the same team.

He'd never said a word when Quinn made the varsity baseball team during his sophomore year. Quinn had been a ghost in the house, and now he lived his life like a demon. All the pain, and for what? A lie?

Gage turned in his chair and gazed at the computer. The blinking cursor seemed to taunt him. *Lies,* it blinked over and over. *Lies, lies, lies.*

So what was the truth?

There was only one way to find out. He clicked on a law-enforcement search engine, then typed in a single name: Earl Haynes.

The ancient, shuddering air-conditioning didn't come close to cooling the attic. Unable to face more painting because it reminded her of Gage, Kari had decided on cleaning out the attic, instead. She'd opened all the windows and had dragged up a floor fan that she'd set on high. It might be hot up here, but at least there was a breeze.

She sat on the dusty floor in front of several open boxes and trunks. Grammy had kept everything. Clothes, hats, shoes, pictures, newspapers, magazines, blankets, lamps. Kari shook her head as she gazed at the collection of about a dozen old, broken lamps. Some were lovely and probably worth repairing, but others were just plain old and ugly. They should have been thrown out years ago.

But that wasn't her grandmother's way, she thought as she dug into the next layer of the trunk in front of her. She encountered something soft, like fur, then something hard like—

"Whoa!"

She jumped to her feet, prepared to flee. There was an animal in there.

An old umbrella lay by the door. She picked it up and cautiously approached the trunk. A couple of good, hard pokes didn't produce any movement. Kari used the umbrella to push aside several garments, then stared down at an unblinking black eye.

"Well, that's totally gross," she said, bending over and picking up a fox stole with the fox head and tail still attached. "All you need are your little feet, huh?"

While she wasn't one to turn down a nicely cooked steak, she drew the line at wearing an animal head across her shoulders. This poor creature was going right into the give-away pile.

The next box held more contemporary items, including some baby and toddler clothes that had probably belonged to her. She held up a ruffly dress, trying to remember when she'd ever been that small.

"Not possible," she murmured.

Below that was her uniform from her lone year as a cheerleader, back in middle school, and below that was something white and sparkly.

Her breath caught in her throat as she pulled out the long, flowing strapless gown. The fabric of the bodice twisted once in front, then wrapped around to the back. Clinging fabric fell all the way to the floor. She crossed to the old mirror in the corner and held the dress up in front of her.

She'd never actually worn it, but she'd tried it on about four hundred times. Her prom dress. Kari squeezed her eyes shut for a second, then stared at her reflection. If she squinted, she didn't look all that different. With a little pretending, it could be eight years ago, when she'd been so young and innocent and in love, and Gage had been the man of her dreams.

Gage. She sighed. She'd been trying *not* to think about him all day. That was the point of keeping busy, because if she wasn't, she worried and fretted, neither of which were productive. Unfortunately, the blast from the past in her arms had dissolved her mature resolve to keep an emotional distance from the situation.

Instead, she remembered her excitement at the thought of going to her prom with Gage. After all, the other girls were going with boys from school, or from one of the nearby colleges. But she had been going with a *man.*

Only, that hadn't happened. Instead of dancing the night away, she'd been on a bus heading to New York. Instead of laughing, she'd spent the night in tears. And while she couldn't regret the outcome— leaving had been the right thing to do—she was ashamed of how she'd handled the situation.

''Too young,'' she told her reflection. ''Of course, if I was old enough to be in love with Gage, I was old enough to tell him I was leaving, right?''

Her reflection didn't answer.

She put the dress down and walked to the stairs. She wanted to call Gage and ask if he was all right. She wanted to go to the station and see him. But she couldn't. Not today. Yesterday all those things would have been fine because he wouldn't have misunderstood her motives, but now everything was different. Now he might think she was pressuring him because of last night and this morning. She didn't want him thinking she was one of those clingy women who gave their hearts every time they made love with a man. She wasn't like that at all. At least, she didn't think she was. Not that she had any experience in that particular arena.

No, the reason she wanted to talk to Gage had nothing to do with their intimacy and everything to do with what he'd just found out. She was being a good friend, nothing more.

The phone rang, interrupting her thoughts. She dashed down the narrow attic stairs and flew toward her grandmother's bedroom, where the upstairs phone was kept.

"Hello?" she said breathlessly. Gage had called. He'd called!

"Ms. Asbury?" a cool, female voice asked.

Kari's heart sank. "Yes."

"I'm Mrs. Wilson. I'm calling you about your résumé. Do you have a moment?"

"Sure." Kari sat on the bed and tried to catch her breath.

Fifteen minutes later she had an interview scheduled for the following week. At this rate she would have a job in no time, she told herself as she hung up. In Abilene or Dallas or some other Texas city.

Just not Possum Landing.

Kari didn't know where that thought had come from, but she didn't like it. She was back in town for a visit, she reminded herself. This time was about fixing up the house to sell it, not reconnecting with anyone. This wasn't about Gage.

She repeated that thought forcefully, as if the energy invoked would make it more convincing. Unfortunately, all the energy in the world didn't change the fact that she had a bad feeling she was lying to herself.

Chapter Eleven

Gage showed up at Kari's door at a little after six. Until he'd walked from his house to hers, he hadn't been sure he would come. He'd nearly canceled a dozen times, reaching for the phone to call and tell her that something had come up. Or that he needed to spend the night by himself to figure out what he was going to do next. This wasn't her problem; she didn't need to be involved.

But every time he picked up the phone, he put it back down again. Maybe he *should* spend the evening thinking by himself, but he couldn't. Not yet. In the past twenty-four hours, he'd come to need Kari. He needed to see her, to be with her, to hear her voice and hold her close. He didn't know what the needing meant and he wasn't sure he liked it. But he acknowledged it.

Kari was a part of his past. Expecting anything more than a few nostalgic conversations and maybe a couple of tumbles in bed was a mistake. *More* than a mistake—hadn't he already fallen for her once?

So here he stood on her front porch, needing to see her and hating the need. He reached out and knocked once.

When she opened the front door and smiled at him, he felt as if things weren't as bad as he'd first thought.

"I come bearing gifts," he said, handing her a bucket of fried chicken with all the fixings that he'd picked up on the way home. "The diner still makes the best anywhere."

Kari laughed and took the container. Her blond hair swayed slightly as she shook her head. "Do you know, I haven't had fried chicken since I left here eight years ago?"

"Then, I would say it's about time."

She inhaled deeply, then licked her lips. "I guess so."

Still smiling, she stepped back to let him in the house. He walked inside, a folder still tucked under one arm.

"What's that?" she asked.

"Information on my biological father," he said. "I did some research today. I'll fill you in over dinner."

She led him into the kitchen. The small table by the window had been set for two. She offered wine or beer—he took the latter.

He watched her as she crossed to the refrigerator and pulled out a bottle. She wore a loose sundress that skimmed her curves before flaring out slightly at the hem. Her feet were bare. He could see that she'd painted her toenails a light pink. Gold hoops glinted at her ears, while makeup emphasized the perfect bone structure of her face.

When she was younger, he'd thought she was the prettiest girl he'd ever seen. Sometimes when they'd gone out he hadn't wanted to do anything more than sit across from her and gaze at her face.

Time had changed her. The twenty or so pounds she'd lost had angled her face and hollowed her cheeks. She'd been a pretty girl before and now she was a beautiful woman. He could imagine her in twenty years…still amazing.

She raised her eyebrows. "Is there a sudden wart on my nose?"

"No. I was thinking how nice you look."

She glanced down at the dress. "I'd say something like 'this old thing,' but it happens to be from an exclusive designer's summer collection. He offered it to me as a going-away present when I was in his show right before I left."

"It's nice."

"It retails for about two thousand dollars."

Gage nearly spit. "You're kidding."

"Not even a little." She grinned. "Suddenly I look a little better than nice, huh?"

"You always do, and it has nothing to do with the dress."

She sighed. "Nice line. Perfect timing, very sincere. You've gotten better, Gage, and I wouldn't have thought that was possible."

He shrugged off the compliment. He hadn't meant

his comment as a line—he'd been telling the truth. But explaining that would take them in a difficult direction. Better to change the subject.

"Are you telling the truth when you say you haven't had fried chicken since you left?"

"Of course." She carried the large bucket to the table and pulled off the top. "I haven't had anything fried. It's not easy staying as thin as I've been. No fried chicken, no French fries, no burgers." She tilted her head. "I've had ice cream a couple of times and chocolate. I let myself have one small piece once a month. Now that I'm a normal person again, I can eat what I want."

"Then, let's get started," he said, putting his folder on the counter and joining her at the table.

Fifteen minutes later, they were up to their elbows in fried chicken, mashed potatoes and coleslaw. Kari licked her fingers and sighed. "I'd forgotten how good this is. Even Grammy couldn't come close to the recipe."

"It's been passed down for several generations. You have the same chance of getting the family recipe out of Mary Ellen as you have of stopping the rotation of the earth. Many folks have tried over the years. There was even a break-in once. Only the recipe book was taken."

"You're kidding."

"Nope. We never did find out who'd done it. Of course, Mary Ellen told everyone who would listen that the fried chicken recipe had been given to her by her mama and no one in the family was ever fool enough to write it down."

Kari laughed.

Gage smiled slightly, but his humor faded. Talk of things being passed down reminded him of his own situation.

She read his mind. "What did you find out today?"

He wiped his hands on a napkin, then reached for the folder he'd left on the counter. After flipping it open, he read the computer printout.

"Earl Haynes is from a small town in Northern California. Like my mom said, he's a sheriff, or at least he was. He's down in Florida now. Retired and living with a woman young enough to be his daughter."

He flipped the page. "He had four sons by his first marriage, and a daughter by another woman. Apparently old Earl likes getting women pregnant, even if he doesn't like sticking around."

"Isn't it a little early to be judging him so harshly? You don't know all the circumstances."

He shrugged. There was no point in explaining that he had a knot in his gut warning him the information about his father wasn't going to be good.

"Let's just say the first reports aren't that impressive," he told her.

"It's interesting that he's a sheriff," she said. "You went into law enforcement and Quinn went into the military. I wonder if that's significant."

He didn't want it to be. The little he'd learned about Earl Haynes told him that he didn't want the man to matter at all.

"What about your brothers?" she asked when he didn't say anything.

He looked at her. "What do you mean?"

"You said Earl Haynes had four sons and a daughter. So you have five half siblings. Four of them are brothers."

Gage hadn't thought of that. He'd always regretted that both his parents were only children—there hadn't been any cousins. Now he suddenly had brothers and a sister.

"Well, hell," he muttered.

"Do you want to get in touch with them?"

"I don't know."

He hadn't thought that far ahead. He didn't want to have any part of Earl Haynes or his family.

"Let's talk about something else," he said. "Tell me about your day."

Kari took a bite of mashed potatoes. When she swallowed, she glanced at him from under her lashes. "I didn't get any painting done," she admitted. "I was too restless. I went upstairs and started cleaning the attic."

"Must have been hot."

She grinned. "It was. Even with all the windows open and a fan going. I found some interesting stuff, though. Old clothes, some jewelry."

She hesitated, then sighed. "Grammy kept a lot of my old clothes and toys. I was feeling very nostalgic."

"What did you see there?"

"My old prom dress. I can't remember how many times I tried it on. I used to put my hair in different styles, then try on the dress to see what looked the best. I wanted everything about that night to be perfect.''

Only, it hadn't been, he thought sadly. She'd disappeared and he'd been left holding a diamond engagement ring.

"I'm sorry, Gage," she said softly. "Sorry for running off, sorry for not telling you what I was so afraid of. Mostly I'm sorry for hurting you and leaving you to clean up my mess."

The words had come years too late, but it was good to hear them. "You don't have to apologize. I know you didn't take off just to hurt me."

"I should have said something. I was just so scared."

"You had a right to be." For the first time he could admit the truth. "You were too young. Hell, I was too young. I'd been so sure about what I wanted that I didn't want to think there might be another side."

Kari leaned back in her chair and voiced the question she'd asked herself over the years. "I wonder if we would have made it."

"I don't know. I like to think we would have."

"Me, too."

Kari studied him—his dark eyes, the firm set of his jaw. Tonight his mouth was set...no smile teased at the corner. He participated in the conversation, but she could tell that he was distracted.

Seeing him like this was such a change. The Gage she remembered had always known his place in the world. While the man before her now was still capable and confident, his foundation had shifted. She wondered how he would be affected.

His pain and confusion were tangible. Impulsively, she stretched her hand across the small table and touched his arm. "Tell me what I can do to help," she said.

"Nothing." He shrugged. "I don't think I'm going to be good company tonight."

The statement surprised her. "I'm not expecting a comedy show," she said lightly. "I thought—"

She didn't want to say what she'd thought. That he would stay with her tonight. That they would make love in her small bed, then curl up together and sleep in a tangle of arms and legs. Even if they weren't intimate, she wanted to be physically close. But Gage was already getting to his feet.

"I'm sorry," he said. "I've got a lot to think about. Maybe we can try this in a couple of days if I can take a rain check?"

As he was already standing, she didn't seem to have much choice. "Sure. I understand."

And she did. The problem was, she was also disappointed.

He started to collect plates, but she shooed him away. "You brought dinner," she protested. "I can handle cleanup."

He nodded and headed for the door. She followed him.

He paused long enough to drop a quick kiss on her forehead and offer a promise to be in touch. Then he was gone. Kari was left standing by herself, wondering what had gone wrong.

Despite the warmth of the evening, a coldness crept through her. They'd made love the previous night and this morning, but tonight Gage hadn't wanted to stay. Their intimacy obviously hadn't touched him the same way it had touched her. He'd been able to withdraw and regroup, while she'd...

Kari wasn't sure what had happened to her. How much of what was happening was due to her personal insecurities and how much of it was Gage withdrawing? Was he really going to a place where she wouldn't be able to reach him?

She hated the anxiousness that filled her, and the restlessness. She wanted to be with him. Obviously, she'd connected more when they'd made love than she'd realized.

That's all it was, she told herself as she returned to the kitchen. An emotional reaction to a physical encounter. There was no way she was foolish enough to let her heart get engaged. She'd already fallen in love with Gage once. That had ended badly. She was smart enough not to make the same mistake again.

Wasn't she?

Kari had barely finished dressing the following morning when there was a loud knocking on her front door. Her heart jumped in her chest as she hurried down the stairs.

Gage, she thought happily, her bare feet moving swiftly as she unfastened the lock and turned the knob.

But the person standing in front of her wasn't a tall, handsome, dark-haired man. Instead, a stylishly dressed woman in her forties smiled at Kari.

"Hello, darling," her mother said. "I know I

should have called and warned you I was stopping by, but the decision to come was an impulse. Your father and I are going to London in the morning. I wanted to come see my baby girl before we left.''

"Hi, Mom,'' Kari said, trying to summon enthusiasm as she stepped back to let her mother into the house.

Aurora presented her cheek for a kiss. Kari responded dutifully, then offered coffee.

"I would love some,'' her mother said. "I was up before dawn so I could make the drive here.''

"You drove?'' Kari asked in some surprise.

"I thought about flying into Dallas and then driving down, but by the time I got to the airport, waited for my flight, then rented a car, it seemed to take as much time.''

She smiled as she spoke. Aurora Reynolds was a beautiful woman. She'd made it to the final five of a state beauty pageant during her senior year of high school before abandoning her plans of fame and fortune to marry an up-and-coming engineer. Like her mother before her, and her mother's mother before that, she'd married at eighteen, had her first child by the time she was nineteen and had never worked outside the home a day in her life.

"I think I remember where everything is,'' Aurora said as she bustled around the kitchen. She spooned grounds into the coffeemaker, then retrieved bread from the freezer and pulled the toaster from its place under the counter.

As she worked, she chattered, bringing Kari up to date on the various events in everyone's life.

"I don't understand why he married her," she was saying. "Your brother is the most stubborn man. I said twenty-three was too young—but did he listen? Of course not."

Kari nodded without actually participating. She was used to fleeting visits during which her mother would drop in, talk for hours about people she didn't know, air-kiss and then take off for some exotic destination. The pattern had been repeating itself for as long as she could remember.

As to her mother's comment about her "knowing" anything about her brothers, Kari didn't. She saw them once every couple of years for a day or so. Theirs wasn't a close family. At least, not for her. She couldn't say what the four of them did when she wasn't around. For all she knew, they lived in each other's pockets.

"How are you progressing with the sorting?" her mother asked after she put bread in the toaster and there was nothing to do but wait.

"It's slow but interesting. Grammy kept so much. I found a fox stole yesterday. It nearly scared the life out of me."

Aurora laughed. "I remember that old thing. I used to play dress-up with it."

"Would you like to have it?" Kari had planned to give the thing away, but if her mother wanted it, she could have it.

"No, darling. I prefer the memory to the dusty reality."

She leaned against the counter, a tall, blond beauty who still turned heads. Looking fresh and stylish in cotton trousers and a crisp blouse, she seemed to defy the heat. Kari knew what small success she'd had as a model came from her mother's side of the family.

"There are some old dresses and other things," Kari persisted. "Do you want to look at any of them?"

"I don't think so. I didn't inherit my mother's desire to save everything. But if there are some photo albums, I'll take a look at them."

"Sure." Kari was eager to escape the kitchen. "Dozens. I have a few in the living room. Let me get them."

She hurried into the other room and grabbed an armful of photo albums covering events over the past fifty years.

"I think your high school pictures are in this one," Kari said, setting the stack on the counter and picking up the top album.

"Hmm." Her mother didn't sound very interested as she poured them each coffee and carried the mugs to the table. Several slices of toast already sat on a plate there.

Her mother put down the mugs, then sorted through the albums. She came across one filled with pictures of Kari from about age three to eight or nine.

"What a sweet girl you were," her mother said with a sigh. "You hair was so light, and look at that smile."

Aurora's expression softened as she slowly turned pages. Kari watched her in some surprise. Her mother hadn't bothered to keep her around all those years ago, so why was she going misty over a few pictures?

She didn't voice the question, but her mother must have known what she was thinking because she closed the album and stared at her daughter.

"You think I'm a fraud," her mother said flatly.

Kari took a step back. "No. Of course not."

"I suppose it's not a big stretch for you to assume that I never cared, but you're wrong."

Clutching the album to her chest, her mother crossed to the table and took a seat. "I remember when you left for New York. Mama was concerned because you had no one there to help you. She was afraid you'd be too stubborn to come home if things got bad, but I knew you'd be all right."

Her mother sighed, tracing her fingers along the top of the album. "I like to think you got your strength from me. That ability to do what's right even when it hurts. Leaving Gage behind wasn't easy, but it was the right thing to do, wasn't it?"

Kari sat in the chair across from her mother and nodded.

"I thought so. I've made tough decisions, too." Aurora looked past her daughter and stared out the kitchen window.

"You were such a tiny thing when you were born," she said quietly. "We had a big problem with colic and you had recurring ear infections. The doctor said you'd outgrow the problem and be fine, but in the meantime your father had been offered a job in Thailand. We talked about me staying with you because you couldn't possibly make the trip. I was terrified to be that far from a familiar doctor."

Kari tried to remember if she'd heard this story

before. From her earliest memories, she'd been in Texas and her parents had been somewhere else. Once, she'd asked to go with them when they'd come to visit. Her mother had said that was fine, but Grammy was too old to travel that far and live in a foreign country. Given the choice between her beloved Grammy and parents who were strangers, she'd chosen to stay.

"I didn't know what to do. You needed me, your father needed me. Then Mama said she would keep you for a few weeks, until things settled down. The doctor was sure you would be ready by the time you were seven or eight months old. It broke my heart to leave you, but in the end, that's what I did."

Aurora sipped her coffee, then opened the album on the table. As she turned pages, she spoke. "Once we were settled in Thailand, we found out travel wasn't as simple as we had thought. Your ear infections continued longer than we expected they would. There wasn't a doctor nearby, so I waited to bring you to join us. Then I became pregnant with your brother." She glanced up and smiled sheepishly. "That wasn't planned, I can assure you." Her smile faded and suddenly she looked every one of her years.

"I didn't want to travel the first few months. Then a wonderful doctor settled in our area. The timing was perfect, I thought. He would deliver my next child and then I could come and bring you home. I waited until your brother was three months old and then I returned here, to Possum Landing."

Her mother turned away and drew in a deep breath. "I'd been gone too long. When I finally arrived, you were nearly two and a half. I walked in the door and called your name. But you didn't remember me. You hid, and when I tried to pick you up, you cried and only Mama could calm you down.''

Kari felt her throat getting a little tight. Nothing in her mother's story was familiar, yet she sensed every word was true. Against her will, she imagined her mother's pain and heartbreak at being a stranger to her firstborn child.

''I didn't know what to do,'' Aurora said. ''I stayed for two weeks, but the situation didn't improve. I think you somehow knew that my plan was to take you away. You wouldn't let Mama out of your sight and continued to run from me. Mama wanted to keep you. She loved you as if you were her own. I couldn't fight the two of you. In the end it seemed kinder to leave you here. So I went back to Thailand without you.''

Kari nodded but found she couldn't speak. Not without tears threatening. She'd always felt she'd been abandoned by her parents, but maybe the truth wasn't so simple.

''Looking back, I can't help thinking I took the easy way out,'' her mother admitted. ''I could have dragged you with me. In time you would have accepted me as your mother. Maybe that would have been better. But I didn't. I can't say Mama didn't love you with all her heart, or raise you perfectly, but I regret what I lost. I never should have left you behind in the first place. I should have found another way.'' She offered a sad smile. ''I suppose that sounds selfish.''

"No," Kari managed to reply. "I understand." She did…sort of. Her head spun. Too much had happened too quickly. She'd come back to Possum Landing expecting to spend a few weeks fixing up her late grandmother's house. Instead, she'd come face-to-face with ghosts from her past. First Gage and now her mother.

"Now I suppose it's too late for things to be different between us," Aurora said casually, not quite meeting her daughter's eyes.

Kari hesitated. "I appreciate hearing about what really happened. It's different from what I imagined." She grabbed her coffee mug but didn't pick it up. "Why now?" she asked.

"The time was never right," her mother said. "At first, I didn't want to take you away from Mama. I always hoped…" She shrugged. "I thought you might come ask me on your own. Eventually, I realized you thought I'd simply turned my back on you."

Kari didn't respond. That had been what she'd thought. Apparently, she'd been wrong.

She thought about what she and Gage had spoken about just yesterday, when she'd told him he would have to forgive his parents if he wanted to make peace with the past. Could she do any less?

"I need some time," Kari told her mother. "This is a lot to absorb."

"That's fine." Her mother glanced at her watch. "Oh dear. I have to head back. There are a thousand and one things to do before we head to London tomorrow."

Aurora rose and Kari did the same. "Do you mind

if I keep this?'' her mother asked, motioning to the photo album.

''Take as many as you'd like. There are plenty.''

Her mother smiled. ''I just want this one of you.''

Kari didn't know what to say, so she gave in to impulse and moved close for a hug. After Aurora disappeared in a cloud of perfume and a promise to ''bring you something wonderful from London,'' Kari returned to the kitchen, where she poured out her now cold coffee.

Just two hours before, her world had been only mildly confusing. Now it was like living inside a tornado where everything was spinning too fast to allow her to hold on.

She didn't know what to make of her mother's story. It shouldn't change anything but her perception of the past, yet somehow everything looked different. Now she had a more clear understanding of what Gage was going through, albeit on a smaller scale.

Nothing was ever simple, she thought, moving to the side window and staring at his house. So much had happened in such a short period of time.

Chapter Twelve

Kari decided the best antidote for feeling unsettled was hard work. She finished painting the second upstairs bedroom, then started on her grandmother's room. The old pieces of furniture slid away from the walls more easily than she had anticipated. She pushed everything toward the center of the room to give herself space to work. She took down drapes, picked up throw rugs and draped drop cloths over everything. By two-thirty she was sweaty, exhausted and in need of a break.

In an effort to get away from her own company, she decided on a trip to the grocery store. As much as she might want to see Gage that night, she figured it was unlikely. So she settled on "chick" food for dinner. A salad, yummy bread, with a pint of her favorite ice cream for dessert.

She'd just stopped by the tomato display to pick out a couple for her salad when something slammed into her grocery cart. One of the wheels rolled into her foot, making her jump. Kari turned in surprise— then wished she hadn't.

Daisy stood behind her own cart, glaring at Kari. "I can't believe it," the petite redhead said, her eyes flashing with rage. "I told you about my plans for Gage, but you didn't care. Well, fine. Try for him if you want, but you're destined to fail. I might have felt sorry for you before, but now I figure you've earned it."

Kari had the urge to tilt her head and wiggle her earlobe. She couldn't have heard any of that correctly.

"I have no idea what you're talking about," she said at last.

Daisy looked disbelieving. "Sure you don't. I told you I was interested in Gage, but you didn't care. You just waltzed into his bed without giving a damn about anyone else. I'll have you know, Gage doesn't like his women that easy. But I guess you already knew that."

Kari opened her mouth, but before she could speak, Daisy narrowed her gaze.

"Don't try to deny it. I saw you leaving his place a couple of mornings ago. I doubt you'd just dropped by to borrow some coffee."

The joys of small towns, Kari thought, trying to find the humor in the situation. She shook her head. "First of all, what I do or don't do with Gage isn't anyone's business but ours. Second, I don't know why you're so put out. You and I aren't friends. In fact, we've barely met. I don't owe you anything. If you were in love with him, I might give your feelings some consideration, but you've already admitted you're not. Your interest in Gage comes from the fact that you think he'll be a good husband and father. While I'm sure he'd appreciate the endorsement, I suspect if he does decide to marry, he's going to want his future wife to be madly in love with him.''

Daisy's eyes flashed with temper. ''I suspect what he'll want is someone who doesn't take off at the first sign of trouble.''

Kari acknowledged the direct hit with a slight wince, but didn't otherwise respond to that comment. ''If Gage is interested in you,'' she said, instead, ''no one else would matter to him, so I wouldn't be a threat to you. If he's not interested, then warning me off doesn't make any difference at all.''

''You're judging me.'' Daisy was fuming. ''But you're no better. You had him and you let him go. How smart was that?''

''I was young and foolish,'' Kari admitted. ''I didn't realize how wonderful he was, but I do now.''

''You're not going to get him back.''

Kari grabbed a tomato and put it in her cart. ''I don't think you get to decide that,'' she said coolly, then pulled her cart from Daisy's and stalked away.

As she walked, she kept her head high, but she was shaking inside. The encounter had rattled her more than she wanted to admit.

As she approached the checkout stand, she thought of half a dozen things she should have said to Daisy, including the fact that at least she'd been smart enough to fall in love with him eight years ago. If Kari thought for a second that she was going to stay around and that he was interested, she would—

Kari cut that thought off before she could finish it. Being annoyed with Daisy was one thing, but acting foolishly was another. She didn't love Gage. She refused to believe she was the kind of woman who would still be in love with him after all this time. She wasn't. She hadn't secretly been waiting to come back to him. The idea was laughable.

No. She had left and she had gotten on with her life. She was still getting on with it. Gage was just a memory. The past, not the future.

Gage pulled into the cemetery and parked by the curb. He waited a long time before getting out of his car. The rational side of him knew that there was no hope of getting answers here. His father had long since moved beyond speaking.

His father.

Just thinking the words propelled him from the car. Ralph Reynolds—the name on Gage's birth certificate. The man who had loved him and raised him and shown him right from wrong. Ralph? No, he thought as he crossed the freshly cut lawn. Not Ralph. *Dad.*

Kari was right. Biology be damned. This man he had loved and mourned was his real father. He might not share the blood that ran in Gage's veins, but he had influenced him and molded him.

He crossed to the simple marble marker. Ralph Emerson Reynolds. There were the dates of his birth

and death, followed by ''Beloved husband and father.''

He *had* been beloved, Gage reminded himself.
Ralph's unexpected death from a heart attack had
devastated the family. Even Quinn had been caught
by surprise.

Gage crouched by the marble marker. ''Hey, Dad,''
he said, then stopped because talking to himself in the
middle of a cemetery felt strange. Then he continued.
''Mama told me. About my biological father.'' He
swallowed. ''I wish you'd told me the truth. It
wouldn't have changed anything.''

He stared at the marble. ''Okay. It would have
changed things. But hearing it from you would have
been better than finding out the way I did. You could
have explained things to me. You could have told
Quinn why he was never good enough.''

Gage stood and paced on the grass. Quinn had deserved to know why his best had never mattered.
Ralph Reynolds had been a great father to Gage, but
he'd been a real bastard to Quinn.

''You shouldn't have done it,'' Gage said, spinning
back to the tombstone. ''You should have treated us
the same. If you could accept me—someone else's
son—you should have accepted him.''

He wanted to rage against his father, but it was
years too late. Maybe that's why he hadn't been told.
Maybe Ralph had pretended; maybe he'd forgotten
the truth. At least for Gage.

Damn. There weren't going to be any sudden il-
luminations that would set his world to rights.

His chest tightened, his throat burned. He looked

up at the sky, then back at the grave. "I still would have loved you, no matter what. Why didn't you believe that?"

There was only silence, punctuated by the background songs of the birds. There were no answers here, there was no peace. His father had long since left for another place. This problem was for the living. Which meant Gage had another stop to make.

In the way that mothers always seem to know what their sons are up to, Edie stood on the porch, watching for him as he drove up. She didn't walk down the stairs to greet him or smile. She stayed where she was, waiting to see his reaction.

He tried to remember how their last conversation had ended, but it was all a blur. Too much emotion, he thought. Too many revelations.

"Hey," he said as he climbed the stairs. He saw the front door was open and that John hovered in the front room.

"Gage."

Edie pressed her hands together. All the energy seemed to have been drained out of her. Her eyes remained dull and flat.

Without saying anything, he crossed to her and pulled her into his arms. She collapsed against him, a sudden sob catching in her throat.

"It's okay, Mama," he said, as she started to cry. "I was really pissed off, but it's okay now."

"I'm sorry," she said shakily. "So sorry. I never meant to hurt you. There were so many times I wanted to tell you the truth."

"I know." He stroked her hair. "I believe you. Dad wouldn't have wanted you to say anything. If he couldn't fix the problem, he pretended it didn't exist. Didn't we used to joke about that?"

She raised her head and stared at him. Tears dampened her cheeks. "He *is* your father, Gage. No matter what, that hasn't changed."

"I know. I lost it for a while, but it's back."

John came out and joined him. He put an arm around Edie and held out his hand to Gage. They shook, then John nodded.

"I told her you'd come around."

"Thanks."

His mother beamed at him. "Do you want to come in? We could talk. There are still some things—"

He cut her off with a quick smile. "I need some time, okay?"

He saw that she didn't want to put off the rest of whatever it was she had to share, but he didn't care if he never knew any more.

"Just a couple of days," he promised, and turned back to his car.

She and John stood on the porch, watching him as he pulled out. He waved and his mother smiled at him.

She thought everything was all right now. That it was all behind them, Gage thought as he headed back to the station. What she'd done…well, she'd had her reasons. Some he agreed with, some he didn't. It would take a long time for him to get over the fact that his mother had thought she was in love with someone else while she was still married to his father.

But what Edie and Ralph Reynolds had done…had survived…wasn't his business. He had to deal with what had had an impact on him.

The truth was that forgiving his mother and making peace with his father didn't change one fact: he was not the man he'd always thought he was.

Kari washed brushes in the sink in the utility room. It was after nine in the evening, and she focused on the task at hand in an effort to keep her brain from repeating the same thought over and over again.

It had been nearly a week since she'd seen Gage.

A week! Six days and twenty-two hours.

Why? She knew that he'd been avoiding her, but couldn't quite pin down the reason. She wanted to believe it was all about his past, but she had a bad feeling that some of it was personal. With everything else going on in his life, the last thing he would want to worry about was her virginity, or how he'd made that disappear. No doubt he thought she would already be picking out china patterns, while he'd simply been interested in getting laid.

Kari turned off the water and sighed. Okay, that was a slight exaggeration. Gage wasn't the kind of guy to only want sex for sex's sake. If he was, he would never have been so careful while they were dating. He would have pushed her, and, as much as she'd been in love with him, she would have given in.

So Gage hadn't been looking for an easy score and she wasn't looking to get married to the first man she slept with. Reality lay somewhere in between.

She set the wet brushes on a rack, then washed her hands and dried them on a towel. Despite the pulsing urge inside her, she was *not* going to cross to the front window and stare out from an opening in the lace curtains. Spying on Gage, watching for when he got home, was way too pathetic. Besides, she'd been doing it too much lately. If she wanted to talk to him, she should simply call, like a normal person. Or go to his house, or even his office. If she didn't...

Kari walked into the kitchen and crossed to the refrigerator. She'd bought a pint of cookie-dough ice cream on her last visit to the grocery, and this seemed like a fine time to have it for dinner. Despite all her logical conversations with herself, the bottom line was that she was alone on a Saturday night, watching for the boy next door to come home and ask her out. This was worse than when she was in high school. She had managed to live in a big city for eight years, have different experiences, even have something close to a successful modeling career. Yet nothing had changed. The situation would be pretty funny if it were happening to someone else.

The phone rang, causing her to slam the freezer door. Her heart rate increased. There were only two types of calls in her current world—Gage, or not Gage. This increased the pathetic factor, but was completely true.

"Hello?" she said, trying not to sound breathless.

"Hi, Kari," Gage said. "What's going on?"

Over the past week, she'd planned her conversation with him dozens of times. She'd had witty lines and blasé lines and casual questions all lined up. Now, of course, she couldn't think of anything but "Not much. I've been working on the house. Just finished painting for the day."

"I've been meaning to get back there and help you."

The road to hell and all that, she thought. "My remodeling job isn't your responsibility," she said. "How are you doing?"

"Okay. Still trying to figure things out."

Silence. She sighed. Things had been so much easier before. Before they'd made love. Before he'd found out about his past.

He cleared his throat. "The reason I phoned is that there's a big dance up at the country club. I've had a few calls from worried parents. They're concerned that the kids might be renting hotel rooms for the night. I did some checking around and it looks like a group of them are planning to spend the night at the Possum Landing Lodge. I'm on my way over to break things up. I was hoping you'd come with me."

She frowned. "To break up a party?"

"Yeah, well, the odds are that some of these teenagers are going to be going at it in the room, and I don't want to have to deal with a bunch of half-dressed girls."

Not exactly the invitation she'd been waiting for, but it was better than nothing. "Sure, I'll help."

"Great. I'll be by in about ten minutes."

"Okay. 'Bye."

She hung up, then flew upstairs to replace her paint-spattered shorts and T-shirt with a crisp summer dress. There wasn't time for a shower or a fabulous hairstyle, so she ran a brush through her hair, fluffing up the ends while she worked. After racing into the bathroom, she brushed her teeth, applied mascara and lip gloss and slipped on some silver hoops. A pair of sandals completed her outfit. She hurried back downstairs and collected her house key, then walked to the front door. She'd just reached it when Gage knocked.

She opened the door and tried not to smile at him. Against her will, her mouth curved up and every cell in her body danced. Talk about betrayal.

Even more frustrating, he looked really, really good. There were shadows under his eyes as if he hadn't been sleeping much, and his uniform was a little rumpled—but none of that mattered. Not when she could see into his eyes and watch him smile back at her.

"Hi," he said. "Thanks for the help."

"No problem."

He didn't move back, so she couldn't step out of the house. They looked at each other. He reached out his hand and lightly touched her cheek.

"I've been avoiding you."

The admission surprised her. She decided to offer one of her own. "I noticed."

"It wasn't because of…" He paused. "I've had a lot on my mind. I didn't want to dump it all on you."

"We're friends, Gage. I'm happy to listen."

"I may take you up on that. I've been doing a lot of thinking and I don't seem to be making any progress."

"Have you talked with your mom? Are things okay there?"

He nodded. ''A couple of days ago I went to see her. She's still trying to tell me more stuff, and I don't want to hear it. I know that I have to listen eventually. But other than that, we're fine.''

She wanted to ask if she and Gage were fine, too. If making love had changed things forever, or if they could go back to their easy, teasing, fun relationship.

''I've missed you,'' she said before she could stop herself.

''I've missed you, too. More than I should.''

Her heart skipped a beat and she felt positively giddy. Man, oh man, she had it bad.

''You ready?'' he asked.

''Sure.''

He stepped back, and she moved onto the porch, closing the door behind her. As they walked to the car, Gage rested his hand on the back of her neck. She liked the heat of him and the feel of his body close to hers. Unfortunately, there didn't seem to be much about Gage she didn't like.

They drove in silence to the motel. When they arrived, several parents were already pacing in the parking lot. Gage spoke to them, then went to the main office and collected keys from the night manager.

''Ready?'' he asked Kari, as they walked up the stairs.

''No, but that's okay.''

It was dark and quiet in the corridor. Voices from the parking lot faded as they moved toward the rear of the motel. Up ahead, light spilled out of an open door. The sound of laughter and loud voices drifted toward them.

"Do you do this sort of thing often?" she asked, trailing behind him.

"When asked. I prefer to come out at the request of the parents and clear things up before they get out of hand. That way I can get everyone home with a warning. If I get a call from the motel management, then it's official and I have to get tough. Most of the kids are mortified to be caught by me and their folks. They don't need much more encouragement to stop."

"For those who need more?"

"They'll be in trouble soon enough," Gage said, glancing at her as he paused near an open door. "Ready?"

She nodded, then braced herself for plenty of shrieking and tears. Gage stepped past the threshold and stalked toward the center of the room.

"Evening," he said calmly, as if he'd been invited.

Several teenagers screamed.

Kari followed him in. Kids were in various stages of undress. Two girls ducked into an adjoining room and quickly closed the door behind them. Two boys were brave enough, or drunk enough, to challenge Gage.

"We're not doing anything wrong, Sheriff," a skinny boy with dark hair said belligerently. "This is private property. You ain't got no right—"

Gage stood directly in front of the boy. "You talking to me, Jimmy?"

The teenager took a step back. His too-long hair hung in his eyes. He still wore a shirt and tie, although both were undone. The color faded from his face.

"Uh, yes, Sheriff. We've been quiet. We haven't made any trouble."

"That's good," Gage said evenly. "Your mama called me because she was real concerned. You're eighteen now, but your girlfriend is still only seventeen. Your mama was afraid you'd have a bit too much to drink and then things might get out of control."

Jimmy took another step back, which brought him in contact with the wall. "My mama called you?"

"Uh-huh. She's waiting downstairs in the parking lot."

One of the other boys snickered. Kari almost felt sorry for Jimmy.

Gage turned to those laughing. "Your mamas are here, too, boys. So let's all get dressed and head downstairs." He motioned to the adjoining room. "You want to see to the ladies?"

Kari nodded. She walked through the doorway and found herself in a living room. This must be the suite the Possum Landing Lodge was always advertising. The decorations were early tacky, with a gaudy red couch and fake oak coffee and end tables. Three velvet paintings decorated the walls.

"At least there's no Elvis," she said, passing a picture of dogs playing poker. She followed the sound of heated conversation.

"I can't believe this is happening," one girl said, as Kari entered the bedroom. "Tonight Jimmy and I were going to go all the way."

"Guess that will have to wait," Kari said, leaning against the door frame. "I realize you don't know me from a rock, but for what it's worth, my advice would be to make that very special occasion a little more private.''

Two girls, both young, pretty and blond, glared at her. She could read their minds. What could an old lady like Kari possibly know about having fun?

As Kari waited, they scrambled into dresses and high heels. When they hurried past her, she went to check the bathroom, where another girl sat on the floor. Her pale cheeks told their own story.

''You done being sick?'' Kari asked.

The girl nodded and slowly got to her feet.

''Want some help?''

The teenager shook her head, then ran out of the bathroom. Kari turned to leave, then stared at the ice-filled bathtub. There had to be at least a dozen bottles of cheap liquor and wine chilling there.

''Great,'' she muttered, and went to find Gage.

She found him lecturing the last of the boys. The teenager escaped with a grumbled promise to think before acting next time.

''At least we got here in time,'' Gage said with a sigh as he closed the door of the suite. ''All the girls gone?''

''Yes. One had been throwing up. She's not going to feel too great in the morning. Apparently, a big party was planned. There's a bathtub full of liquor in there.''

He headed for the rest room. ''Let's dump it, then we can head out of here.''

''You don't want to keep any for yourself?'' she

teased, as he bent down and grabbed a couple of bottles.

He glanced at the labels and shuddered. "My tastes have matured." His gaze slid to her. "In nearly everything."

She wasn't sure what he meant, but she liked that he finally seemed to have noticed she was there.

Gage poured while Kari handed him bottles. They worked quickly and soon the bathroom reeked of cheap liquor. It was only when they finished and moved back into the bedroom that he realized where he was.

The honeymoon suite.

The big round bed dominated the floor space, leaving little room for much more than a small dresser and a TV on a stand. Thick drapes kept out the night. The wood paneling had seen better days, as had the carpet. But eight years ago, Gage had thought this was just the place to secure his future with the woman he loved.

"What are you thinking?" Kari asked. "You have the strangest expression on your face."

He shrugged. "Ghosts."

"Ah. You liked to bring your lady friends here for a big seduction scene?"

"Not exactly. But I had planned to bring you here. I was going to propose, and after you said yes, I was going to make love to you."

Kari's smile faded. Several emotions skittered across her face, but he couldn't read them. Or maybe he didn't want to. Maybe it was better not to know what she was thinking. After all, she'd skipped town rather than marry him.

"You had it all planned out," she murmured.

"Down to the smallest detail, including proposing *before* we made love so you wouldn't think it was just about sex."

"I wouldn't have thought that. Not about you. I know the kind of man you are."

"Yeah, well..." He suddenly felt awkward and stupid for mentioning anything and headed for the door. But before he got there, Kari spoke again.

"Daisy and I practically had a fistfight over you in the produce aisle."

That brought him up short. "What are you talking about?"

She smiled. "Your wannabe girlfriend tried to warn me off. She said you weren't interested in me and that I could never have you back."

"What did you say?"

"A lot of things."

Which told him precisely nothing. Before he could figure out if he wanted to continue the conversation, she crossed to the nightstand and flipped on the clock radio. Tinny music filled the room. She fiddled with the knob until an oldies station came in, then crossed to stand in front of him.

"Dance with me," she said.

Then she was in his arms, and he found he didn't want to refuse her. Not when she felt so right pressed against him. Whatever might have gone wrong emotionally between them, physically they'd always been right together.

They moved together, swaying in time to the old ballad. He thought about what should have happened in this room all those years ago.

"I'm sorry you never got to your prom," he said, resting his cheek against her soft hair.

"Me, too. I would have liked to have those memories." She sighed. "I'm sorry I ran away. You were so good to me. I should have realized I could talk to you about anything—even being scared."

Past and present blurred. Gage closed his eyes. "Nothing is easy," he told her. "If I didn't know it before, I'm learning it now."

"Because of your mom?"

"Yeah. She loved her husband. I know she did. Yet there was this other man. She loved him, too, and I never figured it out. I want to be angry, but if she hadn't gone back to him, Quinn wouldn't exist."

"Sometimes life isn't as tidy as we would like."

He agreed with that. His life had changed forever. What had once been taken for granted wasn't a part of him anymore. A single piece of information had changed him forever. Changed him in a way that made everything else different.

He pulled Kari closer, enjoying the familiar heat of her body, the way she felt and the scent of her skin. Being with her allowed him to forget the issue of his father, for at least a short time. He could get lost in the past, in remembering something much sweeter. How he'd loved Kari more than he'd ever thought he *could* love someone. How he'd loved her long after she'd left, when he should have let go. The things he'd loved about her hadn't changed—her spirit, her generosity, her determination. She was the same woman—more mature, more experienced, but fundamentally the same.

The information could have been dangerous. Under other circumstances it would have been. If things were different he might think the reason he'd never been able to fall for anyone else was that he was a one-woman man and Kari was that woman. He might have worried about falling in love with her again.

But not anymore. Seeing her now, having her back in town, reminded him of all that might have been, but couldn't be now. Even if she wasn't leaving, they couldn't possibly be together. Everything was different now. Himself most of all.

"I'm glad we didn't get married," he said.

She raised her head and looked at him. "What are you talking about?"

Wasn't it obvious? "What if we'd married and had kids together? Eventually, I would have found out about my father."

"So?"

"It changes everything."

"Not for me. I feel badly that you're in pain and I want you to get your questions answered, but aside from that, it has no impact on anything. You're still the same man I knew eight years ago. If we'd married, you'd still be my husband and the father to my children. I would still love you."

Her blue eyes held his gaze. He could read her sincerity. She believed what she was saying, even if she was wrong.

"It changes everything," he said.

"You are the most stubborn man. I can't decide what to do with you."

Then she raised herself up on her toes and kissed him.

Chapter Thirteen

The soft pressure on his lips stunned Gage into immediate arousal. Need pulsed through him in waves that threatened to drown him in desire. Without thinking, he pulled her close and deepened the kiss, plunging his tongue inside her mouth, tasting her, teasing her, stroking her, *wanting* her.

She responded in kind, her body pressing against his, her hips against his arousal. She rubbed against him, as if they weren't close enough. When she closed her lips and sucked, he thought he was going to lose it right there.

"Oh, Gage," she breathed, making it clear that the heat wasn't being generated all on one side.

He'd made love with her enough times to know the joining would be spectacular, but not enough to have expectations of a sure thing. Kari's obvious interest excited and pleased him. She'd been a virgin their first time and he'd worried later that things hadn't gone well for her. Clearly, she'd decided she very much liked the act of making love. He started to back her toward the bed.

The bed. He raised his head and stared at the round mattress. How many times had he imagined them together here?

She turned and saw what had caught his attention. ''Is it too weird to be here?''

''I don't know,'' he admitted.

''Do you want me to convince you, or just stop?''

He swung his gaze back to her. ''Are you offering to seduce me?''

Color bloomed on her cheeks. She cleared her throat. ''Yes, well, I'm not saying I could—just that if you were intrigued by the idea, I would be willing…'' Her voice trailed off. ''You did say you liked to watch.''

Desire slammed into him like a truck going eighty. He didn't know why every single man in New York hadn't begged her to marry him, but somehow they'd missed the amazing jewel glittering in their midst. Somehow he, Gage, had gotten damn lucky.

Not only had Kari never been with another man before making love with him, but she was now offering to seduce him. As if he needed encouragement or persuasion.

He reached for her, determined to show her exactly what she did for him without even trying, when reality intruded.

"I don't have anything with me." He groaned. "Damn."

A slow smile teased her mouth. "Are we talking protection?"

He nodded.

Her smile broadened. "Our young friends might have been foolish about some things, but they were well prepared for others." She motioned to the television. "Exhibit A."

He turned and saw what he'd missed before. Sitting on top of the television was a jumbo box of condoms. There had to be at least a hundred inside.

"Somebody was planning on getting lucky in a big way," he said, pulling her back into his arms.

"Looks like it's going to be you."

"Looks like."

He lowered his head and kissed her. Despite the raging need inside him, he was determined to be gentle and take it slow. That mental promise lasted right up until Kari gently bit down on his tongue at the same time she slipped a hand between them and rubbed his arousal. He swore.

Kari shivered slightly at Gage's explicit language, but not out of shock. Instead she felt bone-melting need. She didn't know if it was the past intruding, or Gage's emotional vulnerability or her own emotional state, but something had happened tonight. Something that made her want to rip both their clothes off and make love to him.

She wanted to be taken. She wanted his body in hers, their hearts beating as one. She wanted the touching, the pleasure, the shared breath, the trembling aftermath. She wanted to bare her soul to him and stare down into the depths of his.

Her need made her bold in a way she'd never been before. When he jerked down the back zipper of her dress, she shrugged out of it as if she spent most of her day undressing in front of him. Before he could unfasten her bra, she did it for him. The scrap of lace slid to the floor. She brought his hands to her breasts, then gasped when she felt the heat of his touch. The ache between her thighs intensified as he cupped her curves while teasing her already tight nipples.

She reached for the buttons of his shirt while they kissed. Her fingers fumbled, but she kept at the task until she could rub her palms against the hair on his chest. From there she went to work on his belt, then his trousers. When she'd undone the zipper, she eased her hand inside his boxer shorts and wrapped her fingers around his hardness.

Such soft skin, she thought, deepening the kiss and beginning to move her hand. Soft skin around pulsing hardness. She eased back and forth, moving faster and faster until he caught her wrist and pulled her away.

"Not like that," he said with a smile.

She delighted in his confession—that she could have made him lose control with a simple touch.

While he stepped out of his shoes and pulled off his socks, she slipped off her panties. He continued to undress while she crossed to the condom box and removed one square packet. She turned to find Gage standing in the center of the room. He was naked.

She looked at him, from his dark eyes to his mouth, then to his chest, his flat belly and finally to his jutting maleness. He held out his hand for the condom. She handed it to him, then watched while he slipped it on.

When he moved to the bed, she followed. He stretched out on his back. "I thought you might like being on top," he said, his expression faintly wicked.

Kari thought about the position—her sliding up and down while he filled her. She thought about his hands on her body, touching, moving, stroking, delighting, and nearly stumbled in her eagerness.

She slid onto the bed, then stretched one leg over him. He filled her completely as she eased onto him.

He sucked in a breath, then instructed her not to move. "We need to get you caught up," he said, then proceeded to show her what he meant.

He touched her everywhere—from her ears to her breasts, down to her legs and between her thighs. He stroked the arc of curves, found secret places of delight and teased her into a frenzy. Tension filled her, making her want to ride him, but he held her back.

"Not yet," he whispered.

They kissed. He moved one hand to her nipples and tickled them until the pulsing inside her grew. Her thighs clenched and unclenched. Her breathing grew ragged. Finally, when she ached and perspiration dotted her back, he moved inside her.

She responded instantly, sliding up and down. On the first round trip, she felt herself falling off the edge. He made sure she went all the way by slipping his hand between her legs and rubbing her dampness until everything shattered.

Her climax overtook her, making her cry out. She

leaned forward, bracing her hands on the bed, riding him faster and faster, each up and down movement sending new waves of pleasure through her. She lost herself and didn't care about anything but her passion and her need.

There was more and more until nothing existed but the feel of him inside her. Then his hands settled on her hips, steadying her movements. His thrusts deepened as he collected himself. Kari forced her eyes open so she could watch her lover's release, only to find him watching her.

Then as he stiffened and called out her name, she saw down into his soul. For that one endless moment in time their hearts beat together. Then the pulsing of his climax carried her off on another mindless round of pleasure, and they lost themselves in the glory of their lovemaking.

When they finally disentangled, Kari expected Gage to roll away. He'd been distant from her ever since he found out about Ralph not being his biological father. But instead of sitting up or reaching for his clothes, he drew her close and wrapped his arms around her.

"Pretty amazing," he said quietly. "Even better than I'd imagined. And I'd imagined a lot."

"I know what you mean. I'm still trying to catch my breath."

He shifted so he was facing her, but kept an arm on her waist. "I haven't seen you in a few days."

She thought about explaining that it had actually

been a whole week, but didn't. "I've been working on the house. And you?"

"Work. Other stuff," he said casually.

"Is that getting better or worse?"

"About the same."

She wasn't sure she agreed with him. Not when he'd made the ridiculous statement about being glad they hadn't married and had children, based on some secret from the past.

"My mom came by for a visit," she said.

"How was that?"

"Weird, as always." She touched the line of his jaw, rubbing her fingers against his stubble. "I always had a very clear view of what happened when I was little. My parents went away and forgot about me. The fact that they kept my brothers with them only seemed to prove my point. But after talking with my mother, I'm not so sure."

She filled him in on the details of how she came to be left behind. "I saw my parents as the bad guys, but what was black and white is now gray. I still think they were wrong to leave me, but I can understand why they did what they did. I want to tell myself it doesn't affect anything, but it does. Still, the fact that my interpretation of the past might be different doesn't change my feelings. Am I making any sense?"

"Yes."

She stared into his dark eyes. "I guess my point is, I understand your confusion a little more clearly. Nothing is different for you, yet everything is different. Information changes perception—but does it change emotion? Am I less angry with my mother now that I know the circumstances that contributed to her decisions? I'm not sure.''

''Me, neither. About any of it.''

She moved her hand to his mouth and traced his lips. ''Don't you dare think you're anything but a wonderful man. You're the best man I've ever known.''

''I doubt that.''

''Don't. I'm telling the truth.'' She made an *X* above her left breast. ''I swear.''

''Thank you.'' He kissed her lightly.

Kari kissed him back. As she did, her words repeated themselves inside her head. Gage *was* the best man she'd ever known. He was everything any woman could want. He was…

Her chest tightened suddenly as she got it. The realization nearly made her laugh out loud. It also nearly made her cry.

She was in love with him. After all this time and all the miles she'd traveled, she was still in love with him.

Why hadn't she figured it out before? The clues had been there—her reaction to seeing him after all this time. Her willingness to make love with him after putting off other men. Her eagerness to spend time with him. The way she worried about him. Her ambivalence about looking for a teaching position in Dallas or Abilene.

''Kari? Are you okay?''

She nodded because speaking was impossible. Now what? What happened when one of her interviews led to a job offer? Did she hang around Possum Landing, hoping Gage would fall in love with her, too? He'd just said he was grateful they hadn't married. Hardly words to hang her dreams on.

The mature solution was to ask him about his feelings, to find out where things stood between them. She opened her mouth, then closed it. Not yet, she thought, burying her face in his shoulder. She needed a little time to get used to the idea of being in love with Gage.

"Hey," he said, stroking her back. "It's okay."

"I know," she lied, because she didn't know anything.

He kissed her head. "Want to come home with me and spend the night?"

She nodded. She loved him—there was nowhere else she would rather be.

Gage didn't have to work the next day, so they slept in late, then went over to her grandmother's house and set to work. They'd just started moving furniture out of the dining room, when there was a knock on the front door.

Kari went to answer it and found Edie waiting on the porch.

"Is Gage here?" his mother asked. "He wasn't home, but his truck is in the driveway, so I thought he might be helping you."

"Sure." Kari held open the front door, then called for Gage.

As she invited the older woman inside, she tried to quell the worry inside her. The past few hours had been magical. She and Gage had slept in each other's arms, only to awaken and make love again at dawn. Her feelings were still so new and tender that she didn't want anything to break the mood between them. Unfortunately, Edie's visit was bound to do just that.

Gage nodded at his mother. "What's going on?"

"You're avoiding me," Edie said bluntly. "I decided if you weren't going to come to me, I would chase you down myself. We need to talk."

Kari's throat went dry. "I'll go upstairs."

"No." Gage shot out a hand and grabbed her wrist. "You don't have to go." He gazed at her. "I'd prefer that you stay."

She nodded and led the way into the parlor. Edie perched on a chair, while Kari and Gage sat next to each other on the sofa.

"If you tell me that you're not really my mother, I'm going to be really pissed off," Gage said lightly.

Edie smiled slightly. "Sorry. You're stuck with me."

"I don't mind."

He reached for Kari's hand and laced their fingers together. She looked from him to his mom and wished this would all just go away.

"So here's the thing," Edie began. "When I went to Dallas the second time, I didn't know what I wanted or what I was feeling. Everything confused me. I just knew I had to see Earl one more time. Which I did. Obviously. Quinn is proof of that. But that's not all that happened."

Kari felt Gage brace himself against more bad news.

"We spent the night together. The next morning there was a knock on the hotel room door. A young woman stood there. She was barely eighteen." Edie shook her head. "She didn't look a day over fifteen, and she had two little babies with her. The second I saw her face, I knew the truth. Earl had been with her, as well. She'd brought her boys to meet their father."

Kari's stomach did a flip. She hadn't thought things could get worse, but she'd been wrong.

"Another conquest," Edie said bitterly. "I realized in that moment, that was all I'd been to him. Any feelings were on my side. I don't know how much of what he told me was truth and how much was lies. It didn't matter. What I had thought was love was infatuation. Or maybe it was just a justification to myself. If I thought I loved him, then sleeping with him didn't make me such a horrible person."

Tears filled her eyes. She blinked them away. Kari tightened her hold on Gage's hand. She was afraid to look at him. For once, she didn't want to know what he was thinking.

"What happened?" Gage asked, his voice low.

"The girl showed him the babies. He didn't deny they were his. He didn't do anything but get dressed and tell her he wished her well. That was it. No offer to marry her or even help out with his sons. I felt so stupid. The girl took off in tears. I ran into her in the lobby and found out her parents had thrown her and her two babies out the day she turned eighteen."

Gage wanted to run. He wanted to run so far and so fast that the words would be erased from his mind. He wanted to close his eyes and have the past disappear. But his mother kept talking, and he couldn't stop himself from listening.

But as she spoke an ugly thought appeared in his brain. This man—this Earl Haynes who used women and abandoned them—was an integral part of himself. Earl's biology was in Gage.

He thought of his own past, his inability to settle down with someone. How easily he moved from relationship to relationship. Was that because of his biological father? Was he a philanderer, too?

No! He didn't want that history, that blood, flowing through his veins. He didn't want to be a part of it.

But it was too late. The past had already occurred and he couldn't undo it. Not now.

Then, before he could make peace with any of it, his mother's words caught his attention.

"I couldn't leave her there alone," she was saying. "So I brought her home. We made up a dead husband and gave her a new last name."

Gage swore as the pieces all fell into place. Vivian Harmon was a close friend of the family. Her two sons, Kevin and Nash, were his age. Both tall, dark-haired, with dark eyes. And no father.

"Kevin and Nash?" he said.

She nodded. "Your half brothers. Vivian and I have talked about telling you four. We've gone back and forth a dozen times over the years. At first, I didn't want to say anything because of Ralph. He didn't want you to know. Vivian and I talked about it again after his death. At that point, I was too afraid to confess the truth. So I asked Vivian to keep quiet. She didn't mind. She'd married Howard years before and he'd been like a father to the boys. She never thought they were missing out.''

Gage felt as if the room were spinning. He didn't just have faceless half siblings in California, he had two right here in Texas. Not that Nash and Kevin lived here now. Nash was a negotiator with the FBI and Kevin was a U.S. Marshal, but they came home on occasion. He and Quinn had played with the twins all their lives. They'd double-dated, been on the same football and baseball teams, worked on each other's cars and shared their dreams with each other. Never had they considered the fact that they might share a whole lot more.

''Vivian's going to tell the boys,'' Edie said. ''Now that you're all going to know, it might help you four to talk about it.''

Gage wasn't sure what they were supposed to say. ''He has a family,'' he told her. ''Earl Haynes. I looked him up on the Internet. He's retired now, but he was a sheriff in a small town in California.''

His mother nodded slightly.

''There are other children. He has several sons from his first wife and a daughter by another woman.''

Edie winced. ''I suspected there was more family, but I wasn't sure.''

''You never asked.''

''I didn't want to know,'' she admitted.

At least she was being honest. "It's too much," he said.

"I'm sorry." She paused. "Do you have any other questions?"

"None that I can think of." He laughed humorlessly. "Just tell me that there aren't any other revelations."

"None that I'm aware of."

"Good."

He could live the rest of his life without any more secrets, he thought grimly.

Edie rose. "You haven't heard from Quinn yet, have you?"

"No. I'll let you know when he gets in touch."

Gage still didn't know how he was going to tell his brother the truth. Nor did he know how Quinn would react. It was a lot to take in.

He released Kari's hand, stood and walked his mother to the door. Tears filled her eyes.

"I'm sorry," she whispered.

He nodded and gave her a quick hug. When she'd left, he returned to the parlor.

Kari stood by the window. She turned to look at him. As they'd planned to work in the house, she wore a paint-spattered T-shirt and cutoffs. A scarf covered her hair, and she hadn't bothered with makeup. She still looked beautiful.

He wanted to go to her and hold her so tightly that he couldn't tell where one ended and the other began. He wanted to breathe in the scent of her and return to that place where he'd felt everything was going to be all right. Unfortunately, that time had passed.

"I know I said I'd help, but I need to head out and—" He broke off, not knowing what he had to do. He only knew that he needed to be by himself for a while.

"It's okay," she said. "I understand."

"I'll be in touch."

"You said that before."

Had he? "This time I mean it. I'll call you to-night."

He walked to the front door and let himself out. He crossed to his own yard and was about to climb the front porch steps, when he heard her calling his name. He turned.

"What's up?" he asked.

She crossed the driveway to stand next to him. "This is wrong," she said, determination blazing in her eyes. "I know you're going through a lot right now, but you can't let it destroy everything."

"What are you talking about?"

She swallowed. "Last time, I was the one to walk away. It looks like this time you're going to walk away. Do you think we'll ever get it right?"

Chapter Fourteen

Gage felt as if he'd been turned to stone. He couldn't move, couldn't speak. Then the sensation passed and he was able to draw in a breath.

Do you think we'll ever get it right?

"What the hell are you talking about?" he demanded.

Kari didn't back down from his obvious temper. Instead, she planted her hands on her hips and glared back at him.

"I'm talking about us. You and me. There's something here, Gage. I know you can feel it. Lord knows, it's keeping me up at night. Eight years ago I panicked. I was too young to tell you I needed time, so I ran. My fears and my desire to experience my dreams kept us apart. I've grown up and you've changed, too, yet whatever we had is still alive. But I'm afraid that this time your past is going to rip us apart.''

He didn't know what to say. While he was willing to admit there was something between Kari and himself, he'd never thought past the moment. He knew about her plans, and they didn't include him. He'd been okay with that. Now she was suddenly changing the rules.

''Are you saying you're not leaving Possum Landing?'' he asked, not sure how he felt about any of this.

''I'm saying I don't know. Last night you told me you were glad we'd never married and had children. You said the fact that Ralph isn't your biological father changes everything.''

''It does.'' How could it not?

She dropped her hands to her sides and took a deep breath. ''See, that's what I'm afraid of. I want you to see that it doesn't matter.''

His temper erupted. ''You're ignoring the obvious. I understand that Ralph Reynolds had a tremendous influence on my life. He raised me to believe certain things and to act a certain way, but those are only influences. What about my basic character? Were you listening to what my mother said about Earl Haynes? He got a seventeen-year-old girl pregnant. When he found out about her twins, he simply walked away. That is my heritage. That is the character of the man who fathered me. I have to live with that and make peace with it, if possible. I may not know much about him, but I know he was a cheating bastard who wouldn't take responsibility for his own children. I'm not willing to take a chance on passing those qualities on. Are you?"

Pain flashed through her blue eyes. Her mouth trembled. "You're not him," she said softly. "You're not him."

"Are you willing to bet your children's future on that?"

"Yes," she said with a confidence that stunned him. "I know you. I've known you for years. You're the kind of man who would put his life on the line for his town because he doesn't know another way to do things. You're the kind of man who looks after other people's grandmothers, and cares for his own mother when her husband dies. You're responsible, caring, gentle, loving and passionate. You're a good man."

Her words hit him like arrows finding their way to his soul. "You don't know what the hell you're talking about," he said, turning away.

She grabbed his arm and stepped in front of him. "I know exactly what I'm saying. You are the same man you were last month and last year. Believing anything else is giving power to a ghost. I believe in you with all my heart."

She stopped talking and pressed a hand to her mouth. Tears filled her eyes. "Oh, Gage."

He watched her warily.

She blinked the tears away. "I just realized, it doesn't matter how much I believe in you. If you won't believe in yourself, there's no point in having this conversation. I can't convince you. I can't make you believe. And loving you won't matter because you won't let it.''

He froze. ''What did you say?''

She lowered her hand. ''I love you. I'm beginning to think I never stopped. You still have every quality I loved before, but you're even better now. How was I supposed to resist that?''

Her words stunned him. She loved him? Now? ''I don't believe you,'' he said flatly.

''I'm not surprised. Worse, I don't know how to convince you. I'm beginning to think I don't know anything.'' She sighed and took a step back, holding out her hands, palms up.

''I love you and I'm terrified you're going to let me walk away because of some ridiculous obsession with the past and what it means to you today. I'm afraid we're going to lose our second chance, and I'm willing to bet there won't be a third.''

Kari's declaration had caught him off guard. Defenseless and confused, he wanted to retreat. *No more words,* he thought. *No more.*

But she wasn't finished. ''It all comes down to making choices,'' she said. ''Are you willing to trust yourself?'' She gave a strangled laugh. ''I guess that's *your* most significant question. Mine is different. Do you still love me? Are you interested in any of this? I've been going on, based on the assumption that my feelings matter to you—and they may not. But if they do, it's your choice. Are you willing to let the biology rule your life? You do have a choice in this.''

She turned away and started for her house. When she reached the driveway, she glanced back at him.

"Let me know what you decide. I hope you have enough sense to see how lucky we are to have found each other again. I think we could be wonderful together. At one time I was set on leaving Possum Landing, but that's not an issue anymore. What I don't know is if you can get past everything you've learned recently. One way or the other, I have to make a decision. To stay or go. When you figure out what you want, let me know."

And then she was gone. Gage stared after her, watching her disappear into the house, feeling his life-blood flow away.

She loved him.

After all these years, after all the waiting—he'd just realized that's what he'd been doing—she finally realized she loved him. She'd come to the same conclusion he had—that all they'd loved about each other was still in place, only better.

The information came a couple of weeks too late.

He might want to be with Kari with all his heart, but did that matter? He had nothing to offer her. Without a past he could depend on, he had no future.

Kari walked into the house to find the phone ringing. At first she thought about ignoring it. There was no way that Gage could have run inside and called her. Besides, if he had something he wanted to say, he would simply come over and tell her.

So she let the machine get it. But when a woman identified herself as someone from the Abilene school where she'd interviewed, she grabbed the receiver.

"Hello?"

"Kari?"

"Yes."

"Hi! This is Margaret Cunningham. We spoke during your interview?"

"I remember. How are you?" Kari wiped the tears from her face.

"Great. I have wonderful news. We were all so impressed, and I'm delighted to be calling you with a job offer."

Kari wasn't even surprised. Of course this would happen moments after she made her declaration to Gage. Fate was nothing if not ironic.

She listened while the other woman gave details about the job, including a starting salary and when they would like her to start. Kari wrote it all down and promised to call back within forty-eight hours. When she'd hung up, she grabbed a pillow from a nearby chair and sent it sailing across the room.

"Dammit, Gage," she yelled into the silence. "Now what? You're not going to tell me what I want to hear, are you. And if you are, you'll take your time, and then what am I supposed to do? I told you I loved you. Doesn't that mean anything?"

She wanted to stomp her feet, as well, but figured that was immature and wouldn't help. She hurt inside. Probably because she'd done the right thing at last and declared her feelings, only to have Gage not respond to them. He'd listened and then had let her walk away. Not exactly the sign of a man overwhelmed by loving feelings.

She sank onto the chair and covered her face with her hands. That's what was really wrong, she thought sadly. She'd admitted she loved Gage and he hadn't offered her love in return. He hadn't offered her anything.

Over the next twenty-four hours, Kari alternately cried, ate ice cream, threw unbreakable objects and slept. She also hovered by the phone, willing it to ring.

When it did, she found herself being offered another job, this one in the Dallas area.

Sometime close to noon the next day, while she cried her way through a shower, she finally got it. It was as if the heavens had opened and God had spoken to her directly.

She couldn't force Gage to love her back and she couldn't insist he live on her timetable. The only control she had was over herself. Her feelings, her goals, her life. Gage was his own person. He had to make the decisions that were right for him.

The realization left her feeling very much alone. What did she do now? Did she keep her life on hold, hoping he would come to terms with everything and realize that they belonged together? Or did she move on, aware that he might never come around?

After her shower, she dressed and fussed with her hair. She applied makeup, then headed out the door.

She found Gage at the sheriff's station. He was talking with one of the deputies, so Kari waited until they were finished. When Gage was alone in his office, she slipped inside and closed the door behind her.

He looked tired. Dark shadows stained the skin under his eyes. While she couldn't read his thoughts, she felt he looked a little wary. No doubt he feared her next confession.

"About yesterday," she said, settling into a chair across from his desk. She really wanted to pace, but figured if she stayed standing, he would, as well. Although the closed door gave them the illusion of privacy, in reality Gage's office walls were glass. Anyone could watch what was going on. Better to have things appear calm. At least no one could hear the thundering of her heart.

"Kari," Gage began, but she held up her hand to stop him.

"I'd like to go first," she said quickly.

He hesitated, then nodded.

Every cell in her body screamed at her to run to him and beg him to say he loved her. She desperately wanted him to sweep her up in his arms, hold her close and swear he would never let her go. She wanted him to declare his love with a sincerity and passion that would keep her tingling for the rest of her life.

Instead, she was going to tell him it was okay for him to let her go.

"I was wrong yesterday," she said. "I shouldn't have confessed my feelings. Or if I did, I should have done it differently. Nothing about this situation is your fault. You have so much going on right now and I just added to your load. For me this is huge, but for you it's just one more piece of the puzzle."

She forced herself to smile and hoped it came out even borderline normal. "You need time to figure out what's going on. You have a lot to come to grips with. I'm not saying I don't love you. I do. I can't imagine life without you. But I'm not going to force myself on you. You need time, and I'm going to give you that.''

Now came the tricky part. She swallowed and twisted her fingers together. ''So, to that end, I'm accepting a job in Abilene. It's close enough that if you change your mind—'' She cleared her throat. ''It would be doable until my school year ended. And if you decide this is… I mean, if I'm not what you want, then I'll be getting on with my life.''

He looked as if she'd sucker punched him. ''Kari, don't.''

''Don't what? Leave? Isn't it the right thing to do?''

He shook his head. She had a bad feeling he'd meant ''Don't love me.''

Pain gripped her. She forced herself to go on. ''Just to keep things from being too awkward, I've hired someone to finish the work on the house. The property management company will take care of selling it. So I'm heading out in the morning. I wanted to tell you that, too. Goodbye, I mean.''

''You don't have to leave because of me.''

It hurt to breathe. He was saying he shouldn't be the reason she left—not ''Don't go.''

''There's nothing to keep me here,'' she said, forcing herself to breathe in and out. The pain would pass eventually. Life would go on. This wouldn't kill her, no matter how it felt right now.

''My family, such as it is, lives elsewhere. With

my grandmother gone, Possum Landing isn't home anymore. She was always the one who mattered. My mother might have given birth to me, but my grandmother was the keeper of my heart while I was growing up.'' She stood slowly.

There was so much more she wanted to say—but what was the point? Obviously her love was one-sided. Not the haven she had wanted it to be. If only...

''Goodbye, Gage,'' she said finally.

Gathering every ounce of courage and strength, she turned and walked out of his office. She didn't look back, not even once. She'd done the right thing. When she'd begun to heal in, oh, fifty years or so, she could be proud of that. Right now, she just wanted to be anywhere but here.

Gage watched her go. With each step she took, he felt a piece of his soul crumble to dust.

She was leaving. She'd said as much and he believed her. Under the circumstances, it would be best for both of them. She would get on with her life and he would try to figure out who he was now that he was no longer one of five generations of Reynolds, born and bred in Possum Landing.

He turned to his computer screen, but the small characters there didn't make any sense. Instead of words, he saw Kari leaving. Again. He'd let her go the first time because she'd deserved to have a chance at her dreams. This time he was letting her go because...

Because it was the right thing to do. Because she deserved more than he had to offer. Because—

He swore as her words echoed inside him. While Aurora was her mother, she wasn't the keeper of Kari's heart. Her grandmother had been that. For Kari, Aurora was nothing more than biology. No yesterdays bound them together. No shared laughter, no talks late at night, no Christmas mornings.

Gage curled his hands into fists as a kaleidoscope of memories rushed through his brain. His father teaching him to ride a bike, then, years later, to drive a car. His father taking him fishing. Just the two of them, leaving town several hours before dawn for a camping trip. Long walks, evenings by the fire building models. Frank conversations about women and sex—Ralph Reynolds had admitted knowing less about the former than the latter. His father had taught him to tell the truth, be polite, think of others. He'd taught Gage respect and courage.

Earl Haynes might have given Gage life, but Ralph Reynolds had made sure that life meant something.

Gage stood up with a force that sent his chair sailing across the room. He raced to the door and out toward the front of the building. He might not have all the answers, but he knew one thing for sure—he wasn't going to lose Kari a second time. Not if she was willing to take a chance on him.

He pushed open the front door and saw her on the sidewalk. "Kari," he called. "Wait."

She turned. He saw tears on her beautiful face. Tears and an expression so lost and empty that it nearly broke his heart. Then she saw him. And as he watched, hope struggled with pain.

"Don't go," he said when he reached her side. He

wrapped his arms around her. "Please, don't go. I can't lose you again."

He cupped her face and stared into her eyes. "Kari, I love you. I've always loved you. I didn't want to admit it, even to myself, but I've been waiting for you to come back. Don't go."

A smile played around her mouth. It blossomed until she beamed at him.

"Really? You love me?"

"Always."

"What about what your mother told you?"

"I don't have all the answers."

Her smile never wavered as love filled her eyes, chasing away the tears. "You don't have to. We'll figure them out together. No matter what, I'll be here for you."

That was all he wanted to hear. He kissed her. "I love you. Stay. Please. I know you have to work in Abilene for a year. That's what you agreed to, right? We'll work it out. I want to be with you. I want to marry you and have babies with you."

She laughed. "I haven't accepted the job yet. I was going to go home and call right now. I guess I'll have to tell them no."

He couldn't believe she would do that for him. He pulled her close again and pressed his face into her soft hair. "I never want to lose you again."

"You won't. I'll marry you, Gage. And we'll have those babies. When you figure out what you want to do about your half siblings in California, we'll deal with that, as well."

He raised his head and looked at her. Love filled

him, banishing the shadows and making everything right. "How did I get so lucky?"

"I could ask the same thing. My answer is that I love you. After all this time, you're still the one."

* * * * *

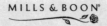

On sale 20th July 2007

CELEBRITY BACHELOR
by Victoria Pade

When millionaire tycoon Joshua Cantrell visited Northbridge College, Cassie Walker was assigned to be his 'minder'. Gorgeous, wealthy men like Josh always made small-town girl Cassie feel inferior, but behind his public image was a down-to-earth man who knew Cassie was *truly* special.

ACQUIRING MR RIGHT
by Laurie Paige

When businessman Lance Carrington bought the company Krista Aquilon worked for, she feared the worst. But was Lance an utterly ruthless corporate raider or a kindred spirit trying to save the firm? One thing was certain – his takeover of Krista was complete.

RIGHTFULLY HIS
by Sharon De Vita

Max McCallister had been the sperm donor for the woman he'd always loved and his brother. But now his brother was dead and Sophie was raising two fatherless little girls alone... It was time to claim what was rightfully his – Sophie and his twin daughters...

THE ROYAL HOUSE OF NIROLI

*...International affairs, seduction
and passion guaranteed*

Volume 1 – July 2007
The Future King's Pregnant Mistress by Penny Jordan

Volume 2 – August 2007
Surgeon Prince, Ordinary Wife by Melanie Milburne

Volume 3 – September 2007
Bought by the Billionaire Prince by Carol Marinelli

Volume 4 – October 2007
The Tycoon's Princess Bride by Natasha Oakley

8 volumes in all to collect!

...*International affairs, seduction and passion guaranteed*

Volume 5 – November 2007
Expecting His Royal Baby by Susan Stephens

Volume 6 – December 2007
The Prince's Forbidden Virgin by Robyn Donald

Volume 7 – January 2008
Bride by Royal Appointment by Raye Morgan

Volume 8 – February 2008
A Royal Bride at the Sheikh's Command by Penny Jordan

8 volumes in all to collect!

Mediterranean Men

Let them sweep you off your feet!

Gorgeous Greeks

The Greek Bridegroom by Helen Bianchin
The Greek Tycoon's Mistress by Julia James
Available 20th July 2007

Seductive Spaniards

At the Spaniard's Pleasure by Jacqueline Baird
The Spaniard's Woman by Diana Hamilton
Available 17th August 2007

Irresistible Italians

The Italian's Wife by Lynne Graham
The Italian's Passionate Proposal by Sarah Morgan
Available 21st September 2007

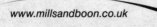

www.millsandboon.co.uk

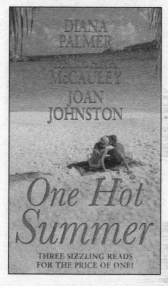